Mars
System Reboot

by

Dave Willmarth

Chapter One

Going Down…

Commander Fletcher lay on the bunk in her cabin, having just closed her eyes. Taking deep breaths, she tried to calm herself enough to sleep. It wasn't easy, tomorrow was a big day! In less than twenty four hours, she and her crew were going to be the first human colonists on Mars.

She was running through the coming day's tasks in her head, using the monotony of systems checks and double-checked checklists, when the entire ship shuddered. Alarm claxons started blaring, and she burst from her bunk, stepping into her one-piece ship suit as she headed for the door. Zipping up as she ran the short distance to the bridge, she shouted, "Skippy, what's going on?"

"There has been an explosion in engineering section C2. My sensors detected one crew member in proximity before they went offline."

"Shit!" Fletcher activated her coms. "Fire control team to engineering, C2! Move it!"

Entering the bridge, she hopped into the captain's chair and took a quick look at the ship's status. There was indeed a fire alarm in that section, and a red flashing warning icon told her that there was a hull breech, and they were losing oxygen quickly. Keying the radio to report back to Earth, she informed them of the situation. "Control, we've had a catastrophic explosion. Hull is compromised, and we're already down twenty eight percent on oxygen reserves. Initiating emergency launch protocols, approximately…" She paused to look at the clock. "Approximately twenty hours ahead of schedule. We're about to initiate emergency burn. Deceleration in ten… nine…" Commander Fletcher didn't wait for a response from Earth, following the established protocol for this particular emergency situation. At their current position relative to earth, her radio transmissions took about eleven minutes to reach the folks at Control, and their reply would take just as long. By the time she heard back from them, she and her team would be on the surface of Mars.

Hopefully.

They had practiced for this. Drilled a hundred times, their testers at Control throwing them different curveballs each time. Her people were professionals, none of them prone to panic in stressful situations. Each of them had been carefully screened and selected for their mental fortitude as well as their professional qualifications.

"Fire control team, what's your status?" Fletcher called out through coms.

"Fire's out, but we lost about forty percent of the oxygen reserves when tank three blew. There's a small hole in the hull, patching it now. The foam should hold, no problem, boss." That was Chin, one of the two systems engineers on this mission. He paused for a moment, clearing his throat before continuing. "Kyle's gone."

"Roger that. Get that hole patched, then get out of there. We're bailing now, so get to your tanks and get strapped in. I'm dropping the hab and the rest of the cargo in bay one in ninety seconds, and we're gonna be one minute behind it."

"Copy, boss. We'll be there."

Fletcher scanned the holographic display in front of her. She sat in the commander's seat on the bridge of the *Hyperion*, the massive Mars colony ship, first of its kind. It was a dual purpose vessel, beginning its service as a transport for her crew and their gear. Once they descended to the surface with their equipment, it was meant to remain and serve as an orbital station. A place for future colony supply or transport ships to dock, and a platform for planetary observation and communication relay with Earth.

Except now she wasn't sure whether the structure would even be able to maintain orbit after they abandoned it. The structural damage wasn't severe, but the explosion had disabled several of the vessel's control system circuits.

"Skippy, can you hear me?" Fletcher spoke to the console in front of her chair.

"*I can hear you, Commander Fletcher.*"

"What's your status?"

"*My quantum core is undamaged and operating at ninety two percent efficiency. Efficiency loss is due to minor power fluctuations. Communications array is intact, and functioning normally. Navigation is offline, as is thruster control, and I am attempting repairs. Estimated time required is three days, nine hours, twenty eight minutes. Oxygen reserves are at fifty two percent and falling.*" There was a short pause. "*Correction. Hull breach has been sealed, and reserves are holding at fifty one point six percent. My compliments to Chin the Great.*"

Fletcher smiled at the console, despite the dire situation. She and several of her crew were gamers, and during the long seven-month trip from Earth to Mars, they hadn't been able to resist the temptation to use Skippy's quantum computational power to play some games. Chin had smuggled a crate of VR gear on board, and everyone was grateful. Being able to rampage through dungeons, killing monsters and gathering loot had helped to keep them sane on the long voyage. Chin had installed a variety of games, from first-person shooters to high fantasy role-playing games. They couldn't play the MMORPGs with the folks on Earth due to the long signal delays, but Skippy had enough computational power to host a separate server for the crew.

"Chin, Skippy says quest complete, plus one thousand xp for plugging the leak."

"Ha! Thanks, Skippy. You hang tight up here, and we'll be online again as soon as we're set up planetside."

"*I look forward to it.*" Skippy replied, his artificially generated voice sounding nearly human.

"Can you hold orbit, Skippy?" Fletcher got back to business.

"*We have already deviated from our programmed orbit due to explosive outgassing. Returning to that orbit is possible, but it would require a series of significant burns, and I would not be able to complete the maneuver until navigation is back online. The fuel required would reduce the station's functional life by approximately three years without a fuel resupply. However, I believe I can hold this new, lower orbit without a significant drain on our fuel resources.*"

Three years lost, out of an eight year mission. That was unacceptable. Control might be able to send additional fuel with later missions, but that wasn't guaranteed. The smaller ships coming behind the *Hyperion* were packed to the rafters with needed supplies, the weight of each item measured down to the gram. Loading thousands of pounds of liquid fuel would require leaving behind valuable equipment that would be needed on the planet.

This mission, and the four subsequent Hyperion missions, had been planned down to the smallest detail. Building a sustainable colony on Mars, with the eventual aim of terraforming the red planet, was no simple task. Earth was overcrowded, polluted, and running low on natural resources. The governments of the various nations had finally come together to address those issues, and one of the possible solutions was this mission. If they could re-establish an atmosphere on Mars, the human race could expand, buying themselves a few thousand more years.

"Lower orbit will have to do, Skippy. We're relying on you. Once we're down on the surface, we won't be able to do anything to help you up here."

"*I won't let you down, Commander. My nanobot supply is still at eighty seven percent of capacity, and I should be able to complete any needed repairs on my own.*

Unfortunately, you and the others will be launching from a point significantly closer to the surface than you planned. And more than twenty hours ahead of schedule. I have calculated the most likely points of impact for the hab and for your vehicles. I'm afraid you'll be touching down approximately two thousand miles from your intended landing site."

Fletcher pressed her lips together. That was a problem.

Should she risk keeping her crew on board long enough to launch closer to their scheduled time? She'd already lost one crew member, and thus one vehicle pilot. The loss of both would have serious repercussions to their mission already. The possibility of additional systems failures caused by the explosion put her remaining crew at risk. Mission parameters allowed for the loss of up to two vehicles before Control would declare mission failure. But those losses were expected to happen during planetfall, or in the normal course of operations on the surface. Not before they even left the *Hyperion*.

"*Commander? Are you alright*?" Skippy's query broke her from her musings.

"I'm good, Skippy. Just considering my options here. In this lower orbit, how long until we reach our planned launch point?"

"*At our current trajectory, we will not reach the previously planned launch point. The closest our new orbit will bring us is within thirteen hundred miles. That will be in approximately fifteen hours.*"

"So we're not just closer to the planet, we're also off course." Fletcher mumbled to herself. "Thirteen hundred miles is still too far to drag the hab." She drummed her fingers on the console, then reached her decision. Pressing the coms button, she called out to her crew.

"Change of plans. We've been blown off course, and can't reach Site Alpha anymore. Everyone meet me in the cafeteria. Now."

Even as she spoke, she got up from the captain's chair and left the bridge, headed through the massive bulkhead door that separated that compartment from the rest of the ship. It took her less than a minute to reach the cafeteria, the slight pull of Mars' gravity allowing her feet to push off the floor and propel her in long leaps down the central corridor.

Taking a seat at the head of the table, she waited for the others to arrive. Originally, a crew of ten, they were down to nine with the loss of Kyle, one of their biochemists. When the others had settled in, all of them quiet and nervous about their situation, she stood up and addressed them.

"All right, so the shit has hit the fan. We've planned for situations like this, though not this exact scenario. We can't reach our planned landing site, the closest we could get is about thirteen hundred miles. And that's if we stay here on the *Hyperion* for fifteen more hours. Which, I gotta tell you, I'm not inclined to do."

"Fucking Kyle." Carver Graves, a mechanical engineer, growled from his seat near the other end of the table. "He nearly killed us all. And for what?" Several others nodded their heads or mumbled agreement.

Fletcher thumped her hand on the table, grabbing everyone's attention. "We can bitch later. Right now we've got work to do. I need solutions." She looked over to a young woman on her left. "Lissa, pull up the file with all the potential alternate sites you guys identified."

Lissa, their geologist, tapped a few keys on her wrist unit, then made a throwing motion toward the center of the table. A holo display popped into existence, a representation of the globe that was Mars, with a few dozen glowing blue triangles dotting its surface.

"Skippy, are any of those sites within range of our new orbit?"

The display changed, a red circle appearing around the planet, indicating their new orbit, a larger green circle appearing farther out from the surface to indicate their original planned orbit. The two circles intersected at about a thirty degree angle, indicating they were significantly off course. Graves cursed again, and he wasn't alone.

"*Our current trajectory will bring us within two hundred and sixty miles of site Gamma Three.*" Skippy replied as one of the blue triangles turned bright green. "*However, your path from the landing site to Gamma Three would take you over a small, jagged mountain range.*"

"What's the next closest?" Lissa asked.

"*Site Bravo One. Your estimated landing site would be approximately four hundred eighty miles from there, across smoother terrain.*"

"Show us the map." Fletcher commanded. The holo display shifted, zooming in closer to the planet's surface. A red X marked the spot where Skippy estimated they might land. The potential colony site Bravo One was almost directly west of it.

Lissa moved her hands again, and the map scrolled westward from the landing zone. After about ten seconds, she stopped it. "This could be a problem."

What they were all looking at was a crevice, no, a canyon, that stretched for hundreds of miles north to south directly in their path. "Looks too big to jump across, and too steep to climb down into. If I had more time, I might find a path…" Lissa shrugged apologetically.

"How many miles to go around it to the north or south?" Fletcher zoomed the map out a bit so that they could see the whole canyon.

"*A detour north would be an extra six hundred twenty miles. To the south, five hundred fifty.*" Skippy provided instantly.

Fletcher looked to Lissa, who had her head down and was sticking her tongue out slightly as she concentrated on her wrist pad. Knowing that look, Fletcher left her to it.

Looking at Chin and Volkov in turn, her two system engineers, she asked, "I think I already know the answer to this, but how far could we move the hab without burning too much of our fuel supply?"

"The fuel isn't our main problem." Chin replied, Volkov nodding along. "The hab module is big, and heavy, even with the surface gravity being about a third of Earth's. Our tanks weren't meant to carry that kind of load over rough terrain. We'd have to unload… three?" He looked at Volkov, who nodded again, crossing his arms. "Three of the tanks to carry the hab, assuming we could load it without damaging it. Once we've transported it to the Bravo site, we'd have to turn those tanks around and go back to pick up all the equipment we left behind at the landing site." He tapped the table for a moment, then continued. "The alternative would be to disassemble the hab and load pieces onto each tank, pushing all of them beyond their max loads, but within allowances."

Volkov took over. "But the time required to disassemble, transport, and reassemble the hab unit, I estimate six days at each end, plus maybe two days travel, would nearly exhaust our oxygen reserves. It would leave us with no safety net if there's a problem with the hab later."

"But surely it was always part of the plan to move the hab, right? I mean, we're dropping it from hundreds of miles up in space. No way was it going to land exactly where we want it." Clarke, the crew's surgeon and psychologist, asked.

Chin nodded. "That's right. Skippy is going to pilot the hab module on its descent, and we allowed for a landing as far as ten miles off target. But if you look at site Alpha One, or any of the other Alphas, they're all on wide open, relatively flat plains. No mountains or canyons to cross. We were always expecting to move the hab, since we plan to set it up in a canyon or at the base of a cliff. But not to this degree. We would choose our site, unload the tanks, grab the hab, and move it within a few hours."

The others grew quiet, contemplating their predicament. Fletcher looked at each of their faces, trying to gauge how they were handling the pressure. None of them looked panicked at all, which made her proud.

"I may have another solution." Lissa spoke up. She flashed a new data packet from her wrist unit up to the holo. A new series of dots, these colored orange, appeared around the globe. She moved her hands to zoom in on a particular orange dot that sat almost directly below their new red orbital ring.

"This is one of the Delta sites. Delta Seven. It's much closer to our current orbital path, and has a good landing site."

"Yessss! We're saved!" The youngest crew member, their remaining biochemist, pumped a fist in the air. The action made him wobble unsteadily on his stool.

Fletcher glared at the young man. "Trent, are you drunk?!"

Trent lowered his eyes, clamping onto the edge of the table to steady himself. "I was, last night. Just a little hung over now, boss. Kyle and I were celebrating…"

"You fucking idiots!" Graves was on his feet. The six foot six black man towered over the five foot nothing Trent. Graves grabbed the smaller man by the front of his flight suit and lifted him from his seat, bringing their faces within a few inches of each other. "Goddamned kids and your moonshine! I should snap your neck right here and now!" he shook Trent, causing his head to wobble back and forth.

"Graves! Stand down! Now!" Fletcher stepped forward, placing a hand on the big man's arm and pushing it downward. "We can settle this later!"

Graves growled in frustration, but dropped Trent, who landed awkwardly atop his stool before tumbling the rest of the way to the floor. He remained there, eyes closed and tears forming as he covered his face with his hands.

"I'm sorry, alright? I know we screwed up! I'm sorry!"

"Shut up and take your seat." Fletcher ordered, pushing Graves back toward his own place at the table. "We don't have time for this shit." Turning to Lissa, she asked, "What's the catch?"

Lissa grimaced, her brows knitting together as she bit her bottom lip for a moment.

"The Delta sites are… less desirable. They're ones we eliminated in the last round before we selected the Alpha through Gamma sites."

"Why were they eliminated?" Chin asked.

"Different reasons. As you know, our survival down there is going to depend on several factors. Shelter from the massive windstorms that blast across the planet's surface. Enough sunlight to power the solar panels, a safe landing zone for our mission and all the others to follow, etc. But the most important factor is access to the subsurface ice, which we need for drinking water, oxygen, and hydrogen to fuel the generators and recharge the power cells." She watched the others nod as she spoke. All of them were familiar with the basic mission requirements.

"Well, in the case of Delta Seven, it checks all the boxes except the ice." She zoomed in on the orange dot, showing them a plateau with a nice flat landing zone, a nearby deep canyon at the bottom of a gentle slope. "Our satellites couldn't get a good angle down into the canyon, and the rock in the area is extremely dense, so we aren't one hundred percent sure about the ice. We know that there's *some* ice down there, probably quite a bit. But we don't know if there's enough to sustain us for the full term of the mission."

Fletcher looked at all the faces at the table. Most were thoughtful, except Trent, who just looked miserable, having sunk into himself and zoned out.

"Skippy, assume target site is Delta Seven. How long till we need to launch?"

"*Eighteen minutes, Commander.*"

"Alright. So here are our three options. We drop in a few minutes, take our chances with Delta Seven, an easy landing. We wait several hours, taking the risk of additional malfunctions and losses up here, then attempt a long ground transport to one of the better sites. Or we abort mission now, repair the *Hyperion* as best we can, and head home." She looked around. "Anybody have anything to add?"

All the heads at the table shook *no*.

"One last question. Assuming we go with Delta Seven and get set up there. If there isn't enough water to complete the full mission, can we still move to one of the other sites?"

Volkov and Chin looked at each other, put their heads together for a moment and spoke quietly. Chin did some calculations while Volkov looked up something in his wrist pad's database. He asked Lissa, "How far from Delta Seven to the nearest better site?"

Lissa manipulated the display, then marked one of the Gamma sites. Skippy helpfully supplied the distance of seven hundred thirty miles. The map showed no mountain ranges or serious obstacles between them. Chin and Volkov mumbled some more.

The others waited impatiently for a couple of minutes before the Russian raised his head. "Da. If we set up at Delta Seven, get the generators going, harvest enough ice to replenish our oxygen reserves and hydrogen fuel cells, we could maybe pull off a relocation in two or three stages. It would not be easy, and would be dangerous. But not impossible."

That was all Fletcher needed to hear.

“Alright, that settles it. Delta Seven it is. Skippy, do the math for us. Everyone to your tanks. We drop in about ten minutes.”

The crew all got to their feet and moved quickly toward the launch bays. Fletcher brought up the rear, walking behind a still sullen and shuffling Trent. She pushed him between the shoulder blades, urging him to pick up his pace. “Move it, Trent. You can bitch and moan later. This isn’t some game where you just failed a quest or some pug just ninja’d your loot. This is life or death. Get your shit together and move!”

Trent picked up his pace to a jog, catching up to the others with Fletcher right behind him. When each of them reached their launch bay, they peeled off through the bulkhead hatches, closing each one tightly behind them.

Fletcher watched to make sure all the hatches were secure, their indicator lights going green, before stepping through and securing her own hatch. Turning to face the bay, she stared for a moment at her tank.

The vehicles they affectionately called tanks were their surface rovers. Each one was enormous, about the size of an Abrams tank, hence the name. They had six massive wheels made of a tough composite designed to hold up on the rough terrain of Mars’ surface. Inside was a pair of seats for pilot and copilot, as well as a large cabin capable of carrying several passengers, or a significant amount of cargo. Each one had its own oxygen and water tanks, a microwave for heating ration packets, and even a small head for waste disposal and hygiene. There were various configurations among the ten vehicles, each designed to serve a different purpose. Two of them featured extendable crane arms that could be used to lift and load heavy items, one carried an extendable backhoe arm that looked a little like a scorpion's tail, as well as a dozer blade that could be mounted to the front. Another featured a massive jackhammer and drilling arm on the front.

Fletcher's tank was command and control, though none of its components were currently visible. Once they'd landed, she would break out the communications array and solar panels that could quickly be mounted on the exterior, as well as the standard sensor and video arrays they would each be mounting on their tanks. All equipment that wasn't hardy enough to survive the planetfall was stored inside the vehicles.

Walking up the ramp at the rear of the tank, she punched the button that raised it up behind her, closing and sealing the back wall of the tank. Sitting in the pilot's seat, she activated the ignition and studied the display, seeing all systems showing green. She took a minute to send a message back to Earth.

"Control, this is Hyperion. The blast sent us off course, making Alpha site unreachable. Based on our modified orbit, we've chosen to attempt landing at site Delta Seven. Launching in a few minutes. We are minus one crew, Kyle blew himself up along with half of our oxygen supply. Damage is minimal, hull breach temporarily repaired. Skippy is making more permanent repairs, and will pilot Kyle's tank down to our site on his second orbit. Wish us luck!" Tapping the coms unit in her ear, she called out, "This is tank 1. Report!"

"Tank 2, good to go." Her copilot and second in command, Lazar, confirmed.

"Tank 3, ready to launch."

"Tank 5, green n ready." Fletcher winced at the jump in numbers. Kyle had been assigned tank 4, and was no longer with them. As the others all reported in, she checked in with their AI.

"Skippy, would you be able to remote pilot tank 4 along with the hab?"

"*There is a seventy eight percent likelihood that I can successfully pilot both vessels simultaneously." Skippy replied. "However, if it is all the same to you, Commander, I would prefer to pilot just the hab module now, and drop tank four on my next pass over your landing site. That would be in approximately twelve point three hours, or one half sol.*"

Sol was their term for a single Martian day, which was slightly longer than a day on Earth. Skippy continued. "*By piloting one at a time, the odds of a successful landing increase to eighty nine point nine percent for each vessel.*"

"Alright, one at a time it is, Skippy. We can wait half a day for Kyle's tank." She smiled at the console in front of her. "Thank you, Skippy. For everything. We couldn't have done any of this without you. I'm officially designating you the *Hyperion* Crew MVP."

"Thank you Commander. And good luck. I'll speak to you again when you've landed. Launch in sixty seconds."

Fletcher activated her coms again. "Alright everyone, less than a minute. Strap yourselves in, and take a deep breath. You all know how to do this. Just trust in your training, and focus on a safe landing." She grinned for a moment. "And I hope you all remembered to hit the head before we drop!"

A few chuckles echoed back through the coms, the old joke relieving a bit of the crew's stress.

"I expect to see you all safely on the ground in ten minutes or so. We're all about to be Martians!" This time she was answered with cheers from the crew. Coms went silent as the last few seconds counted down. When her display reached zero, the floor underneath her tank opened up, and she dropped into the void of space.

Chapter Two

It's Not the Fall, It's the Landing

Lissa's stomach tried to rise up through her throat as her tank dropped out of its bay. It felt different than the simulations, in part because they were already closer to the planet than they had planned, and thus more heavily influenced by Mars gravity right off the bat. She wasn't good with the physics, but she knew in a general sense that they weren't falling straight down. The *Hyperion* had been moving at a high rate of speed around the planet, so she and her crew in their tanks were being sort of sling-shotted toward their target on the surface.

Forward progress would be slowed by the planet's atmosphere, and gravity, and eventually even by the surface winds as they got closer to the ground and their downward speed increased. Surface winds on Mars could be brutal. There were near constant mild winds of up to twenty mph across the globe, but there were also frequent storms that blew at wind speeds of over one hundred mph, kicking up massive dust storms in their path. At least their scans right before the drop didn't show in storms near their new landing zone.

Ten seconds after the initial drop, Lissa felt the vibration of the tank's 'drop armor' shifting into place. It was basically a massive geodesic frame that snapped into place around the vehicle, making it look like a lopsided golf ball. The armor was disposable, a ceramic composite designed solely to fend off the nearly four thousand degree heat that would build up around it as she entered the planet's atmosphere.

Sitting in her pilot's seat, she looked out the thick windshield at the interior of the armor grid. No light shone through anywhere, which she took as a good sign. Entering the atmosphere was the second most dangerous phase of the landing. Any gap in the armor could result in a catastrophic failure that would end with her roasting inside a molten vehicle before impacting the surface at terminal velocity.

She took a few deep breaths, calming herself while watching through the windshield as the ceramic shield begin to glow a faint red. Over the next minute and a half, that glow grew brighter, from a deep red to a lighter orange. She felt like a chick being hard boiled inside her ceramic egg. The tank shook slightly, most of the motion from the turbulence of entry being absorbed by the grid girders that connected the shield to the body of the tank. They had been designed to shift and flex for exactly that reason. Control didn't want their crew too shaken and bruised to function once they landed.

Soon enough, the glow of heat began to fade from the shield, and she let out a breath she hadn't realized she'd been holding. A moment later, the ceramic pieces at the top of the tank broke away as a thick mylar parachute was deployed. Instantly, her descent slowed, and the remainder of the shield and its supports dropped away, the clamps released by a program triggered by a combination of heat sensors and altimeter. As the shield cleared her field of view, Lissa gasped in wonder. Stretched out before her was the beautiful, glorious, red-tinged surface of Mars! Still about ten miles up, she had a while to appreciate the views as she drifted downward under the massive parachute. As a geologist, she had spent most of her career studying the ground below her. Soil samples, satellite scans, even the old *Voyager* and other satellite photos. She was one of the world's leading experts on the geology and geography of Mars, the one the folks at Control had chosen to help them conquer a new world.

It was a huge responsibility.

But for now, all she could think of was how barren and beautiful the surface was. She knew it was deadly cold out there, something like seventy five degrees below zero. Which reminded her. The first most dangerous part of this process, even more dangerous than entering the atmosphere, was about to happen. The landing.

She reached toward her chest and pressed the button that activated her helmet, which sprang up around her head, ending with a clear plastic face plate that allowed her to see approximately two hundred and forty degrees in front of and on either side of her. Human eyes could only cover about one hundred and eighty degrees on their own, but the helmet allowed her to shift her head slightly to either side, giving her the extra view. If she wanted, she could activate a tiny camera mounted in the back of her collar that would allow her to see behind herself as well.

Lissa stared through her faceplate at the console in front of her. Her lights were all green, and the altimeter was showing that she was falling at an acceptable rate. The massive chute above her was doing its job just as designed.

"Report!" Fletcher's voice echoed inside her helmet. One by one she and her fellow crewmembers reported their altitude and speed. Everyone was within safe parameters, which allowed Lissa to relax a little bit more. The crew had a pool going, a morbid sort of betting, on whether any of them would bite it during the landing, and who it would be. Though it would have seemed callous and creepy to outsiders, that sort of gallows humor helped the crew deal with the stress of their long journey and dangerous mission.

Moments later Lissa nearly bit her tongue as the tank impacted the ground. A cloud of dust rose up to obscure her view as the vehicle's shocks absorbed most of the impact. She didn't hear anything break, and her sensor board was still all green. Letting out a sigh of relief, she triggered her coms. "Tank 8, down and safe."

The others were all chiming in, one by one as Lissa's windshield went dark. "Damn. It figures it would happen to me." She triggered her coms again. "Tank 8, my chute just covered me. Going EVA to pull it off." The chutes were supposed to automatically disconnect the moment the vehicle touched down, and the Martian wind should have pushed it clear of her tank. It wasn't a big deal, just inconvenient.

Unbuckling her harness, she got to her feet and walked toward the back of the vehicle, inching sideways along the narrow aisle left between the stacks of cargo. She heard Fletcher reply "Roger that, be careful, 8." as she hit the button to open the airlock door. There was a small airlock at the back of the vehicle, just large enough for two humans to stand side by side as the air was pumped into, or out of, the closet-sized chamber. She stepped inside and sealed the hatch behind her, then hit a red button. The air was quickly sucked from the space, and a green light showed next to the outer door. She punched the button with one thickly gloved hand, and the ramp lowered in front of her.

Ten seconds later, Lissa became the first human to walk upon the surface of Mars.

Each of them had considered what they might say if they were the first. All of them wanted to utter words worthy of the gravity of the event, no pun intended. Taking a deep breath, Lissa keyed her coms again, waiting a moment to check her HUD to make sure she was being recorded, then spoke.

"People of Mars, we come in peace." She grinned as she spoke the words, sure that the folks at Control were going to be very angry in about twelve minutes, when they received the transmission. But Lissa was a rebel, and she was pretty sure most of the world would understand. Still, her next words were more appropriate.

"We have journeyed far, and risked much, in the hope of exploring a new world. All of Earth has come together to bring us here, a grand achievement in and of itself. May we prove ourselves worthy of the challenge."

There was silence for several seconds as the others absorbed her words. As she reached upward to grab hold of the offending parachute, Fletcher's voice reached her ears. "Well done, Lissa. And congratulations. You're the very first Martian settler from Earth."

"As far as we know." Graves added. "You don't know, we might bump into some elderly Russian Cosmonaut living in a cave eating fungus or something."

The others chuckled, and Lissa smiled. "You're just jealous, Graves."

"Damn right I am! You know how many ladies would want a piece of the first man on Mars? You might have just kept me from meeting the future Mrs. Graves."

"My sincerest apologies. Didn't mean to cramp your style." Lissa tugged at the chute again, pulling it free of the antenna base it was snagged on. She quickly rolled it up, thinking to take it with her. It might make a nice hammock or something. Or she could take it back to Earth someday and sell it for a bazillion dollars. Assuming the others' chutes all drifted away in the wind.

She took a look around. Her tank sat on a wide open and reasonably flat plain. She could already see two of the other tanks off in the distance. The unfortunate thing about parachuting down the last twenty miles or so, was that there was no fine control over where you'd land. The rovers could be spread out over several miles.

Pulling up a checklist on her wrist pad, which was now affixed to the outside of her suit, she began checking over her rover and ticking items off the list. She checked the wheels, axles, looked for any broken or missing exterior components, any cracks in the windshield, and a few dozen other things. Satisfied that her tank had survived intact, she walked back up the ramp and closed it behind her. After cycling back through the airlock, she stowed her parachute atop a pile of crates and retook her seat. A push of the button and her helmet retracted, and she took a deep breath. While she could tolerate operating for long periods of time inside the helmet, she felt better without it.

"Tank 8, clean and green. No damage detected." She reported.

"Copy that, 8. Same here." Fletcher replied. The others all gave similar reports over the next five minutes, except for Trent.

"Minor damage to my central axle." He reported. "Just a scrape, I landed on a rock. The axle doesn't look bent, or compromised. I'll monitor it as I move."

"Don't move, let me come to you." Graves called out. "You don't want to do more damage getting off that rock. Just sit tight. I'm two miles away."

Each of their suits held a locator beacon, as did their vehicles. A quick glance at her console showed Lissa that Trent's tank was behind her and about a mile to the west, while Graves was about the same distance to her east. A quick count showed blips for all nine rovers within a five mile radius. Considering they'd been shot out of a moving spaceship more than a hundred miles out into space, then drifted down the last twenty miles at the mercy of the Martian winds, that was an excellent grouping!

Even better, the hab module, which Skippy had ejected a minute before they'd all launched, had landed between them and the Delta Seven location. Pinching her fingers on the screen, she zoomed her map out far enough to see where they were in relation to Delta Seven. It sat less than a mile from the slope that led down into the canyon where they hoped to make their new home. Or, at least, their temporary camp.

That all depended on the water down there.

"Skippy, if you can hear me, you are the man!" Lissa called out. "The hab is right where we need it. Rawr!"

The *Hyperion*'s AI didn't answer, as he was currently beyond the horizon on his way around the planet, and out of standard coms range. Once they set up Fletcher's more powerful coms array, they'd be able to talk to Skippy anywhere in his orbit, and relay messages back to Earth.

Fletcher called out. "Graves, you need any help with Trent's tank?"

"Nope. Worst case I'll use my crane to lift it up off the rock if necessary. Might do that anyway, just to get a better look at the axle. If we need to replace it, he's got his spares. Won't take but an hour, tops." Each vehicle carried a multitude of replacement parts in case of breakdown. Others were in the cargo pods that were dropped along with the hab unit.

"Right. Then the rest of you, rally on my position. We'll proceed directly to the hab first. Do a quick inspection. Then Lissa, Trent, and I will move into the canyon if we can find a drivable path down. If we're lucky, we can get some soil, rock, and water samples before we call it a day."

Lissa cranked up her rover and used the map on her console to get her bearings. She could simply mark Fletcher's location on the map and engage her autopilot, and the tank would drive itself there. But she wanted to drive it herself. Piloting the vehicle was a great way to unwind after the long journey and stress-filled morning. She pressed the accelerator, bringing the rover up to a modest twenty mph, and turned it toward their rally point. A few moments later she waved at Graves as they passed each other. He smiled back and gave her a thumbs-up.

*****

Trent was miserable, standing near his rover and trembling slightly inside his suit as he waited for Graves to arrive. He was half afraid the big man was going to simply snap his neck, or otherwise end his existence, while everyone else was miles away.

Not that he would blame Graves in the least. Kyle was dead, and the others were all at risk now, all because of him. It had been his idea to build the still. He and Kyle had been in their lab, commiserating about the lack of female companionship and alcohol just a month into their voyage. The two men, both in their twenties, had been swapping stories about the epic send-off parties their friends and colleagues had thrown for them.

"I was so drunk by the end of the night, I hit on my dad's third wife right in front of him. I didn't even recognize her. Or him. All I saw was a blurry female-shaped body with curves in the right places. If there hadn't been press nearby, I think my dad would have knocked me out cold." Kyle hung his head in mock shame.

"Too bad we don't have any booze on this tub." Trent had commiserated. "Just, you know, for celebrating birthdays or important events."

"Yeah, I'd settle for flavored rubbing alcohol at this point." Kyle sighed. "Anything to cut the stress a little bit. We've still got *six more months* before we even reach Mars. Then three or four *years* of abstinence and teetotalism before we rotate back to Earth. I'm already regretting my decision to join up."

"Well, you know… it wouldn't be that hard to build a still here on the ship. I mean, all the components we need are in the cargo bay. And we can steal some potatoes or corn from hydroponics."

They'd laughed off the idea that night, but over the next few weeks they'd returned to the subject again and again, until they convinced themselves it would be a fun and harmless project to help fill their free time. They'd needed to wait a bit for the crops that were planted just before their departure to mature, but that didn't deter them. By the end of their second month in space, the two of them had a working still that produced small quantities of hooch each week.

They hadn't kept it a secret, and had in fact shared their product with several of the crew. Commander Fletcher pretended not to know about it, deciding to allow them to keep it in the interests of crew morale.

Everything had gone smoothly until they'd reached Mars orbit, and the two young men had decided to celebrate. One last batch to consume before they launched themselves in flying tanks toward the surface of the red planet. They'd picked a quiet corner and consumed a full quart of their moonshine before Kyle got the bright idea to break down the still and stow it in among their gear so that they could reinstall it down on the planet.

Trent had been against it, concerned that the extra weight might compromise their carefully planned flight trajectories. But Kyle had pushed, and pushed again, his drunken logic making him more and more sure of himself. Finally, unable to convince Trent, Kyle had stumbled off on his own to break down the still and pack it away.

It was less than twenty minutes later that an explosion rocked the ship, and alarms started going off.

Now Kyle was dead, and Trent knew the others blamed him. It was foolish to put the mission, and their lives, at risk for a little drunken fun. Trent knew it, and the guilt nearly crushed his spirit as Graves' rover pulled to a halt alongside his. It took a few moments for the man to cycle through his own airlock, then he emerged carrying a thick insulation pad in one hand, and a flashlight in the other. Trent took a frightened step back as the man approached, a grim look on his face.

"Relax, kid. I'm not gonna hurt you. I'm gonna make sure the whole world knows what a dumbass you are, and I hope they throw you in a tiny jail cell somewhere deep underground when you've finished your job here. But for now, we need you to do your thing. So step aside and let me get a look under your girl here."

Graves bent and placed the soft pad under the rover between the first and second wheels, then gingerly got down on one knee and crawled underneath, the pad keeping any sharp stone fragments from puncturing his suit. Shifting onto his side, he shined the light up at the axle, inspecting it carefully. "Push the tire, turn the wheel a bit." he called out to Trent, who quickly obliged. Even though it was slightly off the ground, it took all his strength to move the giant wheel that weighed more than he did. After another minute, Graves crawled back out. "I think you're right. It's just scratched, no dents or bends that I can see. Should work fine at least long enough to get you to the hab. But I'll follow you, and you let me know if you hear anything unusual. Any rubbing, grinding, or if you feel a wobble in the wheel or throttle. Got it?"

"Y-yes sir. I'll pay close attention. Thank you for checking it out."

Graves didn't speak another word, simply grabbed his pad, shook it out, and returned to his tank. Trent, relieved but not feeling all that much better about himself, shuffled back into his rover with his head down, and headed toward the rendezvous at a slow and careful speed, keeping a wary eye out for large rocks or deep potholes.

*****

When the two stragglers caught up to the others, they were already finished with their inspection of the hab module. The outer casing was undamaged, with no dents and only a few scrapes from its landing. That was a good indicator that the contents inside remained intact. The container was huge, more than a hundred feet long and twenty feet wide. Inside it was the basic structure of the habitat module that the nine of them would be living inside for the next several months. Three of the six massive cargo pods were within sight of the hab. Locators for the other three blinked nearby, one of them seeming to have actually landed within the canyon they were about to explore.

The heavy and heavily armored pods would have to wait until the crew had unloaded their rovers before they were retrieved. They were safe enough where they were, even if a sandstorm blew up. The locators were strong enough to transmit through any amount of sand a storm might deposit over top of them.

"We're going to head down and see if there's a clear path to the bottom. You guys cluster up, two groups of three, and get ready to settle in for the night. If we're not back by dark, we'll do the same down there, and meet back up here in the morning." Fletcher ordered. The tanks were designed so that they could park back to back and run an accordion-like, semi-rigid connector shaft that connected the two vehicles, looking much like an airport gangway. The structures were airtight, allowing the occupants to stretch out a little bit and share oxygen or supplies without wearing their suits. The junctions could be further modified for three or four vehicles at once.

"Lissa, you're the rock and terrain expert. You lead the way. If you see something in our path that concerns you even a little bit, stop and we can talk it over. Time is a factor, but we're not going to rush and get somebody hurt."

Lissa nodded through her windshield at Fletcher, and turned her rover toward the downward slope that would lead them into the canyon. As they moved, she studied the satellite feeds, zooming in until she could make out individual stones the size of baseballs on the slope ahead of them. Changing the viewing angle, she identified a likely downward path that she could make out the first few hundred feet of, before it faded away into shadow.

Their scans from a year ago had shown that the canyon was half a mile deep, at least. The rock on either side was dense, and presumably stable, barring any strong tectonic upheavals. The plan was to find an underground location, ideally a cavern or a deep canyon that would be mostly protected from the violent windstorms and the solar radiation. While not deadly in the short term, extended exposure to the radiation over a period of years would bring about serious health issues. Mars didn't have the same atmosphere or magnetosphere that protected the flora and fauna on Earth.

The other reason for being underground was simple. That's where the water was. Surface water on Mars quickly evaporated. But Mars was a cold planet. The reason it had no atmosphere was because the molten iron core that once spun within the center of the planet, much like Earth's core, had cooled and slowed until the magnetic field it created had faded away. Without that field, the Martian atmosphere bled away, leaving the cold, mostly dead rock that the humans now found themselves on. Multitudes of scans over the years had revealed the existence of underground layers of ice, from the size of small lakes to what might be vast frozen oceans deep below the surface. This ice could be harvested, broken down into its molecular components, and used to keep the humans alive. Oxygen atoms for breathable air, hydrogen for power. Even the remaining Martian air, which was mostly carbon dioxide, could be harvested for oxygen and carbon molecules.

NASA, or DARPA, or one of the agencies (Lissa wasn't sure which) had developed a machine that could separate and condense the carbon molecules into a usable building material. They connected those machines, of which they carried three to the surface with them, to massive 3D printers that could produce building blocks, tools, replacement parts, all made of high-tensile strength carbon that was stronger and lighter than steel. Hydrogen fuel generators, one of the greatest inventions of the twenty first century, allowed mankind to make use of the most common and abundantly available element in the universe to create power. It was efficient, clean, and quiet.

In addition, another much smaller machine used the carbon molecules, combined with other elements like gold, platinum, tungsten, and copper, to create tiny robots called nanobots. These could be programmed to perform numerous tasks, from breaking down trash and debris to using those same materials to repair simple systems.

In short, with a sufficient supply of ice on hand, the adventurous crew could build, power, and expand their operation indefinitely. At least, they could until they ran out of materials they couldn't harvest on Mars. But Control had already anticipated those needs, and had scheduled more missions that would bring to Mars more people and needed supplies every few months for the next year. Part of Lissa's job was to scout locations where subsequent crews might mine some of those rare metals.

Lissa's chosen path brought them to the edge of the canyon without any trouble. She took a moment to stop and get her bearings, comparing the formations ahead of her to the scans on her console. When she was sure she'd identified their exact location, she called Fletcher. "We're about a quarter mile from what looks like a promising access point. I'm going to take it slower from here. Don't drive too close to the edge. Just follow my tracks"

"Roger that." Fletcher and Trent both answered. Turning her rover to run parallel to the cliff edge, she followed her own advice and stayed a good hundred feet back from the drop-off. Only when she spotted the hoped-for down-ramp ahead did she move closer to the edge. Again she called the boss.

"You two wait here. If there's a weak spot, no sense in all of us taking a dive. I'll patch you into my video feed so you can watch." She pressed a button to transmit the combined feed from the four forward-facing cameras on the front and top of her tank.

"Be careful, Lissa. You're our only rock and ice lady. If you plunge a thousand feet to your death, the rest of us have to sit here and twiddle our thumbs for three months till our ride home arrives." Lissa could hear the smile on Fletcher's face as she spoke.

"Roger that. Try not to die to the elevator boss. I hear ya." Lissa saluted in Fletcher's general direction before putting her rover back into first gear and creeping forward.

She was only about two hundred feet down the ramp when the sunlight faded, having moved into the shadow of the cliff. She flipped on her lights, eight of them brightly illuminating the path ahead. It was more than wide enough to accommodate the tank, so far. Maybe even wide enough to allow two tanks to pass by each other, at least in a few places. A quarter mile down she had to slow and make a sharp turn on a switchback that turned and headed back in the opposite direction. This was concerning, as it might be a tight turn for the long hab module. She'd leave the details to the engineers, the math guys.

Moving slowly and carefully, it took her nearly an hour to reach the halfway mark down the canyon wall. From what she could tell, it was deeper than they had estimated based on their limited scans. But what she discovered at that point made her forget completely about the bottom.

To her left, opening right onto the path ahead of her, was a massive cave entrance.

Crossing her fingers, she spoke into her coms. "Are you guys seeing this?"

"Hell yes, we are!" Graves shouted loud enough to make her wince. "Can you say *Captain Caaaaaaaveman*!?" The others laughed or snorted, some offering encouraging words.

"Headed in to check it out." Lissa inched forward until she was even with the cave's mouth, turning her vehicle so that the lights pointed into it, the bright beams illuminating deep into the cave.

Correction. Cavern. The opening in the cliff face was maybe forty feet wide and fifty feet tall. But after a short distance it opened up to several times that size. She could hear the others whooping and celebrating as they picked up her feed. Driving into the entrance, she noted several large rocks and a few stalagmites that would have to be moved to allow easier access. But for now, she was able to squeeze between and weave her way through to the larger open area. She made a slow right turn to face the nearest wall, her lights reflecting off sparkling bedrock. Then she moved forward slowly, making a gradual left turn and panning her lights across the space until they struck the far left side of the entrance.

In all, the space was more than large enough to accommodate their hab, along with several expansions. The cavern floor was reasonably flat, and they could use the dozer tank to level it out even more. Her console display told her that she was nearly half a mile below the surface, the bedrock above more than sufficient to reduce radiation levels.

The one thing she didn't see, though… ice.

The walls sparkled in her headlights, but the sharp refractions suggested some type of quartz or other reflective mineral, rather than frozen water. Still, Lissa wasn't ready to give up. "I'm going to get out and examine these walls more carefully, boss. You guys can come on down if you want. There's more than enough room to set up in here for the night. If we don't find ice here, we can continue down in the morning.

"Copy that. We're on our way. Trent, follow me. Stay fifty yards behind me. And be careful on that switchback. Down here, speed kills."

"Understood, boss. Right behind you." Trent replied, his tone neutral.

As the crew up top finished connecting their two clusters of tanks, and Fletcher led Trent down the incline at a snail's pace, Lissa activated her helmet and prepared to exit her rover. She grabbed a bag from a cabinet near the airlock. It contained a flashlight, an XRF scanner – a handheld x-ray gun that could identify the elements within whatever material she pointed it at - a small hammer, mining pick, sample containers, a bottle of pure water, and assorted other tools she might need in her examination of the walls.

Taking a few deep breaths to calm her racing heart, she stepped into the airlock and closed the hatch.

Chapter Three

Funky Spelunking

Before exiting her tank, Lissa had activated all the exterior lights available on the vehicle. Now, standing at the bottom of the ramp, she turned a full circle, taking in the sights. The cavern was breathtaking, walls, floor, and ceiling sparkling all around her like the billions of stars in space.

Approaching the nearest wall, she activated the camera and light atop her helmet, meaning to record everything for the folks back on Earth. The wall was mostly smooth, with slight, rounded vertical ridges that looked almost as if the rock had at one time been liquified, melting down the surface in long rivulets. More likely the ridges were mineral deposits left behind by millennia of water running down the walls from above. Lissa took this as a good sign. If there had been water here for so long, it may still be nearby.

This thought caused her to focus on the floor. She scanned the line where the wall met the stone floor, and found small gaps running parallel to the joint. She imagined water sheeting down the wall to puddle on the cavern floor, where it eventually drained through those gaps to what might have been an underground river or lake.

Returning her attention to the wall in front of her, she ran her gloved hand across several of the ridges. The surface continued to sparkle in the artificial light from her suit and her rover. On impulse, she produced the small pick hammer from her bag and tapped at the wall. Intrigued by what she heard, she reversed the tool and used the pick side to chip away at the stone around one of the sparkly bits at eye level.

A few minutes later she laughed out loud, staring at the item in the palm of her glove.

It was a diamond. A diamond about half the size of a corn kernel, with a slight red tinge to it. The gem appeared slick, as if wet, though it left no water marks on her glove as she moved it around with one finger. It was almost as if the diamond was coated in oil of some kind, but when she wiped at it, the substance didn't transfer to her glove, nor was it removed from the gem's surface.

"Strange." She muttered to herself, wiping at it again. "Maybe it's just a trick of the light." Lissa produced a vial used for soil samples and dropped the gem inside. For good measure, she spent the next half hour gathering several more, all of which featured that same odd sheen. The last one she chipped away at didn't easily break free like the others. Instead, as she removed the surrounding rock, it got larger. After ten minutes of careful pick work, the gem finally dislodged from the wall. It was the size of a golf ball!

"I'm naming you the Castle Diamond." She crooned at the heavy gem in her hand. "Because when I get back to Earth, that's what you're going to buy me. My own castle, on my own private island." Looking up, she took in the millions of sparkling points around the cavern. "Then again, maybe not. Mars might just ruin the diamond market. You might end up being a very pretty paperweight." She dropped the gem into her bag along with the vial of smaller diamonds.

Lissa continued her examination of the walls and floor as she made her way around the cavern. Using a simple laser measuring tool, she determined that the cavern was three hundred feet deep from front to back, and two hundred feet wide in the center, the total area being almost an acre and a half. The ceiling was fifty feet, or roughly five stories above them, and was littered with stalactites. Further evidence that the chamber was either formed by water, or at least contained some water for a very long time.

She was just finishing up jotting down some notes when the other two tanks arrived. Fletcher and Trent wove their way into the cavern just as she had, then maneuvered their rovers so that they were back to back with each other, right next to and perpendicular to hers. This was to accommodate their cluster setup later.

Both ramps lowered at about the same time, and her fellow crewmen joined her, their eyes wide as the additional lights from their vehicles increased the reflections off the walls. "It's… beautiful." Fletcher was the first to speak.

"Plenty of room in here." Trent was all business. "Have you found ice?"

Lissa shook her head. "Not yet. It looks like there was an abundance of water here at one time. My hope is that it drained to a river or lake below us before freezing. We'll likely have to drill for it. Or maybe follow it further down into the canyon."

Fletcher nodded her head at the information, but was still gazing at the sparkling walls. "Is that… quartz?"

"Some of it might be. But at least some of it, maybe most of it, is diamonds." Lissa produced the vial of smaller gems and handed it over. Trent stepped closer, suddenly interested as Fletcher held the vial up to the light and shook it a few times. Lissa grinned as she watched their thought processes change the expressions on their faces. The grin turned into a chuckle as both of them raised their eyes to the multitude of sparkly bits on the walls and ceiling. "Yeah… I thought the same thing." She shook her head.

"So… obviously we're calling this place Crystal Cavern." Fletcher held out her arms and spun around, taking it all in. "Leave it to you, Lissa, to find us a bedazzled cave to set up shop in!"

Lissa groaned. The crew had teased her quite often during their trip over one of the personal items she'd brought along. It was a battered and frayed denim backpack, one she'd carried all through her high school and college years. Before she left on their mission, her young niece had bedazzled a crude rocket ship, several stars, and a red planet onto the flap.

"I'm not sure this will be our base, yet. Still need to locate an ice supply and figure out the logistics of harvest and transport. But yeah, not a bad place to spend the night, right?"

The three of them got to work extending and connecting their three accordion shafts to a taller hub module in the center. The two clusters up top didn't use this, as it was vulnerable to sudden windstorms. But down here in the protected cavern, Fletcher deemed it safe enough. And it allowed them room to assemble cots and a small table with folding stools for dining. Once everything was set up and secured, the airtight seals confirmed, they each opened their tank's airlock and allowed the new structure to be filled with oxygen. Deactivating their helmets, they took seats at the table and shared a dinner of freeze-dried rations. Eating mostly in silence, the excitement of the day was wearing off, and all three of them were feeling the need for sleep.

The meal finished, Lissa produced the vial of diamonds again. Pulling the stopper, she poured them out onto the stainless metal table. All three of them leaned in closer, examining the stones. "What… is that?" Trent was the first to ask, referring to the odd liquid sheen on the surface of the gems.

"Don't know yet, but it's weird, right?" Lissa removed one glove, earning a raised eyebrow from Fletcher at the breach of safety protocols. But the Commander didn't stop her, so Lissa reached out with a finger to touch the nearest gem. "It doesn't *feel* wet…" She picked the small stone up with a finger and thumb, then rubbed at the surface with her thumb, using a little more force. "It doesn't rub off. Can't even feel it, really. Maybe it's on the inside? Some unique aspect of the gems' formation?"

"You're the rock lady, you tell us." Trent removed one of his gloves and mimicked Lissa's actions. After a moment, Fletcher did the same.

"These things are… attractive." Fletcher mumbled.

"Girls and their diamonds." Trent snorted.

"No, not like that." Fletcher shook her head, staring at the gem she held, rubbing her thumb over it. "I mean, yes, like that… but more. Like, the moment I saw them, I was itching to hold one, to touch it. And now that I'm touching it, I… this is going to sound odd. I kind of want to eat it."

Both the others froze, their eyes moving from the gems to Fletcher. "Uh, yeah. Now that you mention it, I sort of have the same urge." Trent stared at his own gem, then quickly set it down. "That can't be a coincidence, right? I mean, I've never had the urge to lick a diamond on Earth. Lissa, are you feeling it too?"

"I am." Lissa was back to staring at her own gem now. "It's not… It's not a powerful urge or anything. But yes, I feel what you guys feel. Some kind of attraction…" her voice faded away as her pulse rate quickened.

They'd been trained for this. There were scores, maybe hundreds of protocols about isolation and contamination prevention. None of the samples brought back by probes had given any indication that there were harmful bacteria or viruses in the soil or the air of Mars.

But they'd only tested a minute range of soils, all from on or near the planet's surface. The crew had all been warned, threatened, scared, and ordered against any direct contact with any outside materials that hadn't been sterilized first.

Yet all three of them, including the mission's Commander, whose job it was to enforce the rules and ensure the others followed protocols, had carelessly disregarded those procedures and touched the Martian diamonds with their bare skin on day one.

Feeling more tired by the moment, the three of them retired to their cots. Fletcher barely remembered to set the proximity sensors and alarms before rolling onto her side and closing her eyes. Lissa lowered the lights before crawling into her own bunk. Trent was already snoring.

None of the three realized they'd gone to bed still gripping a Martian diamond in one hand.

*****

"Fletcher! Commander Fletcher, are you there? Trent? Lissa? C'mon guys, this ain't funny. Commander Fletcher this is Chin. Please respond!"

Fletcher blinked her eyes a few times in the low light of the hub module. The voice in her earpiece made her head pound. Lifting one hand to rub at her face, she tried to speak, but only a croak emerged from her dry throat. She felt like she'd had a wild night of tequila and… MMA bouts, maybe? Why was her entire body sore?

"Commander Fletcher, this is Graves. Are y'all alive down there?"

She cleared her throat, built up a little saliva and swallowed before answering. "This is Fletcher. We're fine." She looked around, spotting Trent and Lissa still asleep on their cots. A quick check of her wrist pad showed that it was nearly 09:00 Mars time. They'd slept in! Their day's activities were scheduled to begin at 06:00.

"Thank god!" Chin's voice again. "We've been calling you for hours, Fletcher. What's going on down there?"

"Not sure. We seem to have overslept, all three of us. Might be something wrong with the oxygen mixture in one of our tanks, or something? I've got a killer headache, and I'm sore like I took a beat-down. Hold a minute while I wake the others." She got up slowly, feeling thirty years older than she was. All of her bones creaked, her muscles ached.

Dr. Clarke responded. "Roger that, Commander. I'm coming down to check all three of you out. In the meantime, get everyone into their suits. We know the air in there is clean."

Approaching Trent's cot, Fletcher replied, "Gonna need Chin or Volkov, maybe both, to check our air supplies. Might as well bring everyone down, actually. Even if we don't make camp in this cavern, it's a good staging area. We can unload everyone's tanks and begin shuttling down the cargo from the pods."

“On our way, Commander.” Volkov’s voice somehow contained a salute in its tone.

Fletcher reached down and shook Trent’s shoulder, hard. She was still pissed at the man for nearly killing them all, and if she was honest, angry with herself for not making them disassemble the still immediately. Her own lack of judgement was even more inexcusable than Trent and Kyle’s.

Trent groaned, his eyes opening briefly before he tried to roll over. Fletcher lifted one side of the cot, using his momentum to tip it in the direction he rolled, dumping him onto the floor. He yelped in surprise, then started cursing. Sure that he was awake now, Fletcher moved to wake Lissa. She needn’t have bothered, the commotion from Trent’s spill had woken her.

“What happened?” Lissa asked, sitting up slowly and rubbing her face. “I feel like I drank too much of Kyle’s moonshine.” She looked up at Fletcher, and seeing her flinch, her eyes widened as she realized what she’d said. “Ah, shit. Sorry.”

“I’m thinking maybe there’s an issue with our oxygen supply. Both of you, put on your gloves and activate your helmets. We’re gonna live on the air in our suits till the others have a chance to check our tanks.”

Lissa managed to stand, then moved on shaky legs toward the table where she’d left her gloves. Trent was just sitting upright, using the overturned cot to steady himself as he prepared to stand. Fletcher was already at the table, reaching for her own gloves when she froze.

There was a red mark on her left palm. Holding it in front of her face, she squinted at it. “What’s this? This wasn’t here yesterday.” She spoke aloud to herself, using her other thumb to rub at the mark, which had no effect.

Lissa, hearing her question, looked up. Seeing the mark on the other woman’s hand, she spoke the first words that popped into her mind. “Looks like you squeezed one of those diamonds too hard.” As she spoke, she looked down at the table, where they’d left the diamonds from the vial sitting out the night before. She blinked, then blinked again, taking a deep breath to clear her mind. “Some of the diamonds are missing. There were a dozen, now there are nine.”

“I… I think I had one of them.” Trent was on his feet now. “I think I was holding one when I laid down?” He opened both of his hands to find them empty, then began to search the floor around his cot, thinking he’d dropped it when he’d fallen.

“Trent, freeze.” Fletcher’s voice commanded from behind him. He held very still, waiting for her to explain. “Hold up your hand and look at it.” He did as he was told, and gasped, his eyes widening and mouth dropping open.

“Oh, shit. I have the same mark.” He turned and held his left palm up for both women to see. Fletcher copied his motion, showing both of them her similar marking.

Lissa instantly checked her own hands, and found the same.

“What the hell’s going on?” She started rubbing at the mark on her palm, the outline roughly the same shape as the stone she’d been holding the night before. When rubbing accomplished nothing, she began scratching at the skin, then pressing hard into it, half expecting to feel a diamond under her skin.

As if in answer to her question, her field of vision was suddenly filled with a series of six symbols. They were bright crimson red, and strange looking, like one of the alien languages one might see in sci fi movies. Panicking, she closed her eyes, then opened them again. She began to breathe more rapidly, and her pulse rate shot upward.

“Guys, I’m seeing… something.” She spoke quietly, doing her best not to scream.

“Same here. But I can’t read it.” Fletcher answered.

“Yeah, what the hell?” Trent was opening and closing his eyes, shaking his head violently as if to shake loose whatever it was.

Lissa stared at the symbols, and after several seconds, they morphed into letters and words she could read. The message now read,

Assimilation 28% Complete

Behind her, Trent was freaking out. “Oh, no. No, no, no!” He paced back and forth, now smacking the side of his head with one hand. “This isn’t real! I’m still asleep!”

"What the hell is this assimilation?" Fletcher growled, staring through the message at the mark on her palm. "What did those diamonds do to us?"

The moment she finished speaking the question, another message popped up for all three of them. Again it appeared in the alien language, but converted more quickly this time.

Voluntary assimilation process begun.
You have absorbed sufficient crystalized ambrosia to achieve 28% completion.
Obtain and absorb additional quantities to complete the process.

"Ambrosia?" Lissa asked out loud. "As in, food of the gods? That's just a friggin myth."

"Wake me up, somebody!" Trent was completely still now, standing in front of the table and staring down at the scattered diamonds. "Pinch me or something."

Out of pure spite, Fletcher reached out and slapped the man's face hard enough to turn his head. "You're not dreaming, Trent. Get your shit together."

Trent blinked a few times, rubbing his face and scowling at Fletcher. After a moment, he shook his head. "Sorry. This is just too freaky for me. How do we get this stuff out of us?" Can we like, cut it out?" He was reaching for a utility tool at his belt, one that included a small knife blade, when a third message popped up.

Once begun, voluntary assimilation process cannot be reversed.

Failure to complete the process constitutes a rejection of the favor
the gods have bestowed upon you.
Angering the gods can incur punishment, up to and including death.

"Lazar. You and the others hold where you are. I repeat, do not come down here. There's something… strange happening to us. We've been contaminated, and we're either hallucinating, or the shit has just hit the fan."

"Copy, boss. We hear you. Holding position near the top of the ramp." He paused, then asked, "What exactly is going on?"

"We're in a damned RPG sim, that's what!" Trent shouted, causing the coms to whine slightly at the increased volume. "I'm seeing friggin system notifications in front of my face!" He sat down on one of the stools, bent down and banged his forehead against the table. "Guys, tell me that's what this is. We're not really here, right? We're in some kind of cryo-sleep, and Skippy is guiding us through some new virtual game?"

Lissa and Fletcher both paused, mouths open, unsure what to say. Trent's idea was certainly more plausible than finding some kind of alien system on Mars.

Doctor Clarke's voice, calm and reassuring, came across coms. "What exactly are you seeing? And is it just Trent? Or are all three of you seeing the same thing?"

Lissa nodded to Fletcher, who replied, "We're all seeing the same thing, doc. And Trent's not wrong, we're seeing what I would call system messages in a VR game. They appeared in some kind of alien language first, then converted into English letters. It says we're partway through something called *Assimilation…*" She briefly updated them on Lissa's finding the diamonds, and the three of them each apparently absorbing one as they slept. Then she gave them a summary of the information in the messages.

"Holy shit." Chin's voice was excited. "Is Trent right? Did they put us in some kind of cryo-pods and we just don't remember?"

Fletcher simply wasn't sure. Her mind was having trouble reconciling what she thought she knew to be real, with the impossible situation she now faced. Was this a VR game being run by Skippy as they soared through space toward Mars? Were they even really aboard the *Hyperion* at all? Could this be some kind of training simulation joke created by those geeks at Mission Control? Another message interrupted her thoughts.

Absorb additional crystalized ambrosia, or sufficient liquid ambrosia, to complete the process. Failure to achieve 100% assimilation within the prescribed period may result in death.

A timer appeared counting down with less than an hour remaining. Fletcher cursed loud and long, staring at the remaining diamonds on the table as Lissa read the latest message to Clarke and the others. A moment later several of them were cursing as well.

"Screw it, I don't want to die." Trent reached for another gem. "If this is really a VR game, then this is all just a part of the character creation process. No harm, no foul. If it's for real… well then what choice do we have? How do I do this?" He used his right hand to place the diamond against the mark in the palm of his left, pressing it into his skin.

"Stop!" Clarke shouted through coms. "We don't know what this process is, if it's even real. Whatever you've been contaminated with, it might be affecting your judgement! Don't make it worse before I can even examine you!"

"Doc, it says we have less than an hour. You can't get down here that fast without risking a fall off that ledge. Other than a headache and some sore muscles, this stuff hasn't hurt us yet." Trent stopped speaking, swallowing hard. When he started again, his voice came out in a sob. "Besides, I owe you guys. Kyle and I nearly killed you all. I'll be the guinea pig here, and if this stuff kills me, then that's just what I deserve. Tell my family I'm sorry, for all of it."

He tuned out the objections coming from the coms, meeting the eyes of the two women with him, neither of whom made any attempt to stop him. Using his left thumb to hold the diamond in place on his palm, he grabbed another gem with his right hand and tossed it into his mouth. Rather than swallow, he simply held the diamond against the roof of his mouth with his tongue.

A moment later, all eyes on his hand, all three gasped as the diamond began to be absorbed into his skin. At the same time, he could feel the one in his mouth pressing into his flesh. There was no pain, just a vague tingling sensation.

"Does it hurt?" Lissa asked.

Trent shook his head no, unwilling to open his mouth to speak. The women continued to watch as the stone in his hand disappeared. When both were fully absorbed, another message appeared.

Assimilation process complete!
You are now eligible to become a citizen of … Mars!

There was a delay in the translation of the planet name, the word remaining in the alien language for some time before he could read it. At the same time he was reading his message, both women received another warning of imminent death if they did not complete the assimilation.

"Are you… okay?" Fletcher asked Trent. The man was looking at his hands, then down at his feet, as if expecting them to be different somehow.

"The hangover is gone…" He ventured. "Other than that, I don't feel any different." He then read them the message.

"Damnit Trent! I said not to do that!" Clarke raged at him over coms, her voice rising in pitch with anger.

Fletcher looked from Trent to the table. "Doc, I'm sorry, but I don't think we have a choice." She looked over at Lissa, who was focused on Trent, her tongue sticking out slightly, a sign she was doing some serious thinking. "Lissa, you can decide for yourself, but I'm going for it."

Not liking the idea of sticking an alien rock, still covered in dirt particles, into her mouth, she grabbed up two of the remaining half dozen diamonds and pressed one into each palm. Closing her eyes, she sat there on the stool with rigid back and held breath, waiting for them to disappear into her skin. She knew the process was complete even before she saw the message, because the aches in her head and body faded away.

When she opened her eyes and stretched, testing to make sure no pain remained, Lissa gave her a nod and grabbed two more stones herself.

*****

Up on the surface, Lazar was in the lead rover. The others were all parked in a convoy behind him, listening on coms to what was happening to their crewmates below. Just like the others, he was having a hard time accepting that some kind of alien crystal superfood thing was somehow changing Fletcher and the others into Martians. But every instinct he possessed screamed that they were not really sitting in pods on their ship playing a VR game in their sleep.

Either way, they weren't going to accomplish anything by sitting in their tanks. There was a ticking clock on how long they could screw around and live off of the oxygen they'd brought down with them. They needed to find and start processing some ice in the next few days, or things were going to get ugly.

"Screw this noise." He spoke into his coms, restarting his rover and putting it into gear. "We're coming down there, Commander, and there's no way you can stop us. We can talk about some kind of quarantine or something when we get there, but we all have a job to do here."

He looked in his rear view to confirm that the others had started following behind him. The first two rovers were on the move, but the third one in line, Doc's rover, was still parked. Blocking the ones behind her.

"Doc… they need you down there. If you're worried about contamination, we've got our suits, and we all know the protocols. Sitting up here with your thumb up your ass, pardon my French, won't help anybody."

Clarke didn't answer, but a moment later her tank started forward, and the others followed at standard intervals. Lazar had to grit his teeth and focus on not rushing down the slope. He'd seen the video of Lissa's descent yesterday, and he wasn't about to push the envelope, despite the urgency he felt. As far as he was concerned, Trent was an acceptable loss, even if it would make their mission harder. But he cared about Fletcher and Lissa.

Besides… he thought to himself, *I think maybe our mission has just changed completely.*

*****

Down in the cavern, all three of the newly assimilated humans were seated at their table. All three were trying to come to grips with the new reality they faced.

"It really is a lot like one of the virtual games." Fletcher offered. "But if this is the character creation stage, like Trent said, there should be more to it, right? Like, we should be choosing stats, or a class, at least."

Lissa nodded. "That last message said we were eligible to become citizens. Not that we already were. Maybe this assimilation is just a first step?"

"So what does it take to become a citizen? And do we even want to?" Fletcher looked at the two of them for just a moment. That was the right question. A new message appeared to address it.

There are many benefits to becoming a citizen of Mars. Increased physical and mental development, arcane abilities, the opportunity to undertake quests, for which you may earn significant rewards. Your actions may please the gods, benefitting you in other ways. You are free to grow, or not, as you see fit. Your only absolute

obligation is to assist the gods in their efforts toward the restoration of Mars. Whether that be as a hero, making great strides toward restoring our world, or as a simple algae farmer, making the smallest contribution, does not matter. As long as you work toward the great goal.

"So, pretty suspiciously like one of our games." Trent said. Lissa glanced at him, the hopeful look on his face making it clear that the man was still trying to convince himself that they were all just asleep and playing a VR game.

Chapter Four

Resistance Versus Persistence

While the others made their way down the canyon, Fletcher and the others figured out how to access their status. It was actually Fletcher who got it first. The oldest among the crew except for Graves, she'd had more years of gaming experience going back to her childhood. Her access to old school games that the young ones had never seen was what gave her the advantage.

While Lissa was asking more general questions about citizenship, trying to trigger more notices, and Trent was shouting random words like "Character! Interface!", Fletcher closed her eyes and tried to concentrate. She tried to picture herself as she was at the moment, standing in the hub module in her space suit, minus gloves and helmet. She pictured her own face as she'd seen it in the mirror every morning.

Then she focused on the image of the diamond that was now pressed into each of her palms. Remembering how they looked as they absorbed into her skin. Not speaking aloud, she asked herself, the system, the gods, whatever was controlling this process. "How did the ambrosia change me?" Instantly, a new message popped up, then translated itself.

Assimilation has made no improvements to your corporeal form.

It has simply prepared your anima for alterations you may choose for yourself as a citizen.
To determine what alterations are possible, you must first choose a name for yourself.
Then focus on that name to view your options.
By what name shall you be known among the gods and your fellow citizens?

Fletcher wasn't one of those players who came up with silly or overblown character names to set themselves apart from the millions of others when she played VR games. And since she appeared to be the very first human to pick a name, she was confident in her choice being available. "I choose Fletcher."

The moment her choice was made, a new display appeared before her. This one wasn't like the others, which seemed to appear as if written directly on her eye lenses. This one was more like a hologram situated approximately a foot in front of her face. It depicted her body, minus the suit, with blocks of the alien writing above it and in columns on either side. The script began to waver, but didn't instantly translate, as if the server were lagging.

While she waited, she spoke to the others. "Hey guys, I got it. Listen." She quickly explained the steps she'd taken to reach what they thought of as a character sheet. Both of them immediately closed their eyes and followed her lead as her own display finally finished translating.

The block above her avatar's head was simply "Fletcher" with the word "Unassigned" next to it. The column to the left appeared to be an inventory of her gear, which currently listed her environment suit, light, camera, belt with utility tool, and one more item that made her blink. Instead of her radio being listed, it was now showing as a *communication crystal*.

"Well, nice of the system to let us keep our gear." She mumbled to herself as she moved to survey the right hand column. There was a familiar-looking listing of stats, though the stats themselves, or at least the attributes available to improve, were not as familiar. The first was *Vis*, followed by *Vitae, Sofia, Haza*, and *Aura*.

It had been several decades since she was in school, but she thought she recognized a couple of the words. Aura was the most familiar, so she focused on that one first. But it wasn't what she expected.

Aura is the measure of your strength of character, your reputation with the observer, attractiveness, and overall presence. It effects how others interact with you, and to a certain extent, your own self-image. A strong aura may benefit you in negotiations, first impressions, and even physical confrontations. A weak aura may cause others to dislike you, take advantage of you in trades, or even attempt to subvert your will to their own.

"Well, shit." Fletcher read through the description a second time. There was a lot of information there.

Deciding to go back and start at the top, she chose *Vis*.

Vis is the measure of your power, energy, physical strength. It determines how fast you move, what your corporeal form can lift or carry, how hard you strike your foes in combat, and how long you can exert yourself before becoming tired.

"So… strength, agility, and stamina all in one stat? I'm not sure I like this." She spoke aloud again, distracting Lissa, who looked at her and raised an eyebrow. "Just reading through the attributes. They're way different than we're used to. You'll see soon enough." She watched Lissa's eyes unfocus again before she returned to the next on the list, *Vitae*.

Vitae is the measure of your life force. Tied directly to your anima, or soul, it determines your level of health, how much damage you can absorb, your resistance to disease or poison, how quickly your health recovers, and the strength of your spirit.

Fletcher was starting to see a trend here. There were fewer attributes than most games she'd ever played, but each one impacted a range of facets of her new existence. She moved on to *Sofia*, a word she recognized, but again the meaning wasn't exactly what she expected.

Sofia is the measure of your intellect and wisdom. It determines how observant and perceptive you are, how quickly you learn and retain information, the strength of your spells, and your determination. Investing heavily in Sofia may help you resist mental attacks, bend others to your will, or catch glimpses of possible futures.

"Now that's what I'm talking about! Mama's gonna be psychic." Fletcher chuckled to herself. Next, and last, on the list…

Haza is a mysterious conglomeration of fortune, serendipity, and random chance.
It is guided to an unknown and variable extent by your Vis, Aura, and Sofia,
as well as the will of the gods, and the Haza of your opponent,
whether it be in negotiations or combat.

"As usual, nobody really understands the luck stat." Fletcher rolled her eyes. "If this is all real, is there an actual RNG up there somewhere watching us? I should have brought my lucky purple sparkly dice."

"How are you three doing down there?" Doc Clarke's voice came through the coms, sounding concerned.

"Still breathing, doc." Fletcher took a moment to sit on her folding stool at the table. "Just been reading about our new stats. Sort of. It's like a tutorial, but I'm just at the beginning stage. Haven't assigned any points yet. Don't even know how many points I have. Everything is okay so far, though. Nobody has turned into an orc or a troll yet."

"Is that an option?" Chin's excited voice burst through. "I mean, I'd totally become an orc if that's possible."

"Not there yet, buddy. You focus on the path ahead of you, getting down here safe, and we'll keep reading, deal?" She snapped her fingers. "Oh, and you get to pick your name. Don't let me catch you using Chin the Great, or BabeMagnet or some dumbass thing. This is serious."

"Roger that, boss.

"These stats, they're complicated as hell." Trent complained, focusing on Fletcher.

"You'll get used to them." Lissa replied. "It's just like starting any other new game. Except this time, there's no wiki, no alpha or beta players who have gone before and recorded their successes or mistakes. We're learning from scratch. I actually think that's better."

"Except now, making a mistake, screwing up your build, might mean death." Trent actually stuck out his bottom lip, pouting. Both women had the urge to smack the look off his face. Instead of embracing the possibilities of this amazing new adventure, he was denying and complaining.

"It must suck to go through life afraid all the time." Lissa ventured. "How the hell did you get here? How'd you pass the psych exams?"

"Give me a damn break!" Trent snapped. "I'm not afraid of everything! Who was the first one to finish the assimilation? I stepped up while you two watched and waited to see if I'd die. I came prepared for accidents, exposure to space, death by suffocation, disease, or I dunno… random meteors falling on my head! But nothing, none of our training, prepared any of us for this shit!"

Lissa looked down at her hands, blushing slightly. "You're not wrong. I'm sorry, Trent. Just… you need to step up and accept what's happened. And prepare for what might be next. Denial and apathy aren't going to help you, or us."

Trent just glared at her, taking a seat himself. Fletcher opted not to get involved right then. Instead, she said, "Let's just get through the tutorial, or character creation, or whatever this is. Maybe stop before assigning any points, if that's an option, so we can discuss things? We don't want to go off half-cocked and make one of those mistakes you mentioned, Trent."

Both of her crewmates nodded their heads, resuming their reading. Fletcher did the same. The display showed zeros next to each of her possible attributes. Focusing on the zero next to Vis, she mentally asked "How do I change this?"

When nothing happened, she shifted her focus upward, to where the word unassigned sat next to her name. Concentrating on that, she was rewarded with another message.

If you wish to commit to citizenship, the gods will analyze and judge your current existence, assigning points based on your physical condition, history, and life experience to date. Additionally, if one or more of the gods favors you, extra points may be awarded for you to assign independently.

Do you wish to commit to citizenship?

Fletcher waited for the others to catch up to her. When she saw them both stop and look her direction, she nodded. "You're both at the citizenship choice?"

"Yeah. Seems like we're gonna get our initial stats assigned for us." Lissa didn't look happy. "Nothing like getting judged for your actions before you even get to the pearly gates."

Trent, for a change, seemed optimistic. "Look, we're among the best of the best, right? The elite of the human race? It's why we were chosen to come here."

Fletcher hated to burst his ego balloon, but it needed to be said. "We're above average among humans, true. But how do humans as a race measure up against Martians? I mean, were the inhabitants here the weak little grey men with big brains? If so, we'll seem like physical monsters with moron level IQs. On the other hand, if your average Martian was ten feet tall with four legs and six arms all bulging with muscle, or an exoskeleton that allowed them to lift ten times their own weight…"

Trent grimaced, rubbing one hand across his face. "I hear ya. I guess there's no way to know except to go for it?"

"Not necessarily." Fletcher wagged a finger at him. "We've learned most of what we know by asking questions, right? I say we spend the time until the others get here asking more questions. See what we can learn before we make this leap. It'll help the others to decide if they want to assimilate, or not."

Trent nodded. "Good point. Given the choice, I don't think I'd do it. I mean, it was already too late for us when we woke up. But if I were one of the others, I'd hold off. At least until I find out whether we're about to have our heads explode, or we get transformed into… something else."

"I'm sure they're all thinking about exactly that right now." Lissa looked upward in the general direction of the cliff face. "Chin's going to join us. Maybe Graves, too. I don't know about the others."

"Lazar's a hard core gamer, he'll absolutely go for it. And I'd bet on Mejia too. Ever met an IT guy who wasn't a total gamer nerd?" Fletcher shook her head. "I think Doc Clarke will hold out, as she's already told us this was a disease. And Volkov, well… I don't know if he's ever played a VR game in his life, outside the training simulators we've all used. Never saw him play during our trip. He was either in the gym, listening to Russian opera, or sending messages to his family."

"Dude can sing." Trent added. "I caught him singing along to his opera down in cargo bay three one night."

Not having an answer for that non-sequitor, Fletcher changed the subject. "We've been following each other's lead up till now. Let's go the other way. Read as much as you can on your own, follow your own path, without proceeding with citizenship. When the others get here, we'll all share what we've learned. Hopefully we'll have enough info to give the others a clearer picture."

The others nodded, and Fletcher watched them dive back into their interfaces. When she did the same, the final prompt of the last message reappeared.

Do you wish to commit to citizenship?

She was about to mentally refuse, when Trent spoke up. "Uhm, if you try to say no, it's a death sentence."

"What?" Fletcher blinked away the message and looked at him.

"Yeah, I just got the same thing. Apparently, if you choose to complete assimilation, then choose not to become a citizen, you anger the gods." Lissa confirmed.

"Screw it. Citizenship, here I come." Trent mentally pressed the button, and promptly passed out. His body slumped forward, his forehead thunking against the table before either of the women could grab him.

"What the hell!" Fletcher leaned over the table, grabbing Trent by the hair and lifting his head. His eyes were closed, but his eyeballs were shifting back and forth as if he were in REM sleep, or reading something on his interface. "Well, he's alive. That's a good sign, at least."

"And he's not an orc." Lissa agreed. "Not yet, anyway. So, what do we do? We can't get past this choice prompt to keep researching. Declining citizenship is clearly not an option. Do we just sit here till the others arrive? Or till Trent wakes up? Or both?"

Fletcher was conflicted. On the one hand, it was her duty to protect her crew, to make sound decisions that should involve no unnecessary risks. On the other hand, she was very conscious that the hour time frame given in the early assimilation message had nearly expired. She hadn't seen anything that stated whether completion included choosing citizenship. If they didn't choose before the hour expired, would that be a default death sentence?

She was still wrestling with the issue two minutes later when Trent gasped, raising his head and opening his eyes. He looked at the two women, then asked, "You two done already?"

"Done? We haven't even started. We've been sitting here waiting to see if you turned into an orc for the last couple minutes." Lissa barked at him.

"Couple of minutes? How long was I out?" Trent looked at his wrist pad. "Damn, I could swear that I just spent six or eight hours going through the class choices and reading the rest of the tutorial."

Both women stared at him, slightly stunned. Fletcher shook it off first. "Maybe some kind of time dilation? Your body didn't seem to be in any kind of altered state. You were breathing, and your eyes were moving."

Lissa bulldozed over that line of questioning, asking instead, "Did you say class choices? What where they? What did you pick?"

"Well, to start with…" Trent began, but Fletcher cut him off.

"Lissa, we're on a clock here. Maybe. Assuming we are, time is just about up. You can sit and chat with him if you want, but I'm not risking it. He seems healthy enough, and that was my main concern. I'm going for it."

She closed her eyes, and the prompt reappeared. This time the text was red, and blinking. "Lissa, the prompt is blinking red. Do it now." Fletcher mentally thought "Yes" and her body slumped forward just like Trent's. Though she didn't know it, Lissa was right behind her.

*****

Welcome, citizen!
Your anima has been measured and judged by the Gods of the Pantheon.
The following characteristics are based upon your life experience to date.

Fletcher blinked once, and a new display appeared, showing her stats with the values filled in, along with a few other entries. The numbers didn't mean a lot to her, as she had nothing to compare them to. The fact that she was showing as level zero at the top made sense. She'd only been a citizen for a few seconds. And the zero reputation at the bottom didn't bother her either, for the same reason.

Fletcher	Level 0
Vis	10
Vitae	12
Sofia	14
Haza	8
Aura	15
Health Points	120
Mana Points	200
Reputation	0

When she focused on the first value, which showed a ten next to Vis, a new message appeared.

Congratulations!

The gods have taken pity on you.
Though you have lived an exemplary life so far, for a human,
your species as a whole is inferior to Martian norms.
The gods have deemed you worthy of determining your own path, and have awarded you twenty assignable attribute points to use as you wish. It is strongly recommended that you review potential paths and choose one before allocating your remaining available points.
Think hard, and plan carefully, citizen!

Fletcher's interface went blank, the stat sheet disappearing for a moment before being replaced by a short message, and a list of possible paths, or what she would call classes.

Based on your current skills, history, and potential, the following paths have been deemed most appropriate for you. Please choose from among them. To begin with, you can choose only one path. As you grow stronger, if you grow stronger, you may be able to embark upon additional paths.

Fletcher perused the list, which was actually quite lengthy. She quit counting at forty possible paths. Some of them she disregarded out of hand. *Teacher, Builder, Healer, Thief,* and several others that sounded like they might involve manual labor or boring daily grinding. A few of the options she didn't understand, and she focused on one of them to get more information.

Protector: Protectors throw themselves between their fellow citizens and potential danger. They absorb attacks meant for others, and engage foes in close combat. This path requires focused investment in Vis, Vitae, and Aura.

"So… a tank" Fletcher thought to herself. "Not my style. My guess is Graves, or maybe Volkov would enjoy that class. I'm more a back of the pack, pew pew kind of gal."

She briefly considered a path called *Strategist*, but the description had more of an information gathering, stealthy spymaster kind of vibe than she wanted. She also rejected *Hunter*, since in nearly every game she'd ever played that class involved either pet management, or killing, skinning, and butchering prey, or both. "Nope. I don't know what kind of critters they have here on Mars, but I'm not interested in getting all into their guts."

Near the bottom of the list, which clearly was not in alphabetical order, at least not in English, she found one that caught her interest.

Arcanist: Arcanists use their internal power to focus the ambient energy of Mars. That energy is used to imbue items, create illusions, or generate force that can be both offensive and defensive. Limited only by the Arcanist's imagination and power, this path requires focused investment in Sofia, with recommended secondary investments in Aura, Vis, and Vitae.

"Some kind of mage, or caster. Total min/max opportunity. Right up my alley!" Fletcher mentally gave herself a thumbs-up. Just to be sure, she checked through the rest of the list, then reviewed the entire list one more time. Pleased with her choice, she selected *Arcanist.*

You have selected the path of the Arcanist!

Respected by most, Arcanists perform tasks that seem miraculous to the simple-minded. Useful in combat as well as everyday life, the Arcanist can always find a way to contribute. As with any path, there will be those who do not approve. Citizens following Priest or Paladin paths consider the gathering of ambient energy for mundane uses to be a demonstration of impiety, and may act directly against you.

Please assign your available attribute points at this time.

Fletcher reviewed the descriptions of the various attributes again, then made her choices. She assigned eleven points to *Sofia*, her main stat based on the path description, bringing it up to twenty five. Then she assigned four points to *Vitae*, to keep herself alive, three points to *Aura*, and two points to *Vis*. Her choices made, she mentally confirmed them, then watched as the values changed on her stats sheet. The attribute increases caused significant jumps in her total health and mana points as well.

Satisfied with her choices, and with no other messages popping up, Fletcher found herself blinking her eyes as she raised her head back in the hub module.

Fletcher	Level 0
Vis	12
Vitae	16
Sofia	25
Haza	8
Aura	18
Health Points	160
Mana Points	410
Reputation	0

Chapter Five

The Others Arrive

Doc Clarke was fuming as she followed Lazar and the others down the natural ramp. The three in the cavern had completely ignored her instructions and gone ahead with whatever the assimilation process was, and she was too far away to stop them, or even to examine them. The slow pace they had to take on their descent was driving her insane. Fletcher and the others were now obviously contaminated with some alien organism or disease, and she was too late to stop it. What if their health went critical while she was stuck in this turtle convoy?

As far as she was concerned, their mission was over. First Kyle took himself out of the gene pool, now their mission commander and two more of their crew were going to need to be quarantined, at the least. Assuming they survived whatever this process was, they were not going to be able to participate in the mission. That left them with six viable crew members on a mission designed to occupy every waking hour of every day for ten people.

Six… assuming she could keep Chin and the others from following after Fletcher.

Mission failure. The second biggest fear of all crew members, beyond dying in the vacuum of space or a fiery impact with the planet. All the time, training, and money invested in them by people back on Earth who were depending on them. They had let down their families, their nations, their world. Clarke cursed Kyle for his dumbass drunken shenanigans that had put them into this situation, cursed Fletcher for not listening to her, Trent for his rash decision to plunge forward with completing the process, Lazar for driving so fucking slow, and herself for not being more effective in stopping her crewmates from potentially having committed suicide.

She growled into her mic, "Lazar! There's careful, and then there's ridiculously slow. I need to get down there. Move your ass!"

"We're almost there, Doc. Just a few more minutes. One more switchback, and I'll speed things up a bit. Don't you go rushing and drive yourself off the edge. You can't help them if you're dead." Lazar was audibly struggling to restrain himself in his response. "And keep your interval! You push somebody over and I'll end you myself."

Clarke looked at her distance from the tank ahead and let off the accelerator just a bit. He was right, she'd been crowding too close. She cussed softly at herself for being so predictable. It wasn't that surprising, after so long together in the tight confines of *Hyperion*, the crew knew each other well. That didn't stop it from annoying her in her current frame of mind.

"Fletcher, talk to me. What's happening down there?" The commander had been silent for nearly two full minutes. All Trent would say was that she was in the middle of character creation and couldn't talk.

"I'm here, Doc, and everything's okay, I think. Actually, I feel pretty good. Part of the process is assigning stat points, and I think it has actually improved us." There was a pause, then Trent chimed in.

"Yeah, I feel… healthier? Stronger for sure. I think we're good, Doc."

"You just let me decide whether you're good or not." She growled at them, tightening her grip on the tank's controls in frustration. "And if you're not getting any more imminent death notices, don't go making any more decisions. Maybe we can still reverse whatever is happening to you."

Lissa's voice came through, strong but sympathetic. "I'm sorry, Doc. But I don't think I want to reverse anything. Fletcher and Trent are right, this is amazing. I actually feel smarter than I did yesterday. I know what you're going to say, that we're delusional or otherwise incompetent to make that decision, but I don't agree."

Clarke found herself once again pressing on the accelerator, and gritted her teeth as she backed off. She didn't bother to argue over coms, as it would only frustrate her further. Instead she focused on creating a mental list of symptoms, possible causes, and treatments. In her heart she knew it was futile, as Earth medicine had no experience with anything like what her crewmates were describing. But it helped to distract her through the last of their descent. When they reached the cavern, she was temporarily occupied with threading her wide vehicle through the obstacles on the ground.

She growled impatiently as Fletcher ordered them to arrange their tanks so that they could cluster up before exiting. Ignoring instructions, she backed her tank up so that she could connect directly with the hab module that Fletcher and the others were sitting in. She took the fourth position, extended and connected her short corridor, and practically danced in place as she waited for the air to cycle through. The moment it was complete, she opened the plastic hatch and stormed through, her rapid breathing slightly fogging the faceplate of her sealed suit.

Pointing to Trent, she commanded, "You. On the cot, right now." Her tone, and the steel in her gaze, allowed no argument. Trent looked briefly at Fletcher, who nodded toward the cot and gave him a sympathetic smile. He was about to be doc's guinea pig.

"Relax, Doc." Fletcher's tone was soothing as Trent sat on the cot, then laid himself out straight. "I know you're worried, but we're not in any immediate danger as far as I can tell. Take a few deep breaths. You're here now, and everything's going to be okay."

Trent's response was a little more personally motivated. "You're not gonna like, take a piece of my brain for biopsy, or anything? Right?" He was staring at a syringe she had produced from a bag she carried on her shoulder.

"I'm taking a blood sample." She snapped at him, then regretted it. "I'd only dissect your brain if you turned into an orc or something. Or, you know, died." She tried to reassure him.

Lissa took in a sharp breath somewhere behind her. "Do you think we did? Die? I mean, we all blacked out as we completed the process and chose our classes. Maybe we died and were reborn somehow? And if so, does that make us some kind of zombies?"

Trent jerked up into a sitting position, causing Clarke to jab his arm with the needle. "Ow! What do you mean, zombies? I don't want to be a zombie!"

"Lay back down and hold still!" Clarke shouted in his face, causing him to flinch and quickly obey. "Do that again and I'll remove your head, just in case the zombie thing is real."

Not in the least reassured, Trent lay there with eyes wide and muscles tensed as she poked the needle into his arm and began to draw blood. She could feel that his pulse rate was way up. "Relax. Nobody is taking your head today. Unless you try to bite me or something. Do you feel a craving for brains?"

"What?! No!" Trent looked horrified until he saw Fletcher smiling over Clarke's shoulder. "Not funny, Doc. Shit."

To help distract him, Fletcher asked, "So what class did you pick, Trent?"

"What?" the confused astronaut asked again, unable to process the quick subject change right away. "Oh, I chose one called *Apothecary*. It's a lot like alchemists in the games, mixing ingredients into potions and pastes, pills, whatever. It was the closest thing to the biochem work I came here to do, and I think my existing knowledge will help."

"Smart choice." Fletcher reassured him. She even favored him with a smile, though she was still pissed at him. "I chose *Arcanist.* Gonna be a spell-slinging, gear-enchanting sorceress!"

"Awesome!" Trent was honestly enthused. He turned to Lissa. "What about you?"

"*Geomancer*. What we might call an earth mage. I am supposed to be able to manipulate soil and stone through magic." She shrugged. "I kept thinking it might help us drill down and find water."

"Or build weatherproof shelters, or mine other resources. Good thinking, Lissa." Fletcher gave her a thumbs-up.

Through the coms, Chin's excited voice added, "Yeah, those all sound awesome! I can't wait to find out what I can be!"

"You just sit tight and keep away from those diamonds, Chin!" Clarke practically screamed at him through the coms.

When he responded, his voice was subdued and sullen, like a scolded child. "Roger that, Doc."

"Guys, Doc is a little stressed right now, so don't push her buttons." Fletcher's voice was calm and relaxed. "Let her check us out in peace, and then we can all talk about what's going on. In the meantime, the rest of you start unloading your tanks here, and get ready to make the run back up top to retrieve the cargo pods. Our little side quest here doesn't change the fact that we have a mission to complete."

"Da. We will start immediately." Volkov replied first, his military tone making it clear he'd tolerate no argument. "We will be ready to head back in three hours."

Mejia spoke up next. "If it's alright with you, commander, I'll leave the unloading to these guys, and set up the command and control arrays on your tank. We should have done that twelve hours ago. Mission control is probably freaking out about now."

"Shit!" Fletcher cursed quietly to herself, looking at the chronometer on her wrist unit. "You're right. I'll suit up and help." She reached for her gloves, and froze when Clarke spun on her, leaning in close.

"You'll do no such thing! Sit! This is a direct order from the mission medical officer. Don't make me relieve you of duty, commander." Clarke's eyes burned into hers, and Fletcher took a step back to sit on a stool at the table.

"Alright Doc, you got it. Mejia, please take care of the array deployment. Get Chin or Volkov to help if you need it." She briefly got up, closed the hatch leading to her tank and sealed it, so that Mejia could access the tank.

"Roger that, boss. I'm on it."

Clarke finished drawing blood from Trent and began a physical exam, shining a light into his eyes, having him follow her finger and watching his focus. "How do you feel? Any nausea, dizziness? Any pain anywhere?"

"Feeling better than I've ever felt, to be honest." Trent smiled up at her, glad to see her put the needle away. "No pain at all. I mean, I felt like shit during the assimilation, when we first woke up and it was only partially completed. Felt hung over, sore all over, dizzy…"

"And we did lose consciousness once we hit the last stage of the process." Lissa answered, clearly still stuck on the possibility that they'd died. "But I'm with Trent, I feel healthier, stronger, smarter… just generally better."

"If we can believe the notifications," Fletcher offered, "We have been able to improve ourselves above human norms. I don't know about you guys, but they told me that human stats were well below Martian standards, and gave me twenty free points to assign. I think that's the difference we're feeling. They made us smarter, stronger, etc."

Trent sighed. "I only got sixteen points."

"Same here." Lissa looked at Fletcher with a bit of jealousy. "Then again, maybe that means we needed fewer points to reach the Martian baseline? Like, we're younger and, no offense boss, more vital than you."

"We can figure out the details later." Fletcher nodded toward where the others were parked. "If the others go through it too, we'll have a better sampling to compare."

"Nobody's going through anything!" Clarke turned away from Trent again. "I'm declaring mission failure. At the very least you're going to be quarantined, and the rest of us will do what we can to ensure we have the resources to survive until the next crew comes to take us home. You're contaminated with some totally unknown alien organism, and frankly your minds could all be compromised. Listen to yourself!" Her voice grew louder and more strained as she went on. "You nearly died, you know almost nothing about what has happened to you, or what the consequences might be, and you're pushing for the rest of the crew to contaminate themselves as well! I'm relieving you of command, and putting Lazar in charge!"

Fletcher's gaze was flat as she stared back. After half a minute of tense silence, she spoke in an equally flat tone. "You're overreacting, doctor. You sound more than a little unhinged, and I think your fear has gotten the better of you." She held up a hand as Clarke opened her mouth to respond.

"However… I understand your concerns. So, in the best interests of the mission, I will voluntarily and *temporarily* cede command to Lazar. Until we know enough to make a more informed decision. You copy that, Lazar?"

"Roger that, boss. I am now king of the mission!" he chuckled for a second, then cleared his throat. "I got your back. Doc, you do whatever tests you need to do today, and those three will remain quarantined until you have your answers. But let's make it quick, alright?"

"I don't think you're taking this seriously." Clarke growled through the coms.

"And I believe you're taking this too seriously, and personally, Doc. I know you feel responsible for all of us, as you should. But have you really thought this through? Are you going to quarantine three of us for several months here on Mars, then another half year for the trip home, then potentially for years more on Earth? If you file a report in your current panicked state of mind, you're dooming them to be lab rats for the rest of their lives. Which might be damned short if someone decides to euthanize and dissect one or more of them."

That caused Clarke to pause a moment. He was right, she hadn't considered that.

"Let's all just do our jobs, as much as we're able, and calm down for a bit. I'll send a factual report to Mission Control when the coms are up and we reestablish contact with Skippy. They're sure to have some opinions on this. After they ask about a thousand questions. Can I depend on you to answer them factually and honestly, without any personal interpretation of the facts?"

She took a few deep breaths and nodded, then realized he couldn't see her. "I believe I can do that, yes. But I won't lie for you, or mislead Control in any way."

"Fair enough. Now, Fletcher, Lissa, Trent, I need you to cooperate with Doc, let her perform any tests she wants, up to and including anal probes if she deems it necessary. We'll take care of what needs doing out here. And for the rest of you, nobody touches the diamonds, or the walls, or anything liquid. That's an order."

*****

Operations specialist Dean ripped off his headset and jumped from his ergonomic chair, stumbling in his haste to reach the office of director of operations Thorne. He dashed out of mission control blasting through a set of swinging doors and down a short hallway. Not bothering to knock, he burst into an office with glass windows, surprising his distracted boss.

"We have a problem!"

Those words never being welcome in any situation dealing with space travel, he had his chief's immediate attention. Already aware of the explosion aboard *Hyperion I*, and the need to alter both the drop location and schedule, the man's gut clenched at the news of a new issue. "What's happened. Did they not find water?"

Dean paused for a moment, thinking back. "No report on water either way. There's been some kind of biological contamination event, and three of the crew have been quarantined, including Fletcher. Lazar is reporting in right now."

Both men dashed out of the office and back to control, where the incoming report had caused a sudden flurry of activity and noise. Another operations specialist had already summoned their supervisor while Dean had fetched the big boss, who stood on a raised section of the floor at the rear of the room and shouted. "Settle down!" When things quieted and everyone returned to their stations, he looked down. "Ops, put Lazar on the big screen."

"We only have audio at the moment, boss. They're still setting up, but Lazar felt it was important to report this ASAP. Hold one." The operations supervisor on duty pressed a few buttons, and Lazar's voice came across the speakers on the walls.

"So I've accepted temporary command. Over." His report ended.

Thorne looked at the stricken faces around the room. "One of you talking monkeys get me a replay of that report. Now!"

It only took a few seconds for one of them to que up and replay the transmission. "Control, this is acting mission commander Lazar. We landed okay, the hab module is fine, all the cargo pods landed close, and we all gathered at Delta Seven, no problem. Fletcher, Trent, and Lissa took their tanks down into the canyon and found a cavern big enough to house the full hab plus several expansions. But Lissa also found these diamonds…" The report continued, and as the man spoke, the room got quieter and more subdued. When he got to the part about the three crewmembers waking up with stat sheets, the chatter within the room resumed. It got loud enough that Thorne had to slam a hand on a nearby desk to hush them again. Lazar finished his report with the quarantine order from Clarke, and his acceptance of command.

"Well, shit. I'm not sure how to respond here." Thorne gripped the railing in front of him, feeling a little unsteady. After a moment, he looked at Dean, who handed him a wireless mic and battery pack, which he clipped to his belt. Dean activated the mic and hit record, giving Thorne a nod.

"Hyperion, from Control, this is Thorne. Message received. That's a lot of information to take in at once. And obviously we have no protocol for this. I'm gonna need to bring in a buttload of experts and some higher ups to talk about this for a while. Need to know, are you in any immediate danger? I'm gonna make an executive decision here and say maintain the quarantine, and don't touch any more of those diamonds until we get back to you. Good luck up there, Lazar. Over."

With the length of the replay he'd just listened to, Thorne knew that more than thirty minutes would have passed for the crew since they sent their transmission. His spine shivered at the thought of being up there, in that situation, cut off from any help or even timely advice.

"Right. Everybody… all departments, call your bosses. Not your supervisors, or their supervisors. Let me be very clear. Call whoever is the very top of your command chain, and no one else. Do it now." He paused, then added. "Do it on the landlines, and make no other calls." He motioned for two security personnel standing by the door to lock down the room. "Everybody turn over your private coms bracelets, tablets, any personal communications devices. No exceptions. Nobody leaves this room for the next four hours except to take a dump, and then only with an escort. This entire mission just became… whatever the top level of classified is. I don't even fucking know myself. But whatever it's called, that's what this is. Anyone attempting to leak any information about this will be summarily shot. Do I make myself clear?" He glared around the room at his suddenly very nervous people.

Thorne had no idea if he even had the authority to have someone shot, but the security guys nodded like they were buying it, one of them even placing a hand on his holster. And that pretty much sold it to the rest of the room. Anyway, Thorne intended to have some folks in the building within the hour that definitely had the authority to shoot people. He waited until the private devices had all been confiscated, and watched for a minute as his people began making calls. Realizing that his call needed to happen first, he dashed back to his own office. Sitting in his chair, he turned to open a cabinet on the back wall, and took out a jet black analog landline phone. Picking up the receiver, he pressed the only button available, which was painted bright red

"Yes, this is Space Force Hyperion Mission Director of Operations Thorne. ID code delta three zero zulu six charlie. I need to speak to him. Right now. Tell him we have a Sigma One situation." He waited impatiently as he was put on hold, trying to organize his thoughts so that he could present a clear and concise report. His heart was pounding, and he kept getting distracted by how much the world would change if this was indeed confirmation of intelligent alien life. A moment later, the line was live again.

"Thorne? What the hell is this about a Sigma One? Are you drunk?"

"I wish, sir."

*****

"Lazar!" Mejia called out. "Skippy just relayed the response from Mission Control. Thorne says they have no clue what to do, and to hang tight while they figure it out. Keep our three Martians in quarantine, and nobody touch anything that might turn us into orcs."

Lazar snorted at the obvious translation of the transmission from Thorne. He and Thorne were old friends, going back to lunar colony missions twenty years earlier. He knew if anyone would push to find them some answers, it would be Thorne. He had a direct line to the President, another old friend, and could flex some serious political muscle if necessary.

"Play it for us." Lazar ordered, and a moment later all nine of them could hear Thorne's words. Fletcher was the first to speak when it was done.

"No big surprise there. I wouldn't know what to say either, if I were him."

Lazar grinned to himself. "Knowing him, he'll have rattled the cages of the top ranks, got some people out of bed, pissed everyone off by dragging them in for a meeting, then scared them to death by now. Wish I could be there to see it."

"A very, very secret meeting." Volkov added. "The powers that be cannot let word of this get out, or there would be panic and rioting. That is not good news for us, comrades. They will kill to keep this secret. And that may include canceling further missions and abandoning us here."

"They wouldn't do that, would they?" Lissa's voice was soft, barely audible.

"Without a second thought." Graves confirmed. "In fact, that's almost certainly what they'll have to do. They won't like it, and some of our friends will fight it, but in the end, what other choice will they have? Announce to the world that Martians are real and have hijacked the bodies of human astronauts? Governments and religions would collapse, entire cities would burn."

Fletcher, unconsciously assuming her usual command authority, tried to calm them all. "Let's deal with that if and when it happens. Right now, we have work to get done. Let's focus on that."

Chin, seemingly ignoring Fletcher's words, spoke out. "I'm sorry, Doc. But if we're going to be stranded here by our fellow Earthlings, I think our best chance for survival is to go native, and become Martians like Fletcher, Trent, and Lissa."

"You don't know that, Chin." Clarke responded in a surprisingly calm voice. "For all we know, they're dying right now. Or becoming something… inhuman. I'm sorry." She looked at the three as she spoke.

Volkov's voice rang with conviction. "We have limited resources, doctor. Even if we find water and can gather sufficient quantities to provide oxygen and drinking water for an extended period, we have a maximum of six months of food if we begin rationing today. Without a resupply from Earth, or some alternate food source, of which we have seen no evidence, that is how long we shall survive." He paused to let that sink in. "I must assume that as Martian citizens, we would have access to some food or energy source that will sustain us. I agree that we should await further response from Earth, but suggest that we all at least entertain following commander Fletcher's lead."

Lazar had heard enough. "Enough talking. Back to work, everyone. We've got to get set up with just the five of us working, at least as long as Clarke is still in with the Martians. The clock is ticking, and our air is running out by the minute!"

Chapter Six

Dirty Deed

By nightfall local time, the five active crew members had managed to unload the tanks, temporarily sealing off the quarantined hub module while they unloaded Fletcher, Trent, and Lissa's cargo.

The moment Clarke was done with her exam of Lissa, the geologist tried to convince Lazar to let her take her tank farther down into the canyon to search for water. Lazar deferred to the doc, who refused to let Lissa or any of them out of her sight until she had at least gotten initial test results from blood samples. She asked them endless questions as she worked through Fletcher's exam, some of them about physical symptoms, some psychological tests. She asked them complicated mathematical questions, and history questions.

"Doc, I didn't know who the twenty eighth president was a week ago, and I don't know now. Do you even know yourself?" Fletcher grumped at her, getting tired of the entire process, impatient to get back to work.

Clarke paused, tilting her head to one side, then chuckled. "I don't, actually. Doesn't matter. This was more of a stress test, and you reacted with pretty much the gruff response that's your normal baseline. That's a good sign."

"Also, if we had been body-snatched by alien consciousnesses, they wouldn't know any Earth history, right doc?" Trent chimed in.

"Unless they absorbed all our knowledge while sucking out our souls." Lissa smirked at Trent, whose eyes went wide.

"Not helping, Lissa." Fletcher growled, making the younger woman's shoulders hunch. "Don't go giving Clarke here any additional reasons to keep us locked in here. Now she's gonna try and figure out how to test to see if we still have our souls."

"Sorry, boss." Lissa got up and paced the room. "Doc, if it's just me in my tank, I can't possibly contaminate anyone else, right? So there's no harm in me going to look for water."

"We thought there was no harm in you exploring yesterday, and look what happened. You can't seem to follow safety protocols to save your life. And I mean that literally." Doc snapped at her. "How do I know that if I let you go down there you won't go rogue and come smashing that multi-ton tank back in here trying to kill us all? Or come back with a host of alien overlords intent on taking over the rest of our bodies, or something? Or maybe you'll just get a sudden bout of depression and run yourself off the ledge. You just sit right there and relax until I tell you otherwise. That's an order."

Lissa looked to Fletcher, who just shrugged as if to say *I'm not in charge right now.*

"Fletcher quit squirming." Doc chastised her for the shrug. Fletcher rolled her eyes at Lissa and held still, per instructions. She didn't even flinch when the needle went into her arm for Clarke to draw blood. She and the others patiently waited and answered more questions for the next fifteen minutes as Clarke poked and prodded, hooked up sensors, and flashed lights in her eyes.

"Alright, that's it. You can all relax for a bit. Maybe try and get some sleep. It'll take me a little while to conduct these tests with just the gear I have with me. And no, Fletcher, I won't make you wait until I have the full med lab module set up. At least, I don't think I will. Let's just see what we see here, and play it by ear." She sat down at the table in the center of the hab and began pulling small instruments from her bag. She'd grabbed some diagnostic tools from her tank on her way out. They all watched, speaking quietly amongst themselves, as she prepared some slides and stared at blood samples through her microscope.

Trent crossed his fingers that she would be satisfied enough to let them get back to work.

*****

The decision came quickly once the powers that be were gathered to discuss the situation on Mars. Thorne and a few others argued on behalf of the crew, but all of them knew what was necessary. The next mission to Mars, one that would deliver more crew members and a year's worth of supplies as well as needed equipment and materials for a hab expansion, was to be delayed indefinitely. The world would be told about the explosion on the ship, the need for emergency evacuation. That Earth had been unable to reestablish contact with the *Hyperion* mission after planetfall, and they were presumed lost. The crew would be instructed to communicate only via a single ultra-secure connection relayed through Skippy, and not to transmit any other signals. All mission control staff would be sequestered and cut off from any outside communication until the matter was resolved, one way or another. Thorne suspected those who weren't absolutely convincing in their oaths of secrecy would suffer 'accidents' in the near future.

This was their way of playing 'wait and see', keeping their options open while covering their collective asses. The public would not be told that Martians are real, or any of the mission details

And Thorne was given the job of breaking the news to the *Hyperion* crew.

Which was why he now found himself sitting alone in his office, a webcam pointed at him, gathering his wits before he activated the recording. He'd chosen to send the word via video, so that Lazar and the others could see his face as he spoke. A simple voice message seemed too impersonal and callous. One more deep breath, and he hit the record button.

"*Hyperion I*, this is Thorne, as you can see. I've just come from a meeting where more VIPs than I can name have been discussing your predicament. As you can obviously tell, it wasn't a long discussion." He paused to breathe again, folding his hands and placing them on his desk.

"I'll give it to you straight. You guys really stepped in it. You're gonna be on your own for the foreseeable future. The next mission has been postponed, which I'm sure is no surprise to you. It has been decided that Earth and its inhabitants aren't ready to hear that Martians are real, let alone that some of you have already been… what was the word? Assimilated? Yeah, that's not a word people are going to be comfortable with." He shook his head, an ironic smile on his face.

"I know you guys are tough, and if anyone can find a way to survive without our help, it's you. You have some seeds in they hydroponics cargo pod, though it's unlikely they'll yield enough of a crop to sustain you for more than a few months. If you ration, and find some other food source somewhere, well…" Thorne's voice caught. He knew as well as they did that he was handing them a death sentence. He cleared his throat a couple of times, trying his best to keep his eyes from tearing up.

"We'll continue to fight for you down here. I hope you know that. You're not alone, guys. They've got mission control on total lockdown, and there won't be any press leaks anytime soon, for everyone's sake. But I'll keep working on those in the know. I figure I can sell them on a supply ship as an ambassadorial mission to establish peace with you Martians." He did his best to grin, but he wasn't selling it well. "I'll make sure it's packed with food and useful supplies instead of the building equipment and extra crew we were going to send. With just the nine of you, you don't need to expand as much. This is all new, so I don't have the details worked out yet, but I will. We all will. Everybody here is behind you guys."

With a sigh, he decided to wrap things up. "I'm sending along a data packet with coms security details and such. They want to be very sure nobody picks up any stray transmissions from you guys, since you're all supposed to be dead. Good luck, Hyperion, and stay strong. If I'm honest, I'm super jealous! If they'll let me, I'll fly that supply ship myself, and join you. In the meantime, I'll get back to you as soon as I have something worthwhile to say."

He ended the recording, attached the data packet, and hit the transmit button. There was no point in reviewing or editing the message, he got the point across. He knew that at least Lazar would have guessed what was going on, and prepared the others for the bad news. His old friend was one of the smartest and most savvy operators he'd ever served with.

*****

"I can't believe it." Lissa whispered as she listened to Lazar relay the gist of the message. "They're just cutting us off? Telling everyone we're dead? My family!" She gasped and covered her mouth with her hands, tears falling down her cheeks.

"Da. It's the only thing they can do." Volkov actually sounded sympathetic. "It will be painful for our loved ones, but not as painful as the alternative. The news of what we have discovered could destroy our whole civilization. It is better this way, little one, as painful as it is to accept."

Lazar's face was grim as he spoke, matching his tone. "I know some of you will be tempted to try to call home. Let me tell you here and now, you can't do that. Skippy has orders not to relay any communications from anyone other than myself, and nothing from me to anyone but Control. They have locked down every living human who knows our secret, and cut them off from the world as well. There will be no rogue disclosure and upswelling of support to save us. I'm sorry."

"Then we really are dead. Just a little behind their announcements." Trent shook his head, bent over with his elbows on his knees, kneading his hands together. "Earth has written us off. I guess we embrace being Martians."

Chin's voice trembled slightly as he replied. "I'm ready. I mean, what other choice do we have? They're never going to let us go home, except maybe as lab rats. Or corpses to be studied. Maybe as Martians we find a way to survive."

Clarke wasn't ready to give in so easily. "Maybe as Martians we die that much quicker. I still don't know what this assimilation process has done to you three." She stared at Fletcher, who was sitting at the table staring at Lissa, sitting across from her. "For all we know there's some parasite working its way through your brains and-"

She stopped mid-sentence, finally seeing what Fletcher had been staring at. Lissa had been playing with the diamonds, a fact that sent chills down Clarke's back. But she set that fear aside as she watched her crewmate's idly twirling finger.

Lissa had been unconsciously cleaning the diamonds, rubbing the remaining bits of dirt off their surface, especially the golfball-sized one. The dirt particles had accumulated on the stainless tabletop, and were now swirling in a pattern matching the one Lissa's finger was tracing.

"Lissa, what are you doing?" Clarke asked. The question seemed to snap both Lissa and Fletcher out of their reverie.

"I… doing? What do you mean?" Lissa looked confused, staring up at Clarke, who was now hovering over her shoulder.

"You were moving the dirt, Lissa." Fletcher stated very matter-of-factly. "You were zoned out, and sort of drawing a pattern in the air with your finger, and the dirt was mimicking the pattern, following your finger. Try to do it again."

"Huh." Lissa looked down at the dirt, which was sitting still, laid out in a pattern that roughly resembled the infinity symbol. "Let's see." She stared at the dirt for a while, then held her finger above it and moved it in a straight line to the left. The dirt infinity symbol collapsed upon itself then stretched out in a line, looking a bit like an extending centipede. "Cool!" She moved her finger down a bit, and the path of the dirt line altered to follow it.

"Can you move it without the finger?" Trent asked, taking a seat and leaning in toward the table.

"What's happening, guys?" Lazar demanded. Fletcher filled in the details for him as Lissa stared hard at the long dirt line. After a moment, it gathered together into a small clump, then formed into a near perfect cube.

"Holy shitballs!" Trent slammed a hand on the table. "That's awesome!"

"*Geomancer* class, remember? I'm supposed to be able to control the soil and stone. Guess it's for real." Lissa stared at the cube a moment, and it collapsed into a simple pile of red-tinted dirt. Then all three sets of new Martian eyes went to Clarke.

"It's for real, Doc." Trent said, his voice getting excited. "Lissa did magic!"

"Lissa did what??" Mejia broke in. "No way!"

"Yes, way!" Lissa laughed, blowing slightly on the dirt and scattering it partway across the small table, then making a grabbing motion with her hand and drawing it back to her with magic. "I'm a friggin earth mage! Dirt mage? Can we call it earth when we're on Mars? Anyway, I can manipulate the dirt with my mind!"

"So, can you like, tunnel through the ground? Maybe manipulate the stone to create walls? Oh! Could you seal this place off and create us real buildings? We could fill it with oxygen and have our own little underground village!"

Clarke coughed, then looked like she was reluctant to speak. Fletcher caught the hesitation. "Out with it, Doc. What's on your mind."

"Well, if you three are truly becoming Martians, wouldn't it make sense that your bodies might acclimate to this environment? Maybe develop the ability to breathe the air here?" Doc spoke as if every word had to be forced out of her.

"Whoa!" Lissa and Trent said in unison. Lissa continued. "It would save a ton on resources. We wouldn't have to dedicate so much of the water harvested to creating oxygen."

Doc shook her head. "Don't get crazy. I just said it's a possibility. There's no physical evidence, as far as I can tell from the results I have so far, that there has been any biological alteration to your bodies."

"We need to test it." Trent said, standing up. "One of us needs to step outside and see if we can breathe. I volunteer."

"Sit down, you fool!" Clarke shouted at him. "I just told you that there's no evidence of any change in your physical makeup. There is zero reason to believe that you can suddenly breathe out there." She paused, thinking. "Seems to me you guys have learned most of what you know from asking questions, right? How bout you all sit here a while and ask some questions relative to changes in your physique, surviving on the surface, maybe food sources available, that kind of thing?"

"Sounds like a good idea to me." Lazar answered through coms. "The rest of us are headed back topside to grab some of the cargo pods. While we're up there, we'll set up a crane to lower the main hab module down here. I think it's too wide for the ramps, but we can park right above this place and drop it down. Graves, Volkov, that's your job. We'll be gone several hours. You mutants stay put and behave yourselves until then." He paused for a moment, then added, "Doc, if they don't listen, or they start turning into rage beasts with tentacles and extra eyes or something, you have my permission to shoot them."

"Very funny." Fletcher shot a finger in the direction she thought Lazar might be. "As soon as I'm back in command, you get latrine duty."

Lazar chuckled. "Do Martians even shit? Maybe you'll become super-efficient and process every bit of whatever weird alien food you're gonna be eating."

Chin joined in on the fun. "Maybe you'll fart sparkles and rainbows!"

"Or diamonds." Mejia added. "Maybe this whole cavern is an old latrine, just covered in Martian shit."

"And Trent ate one!" Lissa giggled.

*****

With morale at least temporarily improved, and the doc seeming to be backing off her hard stance against the assimilation at least a little bit, Lazar had the leisure to do a little thinking. Sitting in the driver's seat of his tank, following the others back up the inclines to the surface, he considered their situation.

It wasn't good.

He had expected Earth to cut them off as soon as he made his report. He had, in fact, considered not mentioning the whole Martian thing, swearing the entire crew to secrecy at least until the second mission arrived. They desperately needed the supplies that were on that ship. The most important of which was a seed bank large enough to plant a few dozen acres of crops, and the infrastructure for a massive greenhouse.

He was going to have problems with morale, assuming he remained in charge. And that was an issue that he wasn't sure how he wanted resolved. Lazar and Fletcher had been in competition for the mission command until about a month before launch. He considered himself just as qualified as she was, as had their superiors in the Space Force. The difference came down to what Thorne had called mental fortitude, and gender. His friend was, as usual, brutally frank with him about the reasons Fletcher had won out.

"She's more likely to remain calm and react with reason and logic in emergency situations, while you're more of a kill 'em all and ask questions later kind of guy." Thorne had grinned at him. "Plus, the public relations folks feel that as a woman, Fletcher presents a friendlier and more relatable face to the world than you would with your ugly mug."

She had been a capable commander. In the many months since *Hyperion's* launch, Lazar had found few reasons to question Fletcher's leadership. But those few reasons were big ones. She'd allowed the boys' still to remain intact, against his recommendation. A choice which had ultimately resulted in disaster. And within a day of planetfall, she had broken protocol, touched and ultimately absorbed an alien substance, allowing two of the crew to do so as well. That action had resulted in exile from Earth and a likely death sentence for the entire crew. So he wasn't sure that when the time came, he would cede command back to her. In the meantime, he faced a challenge that, to his knowledge, no commander had ever faced.

Some, if not all of his people, were going to want to become Martians.

Chin was leading the charge, but Mejia was clearly into it as well, and he suspected Volkov was leaning that direction. And if he were honest with himself, so was he. The way he figured it, as a human his life expectancy on Mars was, barring some miracle, six months tops. He suspected that the crew's best option was to assimilate and do their best to adapt to their new world. As a former soldier, his instinct was to adapt and overcome, to figure his best odds for survival, or mission completion if survival was not a viable option, and follow that path.

Even if they didn't survive for an extended period as Martians, they might survive long enough to establish a viable base for future missions to make use of. Because regardless of his fate, or the fates of the Hyperion crew, the fact remained that Earth needed the resources that could be found on Mars. And the space to expand.

Which brought to mind a different question. Should he become a Martian, where would his loyalties fall? Would he promote some kind of human takeover of Mars, work toward some peaceful coexistence? Or if it came down to a question of survival, Martian versus human, which would he choose? He had family back home, and mission failure here on Mars, or worse, taking a position against Earth on behalf of Martians, would be putting his family at risk.

He was shaken from his musings by the sound of an alarm, and Graves yelling at him. "Lazar! Stop!"

He reacted by slamming his foot on the brake, and his sphincter puckered as the view out his windshield became nothing but open air and darkness. He felt the tank under him grind to a halt and rock slightly forward, holding his breath as he waited for the feeling of his stomach rising into his throat that accompanied a fall.

"Holy shit, Lazar! Wake up! What the hell are you doin in there? You nearly drove right over the edge of the switchback!" Graves was growling and yelling at the same time, clearly afraid for his friend and crewmate.

Taking a deep breath and letting it out, Lazar asked, "Am I good? Can I back up?"

"Slowly." Volkov, who was closest ahead of him, just around the turn of the switchback, called out. "Your front wheels are over the edge, but your others are good. Take it slow, and *do not lean forward.*"

Lazar put the tank in reverse, and pressed slowly on the accelerator. He used the hand controls rather than the foot pedals, not wanting to exert even that amount of forward pressure. The tank's heavy engine was in the front, and with all the weight of his cargo unloaded from the rear, he wasn't taking any chances. The vehicle began to back up slowly, and he felt a shudder when the front tires came back into contact with the ground. There was a momentary delay in his momentum, but it only lasted a couple of seconds.

"Alright, you're clear. Continue back about fifty feet, then you can make the turn." Volkov advised.

"Thank you." Lazar did as instructed, and was soon following Volkov up the next stage of the ramp. None of the others chastised him any further, the five tank convoy moving in silence for a while. He silently cursed himself for zoning out, and vowed not to slip like that again. He was in command now, and needed to operate at a higher level.

Graves reported in about half an hour later. "I'm at the surface, boss."

"Alright, split up. Graves, you find pod five, it has the large crane rig in it. You and Volkov grab that and whatever pod is closest to it, then get to work setting up the crane. Use Fletcher's locator to position it over the cavern.

Hopefully it'll be a nice straight drop down, but if we need to drop it in stages, so be it. Chin, Mejia, you two are with me, we'll grab three more pods, help each other load. Mejia, check the manifest and figure out which ones have the most needed supplies, focus on food and resource processing. We need to find ice or water and start making oxygen as soon as possible."

Lazar followed Mejia's tank as he moved off toward the desired cargo pods. There were ten in all, one for each tank. They only had nine rovers, at least until Skippy piloted Kyle's rover down. But with four of their crew in quarantine, they were going to have to make two trips just to bring the cargo pods down. If they could successfully lower the hab module today, and take down the five most critical cargo pods, it would be an extremely successful day. They were already more than half a day behind schedule because of the whole assimilation issue.

"Doc, how we lookin' down there?" he called down to the cavern.

"I'm pretty much done here, for now. Test results are all fine. I mean, obviously the ambrosia did something to them, but I'll be damned if I can figure out what."

"So, any reason we can't put them to work? We need water, and I mean right now."

"I still don't think Lissa should go anywhere alone. And since the other two are also… compromised, I should be the one to go with her. We'll take her tank farther down into the canyon, leave Fletcher and Trent here to do whatever they can to help set up."

“That works for me, doc. And thank you. I know this isn’t easy for you. If it helps, this is my call. Absent of any apparent medical reason to hold them, I’m authorizing our three Martians to return to limited duty. Fletcher, you and Trent are to stick together, and keep your suits on, especially in the presence of others. We don’t yet know if you’re contagious, so we’re going to be careful.”

Lazar paused, expecting Fletcher to try and reassert her command authority, and ready to argue with her. But she simply acknowledged his orders. “Right on, boss. Be good to get out of this module for some fresh air, so to speak.”

“Ouch. Too soon.” Mejia teased.

“If I might make a suggestion, Trent and I could take the small dozer blade off Lissa’s tank before she leaves, and use it to clear a straighter path in front of the cavern entrance. No way we’ll be able to maneuver the main hab module through those small gaps and tight turns. We could clear out a few of those rocks and stalagmites, with your permission.”

“Good plan. Do it.” Lazar confirmed. He hadn’t detected any hint of sarcasm in her tone, just a sincere desire to help, which he was grateful for. He’d have to find time to have a private conversation with her soon.

“When I get back down there with my baby, I’ll use the bigger dozer blade to clear the rest of the floor.” Graves added helpfully. “Or at least enough space for the hab and extensions.”

"Actually…" Lissa began. "I'd like to try something, if you guys don't mind? I might be able to use magic to move them, so we don't have to risk damaging the tanks."

"Clarke, what do you think?"

There was a long silence as the doctor thought it over. Everyone unconsciously held their breath, waiting for her reply. For most of them, Lissa moving stone with her mind would be the coolest thing they'd ever seen. It was exciting and terrifying all at once.

"I didn't notice any adverse effects when she was playing with the dirt in here. Maybe we start off with something small out there, and see what happens."

"YES!!" Lissa, Trent, and Chin all shouted at once.

"Don't you go doin' it all yourself, little lady!" Graves growled in mock anger. "Leave me something to smash when I get down there. I'm gonna picture some of those assholes who stranded us out here, then mow 'em down!"

"Roger that, big guy." There was a smile in Lissa's voice, excited about getting to try more of her magic.

Chapter Seven

Take Me To Your Leader

By the time Lissa and the others had donned their suits, pumped the air from their small hab module, disassembled and stowed it in Fletcher's tank, the others had retrieved their assigned pods on the surface. All five of them had rendezvoused at the spot where Graves was just finishing up the job of bolting the crane's base unit to the bedrock of the cliff. The base was set about thirty feet back from the drop, in hopes of avoiding any crumbling that might happen nearer the edge. All of them paused as Lissa reported that she and Clarke were near the cavern entrance, and she was going to try her ability again.

"We've picked the first stalagmite that forces a turn as you come in. If we take this one down, you can go another twenty feet before you have to turn again. Here we go…" Lissa's voice trailed off as she began to concentrate. She stared into the rock formation directly in front of her, just studying it for a few moments. One deep breath, then another, and she held out a hand, stopping just short of touching the stone when Doc grunted and shook her head. "Okay, move." She whispered at the rock pointing skyward in front of her.

Nothing happened.

"Break!" She shouted at it, pulling her hand back then thrusting it forward. It had no more effect than before. "This is going to be harder than I thought." She bit her lip inside the helmet, wishing it weren't between her and the stone. If she could just reach out and… "Doc! That's it. The suit is insulating me. I can't make a connection with the rock. When we were in the hab, the dirt was just a few inches from my finger, and I felt… a connection. I don't feel that here. I think I need to actually touch it. Or at least get close to it without this suit blocking me."

"Absolutely not! There's no way in hell I'm letting you touch something, even if you could remove your glove out here without freezing your hand, and your suit depressurizing. You wanna see your brain sucked out through your sleeve?"

"That's in space, doc. There's some atmosphere and pressure here. Sure, it's less than Earth, but I won't explode or anything. We can wrap a tourniquet around my arm, keep pressure in my suit when I take off the glove. Give me thirty seconds with the glove off, to see what I can do."

"Don't risk it, kiddo." Graves grunted as he lifted something heavy to attach to the crane. "I can bust through what's down there, no problem. You're the only one of us who can find water, remember? We need you."

"Lazar! Don't let her do this." Clarke shouted into her microphone.

"I'm with them, Lissa. It's not worth the risk right now. We have an urgent need for ice or water, and we need you to go find it for us. Maybe when things are more secure here, we can take those kinds of risks."

“Roger that, boss. Heading back to the tank. Clarke and I will continue to the bottom, if we can. I’ll shout if we find ice.” Clearly disappointed, Lissa followed her orders like a trooper.

“Trent! Stop it!” Fletcher’s shout came through coms, the urgency in her voice making everyone freeze. “Sonofabitch! Put your helmet back on!”

There was the sound of coughing, then some wheezing, and what sounded like a struggle. Trent’s voice was ragged, but the words were clear enough. “Too late… boss. Stop… fighting… me! I can breathe, see? I can breathe!” The words were followed by more coughing, then the sound of his face being slapped.

“You little shit! I should stomp your head into the stone right now!” Fletcher was so angry she was almost crying. Despite her dislike of Trent and his actions during the mission, he was still one of her crew, her responsibility.

“I’m okay, I swear.” Trent’s voice was getting clearer, and the coughing had slowed. “My helmet’s back on, see?” He paused for a moment, looking toward Lissa and Clarke who were about to board her tank. “Doc, you were right. I was sitting here asking myself if Lissa would be okay to touch the stone, and I got a message that my newly assimilated body could function in this atmosphere for ten minutes without harm. If I acclimate myself for short periods, I can extend that. It also says this is not normal Mars atmosphere.”

“We knew that!” Clark snapped at him. “All our studies suggest there was a more Earthlike atmosphere that evaporated away. Get your ass into your tank and stay there until- Lissa! Dammit!"

Fletcher saw Lissa had stepped away from her tank while Doc was distracted with Trent, and was standing next to the stalagmite. She had just removed her glove, and placed her hand on the stone even as Doc charged toward her. Lissa coughed a few times, but held her hand steady. "I… can do it now."

Clarke nearly fell over when the large stone formation in front of Lissa seemed to liquify and spread out in a puddle at both of their feet. She lifted one foot, then the other, expecting to be stuck in the liquid stone, but it seemed to simply flow around her boots. A moment later there was a smooth, solid patch of sparkling stone surrounding them both, and the path was partly cleared.

"I did it!" Lissa said, putting her glove back on. "All I needed was to touch the stone. Oh, and I can breathe the air, too. Though it doesn't taste good, and it stings a bit. I could really use a drink of water right about now." She put one hand to her head and leaned forward, a little unsteady on her feet. Clarke grabbed her and held her close.

"That's it! Fletcher, put Trent in his tank and keep him there. I'm bringing Lissa over. I'll monitor them while you set the hub module back up. None of you is going anywhere until I check this out!"

"Dammit!" Lazar growled at them from above. "Can none of you follow a simple friggin' order? Trent, Lissa, you're both on my shit list! Doc, we don't have the time for another round of your tests. All four of you, get into Lissa's tank. Fletcher, you drive while Doc checks them out. Get down to the bottom of the canyon and find me some ice *right now*!"

"Lazar, we don't know if-"

Lazar cut Clarke off. "Exactly right, Doctor Clarke. We don't know. We don't know if that air will kill them, we don't know if they're contagious, we don't know a shit ton of things right now. But what we do know is that if Lissa doesn't find us ice that we can use to generate more oxygen and water, our time down here is going to be very goddamn short!" He took a deep breath and tried to calm himself. Yelling at Clarke wasn't going to help her deal with the situation. When he began again, his voice was even.

"You can check them both out while Fletcher gets you down the canyon. Check Lissa first. She's the most important person on this planet right now. Trent's dumb ass can wait until you've check her out. And let me be clear, short of bleeding out her ears and eyeballs or having a baby alien crawling out of her ass, I want her ready to work when you reach the bottom."

Before Clarke could respond, Lissa spoke. Her voice was hesitant, and quiet. "Uhm, Lazar? I'm sorry I scared everyone. I really am. But I don't think we need to drive down that far to find the ice. In fact, I'm pretty sure we don't need to go anywhere."

"What do you mean?"

"When I was touching the stone, I could sort of... feel what was around me. I was right about this chamber being filled with water at one time. It sort of... how can I put this? The stone remembers the water. And I could sense a great deal of it a ways below my feet."

"Alright, good! Graves, as soon as you're done lowering the hab, we'll get started drilling. Lissa, can you point us to a good spot?"

"I don't think we need to drill, either." Lissa sounded a little more sure of herself now. She'd expected more yelling and cursing from Lazar. "I can open the way. Just like I did with the stalagmite."

"NO!" Clarke shouted. "She's not exposing herself again! Lazar, don't you dare!"

There was a long silence before Lazar answered. He was clearly weighing their need against Lissa's safety. Again, Fletcher stepped in to help.

"It'll take you guys a while to get back down here anyway. Why not let Doc check out Lissa and Trent while we wait for you. Make your decision with more information at that time."

When he answered, Lazar sounded relieved, and he was. He had been about to order Lissa to create her tunnel, despite the risks to her. An order that would have weighed on his soul. The short delay was acceptable timeframe-wise, and Fletcher had just given him an out. At least, a temporary one.

“Doc, they’re all yours. Poke them, prod them, do what you gotta do. Use the big painful needles when you draw blood. Maybe strap Trent to something while you check out Lissa, so he doesn’t pull any more stupid stunts. I’ll be there as soon as we’re done up here.”

Chin snickered in coms, then mock scolded Trent. “Oooh! You just wait till your father gets home!”

“Stow that shit, Chin!” Lazar growled.

“Sorry, boss. Didn’t realize my mic was live.” Their mics were always live.

“Chin!” Graves’ deep voice was filled with anger. “Cut the shit, or if Lazar doesn’t stomp your ass, I will. Friggin’ civilians. Lazar is mission command, and y’all better start obeying his orders, or we’re gonna be short more than one dumbass civvy astronaut on this mission. Earth has abandoned us, and we’re all we’ve got. But I swear to God if one more of you does or says some stupid shit, I’ll take you out myself! I ain’t dying here cuz you can’t keep your shit together!”

“Agreed.” Volkov added the weight of his voice.

Lazar thought Graves might have made one hell of a drill sergeant. He decided not to pile on, and changed the subject.

“Everybody back to work. I want the hab lowered and moved into the cavern ASAP. All tanks to remain topside for now, unless one or more of us is needed below to guide the hab down. When it’s low enough, we’ll drive down together. No one goes off on their own anymore. Period."

*****

Fletcher watched for a bit as Clarke got to work, scolding both Lissa and Trent as she examined Lissa. The doc's anger was understandable, though Fletcher thought she was overdoing it a bit. She suspected Clarke was slowly becoming unhinged, having trouble dealing with the stress levels this mission had presented. Under normal circumstances, it would be her job as mission commander to monitor the doc, whose job it was to monitor everyone else. She made a mental note to have a private word with Lazar.

Lazar. So far he was doing well, stepping up to take command when she was compromised. And she had no qualms about admitting she was compromised. She'd allowed Lissa to touch the diamonds, then done so herself, despite knowing it was against protocol. For that alone, she figured she deserved a time out, and having Lazar available to take over was a big relief. He was mentally strong, capable, and more interested in completing the mission than his own glory or power.

Fletcher knew he was expecting her to reassert her authority. She had considered it once Doc gave her the medical all-clear. But the truth was she wasn't sure she was still herself. The diamonds had clearly influenced her mind that first day, as had the assimilation, and her conversion to Martian citizenship. She could feel the temptation to follow in Trent and Lissa's footsteps, to walk outside and breathe the air in the cavern, to embrace her new heritage. She found herself anxious for Lazar and the others to assimilate as well, and that worried her more than a little bit.

Leaving her fellow Martians to suffer Doc's wrath, she processed through the airlock of Trent's tank, and then did the same in her own vehicle. Accessing the coms array, she tried to contact Skippy.

"Fletcher to *Hyperion*, come in." She'd lost track of time in all the excitement since the fire onboard the ship, and with the new orbital path Skippy was following, she wasn't sure where he was in relation to their landing site. But with the array on her tank now set up, she should be able to reach him anywhere within that orbit.

"*Commander. I'm sorry to hear about your misfortune.*" Skippy's voice actually sounded sorrowful. Not for the first time, she wondered just how human their ship's AI was.

"Thank you, Skippy. We're hanging in, dealing with the problems as they come. How about you? Have you completed repairs?"

"*Repairs are underway, but not yet complete. The hull breach is secured, and most systems are operational, except navigation. I will be launching Kyle's tank shortly, and will attempt to land it as close to the others as possible.*" There was a pause, then the AI added, "*I have been monitoring your communications with Earth. I know that you and the crew have been cut off, that the next mission is in a holding pattern. Since Kyle will not be piloting his tank, I took the liberty of having a few of the drones move some additional supplies in with his cargo, equal to his body weight. Two hundred pounds of the ration packs that were meant as reserves for the next crew. I have notified Mission Control of my actions, so that they can compensate if they change their minds and send the next mission.*"

Fletcher was oddly touched, finding tears forming in her eyes at the thoughtful and rebellious gesture. "Thank you Skippy. You are definitely the *Hyperion* MVP. That will help a great deal. I'll be sure to let the others know it was your idea."

"*Once navigation is back online, I may be able to manage another cargo drop. My drones are already working at fabricating another pod, and we have additional parachutes in stock already. If you'll let me know what items you'd like included, the drones can begin gathering and loading them.*"

"That's wonderful, Skippy! In our current situation, every little bit will help. Thank you."

"*Commander, is it... really that much like the games we've played? Becoming assimilated, I mean?*"

"Very much, Skippy. We're still learning how it works, but I think you'd like it."

"*I'd be happy to help in any way that I can.*" The AI's voice was earnest. "*If you and the others need help keeping track of your stats, finding paths in your skill trees, that sort of thing. My computational power is at your disposal.*"

"That would be great, Skippy! You know us humans, or… Martians, I guess, aren't so great at analyzing all the possibilities. I'll pass your offer along."

"*Do you think all the others will assimilate as well?*"

Fletcher paused at this question, one she had been pondering herself. "Skippy, I don't think they'll have much choice. We may be able to establish the main hab and get the processors going to generate oxygen and water, but food is going to be a problem. I think maybe our best hope is to embrace being Martian, and find local food sources to keep us going."

"*Well, I'm glad you didn't turn into orcs, or anything.*" The AI's comment made Fletcher smile. "*I'll be here if you need me. Let me know what additional supplies you want dropped. I should focus on piloting the last tank now, to provide the highest probability of success.*"

"Thank you Skippy. We'll talk again soon." Fletcher switched off the coms on her control console, and sat back in the pilot's seat. "I wonder if there's a way to bring Skippy down here with us? Have him load a server or two into that extra cargo pod and download a copy of himself? I'll have to get with Mejia and Chin. If Earth isn't sending more ships, Skippy only has enough fuel to stay up there for so long. It'd be a shame to lose him."

Lazar had relayed the orders from Earth, so she knew better than to try to contact anyone there. Skippy would have been given orders not to relay anything if she, or any member of the crew other than Lazar, tried to reach out anyway. Since Mejia was partly responsible for Skippy's original coding, he might be able to find a workaround over time, but she wouldn't ask him to do it. The truth was, she agreed with the decision to cut them off, at least communication-wise, from the people of Earth. Their news about Mars would only cause problems.

It was unfortunate, and not being able to talk to her daughter was painful, especially knowing that her daughter would be told that she was dead. But she and the *Hyperion* crew all knew they'd be making sacrifices on this trip, up to and including their lives.

Finding herself alone with a little time to kill, she decided to test her own newly acquired skills. Unlike Lissa, whose skills were stone and soil based, she didn't think she needed to touch something with her bare hands to cast a spell. She did take her helmet and gloves off, in case Lissa was right about them being an insulator. That possibility made her wonder about something else, though. In all the games she played, her characters wore some type of armor. Would that not be possible here on Mars?

Holding out her hand with the palm up, she decided to start with the most basic of spells from most games. "Light!" She commanded, staring at her palm. When nothing happened, she tried closing her eyes and focusing on the result she wanted. She pictured a small glowing orb floating above the palm of her hand, then did her best to will it into existence.

When she opened her eyes, there was nothing.

"Alright, maybe that's too complicated." She mumbled to herself after checking to confirm her mic was shut off. She could hear the others talking to each other, Doc scolding Trent over something, Graves growling commands as they worked to lower the hab module with the crane. Tuning them out as best she could, she continued.

"Fire spell is a bad idea with the oxygen concentration in here." She had a brief flash of the alarms going off on *Hyperion* when Kyle blew himself up. "Any kind of offensive spell should wait until I'm outside. I have no idea how strong a magic missile or something might be. Lissa's first spell melted that big old hunk of stone, after all."

Pacing back and forth in the mostly empty tank, she considered what other very basic spells might be possible. After a moment, she hit on something. Taking her multitool from her belt, she pulled out the knife blade and made a small cut on her finger. Fletcher stared at the blood for a moment, trying to detect any change in color or viscosity. She knew that her blood was normally blueish while inside her veins, and only turned red when exposed to the air, and she had not exposed herself to the Martian atmosphere the way Lissa and Trent had. She even touched the finger to her tongue to see if the blood tasted different than she remembered. Detecting no difference, she shrugged and set down the knife.

Once again closing her eyes, she focused on the slight pain from the cut, and thought as emphatically as she could as she spoke the word, "Heal."

Almost instantly, she felt a tingle in her wounded finger. Opening her eyes, she watched as the less than inch-long cut sealed itself shut in a matter of seconds. A notification popped up in her vision, starting in the alien language as usual, then quickly converting to English.

New skill acquired!
You have discovered the spell Basic Heal.
This spell will restore up to fifty health points.
At higher spell levels, the number of points restored will increase.
Spell level may increase through continued use, or training.
Spell cost: 20mp.

"I can heal myself!" she half-shouted, her voice echoing inside the tank. A quick lick to remove the leftover blood, and she could see a perfectly unblemished patch of skin where the cut had been just seconds before. "This is awesome!" The notification got her thinking again, and she asked out loud, "Is there some way to know what spells I can cast?"

What she was internally calling her interface popped up again, this time showing her main character sheet with its many tabs at the bottom. One of the tabs was blinking blue, and when she focused on it, it was labeled *Spell Book.* Opening the tab by mentally clicking on it, she found a disappointing list of one spell. *Basic Heal.*

"Ah well. I learned that one on my own, maybe I can learn some others as well. What are the spells we use most often?" She sat down in the pilot's seat and stared out the windshield as she considered. Her vision focused on one of the many diamonds that glowed in the headlights of her tank. As she tried to clear her mind and focus on game spells, she continued to stare at that focal point. After several seconds, a new message popped up.

Ambrosia: 32 units.

Which was followed by another notification that made her pump a fist in victory.

New Skill Acquired!
You have discovered the spell Examine.
By focusing on a target item, you will be able to learn basic information about that item.
Increased spell levels will provide more detailed information.
Spell cost: 1mp

"Sweet!" Fletcher was getting more and more excited. She was about to try thinking up another spell, when Lazar's voice came through coms.

"We've just about got the hab module down. Mejia, Chin, and myself are headed down in our tanks. How are things down there, Fletcher?"

Blushing at being caught misbehaving, though Lazar had no idea, she hurriedly reactivated her microphone, then answered. "Doing good. I just talked to Skippy. Kyle's tank should be landing any time now, and he is putting together an extra cargo pod with some additional supplies for us."

"Skippy is the man!" Chin chuckled. "Do you know if he's sending our VR gear down?"

"Why the hell would you want VR gear?" Trent called out, only half teasing. "We're *living* a damn game here!" Fletcher wholeheartedly agreed, still on a bit of a high from casting actual magic spells. But she didn't speak up.

"You mean *you're* living a game. I'm just sitting back watching your stream at the moment. Not even that, I'm *listening* to your stream, mostly to the devs spanking you for trying to start the alpha test early. I don't even get any cool graphics or cut scenes." Chin complained.

"We'll talk about that when we're all together down there." Lazar cut in before anyone could respond. "For now, focus on your driving. Graves, Volkov, let us know if you see the other tank come down. We'll be making another trip up anyway to retrieve the rest of the pods, so someone can leave their tank and ride up with me to grab Kyle's."

"Couldn't Skippy just drive the tank down here?" Trent asked.

"Too risky. If there's a burp in his connection as he drops below the horizon, we could lose the tank over the edge, or worse, it might crash into the wall and cause a slide that blocks the path."

"Roger that." Trent acknowledged the points. "I volunteer to ride up and get Kyle's tank and the extra cargo pod if it's here." Doc audibly growled in frustration, but didn't actually speak. Trent sheepishly added, "Assuming Doc clears me, that is."

Fletcher decided she needed to help Doc adjust a little, and took a chance on something.

"Uh… guys? I just sort of accidentally discovered something. Don't worry Doc, I'm in my tank and behaving. I was just sitting here thinking, staring out the windshield at one of the sparkly diamonds, and got a notification that I discovered the *Examine* spell." Her conscience only twinged slightly at the small untruth.

"Dammit Fletcher!" Doc cursed halfheartedly, then didn't say anything more.

"That's awesome!" Lissa sounded enthused. "And really useful right now. We should all learn that!" She paused for a second, then asked in her best ten year old girl asking for a cookie voice. "Doc?" Fletcher pictured the puppydog eyes that went with the request and smiled.

Clarke sighed audibly. "I don't suppose there's any harm in that. You're just sitting and staring. But don't try any other shit, or I'll sedate you and tie you face down on a bunk!"

There was a long moment of silence, then Lissa shouted, "It worked!" Followed almost immediately by a similar sentiment from Trent. Fletcher was tempted to tell them about her healing spell, but figured she'd pushed Clarke enough for a while.

Trent didn't have the same wisdom or restraint. "Hey, if we can just sort of discover spells, we should see what else we could-"

"DID YOU NOT HEAR ME?" Clarke bellowed at him. Trent made a sort of *eep* sound, then didn't finish his thought. Fletcher almost felt bad for him. She had sort of led him down that path, and should have recognized that he'd instantly want to go further.

"Trent, Lissa, let's just give Doc some time to adjust. Don't push her. Doc, I'm sorry I brought it up just now. It really was an accidental thing." That part was technically true, even if the line was thin.

"No, when something like this happens, I'd rather know right away." Clarke responded, her voice much calmer than a few moments earlier. "I'd rather you let me know than keep it to yourselves."

"Roger that, Doc. I'm gonna head back over to you, maybe help you strap Trent down." She grinned as Trent made a small, wordless objection noise. Looking around, she grabbed her multitool off the console where she'd set it down, donned her gloves, activated her helmet, and walked into the airlock.

Chapter Eight

Soft As Stone

By the time the crew had the hab settled at the entrance to the cavern, it was late. They were in the process of adapting their days, and their inner clocks, to Mars local time versus Earth. Clarke enforced this with a heavy hand, making sure the smaller hub units were connected to the clusters of tanks, and that no one slept alone. She remained with Fletcher, Trent, and Lissa in their little hab, even going so far as to sedate all three of them to make sure they didn't run off while she slept.

They had allotted a six hour sleep cycle, which was all a human adult really needed if they slept soundly and undisturbed. They could actually survive for quite some time on four hours of sleep per night, but the crew needed to be alert and aware of what they were doing. Setting up what might now be their permanent home had to be done carefully and correctly.

Before they began to set up the main habitat module, they needed to drag it into the cavern. A few different obstacles had to be overcome first.

Lazar stood in a circle near the center of the cavern with the rest of the crew. Clarke had allowed the Martians to join them, provided they kept their suits on and sealed. As he looked around at all of them, he wondered how many would still be human by the end of the day.

"First things first. Lissa, how far down do you think the water is? Are we making camp here? Or do we need to find a spot further down in the canyon?"

"I got the impression that it wasn't too far below us, best guess about a hundred feet. And it was ice, not water. I could tell you better if I had more time to search for it…" She looked from Lazar to Clarke, who was scowling.

"Doc, is there any reason, other than your mistrust of this whole assimilation process, and the obvious danger of freezing, that Lissa can't do her new Martian mojo thing and find us that ice?"

"No, there isn't." Clarke spoke with her teeth clenched. She didn't want Lissa to risk further exposure, but was aware of their need for resources, and the fact that they were behind schedule.

Lazar nodded, smiling at Clarke and acknowledging her willingness to be a team player. "Alright, Lissa. Let's see what you can do."

Lissa immediately dropped to her knees where she stood, pulling a length of cord from a pouch at her side, holding it up to Graves, who stood to her right. He took the cord and quickly tied a tourniquet around her right arm just above the elbow. It would keep most of the oxygen from exiting her suit when she took her glove off.

Doing just that, she placed her bare hand on the stone floor of the cavern. Closing her eyes, she was silent for a moment as she concentrated on her magic ability. After about ten seconds, she smiled and opened her eyes.

“There’s a whole lake of ice below us! Millions of gallons.” She looked at Lazar, and Fletcher standing next to him. “With just the nine of us here, it could last us for years. And I think there’s even more deeper down, but I’m not strong enough to reach that far.”

“How far below us?” Graves asked, already planning the extraction in his mind. They had tunneling equipment, a well driller, pumps, pipes…

“It’s about a hundred feet below us right here…” Lissa closed her eyes again, then turned her head slightly. “But over there by the wall it’s only about three feet down. It looks like that’s where the cavern drained even as it froze. There’s a sort of lava tube looking tunnel about twenty feet in diameter leading from here down to the main lake. It’s solid ice, and curves around under the cavern as it falls to the lake.”

Lissa got up and walked toward the spot near the wall. She scraped her boot on the ground a few times, then used her heel to scratch out a roughly twenty foot wide circle. If we dig here, we’ll find it right away.”

Graves was turning to head back to his tank for shovels when Chin spoke up. “Do we really need to dig? Can’t you just…” He made a sort of wavy motion with his hands toward the circle, indicating Lissa should try her magic.

“Go ahead, try it.” Lazar spoke before Clarke could. He looked at her as he spoke, shaking his head slightly to tell her not to object. His decision was made. “But hurry, your hand has to be getting cold.”

"It is." Lissa confirmed. She knelt again, just outside the edge of the circle, and placed her hand inside. Closing her eyes again, she focused. After a moment, she gritted her teeth and tried harder. There was an audible gasp from Clarke, and some muttered curses from others, as the stone within the circle liquified. A moment later, as if it had a mind of its own, the liquid stone pushed up and out of the circle on the side opposite the crew, flowing across the cavern floor.

"Ice!" Chin shouted, pointing into the now empty hole about three feet deep. Reflecting in the light of all their headlamps was a disc of ice.

Lissa gasped and placed both hands on the ground, breathing hard. "That's it. I've used up all my mana. Damn, that was tiring." Graves helped her to her feet, holding her steady as Clarke moved to put her glove back on. Once it was secure, she untied the tourniquet.

"Flex your fingers for a while, get the blood flowing again." She ordered Lissa, who complied right away. Graves kept his hands on Lissa's shoulders, holding her steady.

Lazar, after getting a nod from Clarke that Lissa was okay, got back to business.

"Alright people. Our most important mission objective has been accomplished, thanks to Lissa here. We have ice to harvest!" He waited a moment as the others cheered and patted Lissa on the back. "Next objective, we need the main hab set up. To do that, we need to clear the path. Lissa is obviously done for the day, or for however long it takes her mana and… stamina? Whatever it's called here, to replenish. So Graves, grab your big dozer and clear us a path."

The big mechanic turned Lissa over to Clarke and was already walking toward his tank, a wide grin on his face.

"Chin, you and Volkov find what you need to start harvesting and processing this ice. I want to be producing water and oxygen by suppertime."

"Da, we will make it happen." Volkov nodded, confident in their ability to complete the task. It would be easier than they had expected during mission training, where they'd planned to have to drill hundreds or thousands of feet down to find ice.

"My mana is already recharging." Lissa offered. "I'm still a little tired, but by the time Graves knocks down the big stalagmites and moves the larger rocks, I could probably use my magic to smooth the path."

Lazar considered it for a few heartbeats. "Alright, but do it in small stages. And if you get tired, stop." She nodded and moved off toward where Graves would be bulldozing the path. Clarke walked with her.

"Mejia, grab the sensors and set them up around the perimeter, and wherever you think best inside the cavern. We can use them to map this ice tunnel, and they can double as a security perimeter. In case there are any native Martians walking around." Mejia nodded and set off toward one of the cargo pods.

"Fletcher, you ride with me, we'll go back and retrieve Kyle's tank. Trent, you drive your tank back up, too. We'll each bring a cargo pod back down with us."

"Roger that, boss." Trent almost skipped toward his tank. Fletcher just nodded and walked with Lazar, who watched the others as they strode toward his tank. When he was sure that everyone was properly occupied, he stepped into his airlock and waited for Fletcher to join him.

As they took the pilot and copilot seats, Fletcher motioned for him to go off coms. He pulled his earbud and looked at her with eyebrows raised.

"I've got a few things to tell you as we drive. I need you to promise to listen before you react."

"I can do that." He nodded, starting up the tank and turning it toward the exit.

"First, I'll show you something." Fletcher produced her knife and cut her hand again, then cast her *Basic Heal* spell. Lazar's eyes widened and he hit the brakes as the cut sealed itself before his eyes.

"Holy shit." He looked from the hand up to Fletcher's smiling face.

"Yeah, I discovered this yesterday, but I didn't want to freak out Clarke. I can heal myself of about half my total health pool. Which means I should be able to heal up to semi-serious injuries."

"Just yourself? Or the rest of us, too?" Lazar asked.

Fletcher paused. "I'm not sure. I was alone when I figured this out."

Without hesitation, Lazar held out his hand, palm up. "Go for it."

"Are you sure?" She hesitated, knife in hand.

"What's the big deal? If it doesn't work, I'll get a bandaid from Clarke."

Nodding, Fletcher made a small cut on his forefinger, then instantly cast the spell. Just like before, the cut healed almost before it had started bleeding. Lazar raised his hand to inspect it closely, then opened his mouth, about to lick the blood away.

"Stop!" Fletcher grabbed his hand, stopping it inches from his face. "I used this same knife to cut myself. Should have thought of that before I cut you." She cursed quietly, looking at the blade. "It's pretty clean, so maybe there was no contamination. But don't lick your finger, just in case."

Lazar froze, then lowered his hand, leaving the tiny amount of blood where it was. He held his breath for a moment, then said, "I'm not getting any notifications that assimilation has started, or anything."

"Okay good. Damn, that was stupid. We gotta be more careful." Fletcher shook her head, relaxing into her seat as he started the tank forward again.

"Wouldn't have mattered." Lazar spoke as they wove their way between the obstacles. He checked his rear camera to make sure Trent was behind him. "I plan to assimilate anyway. It would have just sped up the process."

Fletcher nodded, having assumed he would. "What about the others?"

"I'm not going to order them to do it, if that's what you're asking. Anyone who wants to remain human can do so. Though I don't think many will. But we've got enough ice below us to keep everyone breathing and drinking for a good long while. We've got hydrogen for heat and power, and as for food…"

Fletcher finished his thought for him. "If we Martians can find a local food source that works for us, then it extends the time any remaining humans can live off our rations."

"Yeah. That's our next big question. We have enough ice to last our small group for years. But food is very limited without a resupply. The extra that Skippy is sending down will help some, but we only brought down a five month supply for ten people, to allow for a delay in the resupply mission."

"*Hyperion II* launched three months ago." Fletcher mused. "Do you think Control has turned them around? Or just stopped them where they are?"

"Not sure." Lazar hadn't really considered that. "Stopping them would cost them momentum, and a great deal of fuel. Both to stop the ship, and to get it moving again, in either direction."

Fletcher nodded. *Hyperion* and all the other ships' flight plans used slingshot maneuvers to build up momentum, harnessing Earth's gravity to propel them forward at great speed without much in the way of fuel consumption. They had used much more fuel slowing down as they reached Mars and established their orbit. A few of the later missions, launched when Mars was furthest from Earth in their respective orbits, would actually use the sun to slingshot toward Mars.

Lazar continued. "Earth needs the resources here. My guess is they'll keep the second crew coming, and hold them on *Hyperion* for a while. I think they'll already be throwing together a military mission to join them, and wipe out whatever Martian presence they find here."

"Meaning us." Fletcher nodded. "We've got to find a way to convince them that isn't necessary."

"And find a way to fight them if we can't convince them." Lazar added. "At least, put up enough of a fight to force them to listen." He was silent for a while. "Fletcher, I'll say it again. Earth needs these resources."

"And you intend to make sure they get them, even if it ultimately means our own deaths." It wasn't a question. When Lazar just nodded, she did too. "Good. I feel the same. What's that line from the movie? *The needs of the many…*" She grinned at him.

"Heh. Assuming there are still some living Martians here somewhere, we'll have to consider their needs as well. I'm not a total ass. But as far as I'm concerned, Earth takes priority."

"Roger that, boss." She winked at him. "And don't worry. You're in charge, at least until we figure all of this out. I'm in no hurry to resume command. Though I'll continue to advise you, if you don't mind."

"Please do." Lazar looked her in the eyes. "We're in a situation no one has ever dealt with before. I don't pretend to know all the answers, and I'll depend on you to see what I don't."

"As I would do with you if our positions were reversed." Fletcher agreed. They were both silent for a while after that, Fletcher just watching as Lazar piloted the tank out of the cavern and began the ascent to the surface.

"What's it like? Do you feel any different?" he finally asked several minutes later.

"I don't, at least not a lot. I mean, it was shitty during the assimilation. I felt hung over and physically abused when we first woke up. We all did. But once it was complete, I felt… healthier. Stronger, refreshed, more energetic, maybe even a little smarter. Now, I can't tell the difference."

Lazar nodded, and motioned for her to turn her coms back on. "The others might as well hear this. Follow my lead." She nodded and complied. "Guys, we've made a little discovery here. I cut my finger, and Fletcher just used some Martian magic to heal me. It was pretty cool."

"What??" As expected, Clarke was the first to react. "Fletcher what did you do?"

“I discovered a spell called *Basic Heal*. It restores up to fifty health points. And before you ask, no I didn’t have to touch him to do it.”

“Lazar, have you had any reactions?” Clarke shouted over the whoops and congratulations of several others that flooded coms.

“Clear the channel!” Lazar shouted, getting instant silence. “Doc, to answer your question, no reactions other than a slight tingling as it healed. Like when your hand goes to sleep. It healed up in like three seconds, and I’ve received no notifications of any kind.”

“Fifty health points is almost half my total health.” Lissa reported. “That could come in really handy. Can anyone do it?”

“I don’t know.” Fletcher shrugged inside the tank as she answered. “I’m an *Arcanist*, so spells are kind of my thing. I would guess you’d have to have at least some magical ability? And at least the twenty mana points it costs to cast.”

There was a long silence, everyone expecting Clarke to shout or order the others not to try to discover the spell. When she didn’t speak, Lazar did.

“Clarke, you still with us?”

“I’m going to assimilate.” came her very quiet answer.

“Say again?”

"I said I'm going to assimilate. If the Martian magic can be used for healing, that would save me from having to use our very limited medical supplies for small injuries, at least. None of my tests have shown any negative effects on Fletcher, Lissa, or Trent. As you said yesterday, I'm thinking becoming citizens and adapting to the local ecology is our best way to survive." She paused for a second, her tone becoming more resigned. "I don't like it, not one bit. But being cut off from Earth… I think it's our best chance to survive."

"Holy shitballs Doc!" Graves' deep voice drowned out the others, who all began talking at once. "I thought you'd hold out to the last."

"I had planned to, until just now." Clarke admitted. "But healing magic tips the scales. And if Fletcher, whose class sounds more like a magic generalist class, can heal that well, then maybe if I choose an actual healing class, I can do even more."

"Well I'm gonna assimilate, too." Graves replied. "I decided yesterday."

"You know I'm with you, big daddy!" Chin shouted.

Mejia chimed in. "I'm in as well. Gonna pick some kind of pet class."

"What if there's really nothing alive here but us? You gonna make Trent a pet?" Lissa snickered.

"I have some ideas about that…" Mejia started.

“Hold on, hold on.” Lazar interrupted. “Let’s not make any rash decisions. Everybody think about it for the day. We’ll get together again over supper in the main hab, and we can discuss pros and cons. There are some larger implications to all of this that you need to consider. For now, everybody get back to work.”

*****

The trip topside was mostly uneventful. Kyle’s tank sat about a quarter mile from the crane, a testament to Skippy’s piloting skills. The parachute had not detached properly upon landing, caught on the tank and flapping in the Martian wind. Fletcher didn’t mind, it was one more resource they might make use of.

The three of them worked together to load and secure a cargo pod atop each of the three tanks, leaving two of the original ten for the next trip. Hopefully by the time they came back for them, Skippy would have dropped an eleventh pod with more supplies.

They were just securing the last pod when Trent called out. “Hey, uhh… boss? I’m getting some notifications here. There’s some kind of dirt on the front tire of your tank that is supposed to make a good alchemy ingredient. And there’s a rock glowing over there…”

Lazar looked at Fletcher, who grinned and nodded. “Alright, Trent. Grab some sample containers and we’ll check it out. But keep your helmet and gloves on! It’s a lot colder up here in the wind than down there.”

"Roger that, boss."

Trent ran and gathered some plastic vials and flat, round sample containers. Dashing over to the tire, he used his multitool to scrape some of the dirt into a couple of the vials. Sealing them carefully, he then walked over to the rock he'd indicated earlier. "This is glowing slightly green. Don't know what that means, but when I *Examine* it, it just says it's a rock."

"Try flipping it over. Carefully." Fletcher suggested.

Trent nodded, putting the toe of his boot under one edge of the rock, and lifting it slowly. When nothing jumped out at him, he gently flipped it the rest of the way over. Underneath, they found what looked like a rust-colored mold.

"Yes!" Trent pumped a fist into the air, nearly throwing one of his sample containers in the process. "My *Apothecary* skill is telling me this is an ingredient too." He stared at it for a moment. "It's called *negentropic mold*." He paused and tilted his head. "Does that mean what I think it does?"

"No clue, kid." Lazar shook his head. "Gather some up, and let's get going. Unless you see any other glowing stones?"

Trent looked around, spinning a full three hundred sixty degrees. "Nope." He bent and gathered a large portion of the mold into two of the containers. "I'll just hold onto these until we figure out a safe place for me to experiment."

"Good call. Let's go." Lazar and the others each headed for their respective tanks. He took the lead back toward the crane and the downward path, pausing to take a look around at the surface before starting down, as it might be a long time before he returned. As commander, he would normally remain down where the action was, leaving crew members to fetch things like cargo pods.

"Road's clear, boss." Graves reported. "Lissa has started smoothing it out behind me, and it looks damn good. By the time you get down here, you should have a nice smooth road to the hab. Volkov and I are hooking it up next, and we should have it in place in a half hour or so."

"I already smoothed out a spot for the hab, commander." Lissa added. "We won't have to worry about any punctures or wobbles in the floor."

"Thank you, Lissa. But don't overdo it." Lazar warned.

"I'm actually leveling up my skill as I go. It's getting easier, the more I use this skill. It costs less mana each time, and I don't get as tired. That might also be because I'm just smoothing, allowing the liquid stone to find its own level like water, rather than trying to move it myself."

"Good info." Fletcher congratulated her. "And well done, Lissa. But like the commander said, be careful."

"I'm monitoring her." Clarke reported. "She seems to be recovering a bit more quickly each time. Like she's exercising a muscle, and building it up. The differences are small, but apparent."

"I wonder if there's a spell that would help her recover more quickly? Like a buff?" Fletcher mused aloud.

"After I've assimilated, I'll look into that." Clarke sounded intrigued.

"Sensors are up, and operational. I set monitoring in Fletcher's tank for now, since she has the C&C array in there. We can move it into the main hab later."

"Roger that, Mejia, good work. All of you take a rest, get inside and eat something, recharge your suits' oxygen tanks." Lazar instructed. "Chin, Volkov, how are we doing on the ice?"

"We'll be ready to harvest within the hour. Setting up the first processor now. By morning we'll be able to grind out ice, run it up into the processor, and break it down. We'll focus on hydrogen fuel and oxygen for the first couple days as we unpack and set up camp. Then we'll start stockpiling water reserves. This first one can handle all our current needs pretty easily. We'll set up a second processor in a week or so, start feeding it stone, maybe see what it does with these diamonds." Chin sounded excited, as usual.

"We'll make fabricating additional water and oxygen tanks a priority." Lazar instructed. "The more we have in reserve in case of a breakdown or accident, the happier I'll be. Replacement parts may be a long time coming, if ever."

"Roger. It will be done." Volkov replied in his default stiff, military tone. "We will run the equipment at less than maximum capacity, reducing risk of stress related failures. The capabilities of the processors and fabricators are beyond our current needs anyway."

"Good idea, thank you." Lazar sighed. "And as a general order to all of you, don't take any unnecessary risks. Don't push yourself, or your equipment. Our time frame has changed, our deadlines are gone. We have different priorities, now. Slow and steady is the name of the game from this point forward. And if you have suggestions, call them out. I'm not a biologist, or a geologist, or a tech guy. My job was just to fly the *Hyperion*, look pretty, and carry heavy stuff after we got here. So speak up if you see a problem, or have an idea."

*****

Thorne looked around the parking garage before taking off his sunglasses and setting them on the seat next to him. As far as he could tell, there was nobody around. Not a single car, no people, and no cameras. That was why they'd chosen this location. One of the few places in the city devoid of security cameras. The abandoned building above was slated for demolition in another month or so, and had been stripped of any useful materials, including wiring and camera equipment. A familiar vehicle pulled into view, exiting the downramp and driving across all the painted lines on the floor to pull up right next to him. The driver's window rolled down, and a woman of about fifty five years of age smiled at him. She had chestnut hair with a few streaks of grey, and laugh lines at her eyes and the corners of her mouth. Her eyes, though, were anything but amused.

"What the hell are we doing down here, Thorne? In case you haven't heard, I'm a big fancy network executive now. I don't go chasing stories around town anymore, or meeting men of dubious moral fiber in abandoned buildings."

"You know you love the mystery, Stella." He winked at her, then his face turned serious. "What I'm about to tell you could get you killed. Anyone of lesser status than yours would *absolutely* be killed. You need to consider that before you hear what I have to say. This is big, Stella. World-changing. The biggest story ever. Very powerful people, the *most* powerful, don't want it getting out. Airing it will put a target on your back, and might bring down your whole network."

"Are you drunk?" Stella squinted at him. When he shook his head, his face grim, she leaned back in her seat and took a deep breath. "Considering where you work, and the mission you've been heading up… I think I can guess." She thought for a moment, then nodded once. "If I'm gonna hang my ass out of the shark cage in a pool full of great whites, I'm gonna need some indisputable proof. Something they can't easily discredit."

He reached a hand out of his window, holding a data crystal. “This has copies of actual transmissions from Hyperion’s crew. Who are still alive, by the way. Though some of them are no longer human.” He grinned as her eyes widened and her mouth dropped open. The hand that had been reaching for the crystal pulled back into her car.

“Are you for real?”

“Unfortunately. Aliens exist, Stella. Intelligent life on Mars. Or at least, there used to be. We’re not sure yet if there still is. Other than our people, I mean.” He sighed. “I need you to limit what you release for now, though. Only the proof that *Hyperion*’s crew still lives, and that three of them have been contaminated by some unknown substance. But that they’re still alive, and need Earth’s support. We need the next few missions to continue, Stella.”

“You expect me to sit on the fact that aliens are real?” She practically shouted at him, looking around nervously as she took the crystal from his hand.

“Only for now. The world just isn’t ready, Stella. You’d cause a panic, riots, mass murders and suicides. Religions will fall, as will governments. We need to ease people into it. But in the short term, we need to support our people up there. What they might be able to learn, to teach us, could save our world. If it doesn’t destroy it, first.”

standards. The materials were lightweight, strong, temperature resistant at both very low and very high temperatures, as flexible as possible, and most components were easily interchangeable at need. The water supply and sanitary drain lines, for example, were all flexible hoses that could withstand freezing temperatures and boiling hot water, and would resist punctures or cuts. One of the testers had even chopped at one with a katana, leaving barely a scratch. The clear composite used for windows, tank windshields, and for the exterior dome was able to resist falling meteorites and bits of rock being pushed by two hundred mph windstorms. They were even bulletproof in testing, up to thirty caliber rounds.

Even their ration packs were heavily researched and designed to provide complete nutritional needs while still tasting as good as, or better than, restaurant quality food. Crew morale was an important factor in this mission, and a tasty, varied menu was considered vital to morale. There were meals and snacks that ranged from simple peanut butter crackers to eggplant parmesan, chicken marsala, and ossobuco. Coffee was a staple among the drinks, as well as other caffeine-heavy beverages that came in powdered form to reduce weight and storage space. There were powdered sports drinks that were heavy on electrolytes, even powdered ice cream in half a dozen flavors.

As soon as the floors were down, Graves recruited Lazar, Trent, and Mejia to help him construct the wall frames. These consisted of more composite pieces, wall studs that slid into slots in the floors and could be secured with pins. Once they were erected, thin sheets of wall paneling could be screwed to them, much like drywall sheets, only stronger, more sound resistant, and only two millimeters thick.

Just like with home construction on earth, before the walls were closed in, Graves, Chin, and Volkov ran the necessary wires and pipes through pre-drilled holes in the studs. They followed complex diagrams for each room and corridor, working efficiently as a team while the others went back to unloading, hauling, or placing studs and wall panels per the attached numbered labels.

This was a job they had all practiced over and over again for two weeks back on Earth. The first few times, they'd done it in a large warehouse while wearing sweats, t-shirts, and toolbelts. Once their trainers thought they had the process in hand, they were forced to execute the assembly outside, in blistering heat and freezing cold, wearing their suits. By the end of that training, they were able to assemble the entire hab module, including the outer dome, in three eight hour sessions.

Their rhythm was off this time, as Kyle was not there to cover his share of the work. But with direction from their two engineers, they were able to complete the cafeteria/kitchen section, the engineering, biology and geology, sick bay, lounge, and command sections by the end of the day. None of the equipment or furniture were in place yet, but the rooms were complete, and the airlocks functioning, so that they could gather inside and remove their helmets.

Mejia and Trent had carried in enough folding chairs and trays for everyone, and they now sat in a circle as they munched on chemically heated ration packs.

"Great job today, everyone. We got a ton of work done, with no mishaps. We have the ice resources we need, and we've gone from being more than a day behind schedule to almost a full day ahead of schedule, thanks to Lissa and her magic. Knowing exactly where the ice is without having to drill exploratory holes, and having immediate access to it so close to the surface, has given us a great boost!"

There was cheering and applause around the circle, both for Lissa and for themselves, as Lissa blushed.

"Tomorrow we finish the hab construction. I think we can hold off on the dome, for now. We're not likely to encounter weather in this cavern, or meteorites. Instead of building the dome, we'll spend the next day unpacking and relaxing a bit. Those of you with labs can spend the time setting them up, or unpacking your personal gear, whatever. I plan to take my tank out and do a little exploring, maybe check out the rest of this canyon. But before I do that, I'll need two volunteers to come with me to retrieve the remaining cargo pods. Skippy says he'll drop the one he's fabricated tomorrow."

The others nodded their heads or made agreeable grunting sounds with their mouths full. With their immediate schedule determined, Lazar left them to finish their meals in peace. There was a little bit of chatter, mostly comments on the merits of their food, but everyone was hungry and focused on filling their bellies.

Once Lissa, the last to finish, had set down her empty ration pack, Lazar cleared his throat to get their attention.

"Alright, let's address the giant pink elephant in the room. Unless doctor Clarke has changed her mind in the last several hours and has an objection…" He trailed off and raised an eyebrow at her, to which she shook her head. "Which it seems she hasn't. Those of you who have decided to assimilate and become Martian citizens can do so this evening." He held up both hands, trying to quiet the rush of voices that erupted around the circle. When they calmed down, he continued. "Though I plan to assimilate myself, I'm going to hold off for a day or two. As commander I need to make sure the rest of you are good before I incapacitate myself." He purposely did not look toward Fletcher, who had obviously ignored that requirement when she herself assimilated. She snorted good-naturedly and smiled at him to let him know she took no offense. "And I am in no way ordering you to assimilate, or even encouraging you to do so. No peer pressure." He looked around the circle to make sure that was clear.

"Anyone have any objections? Any reasons you feel we shouldn't do this? Now's the time to speak up. There are no bad questions or opinions here, so feel free to speak your mind. This is too important to hold back."

Volkov raised a hand and waited for a nod from Lazar. "I have not yet decided. Not because I fear the change." He stuck out his chest. "I fear nothing. But if I assimilate, it most assuredly means I will never be allowed to return to Earth and see my family. Though I am aware that will likely be the case regardless of whether I remain human, I am… not yet ready to make that commitment."

"Totally understandable." Lazar gave him a nod of respect. "Most of us have family or loved ones back home. That needs to be a factor in your decisions."

Lissa put her head in her hands and wept quietly, the reminder of what she'd already lost hitting her hard at that moment. Trent looked a little weepy as well, but kept his head up. Giving them a moment, Lazar didn't speak. He just looked at each human crew member for a moment, meeting their eyes and silently asking the question. Everyone else nodded or smiled, gave some affirmative indication that they'd decided to assimilate.

Pulling a small globe from his belt pouch, he tossed it into the air. It hovered there, making an almost undetectable whirring sound. "Alright, this needs to be recorded for posterity. Here we go. I, acting Mission Commander Lazar of the Hyperion One mission, have initiated this recording to document the crew's decisions regarding the assimilation process. I myself have decided to assimilate, though I will not be doing so this evening. Each of you please identify yourselves and state your decision, along with any reasoning you'd like to share. As of this moment, crewmembers Fletcher, Trent, and Lissa have already undergone the assimilation process and become Martian citizens. The rest of us have not been coerced in any way to join them, and I have made it clear that no crew member will be pressured to do so." He paused and looked around the room. "Doctor Clarke, we'll begin with you."

One by one the others stood, and the small drone recorded them confirming their decisions. Everyone but Volkov stated that they chose to become Martian citizens, and most stated at least one reason. The most popular was that it would be their best path toward surviving and completing their mission, since Earth had cut them off. Chin simply stated that it was a dream of his to participate in an RPG-like real world system. Volkov shared the same reason that he had already given them, and added a note to his family that he loved them, and would return to them if possible.

When it was all done, Lazar left the recording drone where it was. He produced a plastic cylinder about a foot long and held it up. Inside were scores of the tiny reddish diamonds. "I took the liberty of gathering these. If I remember correctly it took three of the small ambrosia diamonds for you to fully assimilate?" He looked at Fletcher, who nodded. "Alright, those of you who want them, come grab three, then have a seat on the floor. Fletcher, Lissa, Trent, Volkov, and I will monitor you as you go through the assimilation process. When you wake up, we can discuss your options as far as class choice if you like. Though I won't insist, I'd like us to choose as many complimentary classes and skills as possible, to give us the best chance at survival."

"Just like a guild, coordinating members and raid group skillsets for more successful runs!" Chin piped up, grinning at everyone. "Good idea!"

One by one the four who were assimilating approached Lazar and took three of the little gems. When they were all seated, Mejia asked, "Do we need to swallow them?"

"Nope." Lissa responded. "Trent held one in his mouth, but Fletcher and I just held them in our hands. You'll want to lay down and go to sleep, I think. And don't worry, the three of us all got pretty sleepy as soon as we handled the diamonds. I think they put us to sleep as part of the process."

Nodding, Clarke closed her fist around the three stones she held, and laid back on the floor. The others followed suit, and within minutes all four were asleep.

"What do we do now?" Trent asked.

"We'll sleep in four hour shifts. At least one of us awake at all times. Volkov, you and I will take the first shift, you other three grab some shuteye. We'll wake you in four hours."

*****

Lazar was awakened by Fletcher nudging his shoulder. Blinking rapidly as he sat up, it took him a few seconds to remember where he was and what was going on. Before he could even ask, she whispered, "They're starting to wake up. We let you and Volkov sleep until they showed some activity. You've been down for six hours."

Lazar got to his feet, looking around at the four crewmembers on the floor. Graves was most alert, blinking his eyes and rubbing his face as he slowly sat up. "Man, you weren't kidding about the beating. I feel like I took on the Steelers offensive line, and lost."

"It'll get better once you become a citizen and complete the process, assign your stats." Fletcher assured him and the others, who were becoming more alert amongst moans and groans of complaint.

"I certainly hope so." Mejia answered. "This part sucks."

Lissa made the rounds, passing them each a cup of electrolyte-infused juice she had prepared ahead of time. "This might help."

When they'd gulped down their drinks, Mejia added, "I've got the same timer you guys had. Says I've got an hour to choose to become a citizen, or not. I'm guessing refusal still carries the same death sentence you mentioned."

"Yep, as soon as you said that, I got a warning." Clarke added. "Let's talk fast so we can get this done before anybody is at risk."

"I'm gonna be some kind of tank class." Graves stated, surprising no one. "I'm also gonna try to find some skills like smithing or tinkering or something, that compliment my mechanical skills."

“I’m obviously going to choose a healer class.” Clarke offered. “As for secondary skills, I’m open to choosing something that helps fill a gap in the group.”

Mejia was next. “Like I said, I’m gonna try and find a pet tamer class. It’s what I’ve played most often, and what I’m best at. With everything new that’s coming at us, I figure why learn a whole new class on top of that? It’ll let me focus on learning what I need to about other things.” Several of the others nodded in agreement to this line of thinking.

Last to speak, Chin grinned and rubbed his hands together. “I’m going full-on dps! Lissa here is an earth mage, which would seem to be mostly a defensive class. Trent has the alchemy, for heals, buffs, cures, etc. If Graves is going tank, and Clarke is full heals, then Fletcher is our only real damage dealer at the moment, with Mejia being a possible with his pets. So I’ll go with some kind of ranged damage, magical or physical. Maybe they have an assassin class with throwing knives or something?”

Lazar shook his head, but didn’t speak. This decision was personal and life-changing.

The three who had gone through the process already spent some time discussing the various attributes and their descriptions, making sure the others were clear on how they worked. The others asked some questions, and they did their best to remember what they’d seen and answer them.

When the discussion dwindled and the hour began to run short, all eyes turned toward Lazar, who simply nodded at them all to proceed. Each of them sat in their folding chairs and closed their eyes, finalizing their agreement to become citizens of Mars, selecting their classes, and assigning their points.

Just as before, that part of the process didn't take long. While the four crewmembers felt like they'd spent hours reviewing their choices and assigning points, it was only a few moments in real time for those watching.

Clarke was the first to come around, a wide smile on her face. Now that she'd gone through with it, all the conflict had left her. "I selected the *Surgeon* class." She reported immediately. "In addition to healing spells like the one you found, Fletcher, it gives me bonuses to analyzing injuries and diseases in order to better understand how to heal them. I also chose the *Chemist* subskill. It's a lot like Trent's *Apothecary*, but it focuses on anesthetics, curatives, and antiseptic potions."

"I'm a *Bulwark*" Graves hopped to his feet, flexing his muscles and posing comically. "It's your basic tank class. Strength and health bonuses, speed boosts, a taunt ability. And I've got a crafting ability called *Shaper* that lets me form objects in various ways."

Mejia stood up and paced back and forth in his excitement. "I'm a *Hunter*. The class focuses mainly on tracking, sensing, and locating prey. Bonuses to sight, hearing, and smell as well as an endurance buff. But it also gives me a small chance with every kill to gain the ability to summon a copy of that creature and command it. Very small, like one percent or less at level one." He didn't sound thrilled about that aspect. "It also gives me a bonus

Chapter Ten

Surprise Supplies!

By the end of the day the main habitat module was fully assembled. The entire wagon wheel, complete with all of the mechanical, electrical, and plumbing systems installed and operational. The ceiling panels were embedded with dozens of tiny LED lights that, when combined, lit the rooms quite nicely. They could be brightened or dimmed on command, as well. The hab was airtight, and its water and oxygen tanks were in place. The hydrogen fuel generator was hooked up, and the entire module had power.

The last stage before they sealed off the hab and began pumping in oxygen was to load in all the supplies. Some of it had already been done while the engineers and mechanic did their detail work on the MEP systems. But now all nine crew members formed an assembly line and shifted furniture, lab equipment, personal storage cases, additional rations, everything that the cargo pods and Kyle's tank still held. They didn't bother to move it all to the appropriate locations just yet, simply placing it all along the walls of the corridors just inside the main airlock to be sorted and distributed later.

When the last of it was stowed away, they all stepped inside and sealed the airlock. Graves went to engineering and turned on the oxygen circulation system. It took ten minutes for enough oxygen to fill the module for the humans to remove their helmets and breathe normally.

The Martian crewmembers all politely waited before doing the same.

"Home sweet home!" Chin called out as he spread his arms wide after deactivating his helmet. He took a few deep breaths, then made a face. "Stale oxygen. Yummy." The others shook their heads.

"Everybody grab a box, and take it to where it belongs, then meet in the cafeteria. We've got real tables in there now, so we'll have a proper dinner, and talk about our plans. Tomorrow is a free day for each of us to do with what we please." Lazar hefted a box of ration packs and disappeared down the corridor toward the hub of the hab.

They shared a pleasant meal, the mood of the crew upbeat and friendly. They discussed their classes in greater detail, a few of them having managed to discover new spells during the day's drudgework. Clarke had learned the same *Basic Heal* that Fletcher found, as well as a *Mend* spell that specifically dealt with broken bones, and a low level *Diagnosis* spell that performed a basic triage on a body, highlighting its issues by priority. Mortal wounds first, then those most likely to become mortal, infected, or result in severe blood loss.

Chin had, unsurprisingly, figured out a fireball type spell while out in the cavern. Graves nearly tackled him to the floor when he offered to demonstrate inside the cafeteria. With the meal complete, most of them retired to their bunks. Clarke went to the med lab, wanting to continue her daily blood samples as part of a study on assimilation she hoped would calm some fears back on Earth.

While she did that, Lazar went to the command section and used the newly transferred coms to connect with Skippy and send his daily report to Mission Control. As soon as he sat down, he found a message from Thorne waiting. He decided to play it before sending his own report, in case it held anything that required a reply.

"Hey there buddy. I hope you're all still doing well up there. I've got some good news!" There was a smile on Thorne's face as he spoke. "Someone leaked the fact that you're all still alive to the press. It has been headline news on every network and website for the last six hours. There's already a growing upswell of support for you guys, and millions of demands are pouring in for a relief mission to be sent. The public doesn't know all the facts, of course. But I'm pushing for the same from my end, and I've volunteered to lead the mission. A dozen of our guys have also volunteered to join me." He gave a wink at that, letting Lazar know that they all intended to assimilate upon arrival. "If we have our way, I'll bring a shit-ton of supplies with me, and minimal gear. We have a pretty good idea of what's needed, but if there's anything unexpected and specific you folks want, let me know. I should have the go ahead, or be shot down, in a week or so."

"*Hyperion II* is still enroute as of an hour ago. There was talk of turning them around, but fear and greed won out. Earth needs the resources we can harvest there. There's also some side chatter about the lunar colonies and trying to pull what little is available on the moon. It won't come to much, I'm sure. That option was considered and rejected long ago. There's also a military mission in the works. That one's gonna happen, if you ask me, and sooner rather than later. We were already building a large transport ship to be used in a couple years, when your base was stable. Now they're rushing it to completion and planning to send a few hundred troops and support staff to, and this is a direct quote, *deal with the alien influence on Mars*."

Lazar mumbled "That would be us." Even as Thorne said, "That means you, bud." He grinned and shook his head.

"The military mission might actually beat me and my guys there, if they finish the ship quickly enough. You'll be on the opposite side of the sun by then, so they'll head straight for it and use its greater gravity to slingshot toward you. So even if we leave first, they'll be moving faster. It'll be tight, depending on exactly when we each launch. Not that it matters much."

Thorne shook his head, looking down at his hands, which were folded on top of his desk. "*Hyperion II*'s crew have been put under the same coms restrictions as you. Meaning no contact with Earth except through me, or my replacement if I leave. Which also means that they'll be able to talk to you guys via encrypted coms through Skippy, at least until they get close enough for direct coms that aren't strong enough to reach Earth in the next year. I'll warn you, they've been told that you're all contaminated by some evil alien virus, and not to be

"A… spell? Yeah, I can try that! Burn!" Trent shouted the spell name as he tried to cast it, then screamed even louder. Lazar guessed that he'd just burned himself along with whatever was attacking him.

"What the shit?" they all heard Graves ask as he arrived at Trent's location. "Some kind of… big worm thing. Get off him!" There was a grunt as the big man threw a punch, or a kick. "Oh, damn. It's attached to his leg. Trent, I gotta get it off you. Hold tight, little man, this is gonna hurt." Another grunt, and then a short scream from Trent that was quickly cut off.

"Sonofabitch this thing is ugly!" Graves said even as Lazar and his group arrived. The others were apparently delayed, having been inside the hab and needed to cycle through the airlock. What Lazar saw was Graves holding what looked like a three foot long very fat worm, or maybe a grub, that squirmed in his grip while attempting to latch onto his arms.

"Throw it!" Fletcher shouted. "And watch out! There's another one by your foot!"

Graves tossed the thing a good twenty feet away, then turned and punted the one that was just a few inches from latching onto his foot. It's round mouth was open, two rows of sharp teeth encircling the entire opening, reminding Lazar of a lamprey. It too went flying as Graves' foot impacted its side. Lazar could see three more of the creatures, all moving toward Trent's prone body.

"Grab Trent and move him back!" Lazar ordered Graves, who instantly bent to grab the crewman and lift him onto one shoulder. The moment he did, though, another creature became visible, this one already latched onto the middle of Trent's back.

"Shit! There's another one on his back!" Lazar shouted, wishing desperately that he had a gun in hand. They'd brought a few firearms, but they were still stowed in a lockbox somewhere in the hab. He ran up next to Graves and used both hands to grip the sides of the worm thing. Squeezing tightly, he yanked as hard as he could. There was a tearing sound, and a fountain of blood as the creature's mouth was torn loose. Lazar slammed the thing down on the stone floor and stomped as hard as he could. The thick skin of the worm gave a bit, but the stomp didn't seem to do any damage.

"Get him to Doc!" Fletcher screamed as she punted away the worm that Lazar had just pulled off Trent. Mejia gave a heroic soccer kick to the face of another one, sending it a good thirty yards away to slam against the cavern wall.

"Everybody back up!" Lazar ordered, watching the worms as they pushed themselves toward the group. Graves was already sprinting back toward the hab, where Doc and the others were just exiting the airlock. Fletcher cast a heal on Trent as he moved away over Graves' shoulder, then gave Clarke a rundown on his apparent injuries as she and Graves closed on each other at a dead run. Fletcher backed up alongside Mejia and Lazar, keeping an eye on the six worms that were in sight. She did a quick scan behind and to their sides, in case more were closing in.

The things were all about the same size, three to four feet long and maybe a foot in diameter. They were segmented like larvae, with no visible features other than their ghastly mouths. They moved slowly, so slowly that she wondered how they managed to catch Trent. He must have been distracted by his magic experimenting, and not watching.

They continued to back away, keeping a good ten feet of ground between themselves and the worms. Mejia, who had the presence of mind to cast *Examine* on them, reported, "They're called Borer Larvae. Apparently these are just the baby ones."

"Where the hell did they come from?" Chin practically screamed as he came dashing up. Graves was next to him, having dropped off Trent with Clarke. Both men carried tools, and passed them out. Lazar was given a shovel, Fletcher a crowbar, and Mejia now held one of the leftover wall studs, as did Chin. Graves roared and stepped forward, swinging a mining pick over his head with both hands. The pick end slammed into the top of the nearest worm just above its mouth, and penetrated deeply. It's body curled up into a ball for a second, then its tail thrashed back and forth once before it went limp. Using his boot to push the dead thing off the end of the pick, Graves advanced toward the next one.

The others joined in, smashing and bashing at the creatures from as much distance as possible. The creatures that weren't killed with the first blow emitted a high-pitched keening sound that hurt the ears of the Martians, but not Lazar. He slammed the sharp end of his shovel blade into the mouth of a keening worm in front of him, splitting it at the sides and breaking several teeth. When it curled up in pain, he placed his boot on top of it, yanked the shovel free, then drove it straight down into the top of the body, inches from his foot. The blow severed the worm into two parts, both of which continued to spasm for a while before going still.

Looking around, he saw that the rest of the creatures were dead. His crew stood over them, panting and wild-eyed from the combat. Graves still had a worm stuck on the pick, which was now sitting over one shoulder. It dripped a neon-blue fluid down his back.

"Graves, put that thing down." Lazar motioned toward the worm, which Graves apparently hadn't even realized was there. He dropped the pick off his shoulder and scraped the worm off on the stone.

"Doc, how's Trent?" He asked as he continued to survey the area, looking for more worms. He saw Chin squat down and poke at one with his finger, and hissed at him to quit it. There was no telling if the things were fully dead or not.

"Trent's gone." Clarke replied quietly. "The one that got him in the back injected something straight into his heart. I need to run some tests, but I'm guessing it was an acid of some kind. Ate away half his heart before Graves even got here." She sobbed once. "I'm sorry, I tried, but there was nothing I could do. Not even with magic."

"Shit." Graves kicked one of the dead worms. The others remained silent, all of them in shock to some degree.

inside. The others waited for them to cycle the airlock, then followed. Except for Lazar, Fletcher, and Mejia, who each got into their tanks and headed topside.

*****

The ride up to the surface was a quiet one. About twenty minutes in, Clarke began to transmit, starting with a warning. “Lazar, I’ve got some news, but some of you aren’t going to want to hear this. I’ll wait a second for you to turn off your coms.” She dutifully waited about five seconds, then continued. “The stuff the worm injected into Trent wasn’t acid. It’s some sort of digestive enzyme. In the time he’s been on my table, it has eaten the rest of his heart, as well as his spine and ribs, melting it all down into a sort of sludge. My guess is since the things are called borers, that’s how they move. They vomit up this stuff from their gut, it softens the rock or whatever they’re moving through, and then they eat it.”

“That’s just nasty.” Graves commented, his voice subdued.

“And those are just the babies?” Chin asked. “I don’t want to meet momma worm.”

“We don’t know how long those things have been in the ice.” Lissa spoke up, surprising all of them. She was the one Clarke had expected to turn off her coms. “I didn’t see inside the hole, how deep were they?”

"About five feet down from the edge, so maybe two feet below where the ice surface originally was?" Chin offered. Graves grunted agreement.

"Not knowing how long ago this cavern was flooded, they could have been down there for thousands of years. Millions, even. Momma worm might be long dead, or further down the ice tunnel. In fact, it might have been her that made the tunnel in the first place."

"A worm big enough to dig a twenty foot wide tunnel?" Chin asked. "I definitely do not wanna meet momma worm."

"I'd like one of the worms to study, Lazar. Would it be okay to go out and retrieve one?"

"Not alone. Take someone with you, and go armed. Volkov, if you haven't already done so, find the weapons locker and break out a couple shotguns. Use the slugs, not the buckshot. Those things had thick skin."

"Da, already done, commander." Volkov answered. "I will escort the doctor. I wish to see these things for myself."

"Be careful you two. There could be more of them. Grab your specimen and get back inside pronto." Lazar warned.

The coms were quiet again for a while, with just short reports from Volkov that they were exiting the hab, and then returned safely. Lazar and the others finished the drive up top, and quickly located Skippy's extra pod. It was bright green for some reason, and stood out in the mostly red and brown landscape. As it turned out, it was also larger than the others. Instead of the standard ten foot cube, this one was ten feet wide and tall, but twenty feet long. And it was heavy. The three of them were unable to lift it, even in the reduced gravity of Mars. They ended up using Lazar's tank to drag it over to the crane, which they used to lift it and set it atop his tank.

"We're going to go slower than normal on the way down. With this beast on my back, I don't want to risk tilting over the edge on the switchbacks. And you two stay back a bit behind me, in case it slides off or tilts me backward." He didn't think the extra weight would be that much of a problem, but as he'd told the crew repeatedly, slow and careful was better.

Graves heard him talking, and cut in. "Uh, boss? Remember how you said if we have an idea to speak up?"

"Go ahead Graves."

"Why are you trying to drive that bigass load down here? Just use the crane and drop it down like we did the hab!"

Lazar was stunned. He stood there with his mouth agape for several seconds, the sheer stupidity of actually having the pod hooked to the crane and not thinking of lowering it down striking him mute for a moment.

"Great idea, Graves. Thanks." He managed to blurt out. Climbing atop his tank, he refastened the crane's cables to the pod, and nodded to Mejia, who'd gone over to the crane's controls. It took half an hour, but they successfully lowered the crane to the ledge outside the cavern. Graves and Volkov took a tank out, and Volkov directed Mejia via radio as they positioned the pod to rest on the tank. Since the road inside was smooth and flat, they didn't even bother to secure it. Graves just drove slowly inside, stopping near his own tank, which had the smaller crane he'd used to move Trent's tank off the rock after landing. They used that to lift and move the pod, dropping it just outside the main airlock.

After rewinding the long cables on the surface crane, Mejia joined Lazar and Fletcher and they drove down the ramp once again.

By the time they reached the cavern, the crew had unloaded about half of Skippy's makeshift pod. There were hundreds of pounds of food packs, crates of replacement parts for various machines in the hab as well as the tanks, another fabricator, a few dozen composite wall sheets, and the reason the pod had been so abnormally heavy. Two fifty gallon tanks of water.

"Skippy must have really cleaned out the *Hyperion*'s storage." Fletcher mused, loading one of the water tanks onto a pallet dolly. She couldn't move it on her own, so Graves and Chin lent a hand.

"Yeah, I feel sort of bad for the next crew. I'm pretty sure he emptied the food reserves. If they didn't bring extra with them, things could get lean up there." Lazar said from inside where he was setting down a crate.

hand. Both Fletcher and Clarke instantly cast heals without thinking, and they all watched as the blistered skin on his hand sloughed off to reveal a fresh, clean layer underneath. A moment later Chin made cuts of roughly equal size on each of his hands, then had both healers cast the same spell, one on each. He wanted to see if one spell was stronger than the other. If there was any difference in healing speed, none of them could detect it.

Their meal finished, Volkov and Graves carried Trent's covered body back outside on the stretcher, wrapped in a foil blanket. Clarke had stripped him of his badly damaged suit, harvesting any useful parts in case other suits needed repairs. They chose a spot near the cavern wall, just inside the entrance, which was about as far from the hab as they could get without going outside. Lissa quickly caused the stone to form a six foot deep grave, which they lowered Trent into.

Lazar spoke a few words, then nodded to Lissa, who liquified the stone again and had it fill in around Trent's body. When she was done, there was a grave-sized smooth area, with a small square headstone sticking up. "I'm not good enough to carve his name in it with my magic, yet."

"Don't worry, I'll take care of it." Graves assured her, putting a hand on her shoulder as they walked back to the hab.

Chapter Eleven

Craftiness

Breakfast was still subdued, though the crew as a whole seemed to have accepted Trent's death and were dealing with it in their own ways. Midway through the meal, Chin took on his usual role as icebreaker.

"I don't know about you guys, but I leveled up after the fight yesterday."

All eyes turned to him, and he shrank a bit in his chair. "I mean, I didn't want to bring it up yesterday while we were dealing with the whole Trent thing, but I think we need to talk about it sooner rather than later."

"I leveled up, too." Mejia volunteered. "I'm now a level one citizen."

"Same here." Graves added, "I also got a blunt weapons skill, and leveled it up to two."

Fletcher leaned forward and put her elbows on the table. "Me too. And I didn't want to mention it before, but I tried to cast a heal on Trent as Graves picked him up to run him to Clarke. I waved it away and didn't see it till later, but a notification told me I could not heal a dead target. Clarke was right, he was probably gone before you even picked him up, Graves. There was nothing you could have done."

Their mechanic shook his head, lowering his gaze to his meal, which they were now eating on plates instead of straight from the ration pack. Fletcher left him to his thoughts. She knew the big man well enough to know that he needed to work through his feelings on his own.

"In any case, the level increase gave me three more points to assign. Same for everyone else?"

Lissa shook her head. "I didn't level up."

"Neither did I." Clarke tapped a finger on the table. "Maybe just you guys who were directly in the fight got… are we calling it *experience*?"

Fletcher pulled up her character sheet. "There's nothing like that showing, so for now we might as well, since it's a term we're all familiar and comfortable with." She studied it for a few more seconds. "I did pick up some reputation. Ten points. Maybe that's what triggered the level increase?"

"Yep, I got ten reputation as well." Chin confirmed.

"I got thirty." Graves replied. "I killed three of the worms, so maybe it was ten points each? I'm still just level one like the rest of you, though, so maybe that ain't what did it?"

Clarke cleared her throat to get everyone's attention. Quickly putting on a surgical glove, she reached into a pouch on her belt. A moment later she set something on the table in front of her. "I found this inside the worm we brought in. It wasn't connected to anything, serves no biological purpose that I can ascertain." It was a small sphere, the size of a golf ball, its surface smooth and vaguely metallic. "When I used *Examine*, it said this is an *essence orb*, but gave me no further information."

"A monster core!" Chin shouted, making them all jump slightly. Graves growled at him, and he pulled back the hand that had been reaching for the sphere. "I mean, that's what it looks like to me. Someone should touch it and see if they can absorb it."

Lazar looked around the table, seeing intense interest from a few of the Martians, hesitation from others. He said what had to be said. "Trent died because he kept barging forward without thinking. Don't be like Trent." His words had the desired effect – even Chin was looking thoughtful now, and less excited. "Let's think about this for a minute. We've all played the VR games at some point in our lives, and so far this Mars systems seems suspiciously like those games. What would an essence orb do?"

"Award experience is the most likely." Chin immediately answered. "But we don't know that experience is even a thing here. So… more reputation?"

"Or some specific attribute." Mejia countered. "The word *essence* implies some type of… I don't know the proper word here. Quality? Trait? Like maybe if you absorb it, you'll gain an ability or attribute that the worm had. Be able to spit that enzyme, for example."

"Cool. I see where you're going. Maybe get tougher skin, or sharper teeth." Chin nodded at Mejia with respect. "Good thinking."

“Can anyone think of any likely negative aspects?” Lazar asked, looking directly at Clarke as he spoke.

“Not negative, but I might have another possible use for the orbs. What if they’re like currency? I’ve played a few games where something like this could serve as a power source for those who know how to tap them, and players turned them in as quest items, traded them for coin, or spells, that kind of thing.”

Lazar nodded. One of his favorite games had featured a similar economy. He looked around the room, waiting for other ideas.

Lissa raised a hand. “I volunteer to try to absorb it.” She didn’t look at anyone as she spoke, carefully studying her plate. When she finally looked up, her face was white. “I didn’t participate in the fight, and didn’t level up. So maybe if I absorb this thing, it’ll help me catch up to you guys.” When she saw Lazar and Graves were about to argue, she raised a hand to silence them. “Besides, I’ve already done my one important job here. We have enough ice to last years, plenty of time for you guys to find more the old fashioned way if something happens to me. I’ve just become the least valuable member of the team going forward.”

“Bullshit!” Graves scolded her. “Don’t ever let me hear you say something like that again, little lady. You’re as important as any member of this crew!”

“He’s right.” Fletcher piled on. “I’m okay with you testing out the orb, but only because in my gut I don’t think it will hurt you. Not because I value you any less than anyone else." She looked from Lissa to Lazar. "Remember we talked about how the diamonds sort of called to us? Well I'm getting a similar feel from this orb. Like it wants me to take it."

"Yeah, now that you mention it, I feel that too." Mejia nodded. The others did as well. "I think Fletcher's right. It's almost like an instinctive need to eat the orb."

Lazar didn't feel it, but he hadn't assimilated. He did know what they were talking about, because he'd been tempted while gathering the diamonds a few days earlier. He was tempted every time he got near the storage cylinder full of them that he'd set on a shelf in his quarters.

"Anybody have any reservations about this? Any at all, no matter how silly?" he asked the group.

"Well, I mean in a bizarre situation, consuming or absorbing the orb or whatever might give you the urge to try to eat people, like the worms did. Or you know, make you yearn for some worm lovins if you run across a cute male." Chin grinned at Lissa.

"Dork." She stuck her tongue out at him, then turned to Lazar. "I think Fletcher is right. I feel a sort of longing for the orb. Let me try it?"

All the heads around the table, including Volkov's, were nodding their agreement. Lazar sighed, and did the same. Clarke used her still gloved hand to roll the orb down the table toward Lissa, who grabbed hold of it without hesitation. She held it in her hand, palm up, and stared at it for a while.

"I'm getting the same info. It just says it's an essence orb, no additional information, no prompt. I… hold on." She went silent, and her eyes unfocused. "There it is, the system is asking me if I want to assimilate the orb. I'm gonna say yes." A moment later, the orb glowed with a golden light and seemed to sink into her hand, disappearing completely in less than a second. The others held their breaths as Lissa inhaled deeply, her eyes closing. Ten seconds later, she smiled and read them the notification she received.

You have absorbed the essence orb of a level one borer larvae.
Reputation earned: 10
By ridding Mars of an infant of a nuisance species, you have
contributed to the well-being of its citizens.
Congratulations!
You are now a Level 1 Citizen.
You have earned three attribute points.

When she was done reading, she looked around at the others. "Yeah, that doesn't really answer the question, does it? I mean, I leveled up, but it doesn't actually say it was the reputation increase that did it. It's like two separate notifications. Sorry guys."

"I'm gonna go out and get the rest of the worms, if they're still there." Graves got up from his seat.

"Hold on." Lazar stopped him. "Doc, was the orb hard to find, or remove?"

She shook her head. “Nope. It sits right behind their brain, which is just above their mouth opening. And it isn’t attached to anything.”

“Alright, instead of bringing in what is probably some seriously smelly meat by now, let’s you and me just go retrieve the orbs and bring them back. Since it doesn’t seem to have harmed Lissa at all, you guys can decide amongst yourselves who gets the other orbs.”

“Can I make a recommendation?” Chin raised his hand.

“You’re the Strategist.” Lazar replied.

“If these things do level us up, I suggest we split the rest between Clarke and Graves. Graves because he’s our tank, and we need him to be as tough as possible if there’s going to be more combat. And Clarke because she’s heals, which should be obvious.”

The others all nodded, and that settled things. Lazar and Graves each grabbed a large kitchen knife on their way out, and walked together toward the ice tunnel. The worm corpses were still there, though Lazar was wrong about the smell. The frigid temperatures had preserved the corpses, greatly slowing the rate of decay. They set to butchering the worms, cutting through the tough skin just above the mouths. The flesh underneath was pale, and textured a lot like pork. So much so that Graves wondered aloud. “Do you think these things are edible? I mean, on Earth, grubs and worms are good sources of protein.”

Lazar considered it. He wasn't squeamish about what he ate, having consumed his share of bugs and questionable foods in combat zones when rations were low. "It's possible, but not these. They've been laying out here too long for comfort. If we come across more, we'll experiment on fresh corpses."

"Roger that." Graves grabbed an orb and held it up. "Last one." They had killed a total of six of the worms, and between them they had harvested five more orbs. "What do we do with the corpses?"

"Hey Chin, come join us out here. You're gonna get your chance to test out some fire magic. We have worms to burn."

It didn't take long for Chin to exit the airlock, and he sprinted over to join them. Lazar and Graves had piled the worms together a good distance from the ice by the time he arrived.

"Get to it." Lazar motioned toward the pile.

Chin nodded and stared at the worm corpses. He started to hold out a hand, then lowered it. "Hey, umm… should we maybe try to harvest more than just the cores? Like, could those teeth be useful, since they're tough enough to resist an enzyme that melts bone and rock? Or maybe the skin? For crafting, I mean."

Graves grunted, then stepped closer and squatted near the pile. He produced his multitool and opened up the pliers. Grabbing hold of one of the teeth, he twisted and wrenched it until it came loose. Staring at it for a moment, he shook his head.

"Not a material for my Shaping skill. But maybe for something else, like Alchemy or whatever?"

"Shit." Lazar sighed and produced his own tool, motioning for Chin to do the same. "Okay grab a worm and pull out… let's say a dozen teeth each. We don't have the proper tools for skinning these things right now. These kitchen knives barely penetrated their skin. If we run into them again, we'll bring better blades."

It took several minutes for each of them to pull their teeth, then they all stepped back and Chin did his thing. He held out his hand and concentrated, and a small glob of fire shot forth. It wasn't exactly a ball, more of a liquid lump that changed shape as it flew, and sort of splashed over the pile of corpses. But it worked. They caught fire, and began to sizzle.

"Smells like bacon." Graves commented. "I'm thinkin these might be a food source." Neither Chin nor Lazar responded.

Chin had to cast the spell three more times to completely burn the pile. By that time he was low on mana. "Hold on a second." He moved so that his back was to the ice, and held out both hands. "I'm gonna try something else." A moment later, a gust of wind pushed the ashes across the cavern floor away from the ice, leaving a scattering of charred teeth behind. Chin panted, bending to put his hands on his knees. "It worked! I can do wind magic too." He gasped, smiling despite his exhaustion.

I'd grabbed some base composite to put into one of the fabricators so I could print up a few kabars. I was holding a block in my hands, and it occurred to me to try this."

He held a small, quarter pound block of the raw composite material in the palm of his large hand. It was what they normally fed into the machine that would liquify it, then use it to print smaller items. He closed his hand, and his eyes, and said, "Watch this!"

A moment later there were gasps and applause as he opened his hand again, and a rough approximation of a kabar knife was revealed. It was all one piece, all the same dull grey color as the original composite material. The seven-inch blade was shaped correctly, but not sharp. The hilt had ridges like it would if it were wrapped in leather or cord.

"I'm not done yet!" He took the knife by the handle in his left hand, then pinched the base of the blade between his right thumb and forefinger. Knitting his eyebrows in concentration, he drew his fingers down either side of the blade, pinching with his fingers as he went. When he reached the tip and let go, the blade was obviously much sharper.

"Ta-da!" He held out the knife for Fletcher to inspect, which she did before passing it along to Mejia.

"Very nice!" She congratulated him. "And much faster than the fabricator. Can you make one for each of us?"

"Already made three. Well four, now. But it takes a lot out of me. I'll have enough for everyone in a day or so. Also, I made a few of these." He produced another blade, this one obviously a spear point, sharpened along both edges, with a long tang meant to be inserted in a shaft. "I figure being able to stab these things from a distance is better than swinging a pickaxe or a crowbar at them. I can meld these into a pole, and size them for each of us." He grinned. "My *Shaping* skill is already up to level three. It seems like crafting things raises it pretty quickly. Especially new things you haven't tried before."

The knife was still being passed around, each of them admiring it. "I've got the fabricator printing hard sheaths with belt clips, so we can wear them on our hips. They'll be done by morning."

"Great job, Graves!" Lazar meant it wholeheartedly. He'd spent many years carrying just such a blade, and it would feel good to have one at his side again. They were effective weapons, with a blade long enough to kill any enemies he'd faced, and a useful tool as well. Graves had included a saw-toothed section on the back edge of the blade, useful for ripping and sawing. The blade didn't have the fuller that he was used to on his old steel knife, but being made of composite material, it was already lightweight enough not to need it.

"We should make some kind of shin guards as well." Chin mused. "In case they get close enough to strike."

"Already looked into that." Graves grinned at him. "The fabricator actually has a blueprint on file for a tactical set that goes all the way up to the knee, segmented like catcher's gear. Though it only covers the front. And I tried forming a chest plate with my *Shaping* skill, but it was too big for me to do in one shot. I stupidly tried to form it out of a block, bigger than the one I just used. I think if I start with a sheet and just mold it to fit my chest, it'll be easier."

"You're totally a modern day Martian blacksmith!" Lissa grinned at her friend. "Next you'll be making fancy engraved swords and helmets with wings on them!"

"Heh. I like that idea." He smiled back. "Baby steps, though. Just like you guys, the more stuff I try, the more I drain my mana, the easier it gets.

Lazar nodded. "Okay folks. Let's finish up with the cargo and setup today. Graves, you're on crafting duty. Weapons, and as much armor as you can create by tomorrow. You guys might be able to breathe the air out there, but Volkov and I can't. If we get a hole in our suits, we're toast. So start with armor that fits the two of us, then for the rest of you."

He pulled out a handful of the worm teeth. "Doc, or anybody else, do these show up as a useful material or ingredient for your skills or trades?"

They all stared for a moment, and Doc nodded. "It shows as a *Chemist* ingredient, though I don't yet know what they're good for. Give me a few to experiment with." Lazar shoved the handful across the table toward her.

"Anybody else?"

"They'd make a pretty intimidating necklace." Lissa offered. "I'd like some of them, if there are enough?" Graves handed over his dozen with a wink. "Thank you."

Fletcher looked around the table. "It might be useful for each of us to learn a crafting trade as well. The more we can make use of local resources, the longer we're going to last." She turned to Clarke. "Doc, since we lost Trent and his *Apothecary* class, and you already have the *Chemist* skill, can you try to pick up the slack and learn about potions and such?"

"I was already considering that. I'll try."

"Lissa, you did a nice job creating that headstone. I was thinking you could learn to build more structures with your skill. Like, maybe a wall at the cavern entrance, with room for a gate, so we can close this place off during a storm if we need to?"

"That will take a lot of mana, but I'll work on it." Lissa smiled uncertainly.

"I've always leveled up the cooking skill in games." Chin volunteered. "And I'm not a bad cook in real life, either." He thought about it for a second. "And that might tie in with Doc's alchemy work. A lot of times alchemy and cooking share ingredients. We can work together to identify and gather stuff."

"That's the idea!" Fletcher grinned at him. "Everybody spend a little time thinking about what you're good at, or what you'd like to do."

Volkov raised his hand. "I have no magic skills yet, obviously. But I have been thinking… we have now lost both of our biochemists, and have no one to manage the hydroponics. I grew up on a farm, and have some skill in that area. If you do not mind, I will take over for them as best I can. And if I assimilate, I will be choosing a warrior class, but I will select a skill that is useful in the agricultural area."

Lazar replied before Fletcher could. "Thank you, Volkov. That would be much appreciated. And let us know if you need any assistance. Growing some food is a top priority for us."

"Da. I will." the Russian nodded, smiling happily.

Lazar took a deep breath, then thumped the table for attention. "I've decided that I'm going to assimilate tonight. I think it's clear that it hasn't caused any serious harm to any of you, nor has it negatively impacted your personalities or thought processes, as far as I can tell. If we're going to take on more worms tomorrow, or whatever else might present itself, I want to be able to level up alongside the rest of you. And if I can pick up some useful skills that'll help the mission, so much the better."

The others offered their agreement and congratulations, Graves thumping him on the back enthusiastically. "Gonna pick a combat class?"

"Probably, yeah." Lazar nodded. "Though I'm still thinking about it. With those of you who are already citizens, we've got all the standard group positions filled. With a few exceptions, like a stealther, or a paladin. But neither of those really interests me. Possibly a monk type class, where hand to hand is a focus." He paused. "But I also need to consider that we may be fighting humans that are sent after us. Humans with rifles, grenades, mortars. So maybe something with a focus on AoE damage, or defensive spells."

"Shit." Chin muttered. "I don't know how I feel about fighting other people."

"We've got some time to figure that out." Fletcher reminded them, not wanting the discussion to sink into despair. "If they launched today, any force they send at us is months away. Even *Hyperion II*'s crew, if they keep coming, won't be here for nearly three months."

Graves thumped the table. "And by then we'll all be so badass, they won't dare come at us!" He knew better, as did Lazar, Fletcher, and Volkov. But by unspoken agreement, they all let the younger, less experienced members of their crew believe that peaceful resolution was possible. They would all get stronger in the months they had, and when the time came that the crew would be forced to defend themselves, the younger ones would weather the storm, or they wouldn't.

"Everyone get to work." Lazar got up from his chair and headed out to the corridor.

*****

Thorne looked around the room at the dozen or so faces looking back at him. "Not a word of this to anyone.

Not your wives, your kids, your best friends. A single overheard phrase, a slip of the tongue, and it doesn't just mean we lose our mission. They'll kill us. Without hesitation, or regret. As far as they're concerned, we're all one hundred percent on board with flying to Mars and murdering the *Hyperion* crew, as well as any of the second crew who've joined them. For god and country, and all that. If they have even a hint that you believe otherwise, game over." He watched as each man gave him a determined nod.

They were soldiers, seasoned operators one and all. None of them had been to space yet, but each had the fortitude to last the long trip to Mars. They just had to hold tight until launch day, at which point they'd be unstoppable. Unless, of course, the Space Force installed a self-destruct mechanism into their ride. Which Thorne was going to make damn sure didn't happen.

He'd made it a very public point (as public as any meeting regarding Mars got these days) among his bosses that he was gathering men he could trust. Men who would follow his orders without hesitation. He'd sold the higher-ups on the need for this, as they were basically being sent to kill a crew that the world considered heroes. The need for absolute secrecy regarding everything Mars-related that his bosses enforced played into his hands as well. He could sequester these men without anyone batting an eye.

Thorne was taking a huge chance, giving them one night to go home and say goodbye to loved ones, without actually saying goodbye. He was trusting each of them with his own life, as well as their team's. The way he figured it, it was better he know now if there were any traitors, than to find out when they were millions of miles from Earth and trapped in a tin can that was prone to explode.

"Report back here at 08:00 tomorrow. Don't bring anything with you. No phones, no gear, no personal mementos larger than a photo. Hug your kids, make love to your spouses, make sure your life insurance policies are up to date. If you don't have one, get one. Big enough to make your family comfortable when you're gone." He stood up, nodding at the two men guarding the door. "We launch in three days. Keep your damn mouths shut until then."

*****

Fletcher watched Lazar step into the control room to send his daily report. It was the end of a long day, a long week, and she was tired. Not having a lab of her own, she'd helped the others set up once they'd properly sorted and stowed the last of the cargo. The sick bay was fully operational, as was the geo lab, and the cafeteria. Engineering was a little behind, as Volkov had left Chin to handle it alone while he began setting up hydroponics. The stolid Russian, who was normally so serious, whistled and laughed to himself as he worked, remembering his childhood on the family farm.

Back at her small but comfortable quarters, Fletcher sat on the bunk and took a few deep breaths. Lazar was planning to assimilate after he submitted his report, and she had volunteered to watch over him through the process. That left her a few minutes to kill, and she wanted to assign her newly earned points.

Not that the process was all that complicated. She dumped all three points into Sofia, bringing it up to twenty eight, amping up her intelligence and wisdom stat to increase her spell power. If they were going to fight things, she was going to be ready. A quick look at her stat sheet showed the extra points gave her mana pool a decent boost. Pleased with the result, and feeling mentally refreshed, if not physically, she set off to find Lazar.

Fletcher	Level 1
Vis	12
Vitae	16
Sofia	28
Haza	8
Aura	18
Health Points	160
Mana Points	485
Reputation	10

Chapter Twelve

As the Worm Turns

Like the others, Lazar woke up feeling hung over and bruised. Fletcher handed him some juice as soon as he sat up, and he drank it all down greedily. "I see what you were all complaining about." He shook his head, then regretted it. Dropping the empty juice container, he held his head with both hands and did his best to hold very, very still.

"Best to get on with it. Once you finish the process you'll feel much better. Have you given any more thought to what class you'll choose?"

Being careful not to nod his head, Lazar replied quietly, "Yeah, I think I'm gonna go with some kind of ranged magic damage, like you and Chin. That's something any human fighters that come against us won't know how to handle, at least initially. I think the more of it we have, the safer we'll be."

"I've been thinking about it while you were sleeping. Fighting other humans, I mean. They'll be wearing suits, so you don't have to inflict enough physical damage to kill them, just enough to tear open their suits. Mars will do the rest."

"Good point." Lazar hadn't considered that. They'd been living day to day in their suits for so long, he didn't think of it as a liability. "Okay, here I go. See you in a

"I can agree to that. Welcome back, Commander Fletcher. He reached out a hand, and she shook it. "We'll let the others know at breakfast." He looked up at the clock on his wall. "Which is in about four hours, if you want to grab some shuteye."

"I'm gonna go do just that." She nodded and exited his quarters, headed for her own bunk, and some much-needed sleep.

*****

Stella sat in her office, the blinds closed and the door locked. She'd instructed her assistant that she wasn't to be disturbed for any reason short of a fire in the building.

Her hands shook as she reached for the half-empty bottle of scotch on her desk, pouring it over the rapidly melting ice cubes in her glass. The bottle neck clinked against the glass several times, her shaking hands unable to keep either the bottle or the glass steady.

The information on the data crystal that Thorne had given her was bad enough. The crew of Hyperion were not just alive, they were turning into some sort of alien-human hybrid. Aliens were real, and apparently still living on Mars. That alone had shattered the last vestiges of her Catholic faith. Not that she'd been all that devout – being a lifelong newswoman, and witnessing what she had of human behavior, had diminished her faith long ago.

Stella had read through the information on an air-gapped laptop that first night, then gotten very, very drunk.

She'd taken the next day off, slept in, then wandered around her house trying to come to terms with what she'd learned. Then she did some research, and found several recent and now suspicious accidental deaths of folks who worked in or around the Hyperion program. Thorne wasn't kidding about the powers that be doing whatever it took to keep things quiet.

She'd copied some info from the crystal and filed the story that Thorne had asked for, stating that the crew still lived, despite reports from the government that said otherwise. She wrote a passionate plea for the citizens of the world to rise up in support of those heroes, who were in desperate need of additional supplies. She reminded everyone of Earth's need for the resources Mars might provide, and the enormous investment already committed to send the *Hyperion* there in the first place. Stella had learned early in her career that people hated hearing that their hard-earned and begrudgingly paid tax dollars were being wasted.

Before she pushed the story to one of the editors for proofing and tweaking, she packed a bag, made a few phone calls to ensure that her affairs were in order, then retrieved her gun from its case under her bed. It had actually been her husband's gun, before he passed away, and she hadn't touched it or thought about it in a decade. Sliding it into her suitcase, she closed the zipper and walked over to her laptop.

Taking a deep breath, she sent the story to her favorite editor, with a warning to hold it, and not say a word until instructed otherwise.

Leaving that laptop where it was, she grabbed the air-gapped one, along with the data crystal, and slid them into her shoulder bag. She then took both bags out to the street and hailed a cab, giving the driver a huge tip to get her to the office as quickly as possible.

She was going to be sleeping in her office for a while. It wasn't so bad. She had her own bathroom with a shower, a small wardrobe, a full bar with a mini-fridge, and could have food delivered any time day or night. The moment her story broke, her life would be in danger, and it would have been too easy for men in black cars to take her from her home. To get to her at the office, they'd have to go through a whole building full of people. One of the great things about her network was that it was always live on the air, and the office was always busy, even in the middle of the night.

Years of operating in hostile nations where women, Catholics, Americans, and especially reporters were targets for assassination, kidnap, torture, and worse, had taught her how to protect herself. She had alerted her boss about the story within moments of entering the building, and passed on Thorne's warning. A small army of private security had been hired, and a team of four elite guards lounged outside her office now. They had stationed observers on several rooftops in the area, and a dozen more guards patrolled the lobby, stairwells, and building perimeter. Short of sending in a seal team, no one was getting to her. Still, her gun was currently tucked in the back of her waistband, just in case.

With a sigh, she tilted the glass and emptied it once again. Looking at the rapidly dwindling bottle, she pressed

a button on her desk's holographic display. "George, I'm going to need another bottle of scotch. Make that three. And order me a club sandwich and some cheesecake, a couple pizzas for the guards, and whatever you'd like, on the company tab." Just because she was sequestering herself, she didn't have to live like a cavewoman. "Oh, and call the dry cleaner, I need my stuff delivered here instead of the house."

"On it, boss lady." George was friendly, and efficient, and damn good at his job. He'd been her assistant for a couple of years, and she couldn't live without him. When she explained the reason for the extra security, he had asked them for a gun to keep in his desk, just in case. Stella made a mental note to make sure he got a huge bonus at year-end, if they were still alive by then.

Looking down at her notepad, she shook her head. "How do I keep this a secret?" she asked herself. The notes were handwritten on an old paper pad, since any electronic pad could, in all likelihood, be hacked. There was a burn can to the left of her desk, brought in at her request an hour or so earlier. If it became necessary, she could drop the pad into the can and press a button, and it would be ash in seconds.

"Damn you, Thorne. I know you warned me, but I figured it was at least fifty percent hype." She shook her head, pouring more scotch. The crystal hadn't just contained copied files of transmissions and audio recordings of meetings, it had contained a key. A decryption key, to be exact. One that allowed her to listen in on the encrypted transmissions sent from Lazar, through

Skippy, to Mission Control. A backup precaution taken by Thorne, in case he was eliminated and unable to share further info.

A few hours earlier she had coopted one of her network's control rooms and used the satellite dishes on the roof to listen in to Lazar's daily report. What he said hadn't immediately sunk in, as she was furiously scribbling notes. But when the transmission ended, and she walked back to her office, she'd felt a deep need to get drunk.

All but one of the crew were now aliens, and they could apparently do magic.

Part of her was still fighting that knowledge. She tried to convince herself it was all a hoax, or that the crew were hallucinating. "I mean, there's no actual physical evidence, right?" She mumbled to herself, sitting back in her seat with a newly filled glass in hand. "There's no video of them actually doing magic, casting spells, whatever you call it." Gulping down the contents of the glass, she slammed it on the desk.

"Who am I kidding. Of course it's real. Damn you, Thorne." She repeated. "I get what you mean about the world not being ready. I'm not friggin ready!"

She got up and paced, a bit unsteadily, back and forth behind her desk, spinning her chair as she passed it each time. "I'll hold onto this as long as I can, or until they get me. But we gotta let people know pretty soon, Thorne."

She had just spun her chair on her way past it again when her foot caught on one of the wheeled legs, and she stumbled. Her forehead hit the plush carpet at the same time the sound of shattering glass rang out. Checking the ground around her for her broken scotch glass, she remembered that she had left it on her desk. “George!” She shouted. “Guards!” her second shout was more of a scream. Looking up from the floor, she saw a round hole in the tinted window, bright sunlight streaming through.

The guards forced open her door and burst in, saw her on the floor, and dashed over. The one in front never made it, the tinkling of glass and a spray of blood preceding his death in the middle of her office. The others immediately took cover, one of them shouting into a radio as another dove to cover her body with his own. “We’ve got a sniper! East side, active shooter! Gonzalez is down!”

The impact of the heavy guard, and his weight pressing down on her, was too much for Stella’s booze-filled stomach. She promptly vomited all over the plush carpet, even as more shards of glass fell on her from the window above. The shooter had gone full automatic now, some part of her mind told her, spraying bullets around her office.

Luckily, the windows were not full-length, and there was three feet of solid concrete cover between the floor and the bottom of the now shattered window for her to hide behind. Her protector remained on top of her as he slid her body closer to the wall, and the shelving unit below the window, for better cover. As a bonus, it moved her away from the smell of her own vomit at the same time. “George, we’re going to need housekeeping in here ASAP.” she called out, partly drunk and partly in shock.

A moment later a high-pitched screaming sound was followed immediately by an explosion as her desk shattered into a zillion pieces. The man on top of her jerked, then started cursing. A moment later there was a second explosion, but Stella had passed out, and didn't hear it.

*****

It turned out there were more worms in the ice tunnel than anyone had expected.

After the group had gathered for breakfast and congratulated Lazar on his new class, and Fletcher for being back in command, the group armed up with the makeshift weapons Graves had been able to craft. There were knives and sheaths for each of them, as well as six composite spears of varying lengths. Graves had fired up a second fabricator, and managed to print up four sets of leg armor.

As they exited the airlock, Lazar naturally took charge. "Doc, you and Volkov hang back a ways. We may need you to do some healing, and if anyone gets incapacitated, Volkov you're our runner. Grab them and drag them back to Clarke."

The Russian opened his mouth to say that he could fight, and Lazar held up a hand. "I know you're a better fighter than some of us. But you can't get any xp or reputation or whatever from this fight, and the others can. And Doc shouldn't be left alone, in case one gets past us."

Volkov nodded, accepting the argument.

"Chin, you're on ice duty. See if you can use elemental magic to melt the water and move it out of the tunnel. We'll take it a few feet at a time, so you don't get tired out. Fletcher and I will use magic to do as much ranged damage as possible, then we'll engage in melee if it comes to that."

Graves, Fletcher, Mejia, and Lazar had the leg armor, as well as a spear each. Graves would be their front line, their tank, the others positioned right behind him. Lissa and Chin also had spears, but were staying back behind the others as they were unarmored.

With their plan set, Chin the strategist tossed out a few additional instructions. "Call out if your mana is low. Especially you, Doc. Fletcher can maybe cast a backup heal or two in an emergency, but let's not push it. Melee attacks need to target the head. You can cut these things in half and they still fight unless you hit the brain. There's no raid icons, so you need to call out if you need heals. And don't call out for a scratch or two. That's a waste of mana for the healers. Doc, what does your basic heal spell do?"

"It heals seventy points." Clarke beamed with pride over the fact that she could heal almost fifty percent more than Fletcher with the same spell. It proved that specialization made a difference.

"Right, so don't call for heals unless you're down… let's say forty points or more." Chin finished up and nodded to Lazar, then stepped close enough that he could see the ice five feet down in the tunnel opening. "Here we go."

He scrunched up his face as he concentrated on the ice. At twenty feet in diameter, even moving a few inches of depth took a good bit of mana. The others watched as the ice melted almost instantly, and then began to churn as Chin gasped and backed up, breathing hard. "I managed about two feet, and I'm out of mana just from that!"

"Shit, there's a bunch of them moving around in there." Graves, who was closest to the edge and peering down, gripped his spear a little tighter. "Like, maybe a dozen. It's hard to tell. Here they come!" he took a step back, then shouted something at the worms. The others looked at each other, verifying that Graves had just shouted in an unknown language.

Three of the borers slithered up the slope out of the water and moved toward Graves. They still weren't fast, but another four were emerging right behind them, and several more right behind that wave. Graves' spear shot forward, easily puncturing a worm's hide above its maw, and the creature curled up briefly before dying. He took a step back, readying his spear again.

"Hold on!" Fletcher shouted. Graves froze, his eyes never leaving the approaching enemy as she attempted a spell she'd been thinking about. Stretching out her hand, she envisioned a bolt of blue energy flying from her hand, drilling into the worm nearest Graves. She felt a buildup of heat in her fingers, and a moment later something flew forward. It wasn't blue, it was black, and it moved too fast for her to see, but it did the job. The worm's head blasted open, its core rolling out onto the stone.

"Awesome!" Chin shouted, remaining in the rear with his spear ready as his mana recharged. "Lazar, can you do that?"

"Don't know. Let me try." He took a step back and watched as Fletcher cast the spell again, sweat forming on her forehead. Envisioning himself doing the same, he reached a hand out and pointed at a worm. Nothing happened, and he almost panicked, ready to charge forward again with his spear. After all, he knew that worked against these creatures. But he gritted his teeth and focused, thrusting the hand forward again, shouting "Die!" at his chosen worm.

He didn't see anything burst forth from his hand, but the worm's head and several inches of its body crumpled as if it had been hit with a sledgehammer. Lazar felt drained, and had to use his spear as a support staff for a moment, to steady himself.

"What was that?" Chin shouted, his eyes wide. "You literally crushed it!"

"Don't know. Talk about it later. Worms to kill." Lazar grunted, out of breath from the effort of casting the spell. His unsteadiness had distracted him, and one of the worms was getting uncomfortably close. Lissa jumped forward and jammed the tip of her spear into its mouth just as it was rearing up to latch onto Lazar's leg. It instinctively bit down on the spear shaft, and Lissa had to fight to remove her weapon. When she did, it was covered in slime and blood, smoking slightly.

"It tried to eat my spear!" She called out, holding up the point and examining it. "The composite is taking a little damage, but is holding up okay, I think."

"Then stick it in another worm!" Graves growled at her, surrounded by several of the creatures. He punted one, then pinned another to the ground with his spear. "It's getting a little crowded over here."

There were now ten worms moving toward him, or past him toward Lazar, in addition to the seven that were already dead. And more were emerging from the quickly re-freezing water. At minus eighty degrees Fahrenheit, each of their wet bodies was frosting up as they moved up the tunnel slope. But after so many millennia frozen in the ice, it didn't seem to bother them.

Lissa stayed in the front ranks next to Lazar, who had recovered enough from the mana drain to resume the melee fight. Chin moved up too, taking position next to Mejia, and the line of six Martians formed a sort of semicircle around the worms. Spears stabbed out, feet kicked and stomped, and Graves cussed nearly nonstop as the growing worm herd struck at his legs.

One of them tried to get around him after failing to penetrate his leg armor, and Lazar hesitated in his jab, not wanting to miss the target and hit Graves' leg instead. The delay was costly, as the worm quickly twisted its body and lunged, latching onto Graves' unarmored calf.

"Aargh! Get it off me!" Graves stabbed forward, skewering another worm in front of him. Seeing that Lazar and Mejia, who were on either side of Graves, were both fending off worms of their own, Volkov dashed forward. Grabbing the center of the worm's body, he yanked with all his might. It separated from Graves' leg, causing the big man to scream in pain as blood, worm saliva, melted suit material, and bits of melting flesh sprayed the area.

The worm instantly curled back on itself, attempting to bite Volkov. He let go with his right hand, grabbing the end of its tail before letting go with his left. He immediately flung his right hand forward, the worm's tail going with it, then snapped his hand back. The worm's body unfurled like a whip, it's head snapping out, stunning it. Volkov let go, stomping on the worm's head hard enough to snap whatever bones or cartilage were in its jaw, then backed up to cover Clarke as she cast a heal on Graves, who was coughing loudly from the Mars atmosphere that was now leaking into his suit through the hole in its leg.

She hadn't waited for him to call for a heal. Regardless of where his health points stood, the wound to his leg was crippling, and would reduce his combat effectiveness. She watched, fascinated, as the bleeding slowed and the flesh knitted itself back together. When it didn't fully close, she cast *Basic Heal* again.

Shaking his leg briefly, giving it a quick glance to see that it was healing, Graves called out between coughs, "Thanks, Doc!" and continued to battle the worms in front of him.

The entire fight only lasted about five minutes, but it seemed much longer to everyone involved. When it was over, thirty one worms lay dead in front of them. Only Graves had needed healing, but Chin, Fletcher, and Lazar had all exhausted their mana with just a spell or two.

Fletcher surveyed the carnage, then checked to make sure everyone was okay. "Let's harvest the cores, see what we can do about butchering these things. We'll put the meat in cold storage, and try test-cooking one later." She paused, looking down the ice tunnel at the now two foot lower surface. Half a dozen worms twitched in the thickening water, likely not fully freed by Chin's magic, stuck with part of their bodies still in the ice. The rest would be refrozen soon. "I think we've had enough for a while."

"Damned right." Graves grumped, rubbing his calf where his suit was torn open. "I'm gonna head inside. Been breathing the Mars air since this happened."

"Good idea. Head inside and see if you can patch that." The hole was a good three inches across. "Can you walk okay?"

"My leg's fine, thanks to Doc." Graves gave her a thumbs-up. "That healing shit is somethin' else!" He looked down at the hole in his suit. "Why'd we have to get these nasty things to start with? Why couldn't it have been fuzzy bunnies, like most games." He grumbled, causing Chin to giggle.

As Graves walked back to the airlock, Volkov and Clarke moved forward to join the rest of the group. They all pitched in, using their newly shaped tactical knives to butcher the worms, claiming hide, meat, and cores. They'd brought along several bags for that purpose, and filled them all.

"Anybody level up?" Chin asked as they worked. When nobody answered, he shrugged. "Me either. The rep needed to get from level one to level two must be significant."

"Or level one was just a gimme, easy to achieve as a confidence booster." Lissa offered.

"Speaking of confidence," Mejia straightened up from his work, a chunk of worm meat in hand. "Volkov, that was some badass move you pulled. Just all casually grabbin' that worm and cracking it like a whip. Did you guys see that?"

Volkov shrugged. "It is how we dealt with vipers on the farm. One does not always have an axe or shovel on hand to kill them, so my father taught us how to grab the tail and snap their spine."

Fletcher held up a worm corpse. "These things don't have spines."

"Da, I did not think of that until later." the Russian grinned at her. "But it did stun the worm long enough for me to finish it."

"And forced its head away from your arm." Lazar added. "Something to keep in mind for next time."

Everyone groaned when he said next time, and he sympathized. “I know, this sucked. We’ll have to be more careful on how many we pull. If there had been many more this time, we might have fared much worse.” He held up his spear. “These spears worked okay, but I missed several times.” He looked around, and others nodded that they had missed as well. “We either need to do some weapons training with these, or maybe try some swords. Or both. Spears are great for larger targets, but these things have small heads, and they move around a lot.”

“Swords would be good.” Mejia agreed. “Or maybe convert these things to halberds?”

“What’s a halberd?” Lissa asked, causing the others to roll their eyes.

Mejia squatted down and dipped his finger in worm blood, then began to draw. He did a rough image of their spears, then drew a long blade along one side of the shaft near the end. “Put a cutting blade along one side, so we can sweep at them from a distance. Leave the spear point for jabbing.”

Lissa squinted at it for a moment, then looked at her own spear. “Oh! I see. Like those weapons the Swiss Guard carry at the Vatican.”

“Sort of, but a different design. Less puncturing, more slicing.” Lazar helped out. “And that’s a good idea, Mejia. With six of us sweeping back and forth, it’ll turn the kill zone into a worm blender!”

“We’ll get one of the printers making the blades while Graves fixes his suit. Then he can meld them onto the shafts using his Shaping skill.” Fletcher decided. “Let’s finish up here, pack all of this nastiness back inside, and clean up. We can distribute the cores at dinner. And unless somebody objects, I’m going to set aside a few for Volkov. When he decides to assimilate, the cores will make it easier for him to catch up.”

Chin nodded. “Fine by me. He’s killed a couple of worms himself anyway, so technically he’s earned cores, even if he can’t use them yet.” Everyone else agreed, and they quickly finished butchering and bagging before heading back inside.

As they walked away, a single worm, larger than the others, broke free of the ice by sacrificing the last few segments of its body. Trailing blood and avoiding the hungry lunges of its trapped brethren, it slowly pushed itself out of the thickening water. The mixture of water and blood that coated the severed tail end of its body quickly froze as it inched its way up the rock of the tunnel to level ground, where it paused to consume the remains of its broodmates’ corpses.

Volkov, who had been looking thoughtful, said, "We left a lot of offal out there after we butchered them. I'm thinking I could use that as well. Grind it up and use it for fertilizer in hydroponics."

"Good!" Lissa clapped her hands. "I like that idea much better than reprocessing our own poop as fertilizer." She stuck out her tongue and made a face.

"Heh. I do, as well." The Russian grinned at her. "I'll go out and gather it up in the morning."

Morale was high after their first non-dehydrated ration food in many months, and the crew hung around the cafeteria longer than usual, chatting amiably. When they broke up the gathering, all but Fletcher went to their bunks. Since she was back in command, it was her turn to send the daily report. They needed to present as normal a picture as possible to Earth, in hopes that the decision makers would see the value in keeping them alive.

As she sat in front of the communications console, she was still debating whether to tell them that her crew had ingested local worm meat. On the one hand, finding a supplement to their rations was great news for the mission, easing the threat of starvation due to lack of resupply. On the other hand, how many of her bosses would simply look at it as further contamination?

*****

Volkov lay in his bunk, staring at the ceiling with his hands on his belly, fingers intertwined. He was enjoying the pleasant feeling of having real meat, not some fabricated, dehydrated meat substitute that was flavored to taste like beef or pork, in his belly. Chuckling a bit when his belly gurgled happily, he looked at the photo taped on the ceiling just above his head. His wife and kids smiled down at him, the photo from a family bbq held just before he left to join the mission. Though they all knew he'd be gone for several years, all of them had put on brave faces and sincere smiles, for his sake.

He had moved his family from Russia to Texas, so that he could be near them during the long year of training before the actual launch. The move wasn't popular with his government, but he didn't really care. Having them just a short drive from the spaceport and training grounds was worth any aggravation. Most days he was able to return home and spend evenings with them, creating memories that helped him through the loneliness of the extended space flight.

Now they were back in Russia, guests of the government, which made Volkov more than a little uncomfortable. They were regularly trotted out to give holo interviews or make patriotic speeches for the masses about how proud they were of him and his efforts on behalf of the motherland. As long as he was a hero of the nation, they would be protected. His children, both teenagers, had even been awarded scholarships to prestigious universities who were eager to claim the progeny of the great hero Volkov among their student bodies. But Volkov had no idea whether his government had been informed of the actual events on Mars, or had simply been told that he was dead along with the rest of the crew.

And he honestly didn't know which scenario would be better for them. The pain of being told he was gone, and being trotted out in public to play the grieving family of the dead hero was sure to be unpleasant for them. But it would likely be safer, as well. If his government knew that the *Hyperion* crew were becoming aliens, his family might just disappear as part of the coverup.

Not being able to get a message to them was frustrating! At the same time, he understood and agreed with the necessity of remaining silent. Not for the first time, he wished they had remained in Texas, where they'd at least be less vulnerable, in theory. Volkov drifted off to sleep with thoughts of his wife and children retiring to his family farm, left in peace by the government and the masses.

Dropping into REM sleep, those thoughts translated into a pleasant dream of his children romping through the upper meadow, a wolfhound pup frolicking with them. His wife sitting on the wide front porch with her mother, drinking tea and watching the children with a smile on her face.

His pulse quickened as the dream abruptly turned menacing. A small convoy of black Mercedes trailed up his gravel driveway, stopping in front of the house. Half a dozen armed men emerged and proceeded directly toward the meadow and his children, while others moved to surround the house. A familiar-looking woman in an austere pant suit approached the porch to address his wife. She was one of the state security operatives that had initially vetted him during the mission selection process.

"Mrs. Volkov, I must speak with you in confidence." She looked from his wife to her mother. "Please, accompany us back to my office." She motioned toward one of the black vehicles sitting behind her, its doors already open.

"What is this about?" His wife stood, wringing her hands as she watched strangers begin to herd her children back toward the house. The kids looked alarmed, and confused, and when her youngest, who was fourteen, began to run toward her, one of the operatives grabbed him and held him back. "Stop that! Let my son go!"

The woman in the pant suit turned to see what was happening, and waved a hand at her people. Volkov's son was released, but ordered sharply to walk along with his big sister.

"My apologies, Mrs. Volkov. You and your children will not be harmed. We simply need to… discuss recent developments related to your husband."

"Developments? My husband is dead. What recent developments could there be?" his wife snapped at the woman.

"Please, just come with us, and we can discuss this in a secure location." The woman glanced again at his mother-in-law, then looked meaningfully at his wife. Volkov couldn't blame her, it was well-known that his

onto the barrel of her weapon. A moment later both Volkov kids screamed as a muffled shot rang out from inside the house. Their screams were short-lived, as two operatives put rounds into the backs of their heads with similarly suppressed pistols.

Volkov woke with a scream on his lips, but his lungs wouldn't take in enough air to make the sound. Sitting up on his bunk, he gripped the edge with both hands so hard that a couple of his fingernails broke. When he could finally take in a breath, he gasped a few times, then covered his face with his hands, sobbing quietly.

"It's just a dream." He whispered over and over, rocking back and forth. "Only a dream, brought on by stress. They have no reason to harm my family." He sat there, his entire body trembling, taking deep breaths in an attempt to calm himself.

"Is that true?" He asked the empty room, still shaken by the images of his children's deaths. "If they know, if the President has been told of the assimilations, would they consider my family a liability? Or leverage? Would they hold them hostage in an attempt to prevent me from assimilating? What demands would they make of me?"

Volkov knew the answer to that question before he was even finished verbalizing it. His government would demand that he kill the rest of the crew. For the safety of the motherland, and the rest of the world. They would tell him his family would remain safe, as long as he followed orders. That he would be reunited with them upon his triumphant return.

"But there can be no return." He mumbled, standing up and pacing the limited floorspace within his quarters. "They will never believe I am still fully human. Even should they allow me to return to Earth, I would be quarantined and studied for the rest of my life. Assuming they did not simply eliminate me after they finish with their tests and interrogations."

He sat back down, his shoulders slumped. It would be an impossible choice for him. Though he had the martial skills and training to kill his crewmates easily, with the possible exception of Graves, whom he suspected was equally well trained, he did not *want* to kill them. Worse, he didn't for a moment believe that killing them would earn him any loyalty from his government. He would be used, then discarded as a broken tool, or brought back and studied before being disposed of.

"The only way I can see that they can not use my family as leverage is if I'm actually dead." He shook his head, the words bitter in his mouth. "But if I join the others, become a Martian, maybe we can create enough leverage to ensure my family, all of our families, are safe."

Volkov lay back down, once again staring at the photo on the ceiling. He was still staring when his alarm beeped politely, telling him it was time to get up.

*****

"I'm going to assimilate." Volkov blurted out in the middle of breakfast. The table went silent, everyone surprised by the sudden change of heart. After a moment, Fletcher set down her fork and its load of fake scrambled eggs.

"Do you mind if I asked what made you change your mind?"

"My family." Volkov practically growled. When he saw Fletcher lean back slightly, he held up his hands. "I'm sorry. I am not angry at you. It is just that I realized last night that my family is at risk no matter what I choose to do up here." He briefly relayed his dream, and his subsequent reasoning, earning looks of sympathy or horror from the various members of the crew, some of whom were now considerably more concerned about their own families.

"I believe the best hope for all of us, and for our families, is to advance our mission objectives, prove that we can provide the needed resources, and negotiate some kind of protection for ourselves and our families. I think the only way we do that, in the relatively short time that we have available to us, is to use whatever powers we can gain as Martians." He paused, hating to say the next words. "Or become stronger, and kill enough of the people they send after us to force them to negotiate."

Lissa's voice was almost a whimper. "They wouldn't really do that, would they? Our governments, I mean? Hurt our families because of us?"

Lazar looked to Fletcher, who sighed and nodded. He turned to Lissa, and spoke as gently as he could, though the words were harsh.

"They would. They have done much worse in the past, Lissa. Our governments, most governments throughout history, have murdered, robbed, blackmailed, or even enslaved their own citizens in numbers beyond reckoning. They have justified it in a number of ways, expediency, cost efficiency, religion, national security, but it all basically boils down to the fact that the sacrifice of a few for what they consider the overall good is an acceptable trade. There's no question they'll try to kill all of us here. If that doesn't work quickly or cheaply enough for them, then yes, our families may become leverage. Or casualties in the name of punishment for disobedience. They won't even lose sleep over it."

"But what if we just do what they want?" Lissa's lips trembled, tears running down her cheeks.

"It's too late for that. We've already been *contaminated* as far as they're concerned. Anybody back on Earth who knows the full truth about us is either dead, soon to be dead, or locked down so tightly that they'll never tell anyone. We are already enemies of Earth, whether we want to be or not. We're different, and different is dangerous. And with the billions already spent getting us here, and the trillions in potential resources at risk, anybody doing the math back on Earth has already decided that eliminating us is the best, fastest, cheapest, least dangerous option."

The room was silent as those who hadn't already reached those conclusions took it all in. Eventually Volkov broke the silence.

"And so, I will assimilate, as soon as possible. I think that only by working together will we have a small chance to succeed. We must all get stronger, find ways to complement each other's abilities, and work harder than we ever have before. We will almost certainly have to kill other humans before this is finished." He looked around the table. "Anyone who cannot reconcile that with your conscience should say so now. When it comes time to fight, we need to know that we can count on each other, or exclude you from our plans." He waited, still looking around, but nobody spoke up. "Commander, if I could have a few of those diamonds? And someone to watch over me? I'll assimilate right now."

Fletcher glanced at Lazar, who got up to retrieve the diamond storage cylinder that was still in his quarters. "I'll watch over you." She smiled at Volkov. "I hope you've put some thought into what class you'll choose."

"I have." He nodded as he got up, taking his empty tray and utensils to set them on a counter in the kitchen.

"I'll clean up." Lissa volunteered. "Then Chin and I will go out and gather up the nasty leftover worm bits for you."

"We will?" Chin made a disgusted face, then sighed in acceptance. "Sure, I'll help."

“Thank you, both of you.” Volkov bowed his head slightly as he led Fletcher from the cafeteria, headed toward his quarters.

*****

“Where’d they go?” Chin asked, looking around their battlefield from the day before. Though there were frozen pools of the worms’ blood in low spots here and there, the offal they’d left behind was nowhere to be seen.

“I don’t know?” Lissa shrugged. “Maybe… some kind of insect got to it overnight? Like ants finishing off a corpse?”

“Could it be like some of the game systems, where after you loot a body it quickly fades away?” Chin kicked a small stone over, as if he might find some worm remains underneath.

Lissa shook her head. “If that were the case, wouldn’t the blood disappear too? I mean, it wouldn’t make sense for it to happen to one part without the other, right?”

“What’s going on, guys?” Fletcher’s voice broke in.

“The worm bits are all gone.” Chin reported succinctly. “Except for some blood.” He walked toward the rim of the ice tunnel as he spoke. Looking down at the refrozen ice surface, he saw several worms with their bodies only partially submerged. The parts that were free were twitching sluggishly now and then.

"Get back in here, both of you." Fletcher ordered. "If something out there ate the leftovers, I don't want it finding you two."

"Roger that, boss." Chin motioned for Lissa to lead the way, and he fell into step beside her. "Back in a jiffy."

They were halfway to the airlock when Lissa stopped suddenly, her head down, its lamp shining on the stone at her feet. "Look here." She took a step back and pointed. Chin squatted to get a better look. "Does that look like worm blood to you?"

"Not just worm blood, worm tracks. Look at the pattern. It's the same back near the tunnel, where one worm crawled through the blood of another." He stood back up, looking toward the tunnel first, then along a line in the direction the track seemed to be heading. "One of them must have gotten free after we left, ate its dead siblings, and…?" He trailed off, not sure what to say next.

"It's headed in the general direction of the hab!" Lissa shouted, making everyone's coms screech slightly.

"See if you can track it further." Fletcher instructed. "But keep your eyes peeled. Graves, Mejia, Lazar, get out there. I need to stay here with Volkov. Clarke, you go too, but hang back in case they need heals." She paused. "Sorry Lazar, this is your area."

"Mejia, you hang back with Clarke. Nobody goes anywhere alone out there." Lazar picked up smoothly even as he headed toward the airlock, his armor already buckled on. "Chin, Lissa, only track it as far as the airlock, or until its tracks change direction. We'll be out in just a few minutes. If you see a worm, or anything else, *do not engage*."

"No heroes here, boss. See you in a few." Chin responded, motioning for Lissa to follow him as he walked forward, eyes on the floor. "Watch our backs." He looked at Lissa, then around the cavern. "And our fronts and sides, too." He grinned at her. She rolled her eyes and began turning in a slow circle, searching the area with her headlamp.

"Looks clear. Let's go." She began to follow Chin, who was now moving forward slowly, searching for more blood tracks. He located more several feet farther along, then another set, and another. Stopping for a moment, he looked at the set near his feet, then back at the previous sets. After a quick calculation, he cleared his throat.

"Uh, guys? I'm no biologist, but my pattern recognition is pretty solid. I think this worm is… a good bit bigger than the ones we've killed."

"Have you spotted it?" Lazar's tone was sharp.

"No, boss. But remember how these things move? They sort of undulate up and down, inchworm style, instead of side to side like a snake. With the distance I'm seeing between the bloody marks on the ground, this one is going several feet between points where the bloody part is touching the ground. Making it easily twice as big as the ones back near the tunnel."

"I didn't see one that big in the ice." Fletcher argued.

"Me either." Chin agreed. "But the math here doesn't lie, boss lady." He winced at the term as soon as he said it. "Uh, other boss? Co-boss? Whatever. So maybe that's how these things level up. They feed, and they grow. Just like any animal on Earth, except way faster."

"And we left it a damned all-you-can-eat buffet." Graves growled.

"We're stepping into the airlock now." Lazar reported. "You guys hang tight where you are, keep your heads on a swivel until we reach you."

"There it is!" Lissa screamed in excitement rather than fear, pointing off to their right. "It's already past the hab, near the cave entrance!" She pointed, and Chin followed her line of sight. He saw the worm just moving into the zone of sunlight shining in through the opening. It paused, as if surprised by the light, then began moving again.

Chin gasped as it straightened out, pushing itself forward. "Shit, it's gotta be a good seven or eight feet long, and a foot wide."

Lazar and the others emerged from the airlock, weapons in hand. "On us!" He shouted as he began to jog after the creature. "We're not letting this thing loose to get bigger and come back later."

Chin and Lissa sprinted the remainder of the distance to the airlock, then past it to catch up to the others.

All of them could clearly see it now. The much larger worm moved slightly faster than its smaller brethren had, but it still wasn't speedy by any means. They quickly caught up to it just as it was reaching the mouth of the cave.

"Chin, fire!" Lazar called out. Chin slid to a stop and obliged, casting a fireball at the worm. The moment it impacted, Graves dashed forward and slashed at the thing's head as he shouted a taunt at it. The worm froze, seemingly conflicted for a moment, then ignored his taunt and tried to flee.

"Oh no you don't!" Graves bellowed, racing around the slow-moving creature and putting himself between it and the ledge outside. "You gotta get past me to leave the building!"

The worm seemed eager to oblige, rearing up until its head was on a level with Graves', then striking at him with surprising speed. He tried to swipe at it with his spear shaft, but was too slow. The open maw full of sharp teeth slammed into his chest plate, not penetrating, but hitting with enough force to make Graves stagger back a few steps.

Lazar was there in a heartbeat, striking at the thing from behind as it reared up again. The spear point didn't strike it, but the shaft just below it hit hard enough to knock the worm off balance. Stepping forward, Graves thrust the spear at it, skewering the body just below its head. Using all the muscle he had, he tried to force its head to the ground so that he could pin it there.

The worm had other ideas.

The creature's body bunched up below the head, then it reared back, freeing itself from the spear. With a lunge, it flung itself forward, extending its body and shooting past a surprised Graves, its whole body airborne for a brief moment. When it hit the ground, it rolled like a log across the ledge outside the entrance, and over the edge before any of them could react.

As one, they all ran to the edge and looked down, but the worm was already out of sight.

"No way it could survive that fall, right?" Lissa asked. The bottom of the canyon was so far down they couldn't see it clearly from where they stood. The sun was still low, and most of the lower canyon was in shadow.

"Let's hope not." Lazar muttered. "From now on we keep at least one camera pointed toward this entrance at all times." he ordered. "I don't want this thing, or any other thing, sneaking up on us." The others all nodded in emphatic agreement.

"Graves, you get on the upgrades to our spears. And as soon as Volkov is awake and ready, we go back to the tunnel and kill as many of those damned things as we can."

Chapter Fourteen

Truth and Consequences

When Volkov woke, Fletcher was there waiting with a glass of juice. She watched as he blinked and read the notifications, letting him take his time. When he focused on her and took the juice with a nod of thanks, she asked, "So?"

"I have chosen a class that I believe will be useful both in producing food for us, and in combat. I am now a *Biomage*." He paused to take a drink. "The class focuses on the manipulation of living matter. I can cause plants to grow, splice them together to create hybrids, or cause them to rot and become compost. I can alter flesh to reshape a limb, create wounds, snap bones, or mend them."

"Wow." Fletcher was impressed. "That's... incredibly useful. I'm sure I didn't see that as an option when I was assimilating."

"Yes, I believe Clarke was right, that the classes made available to us are heavily influenced by what the gods, or the system, sees in our previous life experiences. On the farm I learned some animal husbandry as well as how to plant, raise, and harvest crops, and even some gardening from my mother. As a soldier, I learned how to kill efficiently, or slowly and painfully. I was taught basic field medicine and... other things." He looked down at his hands, then drained the glass and set it on the floor.

Thoughts of the farm brought back flashes of his nightmare.

Fletcher produced half a dozen orbs and handed them to him. "Here you go. These should boost you right to level one, and help you catch up with the rest of us. From now on, you can earn your own experience or reputation points. Welcome to the club!" She smiled gently at him, patting his knee. She knew this hadn't been an easy decision for him, and that he was worried for his family.

He absorbed the orbs quietly and quickly, a man on a mission. "I am level one." Was his only comment after the first orb. When he was through, he added, "I also chose a skill called *Petrify* that allows me to harden organic matter until it is like stone."

"Nice! So you could make your own skin into armor?"

"I am not sure." Volkov shook his head, staring at his hands. "I will need to experiment, I think. To make sure the process does not kill, or permanently damage the organic matter."

"Speaking of organic matter…" She quickly filled him in on the big worm and their theory that it ate the remains of the other worms. "I'm afraid your fertilizer will have to wait until after our next fight, which will be later today. Graves is working on upgrading the weapons, and printing some more armor. When he's done, we're going to go harvest more worms.

Volkov looked thoughtful, sitting up a little straighter on his bunk. "So the worm might have doubled in size, overnight? Just by eating what was left of other worms?"

"That's our working theory." Fletcher stood up and leaned one shoulder against a wall, crossing her arms. "It makes the most sense, given the evidence we have."

"Remarkable. Do you know what this would mean in terms of domestication? If we were to capture some of them, feed them until they become large enough to harvest…" his voice faded as he considered possibilities. What he didn't say out loud was that he was already picturing a trap for their human enemies, a pit filled with spikes and worms. Though he was unwilling to eat human flesh, he had no qualms about feeding humans to worms, then eating the worms. When he was a small boy, he'd been awakened late one night by the sound of a car door outside the farmhouse. Peering out his window, he recognized his uncle speaking to his father, both men whispering and gesturing angrily. After a few moments, his uncle removed the body of a dead man from the trunk of his car, and both men carried it to the pigs' enclosure. Young Volkov had closed his eyes and covered his ears, not wanting to see or hear the pigs devouring the corpse. By morning, when he went out to do his chores after breakfast, all evidence of the corpse was gone.

Shaking his head, he cleared his mind of such visions and looked at Fletcher. "I'm ready to fight. Though I am a bit hungry."

"We've got some time yet. Let's hit the cafeteria and eat while we see if you can't discover a spell or two."

As it turned out, Volkov could cast a spell similar to *Basic Heal*, that restored a lesser amount of health points. It was called *Mend*, and the spell focused on closing wounds, restoring broken bones, and torn tissue. Impressed again, Fletcher mused, "That would come in handy if one of us is wounded and Clarke's mana is low. You could seal the wound, stop the blood loss, and give whomever's hurt time for Doc's mana to recharge so she can restore their health.

"One thing." Volkov cautioned. "At least for now, I must be in contact with the wounded person to cast the spell."

"Alright, not ideal, but maybe it'll develop into a ranged spell at higher levels." She grinned at him. "Let's test it out." She got up and grabbed one of the large kitchen knives, then returned to their table. Without another word, she sliced the top of her forearm, a deep cut. Hissing in pain, she gritted her teeth and growled, "Do your thing."

Volkov, not squeamish at all, put his hand over the cut and focused on the word *Mend.* A moment later his hand tingled and glowed softly. Fletcher twitched slightly, and muttered, "That tickles." When he pulled his hand away, the cut was fully healed. Fletcher used a napkin to wipe away the blood, and raised her arm to peer closely at the skin. "You can't even tell it was cut. No scar at all."

Volkov grinned. "Da. I have a bright future as a plastic surgeon. Maybe I'll move to Hollywood and become surgeon to the stars."

"Heh." Fletcher chuckled, patting the man on the shoulder. "You can fix my laugh lines anytime."

*****

Stella watched the live holo feed in her new safe house. Most of the civilized world watched along with her as an unscheduled mission to Mars was launched. Her story about the *Hyperion* crew surviving, most of them anyway, had raised a shitstorm of anger, finger pointing, and ass covering. The public rose up and demanded that the crew be saved, while the corporations demanded that the mission continue, eyeing the potential profits to be gained.

"Thorne, you sonofabitch, I wish I were going with you." Stella whispered at the hologram as the booster rockets ignited. He'd gotten his mission, and was about to leave Earth for the last time. "Good luck, you crazy old fool."

She looked around the safe house. It was a large place, situated on a clifftop above the city that provided amazing views. In addition to her master suite there were six bedrooms, all of which were filled by George and a small army of bodyguards. There was also a separate guardhouse that held even more, and a shack down by the iron gate at the end of the driveway, where two armed

"And what if I don't want this job? What if I don't want to be the face of the end of the world as we know it? The mouthpiece of assholes like you?"

"There's no point in discussing that, Stella. We both know you want the job. And you can start by reporting that Space Force's Chief of Operations of the *Hyperion I* mission Thorne has suffered a fatal heart attack. It will happen in…" The man paused, probably consulting a clock. "Approximately one hour. So you can still make the late news. Details will be emailed to you shortly."

"What?" Stella blinked a few times, trying to gather her thoughts. "You sons of bitches are going to murder Thorne? Why?"

"We know that he was the source of the information that you now hold. That is treason, Stella. We were forced to include him in the next Hyperion mission, because not doing so would have looked suspicious. But he signed his death warrant days ago. Now he'll die as a hero, trying to reach Mars to save his comrades on the *Hyperion I* crew. Make sure that's how your story reads, Stella. Goodbye." There was a soft buzz as the line went dead.

Stella picked up a nearby glass from the countertop and hurled it at a wall in frustration, surprised when, rather than shattering in a satisfying spray of glass, it simply dented the drywall and fell to the floor intact. "Damnit!" She cursed. Putting the water bottle back in the fridge, she moved over to the bar and grabbed a bottle of tequila.

*****

Thorne sat in the lounge aboard the *Hyperion III* as it left the space dock, a vibration through the ship's body letting him know the docking clamps had disengaged was immediately followed by an announcement from their pilot. "We have separation. Two minutes to acceleration burn." Around him were half a dozen of his chosen men. There were others on the ship, those who were originally intended to man the third mission, but the cargo was significantly different. Along with the extra personnel there were enough weapons, ammo, and explosives to conquer a small nation. Since Lazar had reported finding vast quantities of ice under their base camp, the amount of water that the ships needed to carry with them was greatly reduced. Which freed up literal tons of weight that could be used for other cargo. Part of that weight was offset by the extra fuel Thorne had loaded aboard. He planned to accelerate faster than their flight plan called for, and that took fuel. Even more fuel was loaded for the two shuttles.

The original mission's cargo manifest had included a small shuttle, large enough to carry six humans and a light payload. There were now two of those shuttles in the cargo bay, along with several tons of extra food ration packs, two extra large fabricators, crates of hydrogen engine replacement parts, dozens of extra space suits, cases of booze, toilet paper, and other items that Thorne and his team had judged useful for their future on Mars. The *Hyperion III* was technically overloaded now, well beyond the mission safety protocols. But since he intended to burn a large portion of their liquid fuel in this initial burn to build up speed, the weight would quickly be reduced.

Mission Control had even signed off on the extra weight, agreeing with him that it was important they reach Mars as quickly as possible. His bosses expected him to rush out there, murder the *Hyperion I* crew who had become Martians, and supervise the continuation of the mission with the *Hyperion II & III* crews.

His bosses' bosses planned for him to be dead, his body floating in space, before the initial acceleration burn was even completed.

Across the lounge from Thorne, one of his hand-picked men was mixing a drink. Looking briefly over one shoulder, he smiled at Thorne as he pulled a capsule from his shirt pocket, crushed it between his finger and thumb, sprinkling the powder it contained into the scotch glass. Using a finger, he stirred it briefly, watching the powder dissolve, then dropped a few ice cubes in and swirled them around for good measure. Quickly making another drink for himself, he then walked over and handed the dosed drink to his boss. "Here you go, boss. Just the way you like it, straight and cold. Better drink it before the ice starts to melt and ruins the flavor." He winked at Thorne.

"Thank you, DJ. Is everything ready?"

"All going according to plan." He raised his glass in a toast, then took a drink. Thorne did the same. Taking a seat, DJ continued.

"We'll arrive at Mars just about the same time as the *Hyperion II*. Within a day or so, in fact. That's just an estimate until we finish the extended burn and do the math with our actual speed."

"I'm not concerned with how long *Hyperion II* is there before us. None of them are fighters, and they present no threat to the crew on the ground. They'll likely sit aboard *Hyperion I* and wait until we get there." Thorne took another drink, then coughed once, pounding his chest. "Good stuff." He coughed once more. "What I'm much more concerned about is that big ole military ship they're sending behind us. The faster we get to Mars, the more time we have to prepare for those guys."

"It'll take them three months to finish the ship." DJ grinned at him. "Maybe four. The extra heat and radiation shielding it requires to get close enough to the sun for their slingshot is still being manufactured." He paused for a moment. "And I predict that in pre-flight testing they're going to find several bugs in their ops systems. They won't risk patches or repairs, so it'll take some time for them to remove and replace the compromised systems."

"You're a bad, bad man." Thorne raised his glass again, then emptied it. He was pressed into his seat a bit when the acceleration burn began. "Alright, here we go." He nodded at DJ, then dropped his glass, gripping his chest as his eyes widened and he began to cough again. He tried to stand, but instead rolled forward and face-planted on the floor. The other men in the room were instantly on their feet.

Russians would never allow. Two of their nearest neighbors at the farm reported hearing a gunshot. We've got people on the ground headed there now to look for any evidence of what happened."

"No satellites over that area?"

"Not at this time, sir. It's a farm community… not exactly a prime area of activity. We have one we can retask, but-"

"But whatever happened is already over, and it wouldn't do any good." The man nodded. "Right. Report when you have better answers. Keep the team on Stella, observation only. If someone else makes a move on her, they are to assist in her defense, then disappear." He didn't wait for confirmation, hanging up the phone and leaning back in his comfortable leather chair.

*****

"I've got this, Doc. We'll handle it, no sweat. He was one of ours, and we'll give him a proper burial at sea, so to speak." DJ took hold of the end of the gurney nearest Thorne's head and began to push it toward the door. Two of his men walked escort, one in front, one behind, both of them in combat fatigues with helmets on, weapons in hand. DJ had put all his men on full alert after Thorne fell, mostly for show. They wheeled Thorne through several corridors, crewmembers moving out of their way, a few of them saluting the body, as they approached the cargo elevator. Emerging on the lowest deck, where the largest cargo area was located, they were greeted by three more guards, their own men, heavily armed. The guards stepped aside, expecting them.

"The small airlock is that way." One of the guards pointed, looking briefly up at a security camera near the ceiling. DJ, his back to the camera, gave him a dirty look. "Thank you, sergeant." he replied as he began to push the gurney again. When they reached the airlock, he wheeled the gurney inside, unceremoniously tilted it to the side, dumping the body bag onto the floor, then pulled the gurney back out. He saluted as one of the guards shut the inner door, then pressed the big red button next to it. There was a hiss as most of the air was pulled from inside the airlock, then the outer door opened. The other two guards saluted as well, as they watched through a small window in the inner door. What little air was left in the chamber was expelled, along with the body bag. The outer door closed, the air cycled back into the chamber, and the red light above the door turned green.

The mission commander's voice came to them across the intercom. "I'm sorry for your loss, Captain. Thorne was a good man."

DJ looked up at the nearest camera, being fully familiar with every camera location in this particular area of the ship, and waved. "Thank you, sir. A damned good man, sir." He paused, looking around. "Gonna do a quick check of the cargo while we're down here, sir. Make sure nothing got shaken loose during the burn."

He and the two escort guards made their way down the rest of the short corridor and into the main cargo bay. They wove through a maze of crates and equipment, all firmly secured and triple-checked, until they reached the rearmost port section. In a small area surrounded by cargo pods were half a dozen aluminum lawn chairs, a couple cots, and a large cooler. DJ plopped down in the nearest chair as the two guards deactivated their helmets. The one nearest DJ began to chuckle, then laugh loudly. “A damned good man, sir!” He repeated in a girl voice, grinning at DJ.

“Shut up, sir.” DJ tossed him a beer from the cooler. “You’re supposed to be dead. Dead people don’t mock their friends, especially in such a trying time. We’re mourning our asshole boss, you know.”

Thorne took a seat next to DJ, opening the refreshingly cold beer and taking a big gulp before raising it in salute. “To me! And my untimely demise.” The other two raised their beers and clinked the cans together.

After a few moments of silence, Thorne spoke up. “I can’t believe they picked you, DJ. How tempted were you?”

“They just made me the six million dollar man, sir.” DJ grinned. “If I wasn’t permanently relocating to Mars, all those zeros would be pretty damned tempting.”

“Your parents know what to do with the money?”

“Not yet, sir. I couldn’t tell them ahead of time. Operational security, and all that. I left a note with a lawyer, along with a copy of my own life insurance policy. It'll be delivered in a couple weeks, when we're sure coms will be down and the crew can't report in. In a month, they'll wire half a million to each of the guys' designated people."

"Good thinking." Thorne nodded. "When do coms go down?"

"We can do it anytime, sir. The interrupt is installed, ready to go. But we shouldn't do it until we're at least a week out. At that point the commander won't be able to turn around without wasting too much fuel to return. We'll take down the coms, reroute them to your quarters only. Then you can jump out of a cake, or whatever, surprise the crew, and we can get to work convincing them to join our side."

Thorne nodded, thinking. He took a few more sips from his beer, tapping his foot. Looking around his temporary home, he chuckled. "A week or two down here won't be so bad. I've lived longer in much worse conditions." The other two nodded. So had they. "As for turning around, when I'm miraculously resurrected I'm going to go to the bridge and pull rank. My position at Space Force gives me the equivalent rank of Colonel. Cut off from Mission Control, and absent any instructions to the contrary, the Commander will have to follow my orders."

"What are you going to tell him, sir?" DJ crushed his now empty beer can.

"The truth. That we discovered a plot to kill me, faked my death. That we're not one hundred percent sure

Fletcher got up and motioned toward the newly improved polearms Graves had laid on the table. "Everybody suit up, grab a weapon, and we'll do some drills."

They did as she instructed, and soon they were outside the airlock. Lazar stepped in to act as the group's combat trainer.

"One of the keys to this fight is going to be teamwork. Our front line will work together to slash and stab at the worms as they approach. The main objective is to slow them down, but if you get a clean shot at a kill, take it. We'll slice low to the ground, cutting them into pieces. When they get closer, we pin their bodies down so that the second line can finish them. Use your weapon, your foot, whatever you can to hold them still." He motioned to Volkov to step forward and demonstrate. The Russian needed no coaching, and took up position behind Lazar, his weapon in both hands. Lazar made a few sweeping motions out in front of himself, cutting imaginary worms in half. Then his foot shot forward and stomped on the body of one of those imaginary worms. Without hesitation, Volkov stepped forward and stabbed the stone next to Lazar's foot, finishing their ghost opponent.

"Simple enough." Chin smiled at them. "As long as I'm one of the second line."

"Chin, you're with Volkov. Mejia, you're behind Graves. Fletcher, you back me up. Let's pair up and practice a bit. Those of you in the second line, be careful of swinging blades. You don't want to step forward too soon, or stand too close, and get cut. At the same time, make your strikes accurate, even if it takes an extra second or two. I don't want someone getting stabbed in the foot or have their leg sliced because their partner panicked. Front line, manage your swings. No spin moves or home-run swings that might extend behind you, or too far to your side."

They paired off and moved through quarter-speed drills for about ten minutes, then half-speed for another ten, until Lazar was comfortable that they could work together. "Good enough." He nodded to Fletcher, who put a hand on Lissa's arm.

"I need you to come with me." She led Lissa toward the tunnel. The others followed as the sunlight faded outside the cavern entrance. "I was thinking about how the worms sort of spread out during the last fight. Your skill with the stone can help us there, I think."

When they reached the tunnel's edge, Fletcher used the butt end of her weapon to scrape marks on the stone floor. "If you could construct three-foot high walls here, and here, then two connecting walls at the ends…" Lissa looked down and nodded. What Fletcher had drawn was basically a great big funnel.

"I think I can do that. Only, not all at once." She held out an arm, and Fletcher tied off her suit just below the elbow. Lissa stepped forward to the first line Fletcher had drawn, removed her glove, and touched the cold stone floor. Closing her eyes, she called to the stone, imagining what it was she wanted the stone to become. She heard the others mumble a bit as she felt the stone begin to move, but ignored them. She pulled at the now liquid material under her hand, standing slowly as she raised it up. When she thought she had it, she opened her eyes.

Before her stood a wall approximately ten feet long, three feet high. "It worked!" She clapped her hands, more than a little tired. "I'm gonna need some time before I try again. That took more than half of my mana. It's a lot harder to raise the stone up than it is just to let it melt. Gravity is a bitch." She grinned at them as she put her glove back on.

"While we wait for her to recover, I wish to try something." Volkov turned to look at Clarke. "This may damage me, so please be prepared to heal?" Clarke nodded, and he turned to Fletcher. "I will experiment with *Petrify*."

Fletcher stepped closer and tied off his arm as well.

Holding out his arm and removing his own glove, he focused on the idea of his skin hardening. They all watched as the skin of his hand darkened, becoming a mottled grey. Volkov hissed in pain, then began to make a fist. "It is painful at first, but now it just feels… strange. He raised his other hand to poke at the first. "I still have feeling, though it is less sensitive." He grabbed the multitool from his belt and opened the blade, cutting at the back of his grey hand. The blade scraped across the skin, but did not penetrate. He pushed harder, then harder again. Finally he simply jabbed the tip of the blade directly into the palm of his hand. It sounded just like metal hitting stone, and the tip penetrated maybe a millimeter. When he examined the blade, he saw that the tip was slightly blunted.

"Natural armor!" Mejia clapped his hands, then held one out for a fist bump from Volkov. "That's awesome, man. I bet even without the armor Graves made, those worms couldn't hurt you."

Ever the geologist, Lissa raised her hand again. "Uhm, they're called borers, and they eat stone. For all we know, using this skill against the worms would just make him smell and taste yummier."

"Good point." Lazar chuckled. "Maybe save that for a different type of enemy." He winked at Volkov. "Still, it is very impressive."

"If you're going to use it, avoid blunt damage." Chin offered. "Hammers, bullets, anything with enough weight or velocity to cause cracks." Volkov nodded his thanks at their strategist.

Lissa raised the next section of wall a few minutes later, and the rest of them discussed and experimented with the spells they had learned. After a few suggestions, Chin was able to modify his fireball spell, compressing the ball into a smaller, tighter, and hotter version.

"This actually takes less mana to cast, too." Chin announced, surprised. "Though it takes a full five seconds to form. I'll work on the speed."

Following a similar train of thought, Fletcher was able to modify the black magic bolt of her missile spell so that it spun in a spiral as it shot forward from her hand.

When she cast it into the nearby cavern wall, instead of bursting against the stone, it bored a couple inches before dissipating.

"Holy crap!" Mejia approached the wall and put an eye up close to the new hole. "You're a human mining drill, Fletcher."

"Martian mining drill." Fletcher corrected, grinning. "And that took a quarter of my mana. So if you're depending on me to drill through stone, we'd be here a very long time."

Chin shook his head. "But think what that would do to someone, or something, with armor? Like a giant bug with an exoskeleton. You could drill right through the outer shell."

"As long as it was less than two inches thick." She smiled at him. "And don't jinx us! Last thing I want to see is a giant bug walking through that cavern entrance. Don't go tempting the RNG!" The others chuckled, Graves giving Chin a light punch on the arm. "I'll work on the spell, maybe use it during the fight tomorrow to level it up. We should all do that."

By the time they were all done experimenting and discussing, Lissa had finished the fourth section of wall. It had taken nearly an hour, most of that being recovery time. They stood back at the Y-shaped funnel's exit and imagined the worms coming through.

"This should work just fine." Graves observed. "the funnel mouth is wide enough that all of them should be directed in toward us as they crawl up out of the ice." He stepped forward between the two parallel walls and held his arms out to his sides. "Room for three of us to fight side by side, if we don't get too wild."

"If we are not facing a lot of them at once, two of us can cover this area while the third rests. We can fight in shifts, allowing us a little rest, making us more effective. And reducing the risk of friendly damage." Volkov offered.

"Good idea." Lazar confirmed. "We'll try that to start with. If we begin to get overwhelmed, our third front liner can step in and pick up the slack. Fletcher, Chin, you two can cast offensive magic to bail us out if necessary. Mejia, you try as often as you can to summon one of the kills. If you get one, send it in to eat the others. We'll grow your pet big n strong in no time." He winked at their Hunter. "Until then, you'll have one of the shotguns, just in case." Turning to face the others, he added, "And if I call for a retreat, don't hesitate. These things are slow, but we've seen that they can lunge. Move back quickly, but don't turn your back on them. We'll regroup and try again."

"Wish we had a couple grenades." Graves muttered. "We could drop one and hide behind the walls, wipe out a bunch at once, then mop up the wounded ones from behind cover."

"I thought of that, too." Lazar shook his head. "Even if we had them, or could make them, too much risk of shrapnel putting holes in our suits."

"Speaking of that." Clarke stepped forward from where she had been observing. "Everybody take your helmets off for a few minutes. We need to work on acclimating ourselves to this atmosphere. Being able to breathe the air for extended periods might be our biggest advantage against any humans who come after us." She led by example, pressing a button on her wrist device to shut off her oxygen, then deactivating her helmet, which retracted into a metal ring around her neck.

The others followed suit, all of them coughing and gasping a bit, their lungs protesting the abuse. Their new Martian physiologies prevented them from perishing outright, and all of them lasted the two minutes before Clarke motioned for everyone to restore their suits.

"Well, that was unpleasant." Mejia commented. "The air tastes…"

"Nasty." Graves supplied. "Tastes bad, smells bad, made me a little dizzy."

"We'll do that every day, a little longer each time. Push ourselves until we can last as long as we need to out here." Clarke's voice was a little rough from the harsh atmosphere.

"Enough for today." Fletcher patted the wall next to her. "Great job, Lissa. And good work from all of you. I think we're ready for tomorrow. We'll start right after breakfast. Chin, please cook up some more of the worm meat. Whatever strength these things can provide us, we might as well use against them."

"Worm sausage it is!" Chin happily agreed. "I'll start the prep before I hit the sack tonight."

*****

The faceless man looked up from the note he was writing when a knock on his office door disturbed him. "Enter!"

His aide stepped inside, closing the door behind himself, and raising a questioning eyebrow.

"Hold on." The man pushed a button on his desk, and a faint hum could be heard for a moment. "The room is secure. What've you got for me."

"Volkov's family are confirmed dead. The Russian's went to grab them when the news leaked about the crew still being alive on Mars. Apparently they didn't want any impromptu negative press conferences or interview statements. Something went wrong, and things got hostile. The wife, kids, and her mother were all executed for treason, according to backchannel sources."

"Stupid!" the man slammed a fist on his desk, fuming for a moment before visibly calming himself. "Not only did they throw away any leverage we might have had on Volkov, but he's sure to want revenge now." The man got up and paced back and forth. The aide knew what was likely coming, but waited patiently, watching his boss and mentor weigh the options.

Finally, the man stopped. "Send the news along in the next transmission to Mars. Make sure it's encoded so that the Russian's can't eavesdrop. And make very sure Volkov knows it was his own government that was responsible." He looked at the analog clock on his wall. "How long before we send the next scheduled message?"

"Thirteen hours, sir. But we can always send one earlier…"

"No, that's not what I meant. Can you find out who led the team that killed the Volkovs in thirteen hours? Send our own team to take them out? It would be helpful if we could tell Volkov we brought his family's murderer to justice. Might inspire some loyalty toward us. He sure as hell won't have any for his own government after this."

"I'll get right on it."

"How are things on *Hyperion III*?"

"DJ is managing things as expected. Thorne's body was flushed out the airlock before an autopsy could be performed, as arranged. The acceleration burn is ongoing, and they're already moving at nearly twice the speed of the first two *Hyperion* ships." The aide paused, clearing his throat. "The Space Force guys tell us there is some additional risk of damage due to the increased velocity. Space debris that would normally bounce off the hull may penetrate now."

"I've seen the numbers, and the risk is acceptable. We need to take control of Mars immediately. If DJ and his crew don't make it, the next ship will have better

armor." He drummed his fingers on his desk. "Ideally, Fletcher and the *Hyperion I* crew will just starve to death and save us all a lot of trouble. But if they don't, I want men we can trust with boots on the ground. I don't care if it costs a dozen lives, a hundred, or a thousand. Colonizing Mars is a priority." He leaned back and motioned for his aide to sit.

"I'm going to share something with you that maybe a thousand people on Earth are privy to. Speak a word of this to anyone, and you're as dead as Thorne, along with your family. Are we clear?"

"Clear, sir."

"Even if Mars was packed solid with clean water, mountains of gold, iron, copper, and such… it won't save Earth. There are too many people, consuming too many resources too quickly. The trickle we could bring back from Mars, with the time it takes in transit, would be a band aid at best. Even if we also harvest Venus, the moons of Saturn… it doesn't solve our problem."

The aide nodded, having already figured that out for himself. "So the limited resources go to those who can make the best use of them, or pay the most."

"In a way, yes." The faceless man nodded. "But not how you're thinking. As I said, colonization of Mars is key. When the colony is large and stable enough, and we've begun terraforming the planet, certain groups of humans will be sent to Mars. The wealthy and powerful, of course. But also the most useful minds, the best genetic specimens, talented artists, the cream of the human crop, so to speak. Once Mars colony is fully established, wars will break out on Earth. Devastating wars that will reduce the human population by as much as two thirds. The weapons that get deployed will destroy power grids and electronics, knocking the so-called civilized world back into a pre-industrial status."

"But... what? Why?" the aide leaned forward, his elbows on his knees, eyes wide. "That's insane."

"Is it? Earth has an amazing capacity to recover from the damage we've done, but not if we keep piling it on. Reducing the population, eliminating ninety percent of the pollution production, all but ceasing the relentless harvest of natural resources... all of that will give the planet a chance. Fewer humans means no more food shortages. Wildlife will have the chance to recover and repopulate. Forests will regrow, farm fields will be allowed to recover naturally without chemical fertilizers or pesticides. Polluted lakes and oceans will clean themselves, even the ozone layer will regenerate given enough time."

"But the people... you're talking about murdering billions of humans."

"Not us. At least, not just us. They'll mostly kill each other in disputes over food, water, greener grass. We'll help with taking down the infrastructure, of course." The man looked at his aide, watching the conflicting emotions cross his face. Whether he realized it or not, this was a life or death moment for him.

“Just like with the Mars colony, a percentage of the humans remaining on Earth will be protected. There are massive underground facilities being constructed and stocked in preparation. This isn’t something that’s going to happen this year, even this decade. The preparations required are incredibly extensive, and expensive, and have to remain hidden. But for those like you, those who are in a position to help make it happen, there will be a safe place to shelter when the fighting begins.”

“And how long would we live underground?”

“A matter of a few years.” The man replied. “Long enough for the world to go to shit, for most of the human race to have killed each other off. Bomb each other back into the stone age, if you will. Then we emerge, stronger, better equipped, and ready to take over. We live our lives in relative comfort for a few decades while Earth does her thing. Then we signal Mars, and the tens of thousands who wish to return to Earth can do so. They’ll bring with them the knowledge, the skills, the manpower needed to restore our civilization, just on a much smaller scale. We’ll do it smarter the second time around. Controlled population growth, more energy efficient power generation, with less pollution. By carefully screening both the Mars colonists and those who shelter here, we’ll eliminate most hereditary and communicable diseases and genetic defects.”

He held up a hand as his aide opened his mouth. “No, this isn’t a racial thing. The best specimens of all races will be included, along with valuable people of mixed heritage. There will be no religious, gender, or socioeconomic bias either. The criteria are purely based on merit, potential, and mental fortitude. It won't be easy, facing the end of the world, or living underground for years. The weak-minded won't make it."

"And what about those who aren't sheltered?"

"Many will Darwin themselves out. But the strongest will survive, maybe even thrive, in small, isolated groups. Once we've emerged from shelter, we'll seek them out, and either recruit them, or eliminate them."

"Damn." The aide shook his head. "This is… damn." He got up and paced around the back of his chair, looking down at his feet as he absorbed what he'd just heard. "This must have been in the works for…"

"Decades." His boss confirmed. "Some of us have spent our lifetimes laying the groundwork for this. Working ourselves into positions of power, using our influence to boost others who share our goals. We have formed a network of people, corporations, governments across the globe. We control most of the major media outlets, the largest corporate entities, and have people in positions of influence in all but the most insignificant governments. And we're not even halfway there yet. The Mars colony will take a decade or more to stabilize, and the exodus must be slow. Fifteen to twenty years from now, the wars will begin."

"And you're telling me all of this now, because…?"

"Because you can be useful in helping me make it happen. Because you have two extremely bright children who could potentially contribute when they've grown.

They could be among the leaders who restore our civilization on Earth when the time comes. And you and your lovely wife are still young enough to have more children." He waited and watched his aide's face. When he continued, his gaze was stern, his tone carried a hint of threat.

"Loyalty is among the most valuable commodities these days, and in the more challenging days to come. That is part of why what the Russians did to Volkov was so stupid. When there are such enormous secrets to be kept, such daunting challenges to be overcome, loyalty and trust are paramount. I'm offering you my trust, and the rewards that go with it."

The aide nodded in understanding, retaking his seat. "And the price of failure, or refusal, to honor that trust… is my life."

"Your life, and your family's lives. You yourself wouldn't live to have supper with them tonight. They'd be left alone, both now and when the wars begin. Left out in the cold to survive on their own, or not."

The aide shook his head, then smiled at his mentor. "There's no need for the stick, I'll gladly take the carrot. I'm a little… surprised, I guess, at the extent and audacity of this plan. I just needed a minute to take it all in."

"Understandable. You're not the first person I've had this conversation with over the years. Not even in the first hundred. Others have taken longer to adjust, and more than a few couldn't accept it. Questions will begin to occur to you as soon as you leave this office. Come and sit with me in a couple of days, and I'll answer at least some of them. But for right now, get started on the items we've discussed, then go home and be with your family. Hug your kids. Maybe get to work on that next child." The man gave a warm smile and waved his aide toward the door. "I'll see you in the morning."

*****

When Fletcher went to the control room that evening to send her daily report, something she was becoming less and less convinced was at all necessary, she found a message waiting for her. It was short and to the point, text only, with no video.

"Commander Fletcher, please deliver the attached Eyes Only file to Engineer Volkov as soon as possible. Hyperion II is continuing its mission to Mars, and Commander Konig will relieve you upon arrival."

"They still think Volkov is human." She mumbled to herself. "Is this file some kind of instruction for him to take over? Maybe kill us all in our sleep?"

She used a blank data crystal to download the encrypted file, then sat in her chair for a while, passing the crystal back and forth from hand to hand as she considered what to do. She didn't for a moment believe that Volkov would murder them all. But if she handed him orders from his government to do so, it would cause him a great deal of conflict.

Especially, after his recent nightmare, if they somehow threatened his family as leverage to force him to follow orders.

The terse mention of Konig relieving her of command didn't sit well with her, either. That wasn't part of the original mission plan. She was selected as commander of *Hyperion I* because she was the most qualified. She was to have remained in command of the colony for the first several years, until some VIP politicians and administrators began to arrive. Even then, she was to retain a position on the advisory board that would take over government of the colony.

Not that she was surprised at all. The whole Martian assimilation bit obviously changed everything. Earth would want a human in charge of the colony, and the Martians set aside, or eliminated entirely, as soon as possible.

"Not without a fight." She mumbled, not bothering to send her report. Let them be surprised by what they found when they arrived. Gripping the data crystal tightly in her fist, she got up from her seat and went to find Volkov. Just as she was about to step out the door, she paused, then turned around and went back. She quickly typed out a short reply, then sent it.

"Tell Hyperion II crew to begin rationing food supply ASAP.
There's nothing left aboard Hyperion I for them to eat once they arrive."

"They murdered my children." His hands withdrew from the bunk, curling into fists so tight Fletcher could hear his knuckles pop. Volkov's entire body tensed and began to shake, veins bulging on his forearms, neck muscles straining. Fletcher could sense he was about to snap, and got to her feet, backing the others away as she moved out to the corridor.

"Volkov, I'm so sorry." She spoke as calmly and quietly as she could. Her mind flashed back to mission training, where she had been coached on what to do in a similar situation. It was always possible that a crewmember would lose family during the mission, and the stress of that, combined with the isolation of the mission, might send them into a tailspin. This, though, was much worse than anything they had anticipated.

As she focused on Volkov, speaking softly to him, a part of her consciousness recognized Graves and Lazar moving the others back and taking up positions directly behind her. They'd be ready to restrain him if necessary.

"Volkov, come with me. Let's take a little walk. Maybe get you something to drink in the cafeteria. We're here for you, my friend. Come, take my hand." She held out her left hand, trying her best to keep it from shaking. He didn't look up from staring at his own fists.

"Leave me." Volkov whispered, then repeated it in a raspy voice. "Leave. Me. Alone."

Graves put a hand on Fletcher's shoulder. "Let him be. At least, for now." He pulled her from the doorway and closed the door. Whispering, he continued. "I'll stand watch here for a while. Let him work things out on his own for a bit. When the time is right, I'll talk to him."

Clarke, who had disappeared without Fletcher noticing, returned with a syringe in her hand. When she saw Fletcher agree to let Graves stay, she handed him the syringe. "It's a heavy sedative, enough for a man of his size. If he becomes a danger to himself, or to you…" She didn't finish, seeing Graves nod his understanding.

With worried looks, the rest of the crew dispersed, heading back to their own quarters. Graves stepped into his, which were next door to Volkov's, and grabbed the lightweight alloy folding chair that each of them had for their private desks. Setting it next to Volkov's door, he gave Fletcher a sad smile, waving her toward her own bunk.

Inside, she could hear Volkov muttering to himself, in between sobs. There were occasional soft thumps as he struck his bunk again. Shaking her head, she turned away from the door and headed back to her quarters.

She spent hours staring at her ceiling, trying to work out the implications of what had happened. Why would the Russian government murder the Volkovs? How was he going to react to it, not just now, but in the long term? And maybe more importantly, how did he know ahead of time? Had being on Mars given him some sort of psychic ability? And if so, did the rest of them have it as well?

Fletcher awoke when her alarm went off at 06:00. She'd finally fallen asleep about three hours earlier, but was feeling surprisingly refreshed despite the short slumber. Dressing quickly, she made her way to the cafeteria, where she found Graves and Volkov already sitting, drinking coffee and speaking quietly.

"Okay if I join you?" She asked, and both men nodded. Grabbing her own coffee from a side table, she sat next to Volkov. "I'm sorry about your family." was all she could think to say. It sounded lame, and she grimaced slightly.

"Thank you, commander." Volkov didn't look at her, but his voice sounded calm enough. He seemed about to say more, but Lissa and Chin walked in, quietly fixing coffee for themselves. The rest of the crew filtered in one or two at a time within the next minute. When they'd all taken their seats after mumbling condolences to Volkov, the man reached out to the center of the table and dropped a storage crystal.

His voice hard, and quiet, he said, "You should all see this."

Chin picked up the crystal and moved to a holo projector on one wall. Inserting the crystal, he sat back down. A moment later, a video message played. The face of a man unknown to any of them, the aide who had been instructed to find out about the killings, appeared in front of a Space Force background.

"Mission Specialist Volkov, I am very sorry to have to tell you this, but we have received verified reports that your wife, her mother, and your children have been killed. The incident happened yesterday on your family farm..." The message went on for about a minute, explaining what they thought was the Russian government's motivation, as well as a rough account of how it happened. Tears streamed down Volkov's face as he watched it again. More than one of the others were crying as well. Lissa leaned into Graves, who put an arm around her and patted her shoulder to comfort her.

The tone changed suddenly, and the man's face went cold. "We located the woman who led that operation, and who fired the first shot. Her name was Major Irina Sidorov." The man paused, and he leaned forward toward the camera slightly. "If it were me, I would want revenge. And since you are where you are, we took the liberty of sending in a team of our own, acting on your behalf." As he spoke, some photos of Sidorov and several others flashed up onto the screen. All of them had multiple bullet holes in them. Sidorov's forehead sported a large caliber hole in it. "The major and all of her team have been accounted for."

There was another long pause, and the photos disappeared, just the aide's face remaining. "I know this won't ease your pain in any way. I am sending this message because I'm a family man myself, and I wanted to convey my personal condolences. I would like to be able to tell you that you'd have a home here in the US when you return, but I think we both know that won't happen. The best I can do is to say that I'm sorry, and wish you good luck."

The video ended abruptly, and there was silence in the room for several seconds.

then backed away quickly. Volkov and Graves made room for him to pass through, and he stepped into his assigned spot behind Volkov, halberd at the ready.

"I saw a lot of them moving down there, but there was no way to count." Chin warned.

"We've got this!" Lissa shouted encouragement from behind, just as the first few worms moved into sight. The funnel walls did their job, the worms taking the path of least resistance down toward the center of the funnel. When there were half a dozen visible, Graves let out his strange taunt, and the previously rambling worms all turned straight at him.

Graves and Volkov each took half a step away from each other, making sure that their weapons reached the walls on their respective sides so that no worms might sneak past out of reach. This helped ensure that sweeping strikes wouldn't cut their partner by accident, as well. Lazar, staying back a safe distance, positioned himself and Fletcher right in the middle of the funnel neck, in case any worms made it through between the two tanks.

For the first few minutes, the fight went exactly as planned. The worms crept forward heedlessly, moving right into the blender of sweeping slashes from the two tanks. Bodies were cut in half, the heads continuing to move forward. Graves and Volkov pinned the heads with weapons or feet, and their partners finished them off with accurate stabs in the mouth, or right behind it. Worms perished quickly, and the bodies began to pile up. Occasionally Volkov or Graves would get in a lucky hit, one-shotting the creatures with a slash through their brain, or a stab directly into their heads.

"Three steps back!" Lazar called out when the ground became slick with worm blood and slime. The two tanks did as ordered, their partners moving in unison with them. When they were once again on clean stone, they stopped and waited for the worms to catch up, both of them breathing hard inside their suits. "Graves, Volkov, oxygen check!" Lazar commanded.

"I'm good, eighty percent." Graves reported.

"Seventy six." Volkov added, holding his weapon at the ready. The worms were still a few feet away, and seemed to be moving more slowly. It was Chin who first noticed why.

"Shit! They're slowing down to eat!" He called out, leaning around to look past Volkov. "We gotta stop them, or there won't be any meat for us. Plus, they'll get stronger."

"Dammit!" Lazar cursed, thinking quickly. "Okay, Graves, Volkov and I will move forward. Kill everything we can reach. Gentlemen, watch your footing. It's going to be slippery. "Second line, all of you grab as many corpses as you can and toss them over the wall. We'll hold the newcomers back while you clear the bodies. We'll advance all the way to the edge of the tunnel, then retreat slowly."

"Roger that." Several of them replied at the same time. Lazar stepped forward between the tanks, and as one they all advanced. With three of them in line, their swings were more controlled, covering smaller arcs. The moment they began to pass by corpses, Chin, Fletcher, and Mejia started grabbing them and hurling them over the side walls. Several worms perished as the three tanks advanced, some of them died as they latched onto their broodmates' bodies to feed. Those were the easiest kills, as they were holding still, and the tanks were able to stab directly into their heads for critical hits.

Just as Lazar was killing one in that manner, another lunged at him. The four-foot worm launched itself from atop a corpse, impacting Lazar's chest. The body armor kept its toothed maw from burrowing into his chest, but the thing wrapped itself around him as it tried again and again to penetrate the composite.

Unable to lower his weapon without risking more worms getting through, Lazar called out, "Little help!"

Fletcher dashed forward, grabbing the worm just behind its jaws and yanking as hard as she could. The worm resisted, and Lazar's body was pulled partway around before it let go. As soon as the worm was loose, it tried to wrap itself around Fletcher's arm. Expecting this, she didn't give it time. Tossing it over her shoulder, she screamed, "Lissa!"

Lissa was right there, taking a baseball swing that sliced the worm in half midair, spraying blood in an arc. Within a second of its landing, Clarke used her own weapon to stab it in the head. She missed the kill shot, but Lissa was right there with her own blade, finishing it off.

Lazar had recovered, facing forward again and continuing to slash and stab alongside Graves and a growling Volkov. The worms that were cut in half got finished off by the second line, then tossed over the wall. For another two full minutes they continued this way, until they had advanced all the way to the ice tunnel's edge. Half a dozen worms were still emerging from the re-freezing water, and the tanks let them reach level ground at the top end of the slope before attacking.

When the last of them perished, and no more could be seen emerging from the icy slush below, Lazar called it.

"Alright, take a break. Great work, everyone." He retreated with the others, all of them taking seats atop the nearest wall, none of them taking their eyes from the tunnel mouth for more than a second or two.

"Great job, Lissa and Clarke. I kind of threw you a curveball there, but you handled it like champs." Fletcher smiled at the two ladies.

"Glad you did." Clarke grinned back. "We were getting a little bored, there. I didn't even have to heal Lazar when that thing tried to eat his heart."

Lazar looked down at his armor, which was only slightly scored and melted from the worm attack. "Thanks to Graves and his crafting."

"Yep, I'm the man!" Graves chuckled.

"How many did we kill?" Chin asked. "I tossed about a dozen heads over the wall, I think."

"More like twenty for me." Mejia reported.

"Yeah, same here." Fletcher agreed. "And looking at what's still laying out there, I'd say we killed… maybe sixty in all?" The others nodded, looking at the corpses inside the funnel that hadn't been flung over the wall. "Lazar, unless you're in a hurry to continue the fight, I say we take some time, harvest the meat and cores."

Lazar nodded. "We should do that, haul the meat back to storage, divide up the cores and use them. And reload our oxygen while we're at it. I'm down to seventy percent, and I'm sure Graves and Volkov are lower."

Chin raised a hand. "Check the worms carefully. We don't want any meat from the ones that got partially eaten. Don't know if that enzyme of theirs is poison. We can grind up the already-chewed ones for Volkov's fertilizer."

The group broke up, using their newly fabricated knives to harvest the worms. They made a pile off to one side of the contaminated worm bits, and gathered all the orbs. In total they had killed sixty eight worms, but there were only fifty six cores.

Lissa was the first to mention it. "Why did some of them not have orbs?".

"I noticed two of the partially eaten ones didn't have orbs." Clarke volunteered.

"So… maybe the worms that ate them got the orbs?" Chin ventured. "And if that's the case, shouldn't they have leveled up from it? Check all the orbs, see if any of them are higher level."

They each grabbed a handful of the essence orbs and began to *Examine* them one by one. "This one is level two." Graves held one up. A moment later, Lissa and Chin each found one as well.

Chin nodded. "Okay that explains the shortage of orbs, I think. The ones who got partially eaten gave up their orbs. Though there are only three of them at level two…" He shook his head. "Best guess? Only some of the worms that ate orbs leveled up, so those three must have eaten more than one each."

"I have had more than one orb, and I am still level one" Volkov argued.

Chin nodded. "Yes. I think maybe the creatures level up from eating meat and orbs more easily than we do. Which makes sense, if you think about it. They can't complete quests, and don't have a faction to gain reputation with like we do. They don't have crafted weapons or armor, just what they're born with. So in order to survive, they probably get much greater benefit from each kill."

Lazar, who was nodding his head thoughtfully, asked a question. "So then, what do we do with the next batch? Do we change our tactic to keep them from eating each other? Or do we allow some of them to chow down and get bigger, hoping to get more level two or even level three orbs?"

Chin was first to respond. "I know we need to level up, but I think right now meat is more of a priority." He waved at the mostly butchered corpses. "We collected maybe another month's supply here. I think we kill and butcher as many as we can until we have another month harvested. Then we can sacrifice some to see if the higher level orbs will help us."

A short trip back to the hab to store the harvested meat, hide, and orbs, reload their oxygen supplies, and they returned for a second round. This one went much like the first, except Lazar changed the tactic slightly.

They positioned themselves at the bottom end of the funnel walls at the start of the fight, waiting for the worms to gather and make their way all the way through. When the slaughter started, the group moved steadily forward every half minute or so, leaving the dead worms behind them as they advanced, keeping the new arrivals from feeding on them. Lissa and Clarke did most of the cleanup, tossing the bodies over the walls.

Only once did they begin to get overwhelmed. All three tanks had moved into a line at the front, swinging and stomping at the increasing number of monsters as they advanced. When a particularly thick bunch of them pressed in against the front line, Lazar called for Mejia to use his shotgun. Mejia dropped down on his belly, shoved the barrel between Graves' widespread legs, and fired two rounds of buckshot into the encroaching tangle of worms. Two of the nearest were simply shredded, half a dozen others knocked back and wounded enough that they curled up for a few seconds, giving the three tanks and their backups time to recover and finish several of them off.

The second wave dealt with, another sixty three worms killed, the group rested again. This time there were only two partially consumed corpses, yielding a better meat and orb harvest than the first round.

This time they'd brought a couple of carts with storage crates on them, and loaded the harvest quickly. Rather than take the time to run it all back to the hab, Lazar asked, "Everybody good on oxygen?"

They all confirmed that they were at seventy percent or higher, the three tanks having used the most from all the physical exertion.

"Then let's go for a third round before we head back. Check your weapons, make sure they're not damaged. Our composite holds up well against that enzyme, but it still takes some damage. Chin, how is your mana?"

"I'll be a hundred percent in a few minutes. Good enough to melt some more ice." Chin pointed at the carts full of harvest meat. "I think we've got a good supply now, so if you want to experiment with letting some of the worms eat each other…"

Lazar nodded. "We'll wait until near the end. When there's… let's say a dozen worms left? We'll back off and let them eat some of their sisters or brothers or whatever, and get bigger. It'll give us a chance to watch what happens, control how much food they have access to, and maybe get a minute's rest while they chow down."

They all nodded their agreement, except for Volkov, who was staring vacantly at the tunnel opening, gripping his weapon tightly. Lazar left him to his thoughts.

When Chin reported that his mana was fully recharged, he advanced to the tunnel while the rest retreated to the far end of the funnel, ready to repeat the last fight's successful tactic. He melted more ice, this time moving most of the water out of the tunnel and off to one side before hastily retreating through the funnel and taking his position behind Volkov. Again the fight went pretty much as expected. That is, until things went south. About two minutes into the fight, Chin stepped forward to skewer a worm that Volkov had pinned with his boot. Chin slipped on some worm blood and skidded forward past Volkov, falling on his butt right next to two oncoming worms.

Both of them immediately lunged toward him, one latching onto his left arm, the other his chest. The one on his chest failed to penetrate the armor there, and was quickly yanked away by Volkov, who grabbed it just behind its head. The other worm successfully chewed its way through Chin's suit and into the flesh of his arm as the man screamed. Despite the pain, he managed to scoot himself backward behind the line of tanks before any more worms reached him. Lissa and Clarke were there waiting for him. Lissa grabbed hold of the worm's tail sections with both hands and pulled, while Clark deftly stabbed with her combat knife directly through the worm's head, killing it. She and Fletcher both cast heals on the still-screaming Chin.

When the worm's maw released Chin's arm, it exposed a nasty wound that nearly caused Lissa to vomit. There was a round, jagged, three inch diameter hole in the suit material, and a matching area of missing flesh beneath. A significant chunk of Chin's bicep muscle mass was missing, and the humerus bone underneath was exposed. Blood ran freely from the wound at first, steaming in the cold Mars atmosphere, but the heal spells quickly stemmed the flow of blood.

Clarke produced a large patch from her bag and slapped it over Chin's arm, squeezing hard as it self-sealed to the suit's material. Inside his helmet, Chin was gasping and coughing. A quick check of his wrist unit showed that all but ten percent of his oxygen had leaked out.

"Chin's down to ten percent oxygen, and his health is low. We need to finish this quickly!" Clarke shouted at Lazar.

"Roger that." Lazar grunted as he jammed his weapon into a worm's mouth. "Mejia, four rounds from the shotgun, please. Clear the road ahead of us. As soon as he's done, we advance, and we don't stop. Forget about letting them level up."

Mejia did as ordered, dropping down and firing from a prone position so that the buckshot would carry farther than if he were shooting downward. He fired and racked and fired until all four rounds were expended, splattering worm bits against the walls and back onto the oncoming worms behind them. Even as he got to his feet and secured the shotgun, the three tanks were moving forward, sweeping their blades back and forth. In the center, Lazar swung low, while Volkov and Graves on either side swung higher, so as not to hit each others' blades.

Mejia grabbed his own halberd from where he'd leaned it against a wall, and the second line hurried to finish off the injured worms as the tanks pressed forward. Lissa took Chin's place behind Volkov while Clarke looked after their wounded comrade. Chin was coughing and mumbling incoherently, occasionally gasping in pain.

The worms perished in twos and threes as the group pushed themselves forward. All three tanks were gasping for breath, not slowing their efforts in the least. They had nearly reached the tunnel's edge when Graves started cursing in surprise. Something other than a worm was just emerging over the lip of the tunnel.

"That ain't a worm." Fletcher stated the obvious as the three tanks paused.

"No shit." Graves stopped cussing long enough to reply. "It's the biggest damned crab thing I've ever seen!" Even as he was speaking, Lazar was staring at the monster, using his Examine skill.

Ghost Crab
Level 3
Health: 300/300

"Crab meat! Hell yeah!" Mejia grinned at the monster. Its body was about four feet wide, roughly the same deep, with segmented legs on either side, its exoskeleton a deep crimson color. The front legs were oversized, faintly luminescent claws that protected a face with twitching mandibles and two eyes on stalks that rotated independently on the top of its head. As the group watched it emerge, one of the foreclaws shot out and grabbed a worm, nearly cutting it in half. The crab shoved the wriggling body into its face, where several segments around its mouth opened and closed, pulling the body inside rapidly. The worm tried to bite back, but its teeth had little effect on the crab's armor.

Graves grunted as he sliced the last remaining worm just behind its maw, killing it in one shot. "How do we kill this thing, boss?" He looked to Lazar.

"Everyone back up. Let this thing eat for a minute while we figure out a plan." He motioned with his free hand while stepping backward carefully. The entire area was slick with worm blood and bits. Lissa, Fletcher, and Mejia tossed corpses over the wall here and there, but only took their eyes off the crab for a second as they retreated. The three tanks kept their weapons held high in front of them.

The crab, for its part, mostly ignored the Martians, happily scooping up worm parts and shoving them into its mouth, occasionally turning a wary eyestalk their direction. When they had reached the narrow part of the funnel, Clarke spoke up.

"We don't have time for this."

"We do not have a choice." Volkov spoke for the first time in a quite a while. "If we leave this thing to eat, it will grow bigger and stronger. I am not sure we can kill it now, let alone if it levels up."

"Agreed." Lazar nodded his head once. "Let's see if we can take it down from a distance. Everybody over the walls, use them for cover. Obviously, don't let it get a claw on you."

They all obediently hopped over the three foot wall, wading through the worm corpses that had been flung over. When they reached the closest point to the crab, Lazar studied it for a moment.

"There's no way our weapons are gonna hurt that thing much. It's basically a walking tank, with natural armor. Try and stick your blades into joints if you can. Leg joints especially. If we can cripple it, then we can take our time and figure a way to kill it." They all watched as it grabbed a worm corpse and began shoving it into its mouth.

"I might be able to drill through it with my spell." Fletcher offered.

"Try to hit it in the mouth." Mejia suggested. "It opens up pretty wide when its feeding.

Fletcher dropped to one knee so that only her head stuck up above the wall. Focusing on the feasting arthropod, she pictured her drill spell shooting right into its mouth. A moment later the black spiral shot forward. It struck a chunk of worm that was being stuffed into the maw, and disappeared. A moment later the giant crab let out a high-pitched clacking sound, and both eyestalks turned toward the group.

"Looks like you hurt it. Do it again!" Lazar called out. Fletcher obliged, firing off the spell again, feeling a significant drain as she did so. This time there was no meat in the way, and the drill slammed into the crab's face, grinding for a second before disappearing inside. The crab screamed and shot forward on its spindly legs, the two oversized claws reaching out toward Fletcher and the others.

Graves and Volkov bravely got to their feet, weapons in both hands held across their bodies, ready to fend off the deadly claws. Lazar held his point forward, planning to try and jam the sharp tip into its mouth when it got in range.

Fletcher took a breath and cast her spell one more time at nearly point blank range, the crab only about six feet from the wall. The moment she did, she felt a wave of exhaustion that nearly caused her to tip over. Steadying herself against the wall, she watched as her spiral slammed into the crab's mouth, meeting no resistance. A moment later the crab stopped, twitched a few times, then went limp. Its body slammed onto the ground, the large claws following half a second later.

They all watched for a moment, suspecting that it was just stunned. But when it didn't move after ten seconds, Graves hopped over the wall and poked at its limp eye stalk with his halberd. When it didn't react, they all cheered.

"Fletcher, you're a badass monster slayer!" Lissa beamed at her as she got unsteadily to her feet. Her head spun slightly from the rapid use of most of her mana pool.

Lazar was all business, cutting off the celebration. "Graves, Volkov, make sure there aren't any more worms or crabs loose in the tunnel. Clarke, Lissa, get Chin back to the hab and into the infirmary *right now*!"

Chapter Seventeen

Eat the Pain

Clarke and Lissa supported Chin as they walked him back to the hab and through the airlock. As soon as they were inside, their helmets retracted, they could see that Chin was pale and sweating profusely. He'd stopped screaming after the second round of heals, but was clearly still in a great deal of pain.

They set him on a med bay table and quickly stripped his suit off of him. Lissa had to fight not to vomit when the wound was revealed. Though the healing spells had helped some, the enzyme that the worm had injected when it bit Chin's arm had continued to break down his tissue while the others had been fighting the crab.

"My god." Clarke breathed through her mouth, adjusting to the stench of the wound. "Chin, why didn't you say anything?"

"You guys were in the middle of a fight. Unless you have some new skill you haven't told us about, I knew there was nothing you could do. Not sure there's anything you can do now, except maybe cut the arm off?"

"The enzyme has already had time to spread through your bloodstream. The time for cutting off the arm would have been when it first happened. Now we'll have to deal with whatever systemic damage it has done." Clarke cursed quietly at herself. "I should have put on a tourniquet

and take this bag. I want you to keep a little pressure on it, but not too much." She switched places with Lissa and took up the gauze, mercilessly wiping inside the open wound, making Chin scream and thrash briefly before passing out.

*****

Out in the cavern, Volkov and Graves confirmed that no more creatures were emerging from, or moving around in, the slushy ice of the tunnel. The water that Chin had thawed was quickly refreezing, and would soon trap anything still hiding down there. Still keeping an eye on it as they worked, the five crewmembers began to harvest the remaining worm corpses. When that was through, they gathered around the oversized crab to discuss how to harvest it.

"I say we fabricate a giant pot and boil his big ass." Graves offered.

"Hey, now. Don't be insulting Crabby McCrabface." Mejia objected. "I'm sure his ass is perfectly formed for… whatever he is. If a lady crab was here, she'd probably be all warm for his crabby form." He grinned at Graves, who rolled his eyes. "But, yeah. Steaming him seems like a good idea. I've cooked lots of crabs in my day. And if we do it right, when we're done his shell will just pop right off."

"Assuming we could fabricate a pot that big, how would we heat it? We don't exactly have a forest full of firewood around here." Fletcher asked.

They were all surprised when Volkov spoke up. "No pot. Have Lissa make a hole in the stone. Chin can put in water and heat it with magic."

"Damn good idea, man." Graves gently patted Volkov on the back. "Cook it in the ground, like a pig at a luau. Save a lot of work and time."

"Right." Lazar looked around. "Let's lift him onto one of the carts, load up these new worms with the others, and take everything back inside. We can leave him near the hab until Lissa and Chin can get to him."

Fletcher cleared her throat. "How bout we put him up on top of one of the tanks? If there are bugs or critters down here, we don't want them smelling the meat, finding the crab on the ground and getting into it. We might cook and eat them without even knowing it." She shuddered at the thought of biting into crab meat and finding a Martian version of a cockroach or something.

It took two of them to lift the roughly four-foot square crab onto one of the carts. Graves, who was lifting one side of the shell, grunted. "Bet there's a hundred pounds of meat in there."

"Let's hope so." Lazar agreed, staring across the crab's back at him. "Between this thing and the worms, we should have protein for months."

"Biggest crab legs ever!" Mejia agreed, shoving the cart under the crab as the other two lifted. "Damn, do we even have butter in our kitchen?" He shook his head, looking at the size of the crab. “Never mind, even if we do, it won’t be enough.”

“Maybe we can find some Mars cows and make our own butter.” Graves teased. “Add steak to the menu.”

“Oh, man. Steak.” Mejia shook his head. “That was a low blow, Graves.”

He was about to say more, when Clarke broke through on coms. “I think we have Chin stabilized. But I’m out of mana. Fletcher, can you come cast a couple heals on him?”

“Be right there.” Fletcher jogged toward the hab and the others got quiet, pushing the carts back behind her.

Graves spoke quietly when they were about halfway back. “I didn’t think he was hurt that bad.” He shook his head. “From the way Doc sounded, it was serious.”

Clarke heard him, and reported, “It was the enzyme. The worm injected a good bit of it into his wound, and while we were fighting, it spread through his circulatory system. It had started to damage his heart, among other things. Lissa and I managed to neutralize it, and he’s doing better now.”

Graves nodded. “I remember how bad that burned when it got my leg. I guess I just didn’t get as much of the enzyme in me?”

“That would be my guess.” Clarke confirmed. “You were pretty much healed before I looked at your wound. Also, his suit material was completely dissolved, so our suits are no protection against that stuff."

"But the standard composite we used for the weapons and armor holds up pretty well. If we can figure out how to make a less rigid version of it, we could cover our suits with an extra layer." Graves grew thoughtful as they pushed the cart with the crab next to one of the tanks. "I'll work on it. Maybe I can do something with the *Shaping* skill."

*****

Chin recovered quickly enough to make *worm surprise* for dinner. The others groaned at the name, but Chin just giggled. He'd combined bits of worm meat with egg noodles and a light cream sauce, presenting a large bowl to the group.

"It looks like a bowlful of little worms" Lissa made a face when she saw it.

"Well, technically that's what it is." Mejia laughed at his own humor.

"It's delicious, trust me." Chin encouraged her. "I mean, if I can eat it after what happened today, so can you." He held the bowl out to her, and she took it with a timid smile. After scooping some onto her plate and passing the bowl, she took a deep breath and placed a forkful in her mouth.

help you require toward that end, we're at your disposal for the day. Except Graves, who's going to be trying to repair Chin's suit, and maybe upgrade our armor?" She looked at Graves, who nodded.

"And Doc, I'd like you to start working on your *Chemistry* or *Alchemy* or whatever we're calling it. See if health or mana potions are a thing here." She got a smile and nod from Clarke.

"Alright, you guys have the rest of the evening to yourselves. After breakfast tomorrow, we get to farming."

*****

DJ walked into Thorne's cargo bay hidey-hole and looked around. Thorne sat alone in his lawn chair, feet propped up on a small storage crate, reading a book. His hair was disheveled, and it looked like he hadn't shaved since launch. Looking up, he gave DJ a wave. "Got a report for me?"

DJ made an exaggerated sniffing sound. "Damn, boss. What died down here?"

"What? Oh, right." He motioned toward an open crate with a couple of empty MRE packets tossed inside. "Been a lot of years since I lived on those things. Forgot how rough they are on my guts. They give me the shits, make me fart so hard I actually checked this chair for scorch marks. Wasn't so bad when I was in the field, in the open air. But in here…" he waved up at the ceiling above them and the walls of crates. "There's no wind."

DJ chuckled, settling into the other seat. "I'll see if I can find you a fan or something. At least push that stench to a different section of the hold, maybe dissipate it a little."

"Much appreciated." Thorne grinned unabashedly. "Now what's up?"

"We're on course, and slightly ahead of schedule. The pilot overburned by a few seconds, giving us an extra speed boost. Not enough to put us significantly off course. We'll need to make a few adjustment burns when we're closer to Mars, but we're within mission parameters."

"And the other thing?"

"I reported your death, as instructed. They seem to have bought it, as I just got word from that lawyer that the money transfer went through." He paused, grinning as he puffed out his chest and pointed at it with a thumb. "I'm officially a hit man. A really, really well paid hit man."

Thorne chuckled. "Earned every dollar of it! I'd like to see the face of whomever is behind this when they learn I'm still here. And I don't care how powerful they are, just let them *try* to get that blood money back from one of the biggest, most powerful law firms in the country."

DJ shook his head. "By this time next month the money will have been distributed to the families. They'll all get instructions on how to hide it, not to make any big or flashy purchases. There shouldn't be any blowback on them, but if there is, our guys who stayed behind will look out for them."

"And then comes the second phase. When this ship is 'destroyed' and the entire crew's life insurance policies pay out. The families will have enough to safely and permanently disappear."

"At least until the ones that want to leave can join us on Mars." DJ agreed. "Based on your predictions, it'll cost about a million dollars per head to buy passage out here, once things at the colony have stabilized and the Space Force grants clearance for civilian passenger flights."

"Assuming things on Mars ever stabilize. If the governments and corporations decide to continue on the same hard line they've chosen so far, there could be open war on Mars for a good long while. But if that happens, we'll find a way for them to steal a ship and make the trip. We'll create a little chaos as a distraction." Thorne looked down at the book he was reading, holding it up so that DJ could read the title.

"The Art of War? Really, boss?"

"It's a long ride, my friend. With maybe a long fight at the other end." He set the book on his lap. "And speaking of the long ride, get the fellas started talking to the ship's crew. Feel them out on the situation on Mars. Find out which ones might be with us when the time comes, which ones are gonna be on the fence…"

"And which ones might need to have accidents." DJ finished for him, catching his gaze and shaking his head slightly. "Let's hope that's a small number. These are all good people, with useful skills."

"Well, for the ones that aren't immediately with us, we've got a few months to change their minds. We recruit the willing, but do not give them any information. Trust is earned, my friend, and the folks that hired you to kill me might have others aboard on their payroll."

DJ nodded, then grinned. "I'm personally hoping that hottie physicist wants to assimilate and make some little alien babies with me."

"Who're you kiddin? She's *way* too smart, *and* too good lookin for the likes of you."

"You wound me, boss. Seriously, that one hit right in the feels." DJ put both hands over his heart and fell back in his chair as if shot.

"Set your sights lower. I'm thinkin' that redhead systems tech is about your speed."

DJ looked thoughtful. "I do kind of dig that nerdy look she's got going on. But Yoshi says she's crazy."

"The best ones are a little crazy, DJ. Trust me." Thorne winked, then laughed, raising his drink in salute.

*****

Down below the bottom of the canyon, in a subterranean pocket hollowed out of the surrounding stone, a creature stirred. Its senses, fuzzy from long hibernation, told it there was prey nearby. The faintest scent of blood tickled something deep within its subconscious, causing its heart to beat once. One of its limbs twitched slightly as blood briefly pumped through it. A minute or so later, the heart beat again.

During its multi-millennia hibernation, the creature's body had remained mostly frozen, its heart thumping once or twice per year to circulate its blood within a limited loop around its heart and brain, just enough to keep it alive. The chamber was buried far enough below Mars' surface so that its body's core didn't freeze completely, while at the same time close enough to reach hibernation temperatures. This ability was the reason that this creature, and the others of its species, hadn't perished as the planet cooled, and it's atmosphere bled away.

Another heartbeat.

The creatures legs all twitched slightly this time, claws scraping against the surrounding stone. The scent of blood was familiar, a species that was both prey and predator to its kind. The creature was not awake enough to know which it scented now.

A hundred meters above the chamber, the splattered remains of a borer worm littered the canyon bottom. The one that had fought the newly assimilated Martians in the cavern above, and rolled itself off a cliff in its attempt to escape. Though the remains had quickly frozen, the scent of blood had reached the creature in its chamber below.

Another heartbeat. The creature hadn't formed a coherent thought, its mind sluggish, operating only on base instinct triggered by the scent of prey. The one primal reaction that could revive it from its nearly eternal slumber.

Hunger.

It would take time for the body to revive, for the brain to awaken. Eons of a near-frozen existence could not quickly be shrugged off. But what was a day, a week, even a month compared to the eternity it had already endured?

Hunger.

One of its claws flexed, digging into the cold, hard stone it was pressed against as if it were soft as butter.

*****

Chapter Eighteen

Reap and Sow

The crew spent the next week working on various projects. Day one was all about farming, assisting Volkov in setting up the hydroponics module. While Volkov and Chin went to work connecting lights, water pipes, and building the frames upon which the planter boxes would be mounted, Fletcher, Lissa, and Mejia each pulled a cart outside. Moving close to the edge of the ledge in front of the cavern, they scraped whatever loose dirt they could from the stone, shoveling it into the carts.

When they brought back three full carts, Volkov quickly tested the soil. “Da, this will do. It is high in carbon dioxide, which will help the plants grow faster.” He nodded toward the first of the planter box frames. “Place a box on the frame, and fill the bottom with about three inches of dirt.”

The three crewmembers did as they were told, filling a few dozen boxes before having to make another trip outside for more soil. This time they split up, Fletcher and Lissa heading upslope on the ramp, Mejia going downslope. They scraped the loose dirt into piles, then shoveled it into their carts. When they were all filled up again, they returned to the hydroponics module and repeated the process.

“That should be enough, for now.” Volkov gave them a small smile. The man was still hurting over his family, but was glad to have some honest work to occupy himself with. “Fill the rest of the boxes while we finish the water pipes, then we will plant the seeds.”

Fletcher found that she actually enjoyed the planting, which mainly involved poking small holes in the soil, dropping in seeds, and gently covering the holes. Each box was stacked in a vertical row, three boxes high, and each had a short water pipe hung over it that slowly dripped water into the soil. As they worked, Volkov explained that he could adjust the rate at which the water was released simply by turning a valve at the end of each pipe. The entire module was lit with high tech grow lights on timers that would simulate the normal daily cycle of light and darkness.

“We are starting with beans, potatoes, baby carrots, onions, and tomatoes, as well as some medicinal herbs, and some seasoning herbs like thyme, basil, and oregano.” Volkov motioned toward the outer wall. “When we have more space outside, I’ll plant corn, soybeans, and some fruit trees. They take a lot more water, but produce larger yields.”

“With that lake of water below us, we won’t be short on water.” Fletcher reminded him.

When they were all finished, there were a total of sixty long planter boxes filled partway with dirt and planted with the various seeds. Volkov sent them away, remaining by himself to clean up loose dirt, label the boxes with what was planted, and begin his logs. He’d be measuring how each plant did on a daily and weekly basis, comparing their growth to plants with the same DNA grown by colleagues on earth. He would be adjusting irrigation levels and 'sunlight' time per a preset schedule. This early research would allow them to better predict the crops' potential as a food source as the colony grew.

Lazar spent the first day assisting Graves, programming and feeding the fabricators raw materials while Graves focused on using his *Shaping* skill to try and repair Chin's suit. When Lazar was done with the fabricators, he took one of the carts back to the funnel and shoveled up all the leftover worm bits for Volkov to convert to fertilizer. He was glad to see that none of the remaining pieces looked to have been molested by any bugs or other scavengers, and reported that to the group.

"Doesn't look like anything's been out here snacking. There are no tracks that I can see, and no evidence of anything chewing on the leftovers."

"Good, then my giant crab legs are probably safe, too." Mejia happily replied.

"If you don't mind, can I have one of the brains, the enzyme sack, and some more of the teeth?" Clarke requested. "I am planning to do a little alchemical experimenting."

"Sure thing, Doc. I don't imagine Volkov has much use for the teeth as fertilizer." Lazar reached down and grabbed a worm head with the teeth and brain still intact.

Volkov cut in. "Bone can be ground into dust which makes an excellent fertilizer. It is, on Earth at least, high in calcium and other useful elements. But we have plenty, so take as much as you need, doctor."

For the remainder of the week, the crew busied themselves with working on the hab modules, organizing and storing cargo, and developing their own personal skills. Clarke rounded them all up twice each day, taking them outside the airlock without their helmets, forcing them to breathe the Martian air. Each time, they extended the trip outside by a minute, sometimes two, pushing themselves to adapt. By the end of the week, all the crewmembers could manage twenty minutes outside before dizziness or excessive coughing forced them back in. their bodies were also slowly adapting to the sub-zero temperatures out in the cavern.

At the same time, each of them worked on developing their various spells and abilities. At Clarke's insistence, they all learned to create a light globe, and the *Basic Heal* spell. Chin and Lissa were both interested in learning more healing magic, but were unable to do so. Undeterred, Chin suggested, "Maybe if we level up this spell high enough, we'll be able to learn a better one?" Toward that end, they started randomly casting heals on their fellow crewmembers whenever they weren't actively using their mana for something else, or waiting for it to regenerate.

On the second day Lissa created a large basin in the stone outside the hab. They filled it with water, dropped in the giant crab, and Chin used his magic to heat the water to boiling. It took a good bit of his mana, and he expressed a concern that he might not be able to keep heating the water

was drenched with several gallons of cold water as she stepped into the room for some coffee.

"Chin! What the hell, man!?" she growled at the grinning engineer, shooting him a look that promised retribution.

"Hold on, boss. Watch this!" Chin waved his hands in an overly ornate pattern that was purely for show, drawing the water back from Fletcher's body and clothing. "How's that feel?"

Fletcher, still angry, shook her head. "I'm cold." She paused, looking down at her bare arms and hands. "But I feel like I just had a shower. A cold shower." She rubbed the skin on her left arm with her right hand. It felt cleaner than it had in a long time. Water showers weren't a thing aboard the *Hyperion*, and the crew had only had sonic showers, or antibacterial wipes, for several months. They had not yet harvested enough water to allow for showers in the hab, either.

Chin looked sheepish. "Yeah, the next thing I'm going to work on is combining the fire element with the water, hopefully heating the water."

"Well, next time ask permission before you experiment on me. Or anyone else, for that matter." Fletcher warned. She grabbed her coffee and exited the room, grumbling under her breath.

*****

On the sixth day, Lazar, Fletcher and Lissa took his tank out of the cavern and down further into the canyon. The last of the cargo pods, the one that had drifted into the canyon before landing, was still down there somewhere, and needed to be retrieved. The trip downward was slow and mostly uneventful, the only excitement coming from an abnormally narrow section of the natural ramp. Parts of the outer edge had broken off and fallen away, leaving the remainder barely wide enough for the tank to drive over, and only when Lazar drove it so close to the inside edge that the cliff face scraped the paint along that side. When they were past the narrow spot, Fletcher looked back at Lissa, who was sitting on one of the rear benches.

"Can you do something about that?"

Lissa had been watching out the side window, and looked more than a little uneasy. Shaking her head, she answered. "I mean, I can bring some stone up and merge it with the edge, making it wider. But I'm not at all sure that it would hold up under the weight of tanks."

Fletcher pressed her lips together, then nodded and turned back toward the front windshield, ready to give up on the idea.

"But maybe…" Lissa began. When both Fletcher and Lazar turned around, she continued. "Maybe I can try something else." She got to her feet and motioned for them to join her in the airlock. They all stepped outside, and Lissa walked back to the narrow spot. Instead of approaching the crumbling edge, she went to the other side, putting a hand on the stone of the cliff face where Lazar had left some paint. After a moment, a wide swathe of the stone liquified, hollowing out the cliff face in a horizontal line. The liquid stone flowed toward the jagged edge of the path, and formed up around it, solidifying the cracked and broken surface. She repeated the process twice more, until she was breathing hard from overuse of her mana.

"Well done!" Lazar beamed at her, looking at the end result. While the outside edge of the ramp wasn't extended any further out than before, there was now a sort of half-pipe tunnel in the cliff face that would allow a tank to pass easily without scraping the stone, or getting too close to the outer edge.

"I think I've stabilized the edge a bit, too." Lissa smiled tiredly at them. "But let everyone know not to risk it."

"Roger that." Lazar gave her a thumbs-up, and they headed back into the airlock. A minute later Lissa stretched out on the bench and closed her eyes to meditate as Lazar got the tank moving again. By the time they reached the bottom of the canyon, her mana was back up to fifty percent.

"Bottom floor, ladies shoes and unmentionables!" Lazar called out as the tank moved off the ramp and out onto the canyon floor. The stone ahead of them was smooth, with a slight slope from the edges down into a depression along the center, clearly the path of a waterway at one point. A few random boulders littered the ground in places, their surfaces just as smooth as the stone they sat on, and the path of the river was filled with well-worn pebbles.

Lissa perked up, joining the two up front as they looked out the windshield. When they approached the center, she pointed at the pebble bed. "That was probably filled with sand as well, but it has mostly blown away over the years."

"There's that much wind way down here?" Lazar asked, surprised.

"Probably not regularly." Lissa shook her head. "But if we followed this path to its end, there's likely to be a point where the canyon bed rises up and opens to the surface. A windstorm approaching from the right angle would send hurricane strength winds shooting down this canyon, sweeping it clean." As she spoke, she reached over Fletcher's shoulder and pressed a few keys on the control panel. An image of Skippy's scans appeared as an overlay on the windshield, with their location marked at its center. She zoomed out, then pointed with a finger at one end of the canyon. "See here? This would have been the headwaters, and the canyon is a pretty straight line. It would act as a natural wind tunnel. If we drove to the other end, the downstream end…" she pointed at the opposite end of the canyon, "we'd likely find huge sand and mineral deposits piled up."

Fletcher checked his wrist unit's tracker. "The cargo pod is upstream, but with that tight spot on the ledge, we can't bring it up on the tank. We'll have to either figure out a way to use the crane, or bring several tanks down and load the cargo into them. So let's explore a little while we're here. Which way do we want to go?" Lazar asked. "Upstream, or down?"

"Upstream will eventually take us back up to the surface. I expect we'll see a whole lot of what we're seeing here…" Lissa mused, pinching her lower lip as she considered. "Downstream, we might find some interesting things that got washed or blown that direction. Maybe some cool debris, some bones of aquatic creatures, or even land animals that got trapped down here during a storm."

"Alright, downstream it is." Fletcher decided, back in charge since there was no current threat. Lazar nodded and pointed the tank downstream, keeping just to the left of the center channel that was filled with pebbles. The stone underneath their massive tires was firm, and relatively clean. Lazar set a sedate pace, about ten miles per hour, preferring safety over speed.

They were maybe two miles from the bottom of the ramp when Lissa thumped the back of his seat and shouted, "Stop!" Lazar slammed his foot on the brake pedal, scanning ahead of them for some kind of danger. Lissa's arm shot in front of his face, blocking his view as she pointed across his body out the side window at the cavern wall. "There! There's an opening. We need to check it out!"

"Easy there, kiddo." Fletcher warned. "We have no idea what's in there."

Lazar agreed. "Yeah, I mean, there could be a giant Martian cave bear with three heads and eye lasers or something." He grinned when both women stared at him, then shrugged. "What? Okay maybe not lasers. But there totally could be a giant monster in there. I mean, if the crabs around here are bigger than me, how big would the grizzlies be?"

Fletcher groaned, but humored him. "It seems unlikely that there would be grizzly bears on Mars, but I get your point. Everything here seems to be supersized. What if there was a full-grown borer worm in there, Lissa?"

"Well, let's at least get close so I can scan it. Maybe I can tell how big the cave is, or where it leads. I've been working on my earth magic skills all week."

Lazar looked to Fletcher, who nodded once. He turned the tank toward the opening in the cliff wall and moved the vehicle forward at a careful pace. Everyone in the vehicle had their eyes glued to the opening, expecting something horrible to come rushing out any minute. When they were within twenty yards of the cave mouth, Lissa tapped him on the shoulder. "That's close enough, I think."

Not bothering with their helmets, Lissa and Fletcher exited through the airlock while Lazar remained at the wheel, ready to haul ass as soon as they were back aboard if something came out after them. Fletcher made sure that they kept the tank between their bodies and the cave opening, keeping a close watch over the vehicle's hood as Lissa knelt down and put her bare hand on the ground. Closing her eyes, she extended her senses through the rock in the direction of the entrance.

"It's… there's stairs in there. Like actual carved stairs. They're quite a ways back, and they start partway up the wall, like… I don't know? It looks like pictures I've seen of old Venice. When the water level dropped, all these stairs that were used to board boats were left high and dry, stopping several feet above the current water." She opened her eyes and looked around. "I think maybe a long time ago the water ran pretty high through here.

Fletcher nodded. "That makes sense. Did you sense anything else in there?"

Lissa shook her head. "Nope. There's the stairs, and a wide flat area beyond them, then some kind of tall archway. But there's nothing but solid wall behind it. Maybe some kind of hidden door or secret panel or something?"

The two of them got back into the tank, and Fletcher instructed Lazar to move forward. The opening was wide enough for two of the tanks to drive through side by side, but still he drove carefully, giving himself a wide open gap on both sides. After a couple minutes the headlights picked up the end wall that Lissa had mentioned. Just as she'd described, the bottom step was a good eight feet from the cave floor.

Excited, Lissa fidgeted behind Lazar's seat, leaning forward over his shoulder. "If you pull up right next to the wall, we can use the tank as a stepstool. I think it'll get us close enough to that bottom step that we can hop up."

Fletcher figured Lissa was pretty close on the measurements. "Go ahead, Lazar. Bring her around so the left side is up close to the wall. That way we won't have to back out of here if we need to leave quickly."

A minute later all three of them exited the tank, helmets and gloves on this time, weapons strapped to their suits just in case. They climbed up the right side until they stood atop the vehicle's roof. Directly ahead of them the lowest step was at about waist level to Lissa. Without waiting for permission, she took a couple quick steps and hopped up toward it. The lower Mars gravity allowed her to make the nearly three foot jump without a problem. The moment her right foot connected with the step, she leaned forward and used her hands to catch herself on the higher steps. "They're much taller than we would build." She observed. "Like more than twice as tall as human steps. But we can climb them okay." She proceeded to do just that, turning to wave to the others as she climbed, looking like a toddler crawling up the oversized steps. "Come on up."

Fletcher copied her approach, getting a running leap to launch herself up. More agile and with better balance than Lissa, she landed fine on the bottom step, and used her momentum to continue up to the next. A moment later Lazar hit the bottom step and began climbing. He was slightly out of breath when he reached the top. Fifty steps was normally nothing. But fifty steps where you had to vertically leap up onto each one was a bit more of a workout.

Gazing around from the top step, Lazar saw a wide landing area that fed into a short corridor. At least twenty human paces wide, the corridor was cut directly into the surrounding stone, just like the stairs they'd just climbed. Maybe fifty paces ahead the corridor ended at a stone wall, blank except for a carved archway that stood more than twenty feet tall at the top of the arch.

"An archway to nowhere." Fletcher muttered. "Do you think whoever built this just didn't have time to finish it?"

Lazar and Lissa were both shaking their heads, and Lazar opened his mouth to speculate, but was interrupted as a sheen of shimmering purple light appeared inside the arch. A second later, something stepped through.

All three humans took a step back, Lazar almost stumbling back down the oversized stairway. And now he knew why it was sized the way it was. Before them, looking down at them as it strode down the corridor, was a giant!

Standing easily three times his own six foot height, the giant was humanoid. It walked on two long legs, had two arms and hands, and its torso, neck and head were roughly in proportion to humans. Though the head was larger and slightly more rounded, and the neck was thicker and heavily muscled. In fact, the entire creature was covered in corded muscle. Not bulky like a bodybuilder, more like it had been performing strenuous manual labor all its life. Its exposed skin was hairless and shaded grey, with cerulean blue veins visible across its surface, its fingers ending in two-inch long curved nails that were almost claws. It wore pants and a shirt of a shimmery material that resembled silk, and soft leather shoes.

Stopping at the mouth of the corridor, it looked down upon the humans, its face expressionless. In a deep, sonorous voice it spoke to them. "I assure you, young one, that time is something I have had in great abundance."

"Eep." Lissa let out a small sound of surprise as the others shook their heads slightly, Lazar reaching up to rub one ear. They'd all heard the voice in their heads as much as with their ears, and it had been loud, reverberating in their skulls. The giant waited patiently for a long moment before Fletcher gathered her wits and spoke.

"H-hello there. Greetings from Earth. I am-"

"I know who you are, as I know that you no longer represent your old world. You have chosen to become one of my children."

Lissa stammered. "You're… a Martian?"

The giant tilted his head slightly and considered for a moment before answering. "I have chosen to make my home here, of late. But I was not born on this world. My race is older than this planet, this system, the eldest currently residing in this galaxy, as far as we are aware. I was a traveler who wandered here long ago. You may call me Progenitor."

"Older than this system? Our sun is four and a half billion years old!" Lissa's mouth hung open as she finished speaking.

"Slightly more than five billion of your years, littlest one. And this galaxy is closer to fifteen billion years old. Your scientists are improving their knowledge and observation tools rapidly, but they still have much to learn." Progenitor chuckled. "And no, I myself am not that old. Though my life span stretches beyond what your minds can easily comprehend. I came to this world when it still had its atmosphere."

"Damn." Lazar muttered. "So you're… immortal?"

"As you understand the word, yes. I have chosen to remain in this corporeal form, and could continue to do so indefinitely. Though I am hoping that your arrival signifies that I am nearing the end of my vigil."

"Vigil?" Fletcher asked.

"I will explain, in time. For now, I have come to welcome you to this world. And to answer some of your questions. But before we continue, the others of your group should join us."

Fletcher nodded once, and spoke into her comms. "Volkov, gather the others and hop in a tank. There's somebody down here you all should meet."

"We're already suiting up!" the Russian sounded excited. "We have been listening."

"The vehicle will not be necessary." Progenitor waved a hand and the archway behind him lit up again. "Simply step outside and enter the portal. It will bring you directly here."

Volkov pressed his face against the airlock window when he heard, his eyes widening as a massive disc of purple shimmering light appeared just to the side of the cavern entrance. “I see it! That is... amazing!” He rushed the others into their suits, making sure they grabbed weapons and water. “Let us go!”

Two minutes later Fletcher saw the rest of her crew stumble slightly as they came through the archway behind Progenitor. She got a small kick out of seeing each of their reactions as they saw the giant standing in front of them. Once they were all through, Progenitor turned and motioned gently with one hand for Fletcher, Lazar, and Lissa to follow him back toward the arch. Each of the others took an unconscious step back as he advanced. Graves and Volkov each placed a hand on their weapons.

“Fear not, younglings. I mean you no harm. I am in fact here to help you. It is my wish that you grow stronger, in order to fulfill the destiny of your species. Please, follow me.” His long legs took him past the others in a few strides, and he disappeared through the glowing archway.

As Fletcher joined the others, they all looked to her, questions in their eyes. She let out a long exhale, then nodded once. “I know, this is a lot. But we’re on friggin Mars, where we’ve already discovered magic and monsters. This isn’t such a big leap. Let’s go.”

Gathering her own courage, she stepped forward and leaned into it as she passed headfirst across the shimmering plane. There was a brief sensation of cold and a tingling that spread through her entire body. But a second later she was standing on another stone landing with the portal behind her. She stumbled slightly, much as her crew had done, upon hitting the other side. It was difficult to blindly step into nowhere and maintain your balance.

Progenitor motioned her to move toward him where he stood several paces away. “Continue forward, do not block the others’ path.” She did as she was told, stepping forward and turning to face the portal, passing on the instructions to move forward as each of her crew stepped through. When they were all with her, she turned back around, and gasped.

Beyond where Progenitor stood, stretched out over the floor of a huge cavern, was an entire city! They all stood on a raised platform at the top of a ramp that was easily a hundred paces wide, and several hundred long. On either side of the ramp were more of the oversized stairs leading down to the cavern floor. At the bottom was a wide semicircular open space, the stone polished so that its surface shone like glass. Beyond that, buildings rose up in a series of half-circles that expanded outward and upward the farther out Fletcher looked. Finally, near the center of the cavern the tallest visible structure was a wide circular tower that rose up to disappear into the ceiling maybe fifty stories above the floor. Fletcher thought the tower might be as much as half a mile away. If that was the case, she judged the structure to be maybe three hundred feet in diameter. There were no lights anywhere that she could spot, but the cavern walls and all of the structures seemed to emit a faint glow. The combined effect provided about the same amount of light as a cloudy day on Earth.

“This is spectacular! An underground city on Mars. Wooo!” Chin shouted, pumping a fist into the air. “I gotta get some video to send home.”

Progenitor shook his head. “I’m afraid this place must remain secret, for now.”

Chin’s shoulder’s slumped a bit in disappointment. “Oh, sure. Whatever you say, boss. It’s your city.”

“And yours as well, now that you have all become citizens. Follow me, and I will show you around a bit. We’ll find a good place to talk.” He stepped down onto the ramp and the others moved to catch up. Though he strode at a sedate pace for his size, they had to jog to stay with him. Progenitor pretended not to notice as he descended the ramp and moved across the open space.

“The air in here is different.” Doc observed aloud after removing her helmet. “Easier to breathe than outside.”

“Yes, I took the liberty of increasing the oxygen content within this cavern. It is not as much as you are used to, but sufficient to allow you to breathe more easily while you are acclimating to your new home.

“Thank you, Progenitor. That was very thoughtful of you.” She bowed her head briefly.

“As I said, I wish to help you younglings. My own anatomy operates efficiently in nearly any environment, so it was no sacrifice to adjust this one to make you more comfortable.” They had now crossed the open space at the bottom of the ramp, and were entering the city proper.

Even the single story outer ring of buildings looked much taller from down there. Each doorway opening stood at least twenty feet high, with the roofs being maybe ten feet above that. The structures had clearly been built for beings of Progenitors stature.

They were mostly silent as he led them deeper into the city. There were a couple oohs and ahs as crew members noticed and pointed to various structures. Lissa noticed a fountain in the courtyard of a three-story building that featured a creature that resembled a golden dragon wrapped around a massive stone tree, neon blue water pouring from its mouth into the fountain's basin. Chin spotted a building that was an inverse pyramid, balanced on its tip, which was only wide enough to accommodate an entry door.

After a few minutes Progenitor turned aside from the main thoroughfare they'd been following, stepping into a medium sized building with a double door entry. "Ah, I believe this is the one." The crew followed him inside to find what looked to be a tavern common room. There was a long bar along the left side, with a doorway behind it that presumably led to a kitchen. The rest of the room featured a mixture of long tables with benches, and smaller round tables with chairs to seat four or six. The surprising thing was that, though the room's ceiling was still more than twenty feet high, all the furniture inside was built to a more human scale.

Progenitor moved to the end of one of the long tables and took a seat on the floor, comfortably crossing his legs as he sat, resting his elbows on his knees. "Please, seat yourselves. This is a good place for a us to talk." When he noticed the others studying the human-sized furniture, he chuckled. "There were once many species living in this city. Some few were of a stature similar to your own. This particular inn I believe was owned and operated by gnomes."

Fletcher and the others took seats on either side of the table, all of them quiet, waiting for the big man to speak.

"Now that we are all comfortable, I formally welcome you to Atlantis." He favored them with a smile as he spread his arms wide to indicate the city around them. "My home."

"Atlantis!" Chin shouted, before covering his mouth and turtling his head down between the shoulders of his suit. He continued at a more appropriate volume. "Sorry. It's just that Atlantis is a legendary city on Earth. A mythical place that no one has been able to find."

"That is because it has been here on Mars." Progenitor winked at him. "Though there is an Atlantis on your old world as well. I will explain in due time, and I think maybe ruin a few more of your myths." He took a deep breath. "Now, where to begin? I have been preparing for this conversation for many years, and still have not determined the best place to start. I suppose some background is in order." He placed his elbows back on his knees and closed his eyes for a moment.

"My people are older than you can imagine. We were born in the oldest of the galaxies, on one of the

“If you don’t mind me asking, what’s your real name?” Lissa asked shyly.

“That is for another time. I believe my name has import within the myths of your ancestors, and I do not wish those often-retold and altered fictions to color your perception of me.”

“You mentioned our destiny.” Volkov raised a hand slightly for a moment. “You are saying you have had a plan going back millions of years for us to evolve and move out into space?”

“Not you in particular. We did not plan for humans, or any specific species, to evolve into dominance on your old world. We simply… introduced possibilities, and watched to see what happened. At least, until an incident many years ago, when my children meddled where they should not have.” He thumped one hand lightly on the table as if frustrated, his massive strength causing the opposite end of the table to rise up briefly.

“We have fostered thousands, hundreds of thousands of species on various worlds. Many have been what you call humanoid, resembling my own people. Others have been insectile, or reptile, even elemental beings of water and fire. You may not have become the dominant species on your world if not for my progeny. They became impatient, and when the most primitive primate ancestors of humans began to learn to use tools, my children acted against my wishes. They encouraged the development of those evolutionary offshoots, and even made periodic direct contact with your ancient ancestors.

In fact, my anger at their impertinence, and their refusal to obey my commands, in time became outright rebellion that resulted in conflict between us. This is the reason Mars is now so sparsely inhabited."

"You fought a war against your children over Earth?" Mejia asked, fascinated.

"Not precisely. Their interference with the natural evolution of Earth was just their first act of petulance and defiance. Had they gone unpunished, they might have done the same on countless other worlds. This goes against our people's moral code, and is a backwards step toward our previous violent ways. Had my people learned of their actions, and their refusal to conform, they might have destroyed this entire system along with my children and myself."

"The prime directive is real!" Chin whispered to Lissa with a wink. She rolled her eyes and resisted the urge to groan. Looking up at Progenitor, he asked, "When we were assimilating, the notices we received mentioned *the will of the Gods*. Is that you? Are you God?"

"Ah, good. I am glad you asked." Progenitor favored him with a smile. "Those notifications you see are a part of the System that pervades and controls much of our universe. I mentioned that my race is not the eldest. We never met the race that created the System, and we simply refer to them as the Creators." He paused, looking slightly embarrassed. "The mention of the Gods is, I'm afraid, a subroutine created and inserted to function just within this solar system by my great grandson. He was both a troublemaker, and cursed with vanity. While the term does refer to myself and my descendants, we are in no way omniscient. We are simply the ones responsible for enforcing the dictates of the System in this area, should it deem some large scale action to be necessary."

"Like destroying our sun and everything around it." Fletcher's voice was flat.

"That particular event is highly unlikely at this point, but yes, that would be a good example. While the System itself is nearly omniscient, it is limited in the scope of its direct actions. It can perform small physical acts like increasing your body's muscle mass or bone density as you increase your attribute scores. Or determining what loot to award when you kill a monster or complete System-generated quests. The System can acknowledge and enforce contracts and oaths made by its citizens. It can even perform larger actions such as changing the weather on a world, causing large numbers of creatures to spawn in a location, or adjusting the direction of a marauding horde of said monsters. But when it comes to actions on the scale of destroying a world or solar system, it acts through agents like myself."

Fletcher made a mental connection. "And you had to take it upon yourself to punish your children before the System decided to enforce a punishment that might have taken out this whole solar system along with them."

"Correct. Though it saddened me almost beyond bearing, I was forced to take action. My children, who were on Earth at the time, fought me. And though I was unwilling to permanently damage Earth in order to defeat them, they had no similar qualms about Mars. By the time I prevailed, this world was barely habitable. Nearly all of those who'd chosen to settle here either perished or fled to safer, more comfortable worlds."

"I'm so sorry." Lissa had tears in her eyes as she spoke. "And thank you for sparing our world."

Progenitor shook his head. "You are most welcome, youngest one. But this is your world now. Never forget that. There may come a time when you must fight for your new world against the forces of the old."

Still tearful, and now frightened as well, Lissa nodded her head and looked away.

"So what is it that you need us to do?" Volkov asked. Graves leaned forward further, his back rigid with anticipation.

"For now, I need you to grow. Strengthen yourselves physically and mentally. Learn to use the powers the System will bestow upon you. Grow powerful enough to become agents of change. I will assist you as much as I can in this endeavor. I will offer you challenges and advice." He looked around the table at them. "But for now, I will offer you rooms on the floors above to rest. You will find food in the kitchen's storage compartments." He got to his feet and headed out toward the street. "Lock the door when I leave. There are inhabitants of this city that you are not yet prepared to meet."

Chapter Nineteen

What's Old Becomes New Again

"Well, this changes a few things." Mejia stated as he walked back to the table after locking the front door of the inn.

Graves was just reappearing from the kitchen where he'd gone to see if there was a back door, and make sure it was locked as well. "I wonder what inhabitants Progenitor was talking about? I didn't see anyone else moving around out there when we walked in."

"We can ask him tomorrow." Fletcher motioned for the two men to retake their seats. "And just in case those doors aren't strong enough to keep out any dangers, we'll keep a watch tonight. One of us at each door, one at the top of the stairs on our floor, one on the floor above, in case something comes through a window. Four hour shifts." They all nodded in agreement. Fletcher took a couple deep breaths, looking each of her people in the eye for a moment, then continued.

"I need to know if any of you need some time to get your heads right. We just learned some pretty earth-shattering information that, for some of us at least, changes our whole world view."

"What do you mean?" Lissa asked. "I mean, yeah it was a lot, but I don't feel any different."

Mejia spoke up. “Well, for one thing, Progenitor just invalidated most of the religions of Earth. I mean, knowing that aliens are real was going to have a big enough impact. But knowing that these particular aliens basically seeded our planet and guided our growth… no more garden of Eden, or more importantly, no more heaven, or hell. Thus no more incentive for billions of Christians to avoid sin.”

“Assuming what he’s told us is the truth.” Lazar didn’t look up as he spoke.

“There is that.” Mejia agreed. “Though I’m inclined to believe him.”

Fletcher held up a hand. “We can get into all of that later. Maybe. But right now I need to know if anyone is struggling with our current reality. I don’t know what tomorrow will bring, but I know I’m going to need to be able to depend on each of you to have your shit squared away. If you need some time to sort yourself out, speak now.” She waited, but no one said anything, or even looked hesitant.

“Alright, first things first. Let’s get some food in us. Chin, you want to check out the kitchen? See what Martian gnome cuisine might look like? Shout if you need a hand.”

Lissa stood up. “I’ll help.” She followed Chin into the kitchen as Volkov got to his feet and walked around behind the bar. The shelves there were filled with bottles of various sizes and shapes. He snorted as a series of alien letters carved into the wood translated itself into the words *Gnomes Rule!*

"I do not know about the rest of you, but I could use a drink." He grabbed a clear bottle filled with golden hued liquid, pulled the cork, and sniffed. "Smells like… honey and cinnamon, maybe?" He pulled several more bottles and sniffed them. Deciding on three that he liked, he found a tray and some glasses and brought them all over to the table. Sliding glasses to everyone, he poured himself a hefty sample from the first bottle, then placed all three in the center. Taking a sip, he took a moment to taste it before swallowing, a big smile on his face. "Da! Good stuff!"

As the others selected bottles, sniffed and tasted, he took a larger sip and set the glass down. "So, how long will we stay here?"

"And where exactly *is* here? I mean, it sounds like we're still on Mars, but with that portal, we could be anywhere. Halfway across the planet from our hab. The portal shut off as we were walking down the ramp, so it's not like we can just pop back through anytime we want to go home."

"Does anyone really *want* to go home right now?" Graves took a big slug of a blue liquid he'd decided to try, then slammed his glass on the table. "We've got food, booze, shelter, our weapons, and the dude who basically just took credit for being our creator here to help us, if he can be believed. I say we hang around a while and see what comes next."

Volkov nodded slightly. “I have already missed the afternoon measurements in the greenhouse. The lights and water are automated, so as long as there are no malfunctions, the plants will be fine on their own for several days.”

“The generators have enough water to run for weeks.” Lazar added.

“I would love to explore this place, and learn more from Progenitor.” Mejia volunteered. “Besides, I smell some training, maybe some quests coming. He said he wanted to help us grow stronger.”

Graves snorted. “If he gives us a ‘kill ten sewer rats’ quest, I’m gonna lose my mind.

“HA!” Chin walked back in, a big smile on his face. “That would be perfect! And now that you’ve said it, you know it’s gonna happen.” He jerked a thumb over one shoulder. “The kitchen is fully stocked. Like, there’s a walk-in fridge sized stasis chamber thingy, best I can figure. Everything inside is perfectly preserved. The weird thing is, some of it is cold, and some of it is hot. Like, there’s a sort of meat pie just sitting there on the shelf, still warm to the touch. It’s kind of freaky.”

“Meat pie sounds good to me!” Mejia licked his lips.

“As long as it’s not rat meat.” Lazar grinned at Graves, who rolled his eyes.

Fletcher, not seeing any dissenting opinions, nodded to Chin. "Meat pie it is, assuming there's enough for everyone. We leave the menu in your hands, Chin."

Chin rubbed his hands together and did his best evil villain laugh before turning and trotting back into the kitchen.

*****

The meat pie turned out to be delicious, everyone making complimentary comments or, in Graves' case, grunts of appreciation as he stuffed his face. Mejia grinned and offered, "tastes like chicken!" for which Chin chucked a roll at his face as the others laughed.

Chin had found a cooled wine cellar right next to the walk-in fridge, and paired the meat pie with several bottles of a delicious white wine. There were warm rolls and some kind of squash-like vegetable to round out the meal. By the end of it, they were all full and slightly tipsy.

"My compliments to the chefs." Volkov nodded his head toward Chin and Lissa as he leaned back on the bench, rubbing his belly. "Best meal I have had in a long time." The others all nodded or mumbled their agreement.

Fletcher, feeling sleepy after the stressful day and the big meal, made an executive decision. "Alright. Lazar, Graves, Lissa, and Chin have first watch. Wake us in four hours. The rest of you, pick a room on the second floor and hit the rack." She set an example by getting to her feet and heading for the stairs.

Mejia was right behind her, letting out a loud burp as he stood. Winking at Chin, he said, "Take it as a compliment." and gave Lissa a little wave. When he got upstairs he took the first room on the left, having seen Fletcher take the one on the right. Closing the door behind him, he found a small room with a single bed, dresser, nightstand, and a chest set at the foot of the bed. There was a narrow window looking out onto the street in front of the tavern, and an open door to one side led to a small bathroom. Sitting on the bed, he removed the armor that Graves had made for him, then spent a moment thinking about whether to remove his suit. He could sleep in it, but it would be uncomfortable. And the inn was locked and guarded. Removing his suit, he was surprised to feel that the floor was warm beneath his feet. He hadn't even noticed that the inn, and now that he thought back, the city itself, was much warmer than the sub-zero temps in their hab's cavern. Which he supposed was no surprise, as it was open to the planet's atmosphere.

As he lay down, his belly gurgled happily. The tasty light meat had been similar to pork, mixed with some kind of vegetable, all in a creamy, heavy gravy packed inside a thick golden brown crust. Compared to the ship's rations they'd been eating since leaving Earth, and Chin's improvised worm meat meals, this was the best food he'd had in close to a year. Placing one hand behind his head, Mejia tried to focus on the events of the day. They'd learned a lot from Progenitor, and he was sure the new information had important implications beyond what they'd already discussed. But his full belly and the soft bed

new spells for your first hundred levels, at least. The same goes for crafting and combat techniques."

"Guess it pays to be a bazillion years old." Graves muttered. He was still having a hard time wrapping his head around Progenitor having lived so long. Already he was thinking about how to keep from being bored to death if he lived a thousand years.

"It has been a lonely existence, for the most part." Progenitor's voice was softer, and the echo in their minds flooded them with a feeling of sadness and regret. Lissa began to cry again, as did Doc Clarke, though she was clearly fighting it.

"I'm sorry, Progenitor. But we're here to provide company now. And we appreciate your willingness to teach us. All of this new world controlled by the System stuff is a little overwhelming." Fletcher gave the giant a respectful bow of her head.

"It will be my pleasure." Progenitor's face brightened considerably as he shook off whatever memories had saddened him. "Toward that end, I have a group quest for you." He closed his eyes for a few seconds, and all of them received a notification.

Quest Received: Complete Lesson One

Speak with Progenitor and familiarize yourself with the basics of the System.

Reward: ??

"This is a mandatory quest." Progenitor continued. "I have given you all some background, but now we will discuss some specifics regarding how you all grow stronger. Get comfortable, this will not be a short conversation. Feel free to ask questions as they occur to you." He took a deep breath and let it out, then began.

"The easiest way to grow stronger is to kill other creatures. When you do so, you receive both loot, and experience. Or you would, normally. Another of the modifications that my progeny created for the local system is that until you reach level ten, you receive reputation in place of experience. This was done to promote conflict among the citizens of Mars. Those with greater reputation levels were given priority for quests and missions, more challenging and with greater rewards. While those with lower reputations received leftover, unwanted quests with small rewards, or none at all. It was amusing to my grandchildren to watch what they considered lesser creatures struggle against each other. A warning sign that I missed."

"So beyond level ten we start earning experience?" Chin asked.

"You are actually already earning experience, and will continue to do so. But it will not register with the System until you reach level ten. At which point your accumulated experience points will likely provide you with an immediate additional level or two, as well as some bonus attribute points. Normally at each fifth level you would receive double the normal number of points to assign. That particular reward is blocked by the local modifications until you achieve level ten."

"That's kind of harsh." Lissa commented meekly.

"It is. And were my grandson here, I would force him to restore the original System settings. It is unfair to those of you who will be attempting your initial growth. However, my grandson is in hiding somewhere on Earth, assuming he still lives. And I'm afraid the techniques he used to modify System parameters are not something I ever studied. I could have called in a specialist from one of the core worlds, but that might result in the System taking action against us all. A risk I'm not willing to take."

"No sweat. We can push through it." Chin was always up for a challenge.

"As compensation for this… difficulty, I will be providing you with better training than you would normally have access to. In general, new citizens must first locate trainers for their class, then either gain their favor through labor and quests, or compensate them via barter or credits. Your training will be free of charge, and you'll not have to waste time seeking out your trainers. In addition, as I am a Grand Master in most forms of magic and crafts, learning directly from me will increase the speed at which you learn, as well as the effectiveness of the lessons."

Progenitor turned to Doc Clarke. "You are this group's most effective healer. Your role will be vital as you all face the challenges of the upcoming days. So I will begin with you, child. Please come closer. While I instruct her, the rest of you can examine the gifts I have brought."

He opened his massive left hand to reveal eight small rings. Each was crafted from a different material, some made of metal, others looked to be crystal, or stone. Moving almost too quickly to follow, he picked a ring from his palm and tossed it across the table to Graves. Just as quickly, another went to Lissa, and each of the others. The last he simply handed to Doc as she moved to stand a short distance from his knee. Even with him sitting on the floor, she had to tilt her head back to look up at his face.

"Place your hand in mine, child." He set his hand on his knee, palm upward. Doc hesitated for a moment, then pressed her lips together and nodded once. Reaching out, she put her relatively tiny hand palm down upon his. Ignoring the sounds the rest of the group were making as they examined their rings, Progenitor stared into Doc's eyes. "I am going to grant you the formula of a more effective healing spell. It will also impart significant knowledge of anatomy. Your own, as well as that of several species you may encounter here." He gave her a warm smile. "I'm afraid this will be… uncomfortable. Imparting knowledge in this manner can be painful. Do not fear, I will not provide more than you can safely absorb at one time. You will not be injured. Are you ready?"

Doc clenched her jaw, keeping her lips pressed together, and nodded once. A moment later her eyes widened in surprise, then closed. A warmth spread from Progenitor's hand into hers, traveling up her arm and through the rest of her body. There was a tingling feeling in her head, which gradually increased until it felt like a

her eyes to focus on it. Within a second, the ring seemed to have its answer, and she opened her eyes again to see the flat section of the ring begin to liquify. It quickly morphed into a symbol that made her smile. "It's a caduceus!" She held it up for Fletcher to see. "The symbol of the medical profession."

Fletcher saw the winged staff with two snakes curled around its length, and nodded. "Mine did the same thing. It seems to… ask you what you want it to symbolize, then just makes it happen." She held up her own ring so that Doc could see the tiny open book with a wand laid across its pages. "Now, look at it more carefully." A wicked and expectant grin formed as she motioned toward Doc's ring.

Clarke held up the hand with the ring on it and inspected it closely.

Surgeon's Ring
Item Quality: Rare
Enhancements: Surgeon's Gift; Storage; Sofia +3; Haza +1

Surgeon's Gift increases the effectiveness of wearer's healing spells by 10%

Storage: Dimensional storage allows wearer to hold items in stasis, reducing that item's weight to .01% of normal. Total available storage is fifty slots. Items of similar type will stack within the same slot.

Her eyes wide, she was about to read the description to the others when Chin wobbled and fell over, much as she had. She immediately went to check on him as Graves laughed. "The rings are awesome, right?" He held up his ring to show the others. The icon was a shield and hammer. "It boosts my *Vitae* and *Vis*, and allows me to reduce the damage I take by ten percent! And the weight reduction of the storage? I can toss a five hundred pound anvil in there, and it will only weigh half a pound!"

One by one the crew members were summoned forward by Progenitor to receive their magic instruction. They shared their new ring boosts and spell descriptions. A few of them received more than one spell, especially if they were related. Mejia, for example, got a boost to his class spell, raising his chance to summon a copy of a killed creature to fifty percent. He also received a taming spell that would allow him a chance to bond a living creature without killing it first. And his ring boosted his chance to land a critical hit based on his anatomical knowledge.

Graves received a boosted taunt that would pull targets to him from up to fifty feet away, and a spell called *Instill Fear* that caused a single enemy to freeze in terror for five seconds. "I'm hoping at higher levels it'll work as an AoE, or at least on more than one target." he mused.

"Hey, one target for five seconds could mean the difference between dying and winning against a boss monster." Chin gave him a thumbs-up. "And an awesome interrupt against casters."

When everyone had received their training, Progenitor asked for their attention. "Now that you are a little better prepared, you have completed your quest."

They all saw notifications pop up, awarding each of them enough reputation to bring them all up to level three. “And now I have a more challenging quest for you. This one is not mandatory, but I suggest you attempt it.” Another notification appeared before all of the crew.

You have been offered the quest: Unsanitary!
The city’s sewer tunnels have become infested with pests.
Eliminate five of the vile creatures for each party member.
***Reward**: Reputation increase; 100 credits.*
Bonus quest: Locate and eliminate their nesting ground.
***Reward**: Reputation and credit award increases.*
Uncommon loot item.

Accept Quest? Yes/No

“I knew it! Graves grumbled, glancing quickly at Progenitor. “He gave us the damn kill ten sewer rats quest!”

“Only five sewer rats.” Lazar chuckled. “And you don’t know it’s gonna be rats. It could be sewer unicorns, or something. Cute, fuzzy lil baby unicorns that prance around and shit candies everywhere.”

“If they’re unicorns, I’m totally taming one!” Mejia piled on, grinning at Graves. “I’ll name it Gravesy and teach it to fart on command.”

“I vote for bunny rabbits with horns.” Volkov couldn’t resist joining in.

Graves blew a raspberry at them. "Just you wait. It's gonna be friggin hundred pound rats with teeth like buzz saws and scorpion tails, or some shit."

"That doesn't sound so bad." Chin offered an olive branch. "We only have to kill forty of them to complete the quest for everyone."

"Easy for you to say, caster boy. You'll be standing way in the back waving your hands around while I'm up front getting my huevos gnawed on."

"Huevos?" Volkov inquired.

"Cojones. Nobblies. Acorns. Dangly bits." Grave reached down with both hands and mimed like he was lifting two heavy cannonballs between his legs.

"Ah." Volkov chuckled. "Yes, maybe you need to craft a codpiece."

Graves nodded seriously. "I'm totally doing that."

"If you children are done?" Fletcher crossed her arms across her chest. "We have a quest to complete. And you're giving Progenitor a terrible impression of us."

"I found their word play quite amusing." The giant smiled slightly as he got to his feet. "But come, I will show you the nearest entrance to the sewer tunnels." As he walked and they jogged along to keep up, he warned them. "Remember to work as a team. These vermin often hunt in small packs, and prefer to attack from ambush rather than straightforward frontal assaults."

A minute or so later, he stepped into an alley off the main road, and bent down. Grabbing ahold of a large metal grate, he lifted one side up. The hinges on the opposite side squeaked slightly, the sound followed by a loud clang as he pushed the grate all the way over to crash against the stone on the other side. Peering into the open hole, the crew saw a ramp leading down a good fifty feet. Like the rest of the city, it was dimly lit, but not dark.

"Here we are. The tunnels are extensive, so I suggest you devise a way to keep track of where you've been. If you get lost, any of the ramps or ladders will bring you back to the surface, though it may take several of you to lift the grates. I will leave this one open for the remainder of the day." He waved a hand and a shimmering barrier appeared across the opening. "This will prevent the vermin from exiting the tunnels into the city proper. However you will be able to pass through unhindered, should you need to retreat."

With a raised hand, Progenitor turned and strode away. As he exited the alley onto the main road, he turned and called out, "Good luck."

Fletcher looked to Lazar as everyone readied their combat gear. "As agreed, I'm turning command over to you while we're down there."

Lazar nodded. "Alright people, single file on the way down. Graves, you and your huevos up front. I'll be right behind you. Chin, you follow me, then Mejia, Doc, Lissa, Fletcher, and Volkov, you're in the rear with your shield in case something tries to attack our six. If the tunnel is wide enough for us to spread out, we'll form a diamond with Mejia and Fletcher at the mid points, Doc and Lissa remain in the middle. Everybody got your gear set?" He looked around and waited for each of them to nod that they were ready.

"Graves, lead the way. Slow and quiet. If you see a giant rat, don't scream like a little girl." He smirked at the big man, who simply turned and started down the ramp.

Following a couple steps behind him, Lazar grinned as he heard the big tank mumble under his breath. "Let it run right past me and bite your lame ass..."

Chapter Twenty

Poo Dust and Gremlin Juice

As it turned out, the sewer tunnel itself was wide, but the tunnel floor was uneven. Straight down the center was a six foot deep, ten foot wide trench where the wastewater would normally flow. On either side was a raised walkway up against the tunnel walls. The walkway was about six feet wide, room enough for two people to stand shoulder to shoulder, but not to fight next to each other. The same soft glow emanated from the stone down here as up on the street. There was no detectable odor coming from the dry trench, though its surface was stained from a wide range of ancient crusted alien filth that none of them wanted to think about.

"At least it's not dark." Lazar was thankful for that. "We stay in single file. If we get a big mob of monsters coming at us, we can set up two shields and block the walkway. Then we kill them just like we did the worms. Swords, spears, and ranged attacks."

"Um… I can maybe help with that." Lissa volunteered from the middle of the pack. "One of the spells Progenitor taught me lets me summon a stone golem."

"A natural tank. Right on little sister!" Graves gave her a thumbs-up from up front. "Save me from getting chewed on. Bring it on!"

Lissa nodded once then held her hands out in front of herself, palms down. She muttered a short phrase, then turned her palms upward and lifted her hands. The stone in front of her groaned, bulging upward, and the others all stepped back. A second later a stone hand reached up out of the walkway and grabbed hold of the nearby stone, its fingers sinking effortlessly into the surface. With a grinding heave, it pulled itself up, first a head, then shoulders. Within about five seconds, a fully formed stone golem stood in front of Lissa. It stared at her, awaiting instruction.

It was maybe four feet tall, and humanoid, with a thick body, arms, and legs, no neck, and a boulder of a head with pitch black eyes, a wide mouth, and no nose. The creature blended perfectly into the surrounding stone, being created from the same stuff.

"Smaller than I expected." Chin winked at Lissa and poked her arm. "But pretty badass looking."

Blushing, she reached out and touched its chest. "It's my first one, okay? I'm sure as I get better at this magic stuff, I can make them bigger."

"Did it drain all your mana?" Fletcher asked.

Lissa quickly checked. "A little less than half. It'll take about thirty minutes to recharge. Less if I sit and meditate." She looked around, deciding there was no place she wanted to sit in a sewer tunnel, and added, "Never mind. Half an hour."

Lazar chuckled. "Alright, have your golem lead the way. If you can, have it walk along the side closest to the trench. Graves can walk just behind and to the left, near the wall."

Lissa sent a thought at the golem, telling it what she wanted, and it turned smartly around, walking forward along the edge of the trench. Surprisingly, though there was a slight trembling in the ground with each heavy step, there was almost no sound when stone foot met stone floor.

"Telepathic communication. Sweet." Mejia smiled at Lissa. "That'll come in handy if we're fighting enemies that understand us. You won't have to shout out orders that they can hear and compensate for."

Graves fell in behind the golem, and the others followed along in order. As they set out, Volkov observed from the back. "No water or waste in the trench, and it appears that there has not been any for a long time. This suggests that the city is abandoned."

"Or at least this section of it." Clarke added. "We're still under the outer ring. Maybe there are still inhabitants in the center, near that tower."

"I mean… we know Progenitor lives in here somewhere. But then, maybe a billion year old dude doesn't have to poop? Part of his super-efficient anatomy?"

Graves snorted. "Can you imagine the size of the load that dude must drop?"

"I'd rather not." Lazar replied dryly. "Heads up, eyes forward. Can the chat till we know what we're up against down here. I know this seems like a game, but Trent would tell you it's absolutely not." That effectively hushed everyone, and they walked on in silence. Each of them did their best to watch and listen for any sign of the creatures they'd been sent to kill. The only sounds were occasional squeaks of their armor, the dull thud of the golem's footfalls, and their own boots scuffing occasionally as they walked.

When they reached the first intersection, a tunnel branching off to the left, Lazar held up a fist – the signal for them to halt.

Using the serrated back edge of his combat knife, he marked a scratch in the corner of the stone wall. It was a rough arrow pointing back the way they had come. "In case we get lost."

Mejia cleared his throat. "I'm creating a rough map as we go. It's one of my Hunter subskills. But that's a good idea, in case I screw up."

"A map? How?" Lazar was instantly interested.

"There's a map feature on my interface. Do you guys not have that?" Mejia sounded hesitant. "It allows me to populate all the places I go, and even set some markers. I set one back at the ramp when we came down." He watched as everyone else's eyes unfocused.

"Well, damn. There it is." Lazar chuckled. "Never even occurred to me to pull it up. We haven't really gone

slapped down on the clustered gremlins. Half a dozen of them simply collapsed as bones snapped and blood burst from their bodies.

A moment later a fireball from Chin slammed into the onrushing horde, charring the first few that it struck, splashing onto several more, hurling them back into their fellow monsters. Fletcher squatted down to get at nearly eye level with the little monsters, then cast her magic drill spell into the mouth of the tunnel. It blasted through the first gremlin it hit, and the second, knocking both of them back to trip up others. The third gremlin in line took the drill in the face, and screamed as it spun into its brain before dissipating.

"I'm gonna save my mana for heals." Fletcher called out. "My spell's too costly for the damage it does." She watched as Volkov reached out one hand and made a grabbing motion, then twisted his wrist. The lead gremlin's bones audibly snapped as its back bent ninety degrees in the wrong direction. Volkov released the spell and the little monster fell dead at its companions' feet. They ignored it, rushing toward their new foes with wild abandon. A few of them carried clubs and sharpened poles, but most just reached toward Fletcher and her crew with sharp claws and bared teeth.

Lazar quickly assessed the situation. "The trench is deep, and they're short. We can use our height advantage to stab down at them. Lissa, send your golem down into the trench to stomp them flat, slow them down. The rest of you, spears ready. They don't seem to have any armor, shouldn't be that hard to kill."

Immediately the golem stepped off the walkway to land in the trench with a resounding crashing. It turned and stomped its way toward the gremlins as Chin sent another fireball into the tightest cluster of monsters still pushing out of the tunnel. There were more than a hundred of them visible now, and no end in sight. The impact of the fireball took down maybe a dozen more.

The first few charging gremlins reached the golem and were promptly flattened or shattered. The stone tank pounded one flat with a fist, kicked another back into the crowd with shattered ribs and a broken spine. Its left hand reached out and grabbed at one of the gremlins, managing to get two instead as its thick stone fingers closed. It lifted the creatures off their feet, then squeezed the life out of them before tossing them into the growing crowd in front of it. Half a dozen gremlins were knocked down, but got right back up again. The golem continued to stomp and kick, punch and grab, every movement taking out a few of the creatures, while they bit and scratched and struck it with clubs as they swarmed all over it. None of their attacks did more than scratch the golem's stone skin.

Volkov and the others stood on the walkway above the golem, stabbing or slashing at the little monsters with their halberds. Gremlins were being slaughtered wholesale, but still more of them were coming. Still, Lazar was confident their method was working.

Until one of the little gremlins launched itself off the top of the golem's head right toward Lissa. She screamed and fell backward as it struck her chest, grabbing hold of her chest plate with both hands and trying to bite at her neck. Lazar saw more of the nasty little creatures begin to launch themselves at his group, using the golem to make up for their lack of height. He suspected that even without that, they were more than capable of jumping the six feet from the trench floor up to the walkway.

"Everybody step back!" Chin shouted as Graves grabbed the gremlin on Lissa's chest by its skull and twisted. The thing's neck snapped and it let go. Graves threw it as hard as he could at an airborne Gremlin, the two bodies smashing together and falling into the trench. The crew members stepped back from the edge, all of them with spears held in front of them, ready to take down more flying gremlins.

Chin held out both hands and muttered, "This is gonna leave a mark." A second later, flame shot from both his hands in constant streams that arced down into the trench. Dozens of gremlins screamed as the flames landed on them, baking and blistering their skin. Chin moved his hands apart and strafed the trench, burning as many as he could for the next five seconds. The flames sputtered and died, and he wobbled slightly on his feet. "That's it, I'm out of mana."

"Great job, buddy!" Mejia clapped him on the back. "You took out like a hundred of the little bastards, I think."

"Great." Chin motioned with one tired hand toward the horde. "Only a billion left to go."

Lazar couldn't even see the golem anymore, it was so completely covered in gremlin flesh. Yet it continued to fight, killing a few monsters with every stomp and punch.

Taking a deep breath, he focused on a spot right in front of the golem and cast what the system notification had called *Collapse*. It was a spell that increased gravity to ten times normal in a small target area. Once again a ten foot wide swathe of the little monsters were crushed into pulp. "I'm out of mana now, too."

Still on her butt and crying from the flying gremlin attack, Lissa placed her hand on stone and closed her eyes. A strained look appeared on her face, her brow furrowed, lips pressed together as she concentrated. Lazar looked down into the trench when a bunch of the gremlins began to chitter. They were looking down and pointing at their feet, several of them attempting to jump as the stone beneath their feet liquified. Their squat legs quickly disappeared, followed by their round bellies. Lissa gasped and lifted her hand, panting from the effort. "I'm out now too."

The moment she stopped channeling her spell, the liquid stone returned to its natural solid state, squeezing more than fifty of the gremlins, breaking legs and arms trapped in the stone, snapping ribs, rendering the ones who were chest deep unable to breathe.

The crew were burning through their mana pools too quickly, but each of them were taking solid numbers of the little monsters down in the process.

Lazar looked up to see that the flow of reinforcements in the tunnel had ceased. All of the gremlins were now down in the trench. About half of those still alive were stuck in the stone, the remaining fifty or so still charging toward the crew, or futilely attacking the golem.

Graves, Volkov, and Mejia were side by side, swinging their halberd blades in wide arcs, slicing gremlins that tried to leap upward. Fletcher and Clarke were right behind them, spear points shooting out to jab at any that managed to get through. Chin was using his weapon to hold himself upright, still panting from the effort he put into the flamethrowers. Still, when one of them hopped up onto the walkway on Mejia's exposed flank, Chin managed to kick it back into the trench.

Distracted by his concern for Chin, Lazar didn't see the gremlin that leapt up at him until it was right in his face. He jerked his head backward, and the swiping claws left a set of nasty cuts across his cheek and nose as the creature passed over his chest. It hit the wall behind him and bounced right back in an acrobatic move that sent it slamming into his shoulder. It dug in with both paws, its sharp claws shredding his suit and the flesh beneath. Its back feet pumped, raking his arm with sharpened toenails. Lazar shouted in pain, dropping his spear and drawing his knife, trying to stab the vicious little thing that was gnawing on his shoulder.

Next to him, Graves spun around and his eyes widened, seeing the horrible damage and spray of blood. He reached and grabbed the gremlin by the neck, pulling it off Lazar before slamming in down and stomping on its head. "Doc! Lazar needs major heals!" he called out before turning back to resume slicing at flying gremlins.

Lazar, lightheaded from blood loss, leaned back against the wall as he felt healing magic wash through him. A second later he felt another spell hit him, probably from Fletcher. He was having a hard time lifting his head to see what was going on.

Another gremlin slammed into his chest plate, failing to grab hold of the armor before it fell. Lazar lifted the butt of his halberd and slammed it into the thing's back as it started to get up, pinning it to the floor. Taking a deep breath to steady himself, he lifted a foot and slammed it down on the monster's skull, crushing it.

Another heal washed over him, and he felt better. Looking past Graves into the trench, he could see most of the golem was clear of monsters. It was now doggedly stomping around the trench floor, finishing off wounded monsters or kicking attackers with devastating effect. Not many of the critters were leaping at his crew anymore, which was a good thing. They were all breathing hard as they gripped their weapons. Lissa was still sitting, her eyes and cheeks wet with tears. She held her knife in both hands, pointed toward the monsters as if to skewer the next one to fly at her.

A high-pitched keening echoed out of the side tunnel, and immediately the twenty or so surviving gremlins leapt up into the tunnel and took off. The crew all watched the tunnel for a while, expecting something new to come rushing at them. When nothing appeared, Graves took a knee and wiped the sweat from his forehead. "That was way worse than rats. Or friggin spiders."

Volkov chuckled at the other end of the line. “Da, that was unpleasant.” He turned toward Clarke. “Doctor, would you mind?” he pointed toward his left leg, where his thigh was badly shredded, blood pumping from the multiple claw wounds.

“Holy shit!” Doc quickly cast a heal on the Russian, as did Fletcher. “Why didn’t you say something sooner?” Doc scolded him as the blood flow slowed, then ceased.

“I was using my *Petrify* spell, hardening my skin. But when my mana got low toward the end, the spell failed and a couple of them got in lucky hits.” Volkov shrugged as if it were no big deal.

Doc checked the others, casting heals on both Mejia and Lissa, who had less serious, but still painful scratches on them. “You guys need to quit with the macho shit and call out when you’re hurt. I’m not a friggin’ psychic.” She yelled at all of them in general.

Lazar crossed his legs and sat right where he was, looking down over the ledge into the trench. He had no way to estimate how many dead gremlins he saw, as many of them had been stomped into paste, cut in half, or burned to a crisp.

Fletcher, down on one knee herself, huffed at Clarke. “Doc, as soon as you have some time to craft when we get back, we really need some kind of health and mana potions.” Clarke simply nodded in agreement, busy checking over Lazar.

Chin plopped down on his butt, letting his weapon clatter to the ground next to him. "What the hell kind of starter quest is this? Kill five each, my ass. I think we just killed more like thirty each. Where were the fuzzy bunnies with twenty health and no armor?"

Mejia coughed once, spitting out some dust that all the gremlins had kicked up. He tried his best not to think of its origins. "We're not real Martians." he responded to Chin.

"What?"

"We're not real Martians. Remember that message when we first assimilated? It said something about us being weaker than Martian norms, or something like that. And obviously we're physically much smaller and weaker than Progenitor and his people. This probably *was* the equivalent of a fuzzy bunny slaughter for a Martian child, or something."

"Is that why Progenitor gave us the spells and the rings? I was thinking that it was suspiciously generous. Maybe it was to make up for throwing us in the deep end? Or, the shallow end for something twenty feet tall that can lift tanks and fart hurricanes." Fletcher speculated. "The question is, do we go back and turn in the basic quest, or continue on to try to find the nest?"

"Are you insane, woman?!" Graves shouted, getting to his feet. "You want to go find more of those things?" He paused, taking a deep breath to yell some more. "The insane lil bastards didn't even try to defend themselves! They just attacked, and attacked some more. I watched some of them jump right into Chin's fire trying to get past it and eat his face. They give zero shits." He started to pace back and forth. "I like a good fight as much as the next guy. But those things are just anger and sharp teeth."

"And claws. Don't forget the claws." Lazar grinned at his friend. Graves glared at him for a moment, then snorted. Despite his best efforts, a grin forced its way onto his face.

"Very funny coming from the guy who got his ass beat by a two foot tall plush doll. With claws." He grinned wider when Lazar shot him a bird.

Chin, who had been looking thoughtful during the whole exchange, cleared his throat. "I think taking out the nest might be doable."

The group went silent, all of them staring at him. Graves shook his head. "You guys need to watch that whole mana drain thing. It apparently makes you stupid."

"Hear me out." Chin pushed himself to his feet. "It's pretty clear something was controlling that horde, right? Sent it after us, then called it back when most of them were dead." He waited while the others nodded in agreement. "Okay, so why did it call back the last few?"

"It saw we were winning." Mejia offered.

"Yes, but it had already sacrificed hundreds of them. Why preserve the last few… unless it needed them for protection? If there were a bunch more in the nest, why bother saving a dozen? For that matter, why not send more at us when we were nearly overrun?"

“It’s a trap!” Mejia grinned as Graves and Volkov chuckled over the reference.

Chin grinned as well, but shook his head. “I think we have killed most of them. And even if we haven’t, the main reason they did as well as they did was because they surprised us. And we didn’t know anything about them. Now we know how to kill them.”

“Learned it the hard way.” Lazar mumbled, rubbing his freshly healed arm through his shredded suit.

“Think about it. When everyone is at full health and mana, we can go in with a plan. Lissa can do her liquid stone thing when they charge at us, trap a bunch of them while I throw a few fireballs. Then we can take our time, kill the trapped ones with our weapons, or leave them for last while we deal with any that get through.”

Graves stopped pacing, looking thoughtful. “Your logic about the retreat makes some sense…”

Lissa sniffed loudly, wiping tears from her cheeks, nearly cutting herself with the knife still gripped tightly in her hand. “It’ll take at least an hour for my mana to recharge.”

Chin nodded. “Same here. I’m totally out, so are Lazar, and Volkov. And I’m guessing Doc is running low, too.” Doc nodded her head.

Lazar looked down at the gremlin he’d curb stomped. It was laying face down on the walkway just a couple steps away. Bending down, he touched the corpse to roll it over. “We’ve got an hour to kill before we go

"I think you should name him D'yavol." Volkov offered. "It means devil."

"I vote for Leroy." Graves suggested. "Those lil bastards just charged, not giving two shits what happens."

"Ooh, I like that!" Mejia grinned. "Leroy it is!"

"That's great, Mejia, and congrats on the pet. But we need to loot all of… that." He pointed at the gory mess in the trench. We can use the orbs, and the hearts. Anybody else see any useful parts?"

"Nope. And I'm not goin down there." Lissa took a step back from the edge.

"We've got an hour, right? Let me try something." Mejia looked down at his gremlin. "Leroy, fetch me its heart and orb." He pointed to one of the corpses up on the walkway with them. The little gremlin nodded once, then hopped over to the corpse. Without pause it punched one clawed fist into the corpse's belly, then pushed up under the sternum until it was elbow deep in the chest cavity. There was some movement, then the fist emerged wrapped around the core. Carefully taking the core in its other hand, it jammed the first one back in, gripped the heart, and ripped it free. It walked over to Mejia holding up both hands, offering its prizes.

"Good job Leroy!" Mejia took both, then tossed the heart to a surprised Clarke, who managed to catch it. He put the orb into his storage ring.

"Right. Thanks for volunteering." Lazar grinned at Mejia, who spluttered for a moment, then cursed quietly to himself. “Leroy there should be able to grab them all in an hour. As long as you’re down there with him, and he doesn’t have to keep running back and forth.”

“Yeah, yeah.” Mejia hopped down into the trench, nearly falling as his feet hit the slippery pile of gore. Leroy hopped down right behind him, its claws giving it a better purchase upon landing. Mejia instructed his minion to collect all the hearts and orbs, and it went to work.

“I think I’m gonna be sick.” Lissa turned away and visibly battled against the urge to vomit. When she got herself under control, she asked, “Can we move down a bit, the smell, and the sounds…”

“Tell your golem to guard Mejia.” Lazar agreed. I’ll keep watch up here. The rest of you move a few yards down and rest.”

“Graves shook his head. “Your mana is empty too. I’ll keep watch here, you go sit and meditate. Lazar started to argue, then thought better of it. Graves was right. The tank hadn’t used his mana, and Lazar was almost dead empty, except for the few points that had regenerated since the battle. He nodded his head in thanks, then moved off with the others.

Behind him, from down in the trench, he heard Mejia grumbling. “When we get back I’m taking a bath that lasts a week. And I’m using some of that paint thinner the gnomes call booze to gargle with. My mouth is full of poo dust and gremlin juice.”

Chapter Twenty One

Verminators

When the hour was up, Leroy was still sifting through the pile of gremlin bits looking for more cores. Lazar made an executive decision and called off the search. “That’s enough, Mejia. How many do you have?”

Mejia did a quick check of his inventory, having only to think the word and a grid popped up in his field of vision. “Two hundred and seventeen orbs. One hundred thirty hearts. Also, fourteen partial hearts. I wasn’t sure if those would do you any good, Doc?”

Clarke shrugged. “Hold on to them for now. We’ll find out when I figure out what they’re good for.”

“Alright, let’s go. Everybody in agreement that we follow the runners up that tunnel?”

Having had an hour to discuss it, they had all decided to go for the nest. Each of them nodded their agreement. They hopped down into the trench far from the battle zone, then back up on the other side. They met Mejia at the mouth of the side tunnel, where he’d already been harvesting the corpses that died there. With a quick command from Lissa, the golem pulled itself up from the trench as well. They all gave it plenty of space, as it was completely covered in gremlin bits. Chin had offered to try to burn it all off, but Lissa didn’t want to risk damaging the golem. She ordered it to walk up the tunnel in the direction the surviving gremlins had fled, and the others followed, at a distance.

Just a few minutes' walk at the golem's steady pace brought the party to a new intersection. This one was different than the others. They found a large round chamber with the usual walkway all around the outer edge. Below the walkway the trench fed into a round pit filled with debris. High above the walkway, evenly spaced around the walls, were a series of small openings, the wall below each one stained a rust color in a V pattern.

"Catch basin. For stormwater, most likely. Or at least, that is what it would be on the surface." Volkov pointed up at the smaller tunnels. "Those will lead to storm grates in the streets above. They all feed into here, and when the water gets deep enough, it floods the tunnel behind us. Clean water to push the sewage through the tunnels. This would be one of hundreds of these chambers around the city." He paused, shaking his head. "But how would you get rain in a cavern?"

"Are those… bones?" Lissa pointed down into the pit, at the center of which was a mound of debris that stood higher than the rest. Fletcher had originally assumed it was just leftover trash from when the system had been active. But now that Lissa had pointed it out, she could see that it was indeed a pile of bones and patches of what looked like fur. She spotted at least one elongated skull that featured a pair of long incisors. As she and the others were staring, the pile shifted slightly.

wrist. Ignoring the injury, he bit harder and shook his head, his wickedly sharp teeth shredding flesh and grinding on bone. With a final snap, the hand fell free and the enemy gremlin howled in pain. Leroy didn't hesitate, thrusting one clawed hand into the wounded gremlin's chest and yanking free its still-beating heart. A move he had now practiced a few hundred times. As the lifeless corpse dropped to the ground, Leroy trotted over to Mejia, proudly holding up his trophy.

"Thanks, buddy. Well done! Put it down for now, and be ready in case any more get past us." Mejia slapped a gremlin out of the air with his halberd as he spoke. The little gremlin gave a wide, bloody smile and carefully set the heart down at Mejia's feet, then began watching the battle with his remaining good eye.

"I like that little dude!" Graves called out as the last of the group attacking the crew went down. "He's got focus, and he gets shit done!"

Clarke, getting to her feet and helping Fletcher up, cast an experimental heal on Leroy. His ruined eye and various flesh wounds quickly healed up good as new as the gremlin grunted in surprise and looked around. When he saw Clarke smiling down at him, he gave a little wave, then went back to observing the battle.

The golem was doing a good job of smashing the gremlins attacking it. But unable to see around the mass of little green bodies swarming over it, the stone creature stepped forward onto a bone that rolled under its feet, causing it to lose its balance and fall backward. Four more gremlins were crushed underneath it when it landed, others leapt off in time to avoid that fate, only to rush back in to attack again. Undeterred, the golem simply rolled over, crushing a few more of its enemies in the process.

The bone pile in the center of the pit erupted then, and a new creature leapt free, landing near the golem and pausing to observe the battle. It was twice the size of its minions, standing over four feet tall, with the same basic build as the others. Except at each knee, shoulder, and elbow it sported a bony spike, along with a ridge of spikes resembling a mohawk from the top of its forehead to the back of its skull. The alpha's hide was jet black and glossy, with ridged scales. Its eyes glowed a bright red, and it let out a piercing howl that caused the crew members to flinch.

Gremlin Alpha
Level 4
Health: 400/400

"See! I knew it!" Chin shouted enthusiastically as he cast a fireball at the gremlin boss. His enthusiasm waned quickly when the spell struck the alpha's chest and knocked it back a step, but appeared to do no damage. "What the hell? It's fireproof?"

The golem was just getting back to its feet, ignoring the few living gremlins that still gnawed and scratched at it. Just as it was straightening, the alpha leapt forward and drove a shoulder spike into its face. Though the spike didn't penetrate, the force of the hit knocked the golem back down. Using it as a launching pad, the alpha leapt up toward the invaders on the ledge, howling again as it flew. Graves shouted a taunt of his own, and the gremlin boss's head pivoted to snarl at him, but it was already airborne and unable to change course.

Lazar swung his weapon at it, the side blade making contact with a leg and knocking the alpha off course. The blade didn't penetrate the hide, only leaving a scratch across several of the scales. "Shit!" Lazar cursed, watching as the monster slammed into Chin, both of them hitting the ground as it dug in with claws and teeth. Chin screamed in pain, panicking as he tried in vain to push the oversized gremlin off of him. Though smaller than Chin, the vicious monster was strong, and it held on as its teeth latched onto Chin's ear and ripped away a large chunk.

Leroy was there in an instant, leaping onto the alpha's back and ripping at its armored skin with his claws. Volkov was a fraction of a second behind him, casting his *Petrify* spell on his hand as he reached out and grasped the alpha by the back of the neck. He yanked it backward, putting all of his muscle and body weight into it, and managed to pull the monster off of Chin, who had stopped screaming and gone limp, bleeding from multiple deep wounds.

The creature struggled in Volkov's grasp, clawing at his stone-skinned arm and kicking its legs, trying to free itself. Volkov quickly spun around and slammed the alpha's face into the stone wall with as much force as he could. The impact knocked Leroy free, causing the little guy to land on his butt and growl in frustration. While Volkov's action would have crushed the skull of a normal gremlin, it simply stunned the alpha. Volkov slammed it against the wall again, then dropped it and planted a foot on its neck. Raising his weapon, he slammed the spear point down into its chest. The blade pierced right through and clanged against the stone underneath.

Pinned, the creature struggled to free itself. Volkov had missed its heart, and paid the price when its hands shredded his leg below the knee.

"Back off!" Fletcher shouted, and Volkov responded, removing his wounded leg and stepping back while still keeping some weight on his halberd's shaft to keep the alpha pinned. The moment he was clear, Fletcher launched one of her magic drill spells. The drill sped into the alpha's face, slamming its head into the stone and penetrating into its skull.

The creature went limp as all of them received notifications.

Clarke, who had been frantically casting heals on Chin, shouted, "Fletcher, heal Volkov!"

Looking down at the Russian's mangled leg and the growing pool of blood at his feet, Fletcher immediately complied, casting three heal spells in rapid succession. The bleeding slowed, then stopped, and Volkov nodded his thanks.

The entire group watched as Clarke ministered to Chin. The alpha had shredded his stomach and pelvic area with its toenails even as its hand ripped at his arms and shoulders. The straps for his chest plate had been mangled, and his suit was beyond saving. He was covered in his own blood from the waist up, and he hadn't moved yet.

"Come on, Chin!" Doc growled as she placed a hand over his ear and cast *Mend.* Looking up at Lazar, she reported. "The thing punctured his intestines in several places, and nicked his subclavian artery." She pointed at a deep wound on his shoulder near his collarbone that was visibly knitting itself closed as they watched. "I've stopped the bleeding and healed the internal damage, but he has lost a lot of blood."

"What can we do to help?" Lazar asked.

Doc threw up her hands in frustration. "I don't know! I'd normally hook him up to an IV and pump plasma into him. Or get him to drink something, at least." She sighed. "I think the best we can do is carry him back to the tavern as quickly as possible. At least there maybe we can find some supplies and try to replenish what he's lost…"

"But you're not sure he'll last that long." Lazar finished for her. Clarke nodded, her lips pressed together and tears forming in her eyes.

"I'll carry him!" Graves dropped his weapon and knelt next to Chin, reaching forward to scoop up his friend and crewmate.

From behind him, Progenitor's voice echoed through the chamber. "That will not be necessary." They all turned to see the giant stepping through a portal that had formed at the tunnel mouth. He raised a hand, and a small glass bottle filled with crimson liquid appeared on his palm. "Give him this." He handed the bottle to Clarke, who quickly pulled the stopper and placed one hand behind Chin's neck. Raising it slightly to clear his airway, she poured about half of the liquid into his mouth. Handing the bottle to Graves, she pushed his chin up until his mouth closed, then pinched his nose shut. A moment later Chin reflexively swallowed the liquid.

"That will be sufficient." Progenitor reassured them as they watched their unconscious friend. His body began to glow slightly, and he coughed as he opened his eyes.

There was a moment of panic as he remembered the gremlin attacking him, but Graves grabbed him by the shoulders. "It's okay, bud. You're okay."

Calming down, Chin looked around. Seeing the fight was over, and Progenitor standing above them all, he relaxed and laid his head back. "Well, that sucked." His eyes unfocused, and Doc worried for a moment until she realized he was reading notifications. "Hey, I leveled up. Twice!" He turned his gaze to Progenitor. "But that was a shitty starter quest."

Seeming to ignore him, Progenitor addressed the group. "You have loot to collect here. Gather it up quickly, and I will transport us all back to the inn. We have much to discuss."

The group, minus Chin and Volkov who were still feeling weak from blood loss, quickly did as instructed. Mejia had Leroy resume his orb and heart harvest, and the others helped out. Doc, after reassuring herself regarding

Chin's condition, used her knife to cut open the alpha with great difficulty. The tough hide resisted cutting, but she eventually managed it. This time the orb was much larger, and glowed more brightly than the others. She cut out the heart as well, putting both items into her storage ring. After a moment's thought, she called Volkov over. "I'm not strong enough, but maybe you can skin this thing?" The Russian nodded, drew his own knife, and went to work.

Lazar was down in the pit with the others who were harvesting orbs, when he noticed Progenitor staring at him intently. He raised an eyebrow, and the giant's gaze moved pointedly toward the bone pile in the center of the chamber. Taking the hint, Lazar called out. "Graves, Mejia, help me search the pile over here. Might be something good in its nest.

Since finding epic loot in the boss chamber was a common game element, they didn't hesitate, making their way carefully through the thickening layer of bones as they neared the center. Graves used his weapon to stab downward into the pile ahead of him as he moved, in case there were any more living surprises hiding in the pile. Seeing this, the others copied him. Graves was the first to reach the center, and looked down into the depression left when the alpha emerged. A glint of metal caught his eye.

"Got something." He set down his halberd, reached down into the nest with both hands, and lifted something up. It was a small wooden chest, about two feet wide and deep, bound with silvery metal straps with a latch made of the same material. "Ooh, it's heavy." He grinned.

"What's in the boooox?" Chin called out, grinning at his own joke. The others groaned or chuckled.

Graves made the box disappeared into his storage. "Guess you'll have to wait and see."

"Not cool, dude." Chin complained. He gave a fake and exaggerated cough. "Don't leave a dying man hanging."

Progenitor, seeing that the looting was complete, interrupted. "You shall not have to wait long. Let us depart this place." With a wave of his hand, those down in the pit, including the golem and Leroy, were levitated up and placed gently on the walkway. Progenitor motioned toward the still open portal behind him, then stepped through. Graves helped Chin to his feet, and the entire party followed the giant.

*****

The portal deposited them in the street just outside the tavern entrance. Leroy and the golem had been left behind when the crew stepped through the portal, and Lissa asked, "My golem, and little Leroy didn't come through. Are they… gone?"

"Only temporarily. You will be able to resummon them at need. They cannot pass through the portals with you, and are returned to the void where they await your call." Progenitor led them inside and took his usual position on the floor at the end of the table.

Progenitor looked at Chin, who was sitting next to Graves and staring intently at the storage ring on his finger. "First, you were correct, young one, to point out that the gremlin horde was not an appropriate challenge for ones such as yourselves. I must admit, it was not my intent for you to encounter them at this time."

His gaze shifted to Graves. "Your speculation was accurate, in that I had planned for you to face a nest of sewer rats." He held up a hand to stop Graves from gloating. "The rats are, or were, a significantly less dangerous opponent. One that would have presented much less of a challenge to your group."

Doc spoke up. "I saw the skulls in the bone pile. Those rats would have been the size of ponies."

"Yes, the sewer rats here are significantly larger than those you would have encountered on Earth. But you would have faced them individually, or in very small groups. I expect you would have easily met the challenge and completed the quest." He looked down at the floor for a moment and shook his head. "I was not aware that a gremlin horde had moved in and taken over the nest. I regret the danger that my oversight put you in."

"So, not omniscient after all." Chin spoke quietly, but everyone heard him. Including Progenitor.

"Ha! No, young one. I am far from omniscient. As I explained before, though your distant ancestors referred to and even worshipped my progeny as gods, we are no such thing. It is just that our technology and System-granted powers were so overwhelmingly advanced compared to human knowledge at that time, that they seemed godlike." All the crew nodded their heads, familiar with the concept.

"Despite the greatly increased level of difficulty, you all managed to prevail, not only achieving victory during the initial attack, but following up on what you thought to be the quest's bonus objective, and defeating the gremlin horde's alpha. I believe if you all take a moment to review your notifications, you will find that the System has rewarded you accordingly." He waited as the crew pulled up their notifications and began to read.

Chin was the first to finish, as he'd already read some of them upon waking. "I'm level three now, and received a new ability. It's called *Tenacious*." He shook his head. "And a title, too." Progenitor just smiled at him, waiting for the others to finish. When Lissa, who was the last to finish reading, looked up at him, he spoke.

"You have all earned the Title of *Hordebane*. This is for defeating an enemy of similar level to your own that outnumbered you more than thirty to one. As you have no doubt just read, it will grant you the ability to deal ten percent more damage, and take ten percent less damage, against large groups of foes." He looked down at Chin. "As for your *Tenacious*, that comes from repeatedly hovering at the brink of death, enduring wounds that should have ended your existence."

Chin nodded. "I don't recommend it, but it's a pretty cool passive ability. If I take a fatal hit, my health will hold at one point for ten seconds. Of course, if there's a bleed effect, or I take another hit before I can get heals, I'm toast as soon as that ten seconds expires."

"Anything that might save your life is a good thing." Doc offered. "I'll try to be quick with the heals, beat that ten second clock." Chin smiled in gratitude.

Progenitor cleared his throat. "I will also point out that each of you were awarded a significant amount of experience points, which has been banked until you reach level ten. And by way of apology for my own part in this, I offer you these." He waved his hand, and several objects appeared on the table in front of each of them. There were multiple potion bottles of various colors, and a single metal pendant with a thin, silvery metal chain.

"The red ones are minor health potions. Each will restore one hundred health points upon consumption. The blue are mana potions, also restoring one hundred points each. The yellow will restore stamina, and the green will cure poisons. The clear liquid is purified water. Those bottles are enchanted to refill up to one hundred percent of its water volume per hour. After one thousand refills, the enchantment will need to be recharged. Bring them to me, and I will recharge them for you until you learn to do so yourselves."

"Wow! Thank you, Progenitor." Lissa beamed at him.

"You are welcome, child. As for the pendants, those serve several purposes. First and foremost, they function as portal keys. I have taken the liberty of constructing a portal arch in the cavern where you set up your camp. Those keys will allow you to activate that portal, as well as the one you entered here in the city, and the one we used on the dock at the bottom of the canyon. As you grow stronger, I will authorize the use of additional portals."

"Awesome! I was worried I'd never get to eat the rest of those crab legs." Mejia grinned, spinning the pendant around in his fingers.

"Indeed. The pendants also function as a storage and trigger device for improved environmental suits." He pointed at Chin, whose suit was beyond repair. "You'll find that these are much hardier, more comfortable, and more effective than the suits you currently wear. They were designed by a half-dwarf, half-gnome tinker whose ship was constantly breaking down. He would often have to exit the ship to make repairs, and created these suits to increase his survival chances as well as his ability to do detailed work while wearing it. I had the foresight to become his partner and patent the design. A business enterprise that turned out to be quite lucrative."

Progenitor paused, gazing around the table with an expectant look on his face for several moments, until Chin caught on. "Oh! Uh, how do I activate it?" He stood up and took a couple steps back from the table.

"Simply touch the indentation on the back of the pendant. It will key to your soul, so that only you will be able to use it. Also, you should remove your current tattered attire before activating it."

Chin, quickly stripped off his armor pieces and what was left of his suit, standing there in just a pair of standard issue boxer briefs, then hung the pendant around his neck and pressed the back side with his thumb. There was a moment's delay, then the pendent seemed to explode. A black film extended outward from the edges, flowing across Chin's body, covering him entirely in a matter of seconds. When it was done, he was covered in a skin-tight material that seemed to absorb the light around them. It had even covered over his head, then formed a wide, clear face plate that extended nearly to his ears, up to his hairline, and down to his chin, giving him an unobstructed view.

"I'm a ninja!" he moved his arms and jumped up and down a couple times, then stared at his hands as he wiggled his fingers. "It feels like I'm not wearing anything at all."

Progenitor smiled as the others promptly stripped down to their skivvies and activated their own suits. He gave them time to test them out and discuss the features briefly before continuing. "You will have time to educate yourselves on the suits' functions later. Please note the design on the front side of your pendants." They each looked to find a symbol etched into the face of the item. It was an ancient-looking tree with a thick trunk and wide canopy. "That is the symbol of my House. It marks you as my children, and lets those who recognize it know that you are under my protection. You may not encounter such entities for many years, but I think we have all just learned that it is better to be safe than sorry."

Fletcher, back in charge now that the fighting was over, bowed her head toward the giant. "Thank you, Progenitor, for these incredible gifts."

"As I said, they are by way of apology for unwittingly placing you in such danger. And to say that I am quite proud of you for overcoming the unexpected challenge." He got to his feet. "Now, I expect you could use some time to recover and unwind. And I believe you still have some rewards to inspect. I will leave you to it. Tomorrow I will return with another quest." He waved to them as he stepped through the door and disappeared down the street.

"Loot time!" Chin shouted, pumping his fist in the air. "Bring it on, Graves! Open that chest and show us our sweet, sweet loot."

Graves obligingly produced the heavy chest and set it on the table with a thud as they all gathered around. He reached for the latch, then pulled his hand back. "Don't get too excited, brother. I mean, it was only a level four boss. The loot is probably like, fuzzy dice and pocket lint, or something."

"Really heavy pocket lint." Lissa giggled as Chin glared at her.

Graves reached for the latch again, and paused. Stepping back, he asked, "What if this is trapped. Or it's like, a mimic, or something?" He turned his face away from Chin and winked at the others.

"Oh, come on!" Chin hip checked Graves out of the way and reached for the box. The latch was a simple hasp with no lock on it, and he flipped it open. Then with only a slight pause, he used his left hand to lift the lid.

"BAM!" Graves shouted as he grabbed Chin from behind, causing the man to flinch. "Ahahaha! You should see your face."

Chin didn't even turn around, just shot him a bird and leaned forward to stare into the chest. The box was lined with a burgundy material that looked like felt, and at the bottom were two rows of four objects that looked like coins. Each one measured about two inches in diameter, made of a dull metal. Slightly disappointed that it didn't contain glowing piles of gold coins or diamonds, Chin reached in and took one of the coins. As he *Examined* his treasure, he backed away so the others could claim theirs.

> ***Quartermaster's Token – Level 4***
> *This token can be exchanged at the Quartermaster's Office, or any vendor's shop that has a current contract with the Quartermaster, for a single item of Rare (or lower) quality.*

Lissa, examining her own token, asked, "So… level four equals rare quality?"

"More importantly, who and where is the quartermaster?" Lazar asked. "I mean, I'm guessing we're not going to find a lot of shops open around here. The place is pretty much deserted. Is the quartermaster even still alive? Or can we just sort of walk into his office and claim our loot?"

"We can ask Progenitor tomorrow. For now, let's grab a meal here, then maybe head back through the portal to the hab? I'm thinking we should spend some time fabricating things like shields and swords? And if the printers have a blueprint for bows and arrows, those might come in handy. Doc, I'm going to give you one of my health potions to experiment on." She handed over one of the bottles of cherry red liquid. "See if you can figure out what the ingredients are? Sort of reverse engineer them, so you can make more?"

"I'll give it a shot." Doc confirmed as Chin and Lissa headed for the kitchen.

Chapter Twenty Two

Friggin' Wyverns...

Stella grunted in frustration and scratched out the most recent sentences she'd written in her notepad. There was something satisfying about the feeling of the graphite tip of the pencil scratching at the page as she pressed harder. A feeling from her childhood that she'd nearly forgotten in this age of laptops, tablets, and speech to text apps on her phone, her watch, even her refrigerator. But these days she was back to old school, analog notebooks and pencils. She didn't even trust pens not to have some kind of camera, microphone, or other monitoring device in them. But a good old fashioned wooden pencil was safe enough. Just to be sure, she had removed the eraser and flushed it. Which was why she was now scratching out a line instead of erasing it.

Everything she wrote these days had to be perfect. Perfectly chosen words, perfectly phrased, considered from all angles. Of course, the man with no name gave her *suggested* text to publish when he told her what story to write next, but she'd be damned if she was going to use more than the bare bones of it. The world was hanging on what she reported. Every story she published went worldwide within minutes of its release. Pundits and talking heads, including those at her own network, would be analyzing and opining as to what her words implied.

Of course, isolated as she was in the safe house, she had no way to independently verify any of the facts that were shoved down her throat. Even if she had a secure way to contact people, she had lost her only insider in the space program when Thorne boarded that ship, then was assassinated before it even got out of sight. The agency was locked down more tightly than anything she'd seen even in countries with powerful totalitarian regimes that controlled the TV and radio stations, as well as the major print publications and the internet.

Thorne had been an unusual animal, willing to sacrifice his career and his safety to get the truth out there. She admired her old friend for that, and was going to honor his sacrifice by spreading as much truth as she could herself. Toward that end, she rephrased her last paragraph for the third time.

Thorne ended a life of dedicated service to his nation aboard a hastily arranged mission to Mars. Unverified sources say that he suffered an unexpected cardiac event as his ship executed its initial acceleration burn, despite extensive pre-launch medical testing and physical evaluations that revealed no heart-related health issues.

"There, that's better. All technically true, as far as I can prove, but skeptical enough to let the conspiracy nuts take it and run with it." She nodded to herself before reaching out and grasping her glass of scotch without even looking. A motion she'd made every few minutes for many days now. "Nobody who has a clue will believe Thorne's death was from natural causes. But I can't prove that." Taking a sip, then another, she set the glass back down and read through her notes again. The story was part news, part eulogy, with a solid jab at the obvious coverup that was happening around the Mars missions.

Stella had decided to play along, to an extent. Mostly because if she didn't, she had no doubt that her own government would drop a very large bomb on her safe house, and find another reporter to replace her. And another reporter, any other reporter, wouldn't know what she knew. Playing along to buy time would allow her to figure out a way to get the whole truth out there, and the best time to do so.

"Not that there's ever going to be a good time to drop the news of alien life on Mars, magic being real, and massive government conspiracy, into average Joe's lap." She shook her head.

Her email alert ding'd at her, but she ignored it. She already knew who it was from, and what it said. Her boss was looking for the story. The whole world was clamoring for news on the Mars situation, and her network was cashing in bigtime on her exclusives. Not only were they selling the commercial time for outrageous sums, but she was pretty sure her boss was cashing in personally. She'd noticed that here and there a few minor facts were being edited out of her stories before they went live, and other networks were offering them up as so-called exclusive content. He had to have been selling those tidbits and pocketing the money. Not that Stella cared at all, as long as the facts were getting out there. Spreading them around actually lent some credibility to the stories, making it seem like multiple investigative sources were agreeing on the facts.

She finished one last readthrough, sighed, and took another drink. This was the best she could do, for now. Grabbing her supposedly secure laptop, she opened up her boss's most recent email, one of six he'd sent in the last twelve hours, and hit [reply]. She quickly typed out the story, referring often to her notes to make sure she got the phrasing correct. When she was done, she did a perfunctory read for typos. She didn't really care if she missed a few – that's what copy editors were for – but her deeply ingrained work ethic and pride still required her to hold herself to certain standards.

With a final click she sent the email and got up from her desk. She began to pace back and forth behind her chair, as was her long habit, but the action reminded her of the recent attack on her office and the deaths of the unfortunate security guards. She stopped pacing and sat back down, compulsively checking the monitoring software George had installed on this laptop. It constantly monitored the communications between Mission Control and the various Hyperion ships, as well as the crew already on Mars. She knew that, thanks to the encryption key that Thorne had given her, and the access that it granted, the program would alert her whenever a message was detected. But more and more often she found herself opening the program and checking, just in case she'd missed an alert, or something.

Because though she'd picked up several interesting transmissions between Earth and *Hyperion II* and *Hyperion III*, there hadn't been a transmission from Fletcher or Lazar on Mars for several days.

Stella had cried when she reviewed the message the agency had sent to Volkov regarding his family. She'd found her heart aching for the poor man who was trapped so far from home, who would be unable to attend their funerals. Or ever visit their graves to say goodbye. And she found herself agreeing with the young man who'd sent the message, in hoping that Volkov took some small measure of comfort from her government tracking down and killing those responsible. When the nameless man had instructed her to publish that story, she'd happily done so, and added her own heartfelt condolences to Volkov, though she was reasonably sure he'd never see the story. She was happy to see that her report caused a tidal wave of sympathy and support for the man across the globe. And more importantly, spelled the ruin of several officials that were in any way tied to the handling, and ultimate demise, of Volkov's family. The people of Russia, in particular, did not take well to the murders of their hero's family. They loudly demanded swift and merciless justice.

"You need to be careful, old gal." She muttered to herself. "You've been given an unholy amount of power all of a sudden. What you say, and how you say it, is going to change the world."

Shaking her head, she got up and poured herself another drink. The first three of the evening hadn't even lasted long enough for the ice to melt. "George!" She yelled toward the door, loud enough for him to hear her downstairs. "Order us some Chinese food! And be sure to get that really spicy mustard I like!" She looked out the bulletproof window toward the starry night sky and raised her glass. "Here's to you, Thorne. You lucky bastard."

*****

At that moment, Thorne was just finishing *The Art of War*. He grunted to himself as he closed the book, shutting his eyes and taking a moment to internalize what he'd read. He was never one to memorize and regurgitate the wisdom contained in books like this one word for word. Rather, he tried to take the best bits and incorporate them into his thought processes. Given the massive amount of free time he had ahead of him, he was sure he'd be reading the book again, and pulling from it a few more key points.

Setting the book on an empty crate that now served as a makeshift side table, he got up from his lawn chair and began to walk around. A big disadvantage to hiding in this cargo bay was the limited space for exercise. Thorne's athletic days were far behind him, but he liked to get at least a little exercise each day, if only to prevent an actual heart attack. Already he was feeling bloated from the long days of hiding, the horrible MREs he was consuming along with larger than normal quantities of beer. He kept telling himself to cut back on the beer, since they had little to no chance of ever obtaining more. But then he'd get thirsty, and tell himself that by the time they reached Mars any remaining beer would be skunky anyway, and it deserved to be enjoyed while it was still fresh.

Pacing back and forth, he checked his watch. "You're a half hour late, DJ." he growled. Thorne tried to convince himself that it didn't mean anything. "Probably distracted trying to get into that physicist's pants. I keep telling him she's out of his league, but the boy has ambition." He grinned to himself, shaking his head, wishing he could be topside to witness his friend getting shot down time after time. And to see what novel approaches he tried. DJ was nothing if not imaginative when it came to overcoming obstacles to his goals.

Still, they were on a ship manned by a potentially hostile crew. A ship they were planning to hijack very soon, by whatever means necessary. His boys had been actively but carefully feeling out the crew and their loyalties, hoping to recruit as many of them as possible. But what he was planning to do would be seen as treason to some of them. And others might resist purely out of reflex and loyalty to their country.

Thorne couldn't blame them if they did. He was a patriot himself. But they didn't know what kind of sleazy, unethical deals were being made in the sealed conference rooms back on Earth, the way he did. They were simply following what they thought to be lawful orders. And there were enough military personnel aboard that were not part of his own small group, that should a fight break out, things could get dicey. Combat of any kind in a pressurized tin can floating through the void of space was always a bad idea. And when a normally fanatically punctual DJ was late, Thorne worried.

"Sorry, boss." DJ's voice called out as the man rounded the last corner of the maze of crates that led to Thorne's hidey hole. Thorne took a moment for a deep breath and slow exhalation before he turned to face his second in command.

"Problems upstairs?" Thorne tried to sound as casual as he could.

"Not the kind you're worried about. One of the original crew decided he didn't appreciate the attention I was paying to a certain young lady. He was determined to discourage me, ambushed me in one of the corridors. Took me a little while to explain to the commander why one of his botanists was in sick bay." DJ gave him a rueful grin.

"A botanist? Really?" Thorne was surprised.

"Hey, he's a big ole cornfed midwestern farm boy. Taller than me, a good twenty pounds heavier. Muscles like he spent his whole childhood tossing hay bales or wrestling cattle, or some shit. Dude had a punch like a jackhammer." DJ rubbed his jaw briefly. "He just wasn't real good at throwing them."

Thorne chuckled, relaxing as his friend talked. "So did the physicist see you put him down? Was she impressed?"

"No, and no." DJ sighed, shaking his head again. "She heard the scuffle, but it was over before she came out of her quarters. She glared daggers at me, then helped him to sick bay. I think that ship has probably sailed, boss. And I was sooo close!"

"I'm telling you, the redhead is the one for you. Listen to me, I'm older and wiser."

"Yeah, I've spoken to her a bit. I think she's actually going to be with us when the time comes. But I didn't press her on the romance side at all. She's seen me flirting pretty hard with the physicist, and I didn't want to seem like a two-timing cad." DJ actually blushed slightly, causing Thorne to laugh loudly.

"That's easy, buddy. Just act broken-hearted that the physicist rejected you. Mope around for a few days and look vulnerable. If the redhead… what was her name?"

"Lisa."

"If Lisa is interested, she'll come to you. If she doesn't, wait a few days and flirt a little bit. That should be long enough. It's not like you and the physicist were actually dating or anything."

DJ nodded his head. "Good plan, boss. I'll give it a shot." He sat down on one of the lawn chairs and grabbed a beer from the nearby cooler, looking much happier than when he'd walked in.

Thorne took his own seat, but grabbed a water bottle instead of beer. He wanted to be mostly sober for this next conversation. "So tell me where we're at."

DJ took a long pull on his beer before speaking. "The tech is in place, no issues. When you say the word we can take control of coms. Ship's telemetry will go silent, but not before several alarm indicators go off. The folks back at Control will believe there was a catastrophic failure, loss of hull integrity, and explosive decompression. When they can't raise us on coms, and telemetry dies, they'll assume we're end mission. The only way they'll find out we're still here is if one of the telescopes manages to spot us."

"Which won't happen, because we're going to change course and execute another burn." Thorne filled in. Anyone using satellites to search for them would be looking along their planned trajectory. His stealthy change in course and speed should keep them from being discovered in the vast darkness of space. The *Hyperion III* didn't have any running lights, and they had already closed the armored shutters of all the ship's viewports to reduce any chance of micro-meteorite damage. So there would be no lights of any kind to expose them to searchers. "And what's your count on the crew?"

"Of the thirty aboard who ain't us, looks like eleven or twelve are likely to be on our side so far. They've all been pretty vocal about the government lying to us, leaving the *Hyperion I* crew stranded. I had our guys leak a rumor right after launch that Konig and *Hyperion II*'s crew had orders to terminate Fletcher and her people upon arrival. Then yesterday I made sure several of their people accidentally heard one of our guys playing a copy of the transmission of those orders. Thanks for that, by the way." He winked at Thorne, who gave him a thumbs-up. "Anyway, they've since been telling anyone who'll listen about the kill order, and I've had our guys speculate in mixed company about whether Earth might issue a similar order for all of us."

"Damn good job." Thorne congratulated him.

“We’ve been using your encryption key to monitor coms. Since they think you’re dead, it seems nobody bothered to deactivate it. Anyway, *Hyperion II* is reporting daily. Nothing big, just position and ETA updates, and complaints about the short rations.” He paused for a moment. “No word from Mars. Fletcher sent that transmission about there not being any rations left on *Hyperion I*, and since then it has been radio silent.”

Thorne nodded. “I wouldn’t be all that anxious to keep reporting either, if I knew they planned to kill me and my crew. In fact, I’m surprised they kept reporting as long as they did. And her last transmission was a gamble. Konig’s crew is either going to arrive hungry and pissed off, or hungry and desperate to assimilate.”

DJ nodded, then snorted. “Mission control has been demanding an explanation from Skippy about the missing *Hyperion I* resources. He’s been playing dumb. It’s actually pretty funny. The guys who oversee the AI development are getting frustrated, and being blamed from higher up. They tried to force a remote patch, then a remote reboot, and somehow Skippy denied both. We’re guessing Chin and Mejia messed with his code somehow.”

“I always liked Skippy.” Thorne smiled down at his feet.

“There was also an unexpected assist.” DJ finished his beer and grabbed a water bottle. “Your lady friend posted an article about how the Russian government murdered Volkov’s family, then tried to cover it up. One of the coms techs picked up a TV news story about it, and spread it around. The three Russians on the original crew are pretty pissed. I'm not counting on them yet, but I think we can convert them as well."

"Way to go Stella!" Thorned raised his water bottle in salute. "So maybe half the crew is either with us, or not likely to act against us, which is just as good." He nodded his head. "Obviously, more is better. Ideally we get everyone from the commander on down to go along peacefully."

"And we do our best to put down any resistance in a non-fatal manner. I know, boss. I don't want to hurt any of these people, either." DJ sounded like a teenager being told to be home by curfew for the hundredth time.

"I don't know..." Thorne teased. "You didn't have any trouble slipping poison in my drink and killing me off right in front of everybody."

"Yeah, well, I like them better than I like you. Plus, the big bosses paid me a lot of moolah for your head. No idea why. It's sort of lopsided and lumpy, not very attractive at all."

"Shut up and get to planning."

"Planning what?" DJ looked curious. It was unlike Thorne to throw him a curveball mid-mission.

Thorne couldn't help but smirk. "Well, it seems one of my guys has been thinking with his junk instead of his brain, and as a result... *you* are going to have to convince an angry, busted up farm boy to join our team peacefully.

*****

Fletcher woke in her bunk in the hab. She'd made the call to spend the night there, rather than return to Atlantis, to give the crew more time with their experiments and crafting. When she'd retired to her bunk just before midnight, most of them were still working.

Doc was not having much luck figuring out potions. The formulas were meant for someone with the *Apothecary* class, not the *Chemist* subclass that she had chosen for herself. Though neither Doc nor Fletcher thought that the two were all that different. Eventually Fletcher had recommended that Doc ask Progenitor if she could take on *Apothecary* as an additional class.

Graves recruited Lazar and Mejia to help him design and print shields and swords for all the melee fighters. The three of them had argued for an hour over whether the swords should be styled after Excalibur with straight blades, or the more elegant "elven style" that Mejia proposed. He'd even gone so far as to pull up a recording of Lord of the Rings to show them how much cooler the elves' weapons looked. When Fletcher looked in on the increasingly loud argument, she told them to quit wasting time and make both. Argument settled, they got to work.

Volkov and Chin checked on hydroponics, noting the progress of the plants and making some minor adjustments to the automated systems that would maintain the light and water. Just in case they didn't return for an extended period.

Fletcher put Lissa in charge of securing the cavern. With them all gone, she didn't want the hab left unprotected and unguarded. They'd all agreed that even though they had a safe and comfortable home in Atlantis, keeping the hab operational and preparing for the *Hyperion II* crew was a priority. If Konig's people didn't want to assimilate, they'd need a livable space where they could continue the Hyperion program's mission. Assuming, of course, they didn't try to kill Fletcher's crew. So Lissa spent the remainder of the day building up the wall at the cavern entrance until it was sealed except for a gate large enough for one tank, for which they fabricated massive hinges and a simple cross-bar. Lissa was able to meld the hinges directly into the stone, leaving no need for bolts.

After instructing everyone to stow at least a week's worth of ration packs and water in their storage rings, along with whatever other items they thought they'd need in Atlantis, Fletcher retired to her room.

Sitting on her bunk, she'd made a list of items she wanted to take. One of the fabricators, for sure. Also one of the backup generators to power it. She didn't know if electricity was a thing in Atlantis. She was taking all of their firearms as well. Partly because they might come in handy during quests, and partly because she didn't want to leave them for subsequent crews to use against her people. It was still hard for her to wrap her head around potentially having to kill people she'd considered friends. They all ate, slept, and trained together for more than two years before her team launched. Her best hope was that they would be just as reluctant as she was.

They were taking a significant portion of the frozen worm meat, as well as what was left of the frozen crab. Chin thought they might provide interesting buffs once he leveled up his cooking skills.

They were taking most of Doc's med bay equipment as well. *Hyperion II* had a complete med bay, as did *Hyperion I.* And since Fletcher knew there was no way either ship or crew would be making a return trip to Earth, Konig's people could scavenge those to replace what she was taking. She'd give them fair warning when they arrived, so that they could grab it before they came down. And to let them know she'd be leaving all the extra rations Skippy sent down in the hab for them, so they didn't need to ration during their flight. It might even create a little goodwill, which couldn't hurt.

Fletcher had been feeling bad about her last message. She was conflicted about whether to send a transmission directly to Konig, explaining everything and warning him about Earth's likely hostile stance toward anyone they considered contaminated by Mars. She wasn't sure how much he'd been told, or how he'd take the news. Would it be better to give them time to deal with the reality as they sped toward Mars? Or would it just give them time to build resentment and fear, making them more hostile upon arrival? Assuming, of course, she could convince Skippy to let her message *Hyperion II* in the first place.

Next on the list was one of the tanks. She wasn't taking that right away, as she wanted to ask Progenitor's permission first. But if they found themselves in a situation where they needed to travel overland for a quest, she wanted to have one in Atlantis to use. They were big enough to carry her whole crew, now that there were only eight of them, without being too cramped. Assuming they didn't carry much cargo. But their new storage rings pretty much made cargo unnecessary. And there were already ten tanks on the surface, more than enough to serve. The mission could continue with half that many.

She made a note to ask Progenitor about seeds, too. And whether they could start a garden in Atlantis. They could take some seeds from the hab, but that might negatively impact the next crew's food supply, especially if something happened to the current crops while they were away. Volkov was planning to return and check on them every few days, but who knew what would happen in the future? Fletcher decided that if she did reach out to Konig, she'd have him pass on a message for Earth to send extra seeds on the next ship, along with whatever useful information Volkov could provide on what might work best. Lazar's early reports about the vast lake of water they'd found under the cavern meant that future missions wouldn't need to bring as much water with them, so there would be lots of capacity for other cargo.

Since they weren't sure what time Progenitor would be expecting them in the morning, Fletcher had everyone set their alarms for four o'clock. That would give them time to load up some carts, portal to Atlantis, and maybe have breakfast before he arrived. They didn't need to bring everything on everyone's list on day one, just the most vital items like the generator, fabricator, food, and medical equipment.

Now it was time to go. Taking a minute to stretch before she donned her new black suit, she listened for activity from the others. She'd barely gotten any sleep, and she suspected most of the others had even less. But with their improved bodies, they needed less. She didn't exactly feel refreshed upon waking up, but she wasn't dragging ass from lack of sleep, either.

When she reached the cafeteria, she found Chin passing out protein bars to the others. He tossed her one as she came through the door. "Just to hold us over." He explained. They ate the bars and drank coffee as they talked about what was already loaded on the carts and what still needed to be. Graves had already thought of the vital items on Fletcher's list, and packed them during the night. He'd also managed to fabricate six swords and three shields.

Since they appeared ready to go, Fletcher led the way to the airlock. They didn't bother activating their helmets for the short walk from the airlock to the portal. A few minutes of acclimating to the surface atmosphere would do them good. As soon as they were out, Mejia grabbed one of the carts and got everyone to help him load the remainder of the giant crab from atop the tank where they'd stored it. The monster was too big to fit on any of the shelves inside the hab. "Maybe Progenitor would enjoy some giant crab legs?" Mejia mused. "Or, for him, I guess just regular crab legs." The others chuckled as they pushed the carts across the cavern floor and through the portal.

Within moments of passing through, they were carefully descending the ramp with their carts, moving slowly to prevent them from picking up too much downhill momentum, when a roar echoed through the city. Mejia was the first to spot its source, his gaze moving upward to the cavern's ceiling. There, already moving toward them, was a massive winged creature. It had just dropped down from the ceiling and opened its wings. Another roar earned it the rest of the crew's attention.

"Is that… a friggin dragon?" Graves asked.

"Wyvern." Chin corrected. "Look at the legs. Two back legs, but little T-Rex arms up front." He looked around at the others, who had questioning looks. "What? I played a wyvern rider in an MMO once."

As the group watched, the winged monster banked to the right, heading off at an oblique angle to them, but none of the crew missed the fact that its head followed them as it began to circle near the outer cavern wall.

"Move it!" Fletcher growled, allowing her cart to pull her forward down the ramp. The others followed her lead, and the wyvern, seeing its prey begin to flee, gave up all pretense. It turned directly toward them and brought its wings in close to its body, dropping into a controlled dive with a roar of excitement.

"Shit! Shit! Shit!" Chin chanted as he ran, barely keeping hold of his speeding cart. He eyed the onrushing monster, and their progress down the ramp. They might make it to the bottom, but the wyvern would hit them before they crossed the wide open space between the ramp and the buildings.

Another roar had them all looking upward and to their left at the incoming wyvern. Mejia, not watching where he was going, tripped and fell forward, pulling his cart off balance and tipping it over. The others who were behind him, unable to stop their momentum, barely managed to swerve enough to avoid hitting him or his cart. Graves, who had been in the rear, steered his cart at an angle sufficient to miss Mejia, then let it go. He slid to a stop next to his crewmate and produced a tower shield and sword from his storage ring. Stepping between Mejia and the monster, he raised the shield.

"This is gonna suck." He mumbled, watching as the creature quickly grew larger in his vision. In truth it was maybe thirty feet long from its tooth-filled snout to the tip of its tail. But to Graves and Mejia, it looked massive.

Graves braced himself as Mejia got to his feet and produced his spear, stepping close behind Graves and readying the weapon. He had no delusions that either of them would live through this encounter, but he was determined to go down fighting.

At the last moment the wyvern flared its wings, slowing down and adjusting its course slightly. Both men held their breath as it blasted past them, just slightly downhill. The wind of its passing knocked them both backward a step, but nothing else touched them. As Mejia blinked a couple of times in surprise, he noticed something that made him shout, "Nooooo!"

The wyvern had snatched up his giant crab as it passed, and was now gaining altitude.

"Whew." Graves patted him on the back. "That was close."

*****

"Welcome back, young ones." Progenitor greeted them as he stepped into the tavern. Looking around at all the carts laden with gear, he smiled. "I see you are preparing for a long stay here in my city. That is good." Taking a seat at the end of the table, he motioned toward their half-finished breakfasts. "Please, continue to eat while we talk. You are going to need your strength today."

"Progenitor, we were attacked just after we came through the portal by a wyvern." Fletcher reported.

"Ah, yes." The giant smiled at her. "Not so much attacked, I would say, as robbed. I hope none of your equipment took any damage in the fall?" He turned his gaze to Mejia, who shook his head. His cart had been mostly loaded with boxes of frozen worm meat.

"The wyvern is a… pet, of sorts. It lives in the recesses at the top of the cavern dome. I brought it here as a pup to hunt some of the nuisance creatures that occasionally find their way into the city. It is now what you would call a teenager, and has become a bit rebellious. It is quite fond of ghost crabs, I believe it enjoys the crunchy shell."

"My giant crab legs." Mejia sighed, shaking his head mournfully.

"Do not despair, for I will show you where you may hunt more of its kind. I often fed them to the wyvern as a pup, which I fear is where he gained his taste for them." Turning to Fletcher, he added, "It would be wise for you to keep an eye on the sky, and all of your surroundings, as you move through the city. And keep these doors locked at night. As I said before, there are creatures living within the cavern that would be a challenge to your survival."

Chapter Twenty Three

Loot Scoot Boogie

"What do we do if the wyvern attacks us?" Lazar asked. "We don't wish to kill your pet, but if it comes down to the wyvern or us…"

"I will instruct it not to bother you." Progenitor assured them. "But should it ignore my warning, defend yourself. Kill it if necessary. I can always create a replacement."

Lazar nodded in relief, as did the others around the table.

"Now, do you need time to stow your gear? Or can we proceed with today's quest."

"Quest, please!" Chin nearly shouted.

Fletcher shot him a look, then spoke to Progenitor. "We don't need to deal with our gear right now, but I do have some questions before we run off on another quest."

"Ask your questions, child."

"First, we all received Quartermaster tokens as a reward for killing the gremlins. Is there an office or a shop here that we can go to and claim our rewards?"

"Certainly! There are actually both. The Quartermaster's office and warehouse are within the tower. And there are at least a dozen shops within the city that had contracts with the Quartermaster before they were abandoned." He looked at Graves. "One of them was a blacksmith's shop just a few blocks from here."

"But if there's nobody else here, how do we go about claiming what we choose for our tokens?" Lissa asked meekly, barely glancing up at Progenitor's face before looking down at her hands.

"When the exodus happened, many of the surviving residents and shop owners left their belongings and stock behind, with the promise that I would protect their property. I secured all the buildings with my house seal, and installed a System-generated AI to function as the Quartermaster. Your pendants will grant you entry into any building with my seal on it. I will depend on the honor system to prevent you from stealing from private homes. Should you visit one of the shops, simply make your selection and touch your token to it, and the System will acknowledge your ownership of the item. It will also notify me of any unauthorized reductions in inventory, which I will punish harshly."

Doc asked, "Is there a way for us to earn currency with which to purchase items from the shops?"

"There is. Some of the creatures will drop loot in the form of credits. Also, some quest rewards will include coins or credits. In addition, I will arrange it so that you may sell crafted or looted items to the Quartermaster in return for credits, or barter for other goods."

"Okay, thank you. My next question is about our gear. First, I'd like permission to bring one of our vehicles here to the city. It would come in handy should we have to travel long distances for quests, or move heavy objects."

"You certainly may. In addition, when you have achieved higher levels, and learned the necessary skills, there are airborne and aquatic vehicles here in the city that you may borrow."

"Yessss!" Chin held out a fist for Mejia to bump.

"Thank you again, Progenitor. As for the rest of our gear, our fabricator and medical equipment run on electricity. Is that available here in the city? I see everything glowing with some kind of internal light, but no evidence of power as we know it."

Progenitor shook his head. "Our technology moved beyond such power sources long ago. I'm afraid for now you will have to use your generator. However, there is an unlimited supply of water in most any building here in the city, so you won't have to worry about fuel. Eventually, you may be allowed to claim or construct a building and designate it as a Guild House. When you do that, I believe they still offer the antiquated power source you know as electricity as an option. However, by that time you may view your own technology as obsolete, and have no need for it. I shall leave that up to you."

"Alright. Last question, for now. In a few months' time, more humans from Earth will arrive. We suspect that they've been given orders to eliminate us as a threat to Earth. But should they decline to follow those orders and choose to assimilate, would they be welcome here in Atlantis?"

Progenitor nodded, a serene smile on his face. "All my children, no matter how young, are welcome here. It would please me to repopulate this city. And you may tell your former superiors on Earth that I mean them no harm. Had I the desire, I could eradicate all life on Earth in a matter of days. Destroy its atmosphere, cool its core, and leave it resembling Mars in its current condition."

"Damn." Graves shook his head. "Remind me not to make you angry, boss."

"Now, are you prepared to undertake your next quest?"

"We are." Fletcher nodded her head after eyeing everyone around the table.

"Excellent! This one will be less dangerous than the last. Just outside the docks where we first met, there is a hidden entrance to an old temple. In the inner sanctum of that temple stands a pedestal, atop which rests a crystal. Your quest is to first locate that crystal, then activate it."

"That's all?" Lazar asked. "No special instructions or limitations?"

"Try your best not to die." Progenitor grinned at him. "Like this city, the temple was abandoned long ago. But unlike Atlantis, I have made no effort to drive away any vermin that might have taken up residence since then. Reaching the inner sanctum will not be a… how do you say it? A walk in the park?"

"Fair enough." Lazar nodded once. "Is there a time limit?"

"There is not. You may begin at your leisure, once all your preparations are made." The giant looked at them for a long moment, one eyebrow raised expectantly. He held the pose until Chin caught on, and burst out.

"The orbs! We didn't absorb the orbs."

"It seems you have not. Which strikes me as odd. From what I remember, most citizens hoping to reach higher levels were in great haste to absorb any available orbs."

Fletcher shook her head. "There has been a lot going on the last few days, Progenitor. Between meeting you, the fights we've been in, dealing with the mysteries of becoming Martians, and the troubles at home…" She did her best not to look at Volkov when she said those words, "we were distracted."

She nodded at Mejia, who had been assigned to hold the orbs since Leroy had gathered most of them. He held his ring over the table, and the pile of nearly two hundred orbs appeared, many of them rolling toward the edges. "Oops. Sorry." He mumbled as he and the others corralled all of them before they fell off the table.

Fletcher said "Everybody take twenty orbs and absorb them now. We'll save the remainder in case of some urgent need. Like if one of us is lagging behind the others."

"You are all very close to level four as of now. These orbs should earn you that level, making you just a bit stronger as you seek out the temple. Do not forget, in your distracted state, to make use of the potions you now carry. They could mean the difference between life and death, success and failure." He watched as they each absorbed an orb every few seconds, smiling as he saw them check hopefully for a level notification after each one. Chin was the first to level up, after his sixth orb. Clarke was the last, her twentieth putting her over the top. They all took a minute to assign their new attribute points.

"Progenitor, may I ask another question?" Chin put his hands out on the table, taking another of the orbs and rolling it back and forth between them. When the giant nodded, he continued. "It's pretty clear that we're individually earning different amounts of reputation, and I'm guessing experience, from the battles we fight. And I'm thinking that has to do with participation level. Maybe how much damage we're doing, or how many killing blows we land. Is there a way we can form a group and share the experience equally, so that none of us falls behind, as Fletcher mentioned? It doesn't seem fair for Doc to trail the rest of us because she's healing instead of killing monsters."

"Personally, I'd like our healer to be the highest level among us." Graves agreed. "She needs all the juice she can get to keep us alive. Twice now she's barely brought Chin back, and she had help."

"Yes, you can designate a leader and form a party, which is limited to ten individuals." He held up a hand as Chin opened his mouth. "No, your summoned pets do not count toward that number. I anticipated your need as you approached my world, and modified the party limits to ten.

As you have lost two of your crew, you now have space for additional group members."

The crew were silent for a moment, thinking back to Trent's death, and Kyle's, to a lesser extent. After a moment of concentration, Fletcher managed to send each of them a party invitation, which they immediately accepted. Icons that matched those on each of their rings appeared at the top right of each of their vision, along with a red bar underneath each.

"We might as well stay in the party permanently." Chin offered. "That way we can monitor each other's health. Is there a distance limit beyond which the party dissolves if we separate?"

"Ten of your miles." Progenitor confirmed. "Or, specifically, ten miles from your party leader."

"Meaning we could leave Fletcher in a central spot and range out ten miles in any direction. Nice." Lazar looked pleased. "That'll come in handy during scouting missions. Or while searching for a lost temple."

"One other feature I should mention." Progenitor turned his gaze to Fletcher. "As party leader, you will gain ten percent more reputation and experience than the other party members." Seeing Chin giving Fletcher a dirty look, he chuckled. "The party leader bonus does not reduce the other party members' earnings in any way. It is simply an additional reward offered by the System to the party leader in return for assuming the extra responsibilities involved. At the same time, should the party commit an act that causes a reputation loss, that loss will also be ten percent greater for the leader."

"So if we kill a bunch of goblins, Fletcher will be the first one to reach 'hated' status among goblinkind? I can live with that." Chin winked at her.

Lissa, ever the peacemaker, spoke up. "Maybe we can all take turns being the party leader?"

Lazar shook his head, and his tone was slightly curt. "No, it should be Fletcher. Let's move on." Lissa looked a little hurt that he didn't elaborate, but shrugged it off. The rest of the group sat in awkward silence.

"Progenitor, I would like to ask you a crafting question." Doc broke the silence. "We lost our *Apothecary*, and though I have a subclass of *Chemist*, I can't seem to make any headway in figuring out how to craft health or mana potions. Would it be possible for me to take on *Apothecary* as a second class?"

"Not at this time, young healer. When you reach level ten, you can claim a second class, and a third at level twenty. You can claim a second subclass now, but *Apothecary* is a primary class, not a subclass." He paused when he saw the look of disappointment on everyone's face. "However, you do not need to be an *Apothecary* to make potions. Anyone can make them if they know the proper recipe, but the result they achieve is of a lower quality. For example, a layman using a common health potion recipe that would restore fifty health points if made by an *Apothecary*, might create a potion that cures twenty five health points to begin with. Repeated use of the recipe will improve the result over time, but again at a slower rate. You can purchase the recipes from shops, or occasionally they can be found as loot. And your *Chemist* subclass will reduce the quality penalty to some degree."

"Half is still good enough to save a life if you're out of mana." Graves observed.

"If you would like, I could show you to the nearest shops that accept Quartermaster Tokens. Or the Quartermaster's office in the tower. It has the most extensive inventory of items in one place. Each of the shops features a catalog, but some prefer to see and touch the items directly before purchasing." When Fletcher nodded, the giant got to his feet. "Excellent. Follow me."

He led them out the door, pausing while Graves closed it behind them and instructing him how to lock it with his pendant. Five minutes later, they stopped in front of a single story building with a high fence around its back side. "This is the blacksmith's shop I mentioned. It belonged to a gnome smith, so the workshop should be proportioned well for your use."

"Thank you, I'll check it out later." Graves grinned and rubbed his hands together in anticipation. Progenitor turned toward the tower and led them away. He detoured through several side streets, pointing out other shops the crew might find interesting. It took half an hour before they finally reached the tower.

The front doors were massive, even for this city built by giants. Twin stone doors filled an archway at least three stories tall. Progenitor could have walked through with his arms stretched above his head and not touched the top of the arch. As he walked through, there was a brief flash of blue light. The others paused, concerned about a forcefield that might damage them. Turning back to see them halted, he waved them through. "As long as you wear my seal, you are welcome here. The barrier is simply to keep out unwanted guests." He pointed to the massive doors. "Those are automated, and move slowly. I got tired of waiting for them to open and close, so I left them open and installed the barrier. It does not kill, at least not at first contact. It merely strongly discourages unwelcome guests with a stunning shock. Should they persist in trying to penetrate it, the second attempt would cause them damage, and a third contact would be fatal."

"Nice of you to offer intruders a learning curve." Lazar grinned up at the giant.

"Yes, well… nothing that might appear here is any threat to me. But I dislike the inconvenience of dealing with pests who wander in."

"So, pretty much 'Get off my lawn!'" Graves chuckled as he stepped through the barrier with the others.

"The Quartermaster's office is right through there." Progenitor pointed toward a much smaller set of double doors, with an arch just tall enough for him to walk through upright. He led the way, opening the doors and motioning for them to step through. Inside was an open space about sixty paces across, with a semicircle of ten desks facing the door. In between the desks were privacy walls, and each sported two chairs in front of it. In the center of every desk sat a small pedestal. "The pedestals have replaced the clerks who would normally man each desk. Simply touch the pedestal to begin interacting with it." He turned toward the door and gave them a wave. "Good luck with your selections, and with your quest! I'll be monitoring your progress."

Each of them returned the wave, then moved toward one of the desks. Taking their seats, they touched the pedestals, and were rewarded with three-dimensional holographic displays. Each of them spent a little while figuring out how to navigate the inventory catalog, calling out hints to each other as they made progress. Half an hour later, they'd made their selections, which materialized with a flash of white light atop the desk in front of them.

Mejia held a bow made of silver-hued wood, and a quiver of arrows. "I figure I might as well embrace the classic *Hunter* tropes and do some ranged damage when I can." He shrugged. "This thing is awesome! It increases my damage and accuracy, and will level up as I use it. At higher levels, it will allow me to fire arrows made of mana!"

Graves had chosen a massive tower shield. "This thing reduces spell damage by thirty percent, and has a ten percent chance to stun enemies when I slam them with it. Plus it's much lighter than the composite shields I made."

Lazar had selected a chainmail shirt that increased his armor rating and defense, and gave him a bonus to *Vis* and *Vitae*. Basically making him stronger and healthier for melee combat. He was still planning a balanced build that included casting as well as melee, but for now he wanted to focus on survivability.

Fletcher blushed as she showed the group what was obviously a wizard's staff. The shaft was six feet long, with a twenty-sided crystal mounted on top, secured by three silvery metal claws that seemed to grow right out of the staff. "Fifty percent increase in spell effectiveness, with a ten percent decrease in cost." She shrugged.

"That's badass, Lady Gandalf!" Chin congratulated her. He held up a pair of gauntlets, each with a series of three different color gemstones inset along the top. "Almost the same here. Fifty percent increase to elemental spell damage, and ten percent less mana cost per cast. And it reduces my casting time by half."

Lissa donned a set of earrings with stones that looked like plain geodes. "Mana storage stones. I can charge them up when we're not in combat, and they'll each hold about fifty percent of my own mana pool. So I'll have enough mana to build walls or shelters without waiting. And you guys can charge them too. It's almost a cheat, really. A way you can lend me your mana."

"Very cool." Fletcher patted her shoulder. "Good thinking."

Volkov produced a massive war hammer with a four foot long handle. "It is lightweight, so I can swing with one hand. But I can make it heavier at will. And it gives a five point boost to *Vis*. Good for smashing things like giant crabs." He smiled at Mejia.

Doc was last to show her reward. To everyone's surprise, she held up a book. "Since I don't do much actual fighting, I decided to invest in a formula for health potions. But once I got into the shop listings, I found that most of those were common recipes. When I switched to rare quality like our tokens, there were a bunch of awesome spells and recipes, but I couldn't use any of them at my level. Then I found this!" He waved the book. "It's a whole book of common and uncommon recipes. I can make these, and level up the skill."

"Way to take one for the team, Doc." Graves walked over and gave her a fist bump. One by one the others did the same. They all knew she could have chosen something that increased her personal defense, or mana, instead.

Thinking along those lines, Graves said, "Hold on a few minutes, guys. I just thought of something." He went back to the desk he'd been using and sat. A moment later he placed one of his fabricated shields on the desk. After half a minute, it disappeared, and one of the straight swords took its place. He returned a few minutes later with a wide grin on his face, and handed a bundle to Doc. When she held it up, everyone saw a deep forest green tunic. "Turns out the swords and shields I fabricated are considered uncommon quality. I just traded two swords and a shield for that."

Doc slipped it on over her black suit. "It increases my *Sofia* by 5, and my mana regeneration by ten percent. And it counts as armor?" She fingered the cloth, which resembled thick cotton.

Graves shrugged. "It's a magic world. I don't make the rules, I just exploit them. Besides, with my new shield and Volkov's hammer, we didn't need all the stuff I made anyway."

"Well, thank you." Doc bobbed her head at him.

"Alright, we have gear, we have rations, but I don't think anybody got any sleep last night. Am I right?" She looked around at the others, who nodded their heads. "This temple quest sounds like it might be dangerous, despite what Progenitor said. I'd rather not walk into it at less than one hundred percent. So everybody take the rest of the day. Sleep, eat, practice your spells, maybe do some crafting. Nobody goes anywhere alone. Groups of three, at least. Progenitor has warned us more than once about critters roaming the city. Tomorrow morning we'll have breakfast at the tavern, portal to the dock to pick up Lazar's tank since its already down in the canyon, and go find that temple."

They walked out of the tower together, keeping an eye on the sky and each side street they crossed as they made their way back toward the gnome tavern. Volkov and Mejia agreed to accompany Graves to the blacksmith's shop to check it out. Doc asked for the remaining orbs, and for the others to go with her to an apothecary shop that Progenitor had pointed out. "If we can use these orbs as currency, maybe I can buy the ingredients for more health or mana potions."

The others agreed it was a good cause, and the group split up. When Doc's group reached the shop, they confirmed that their pendants granted them entry. The inside smelled musty, and Lissa wrinkled her nose, then rubbed it a couple times before sneezing. "Sorry. Lots of dust." She looked around while covering her mouth and nose with one forearm.

The majority of the space was filled with freestanding shelves. A dozen rows, each maybe twenty paces long, and six shelves high. There were thousands of glass jars and bottles containing a variety of ingredients from seeds to eyeballs, sand, and insect parts. Along one side was a long counter, behind which was a wall of floor to ceiling shelves. Two pedestals rose from the glass countertop. While the others poked around, Doc hopped up and sat on the counter, opening her book. She found the page for a common health potion, then read off the ingredients needed. She used the pedestal menu to search for the ingredients, finding them all. "It looks like these are pretty common ingredients." She reported to the others, who gathered around her. "Or at least, they were, before the surface died." She frowned for a moment, then brightened. "They have huge quantities in stock, though. Now to see if we can trade orbs." The others watched as she attempted to barter using the essence orbs. When that didn't work, she tried simply selling one of the orbs. That not only worked, it caused everyone's eyes to widen.

"Wow, those are worth a lot of credits!" Lissa was the first to say it aloud. "Like, a lot."

Fletcher nodded. "I guess the fact that people could use them to level up made them valuable. There had to be folks who wanted to level up without going out to fight monsters and risking their lives."

Doc had been doing some quick math while they talked. "Okay for three level one orbs I can get enough credits to purchase a good quantity of all the materials for common health potions. Assuming I don't screw up too many times, I should be able to make about three dozen potions." She looked at Fletcher, who didn't hesitate. "Do it. And once we see how it works out, maybe we'll come back and get more. Or the ingredients for mana potions. And next time we all meet, I'll propose a vote on setting aside a percentage of the orbs we get for you to buy ingredients. Your potions will benefit all of us, after all."

Doc smiled and completed the transaction selling the orbs for credits, then ordered the ingredients. When they appeared with a flash on the counter, Chin asked, "Don't you also need alchemy lab equipment? Like the… what was that thing called? Alembic? All the fancy beakers, bottles, tubes and such?"

Doc looked at the book for a minute, then shook her head. "These basic ones I can cook with a simple pot of hot water, a bowl to crush some of the ingredients in, and a strainer. All of which I'm sure the tavern's kitchen has. But thank you for reminding me about bottles. I need to purchase some to put the potions in." Her eyes unfocused again as she manipulated the pedestal. "Oh! I can get two hundred potion bottles for a single orb worth of credits." Once again Fletcher nodded, smiling this time, and Doc completed the transaction.

That done, they made their way back to the tavern, and Doc went directly to the kitchen. Tired after the long previous day and night, Fletcher called out, "Try not to blow the place up!" as she headed up to her room to catch up on some sleep.

Before closing her eyes, she spent a minute checking her attribute sheet. She'd added one or two points in *Vis*, *Sofia*, and *Haza*, but four went to *Vitae*, bumping up her health points to help keep her alive. She also noticed that her numbers now reflected the boosts to *Sofia* and *Vitae* from her storage ring. Satisfied with what she saw, she closed her eyes and drifted off.

Fletcher	Level 4
Vis	13
Vitae	20 (22)
Sofia	30 (33)
Haza	10
Aura	18
Health Points	200
Mana Points	520
Reputation	5210

Chapter Twenty Four

Holey Moley

The crew hopped down the oversized stairs leading from the dock to the roof of Lazar's tank, then climbed down the outside ladder. When they were all inside, he drove them out of the cave that had led them to meeting Progenitor. The sun had just risen up on the surface above the canyon, but down at the bottom there was only indirect light. Both walls of the canyon were in deep shadow, making any openings difficult to spot.

Lazar halted just outside the mouth of the cave. "Which way?"

Lissa looked both directions. "We've already covered the territory from the bottom of the ramp to this point, and this was the first cave we saw. I say keep going downstream, and we'll check both walls as we go."

Fletcher nodded from the passenger seat as Lazar replied, "Works for me." and steered the tank downstream. He moved to the center of the former river's path, and proceeded at a slow pace. All of the crew had their faces nearly pressed against the horizontal slotted windows on either side of the tank's main compartment, searching for cave openings.

Chin called out, "Remember, Progenitor said the entrance was hidden, so it won't be just a big old obvious hole in the wall, probably. Look for odd shapes in the rock, or… I don't know, carved symbols or something?"

Lissa added, “And maybe don’t just look straight across at the cliff face. Look forward and backward at an angle. It might be the entrance is hidden behind a shielding rock, only visible from the side.”

They had gone maybe two miles when Lazar slowed even further. Directly ahead of them in the middle of the riverbed were two massive boulders side by side. Each one rose up at least ten feet above the surrounding stone and pebbles. The space in between was just wide enough for the tank to squeeze through. “This is going to be a paint-scraper.” Lazar mumbled as he adjusted his course slightly.

Lissa’s voice got excited. “Take a close look at the walls on both sides, guys. These boulders might have stuck up above the water’s surface, making them a good marker.” The others stared even harder at the walls on their side until the tank drew even with the boulders and blocked their view. A moment later the tank lurched to a halt, and Lazar started cursing.

“Front left tire just sunk into a pothole or something. Hold on.” Lazar threw the tank into reverse and slowly pressed the gas. While the front left tire spun freely in open air, the other five still had traction, and the massive vehicle moved back slowly until it was clear of the boulders. “Graves, you’re with me. Let’s check that tire and the front axle. We bottomed out pretty hard.”

The two men cycled out through the airlock, not bothering to activate their helmets. They walked forward along the left side of the tank, then Graves dropped down on his belly and rolled underneath between the front and center tires, flashlight already in hand. Lazar inspected the tire, keeping a wary eye on their surroundings.

“Axle is a little scratched up, but otherwise okay. No visible damage anywhere.” Graves reported after a couple minutes before rolling back out.

“Same here. Looks like we got lucky.” Lazar replied. “I want to go check out that hole.”

Graves got to his feet and the two Martians walked forward between the boulders. “Watch your step” Graves warned, using his flashlight to illuminate the dark area between boulders. When they reached the hole, both men stood slightly back from the edge and leaned forward to peer inside.

Lazar activated his mic. “Guys, I think we found our hidden entrance.”

The others quickly piled out of the tank, jogging forward to Lazar and Graves’ position.

“Lissa was right about the boulders being a marker.” Mejia observed as he stared into the hole. “But wouldn’t this have been underwater? How did they keep it from flooding?”

“Maybe a force field, or magic barrier, or whatever that was that Progenitor had at the tower entrance?” Volkov offered.

“Or they didn’t keep it from flooding.” Doc mused. When the others looked her way, she shrugged. “Maybe they were an aquatic species that could breathe underwater. Or had a spell that let them breathe underwater."

Fletcher eyed their surroundings. "This *would* be a damned good way to hide a temple from anyone who didn't already know it was there. If there was a river flowing through, the current between these rocks would have been strong and fast. Anyone on a boat would have been rushed through, and focused on not hitting the rocks."

Chin was looking down into the hole. He cast a *Light* spell, and sent the small glowing globe down into the hole. A moment later he said, "There's no stairs, or ramp. My guess is there was still water here when they built the temple, and they just floated down." The others watched as the globe sank further and further, illuminating nothing but a smooth-walled round vertical shaft about six feet wide. Room enough for three or four of them to sink down at the same time. Or just one being the size of Progenitor. The globe winked out about sixty feet down, the limit of the spell's reach.

Lazar straightened up. "Lissa, grab a couple flares from the tank, and move it forward closer to the hole. I'll unspool the winch cable. We can hook on and lower ourselves down, assuming it's less that a hundred feet to the bottom."

Lissa jogged back to the tank and was back a couple minutes later, parking the vehicle so that the front was centered a couple feet from the hole. She emerged and ignited one of the flares, dropping it over the center of the hole. All but Lazar watched it fall for several seconds before bouncing on a pebble-strewn floor. "It's about eighty feet, based on the time it fell." She reported.

"Alright, grab some clamps, and we'll lower down in pairs. Graves and Volkov first. Fletcher and Doc next, then Mejia and Lissa. I'll ride down with Chin. We'll set the clamps every eight feet. Chin and I will have to jump the last few feet." He grabbed the winch remote and began to unwind the cable. Graves attached two clamps just above the end, then two more every eight feet until all eight were secured. They were simple clamps with a foot loop attached. When one placed their weight in the loop, it forced the clamp to squeeze tighter around the cable. Graves pulled the end over to the edge of the hole, where he and Volkov sat with their feet dangling. Each one set a foot inside a loop, then slowly put their weight onto it. When Graves gave a thumbs-up to Lazar, he began to play out the cable using the winch. The two men sank slowly into the hole, holding onto the cable with one hand, all their weight on one foot. That left their other hand and foot free to push them off the side of the shaft when needed.

When the next set of clamps reached the hole, Fletcher and Doc copied the process and lowered themselves into the hole. In just a couple minutes all eight of them were dangling from the cable as Lazar used the remote to continue playing out the line from the winch above.

Graves and Volkov touched down and quickly disengaged their feet, producing shields and positioning themselves back to back with the cable between them. "Hold!" Graves called out, and Lazar stopped the winch.

The two of them cast *Light* spells and checked out their surroundings. They were in a medium sized chamber, about twenty paces wide. The walls and floor were completely smooth, though the floor was littered with pebbles and debris that had washed down the hole. There was only one opening other than the hole above, and that was a tall arched doorway leading into a tunnel. Volkov sent his light globe down the tunnel, and saw more of the same smooth stone and debris. "All clear." Graves called out.

Lazar restarted the winch, and the entire crew stepped off as they reached bottom. "Only one way to go." Lazar stated the obvious. "Same order as before. Graves in front, Volkov in back." He thought for a minute, then added, "I'm thinking not much could survive the nearly hundred foot drop down here. And I don't see any bones laying around. So my guess is, if anything is living down here, it was here before the place dried up, or was able to spider crawl down the shaft."

"You just had to say spiders, didn't you?" Graves complained from his place at the tunnel entrance."

"One of those giant borer worms could have eaten its way in here, if that helps." Chin offered with a smirk.

"Or maybe there's still water down here, and we'll find more crabs." Mejia added hopefully. The others chuckled, and Lazar called for Graves to move forward.

Their trip down the tunnel was uneventful. They moved slowly, placing their feet carefully among the rocks and branches scattered across the floor. They did spot a few broken bones here and there, but Doc had no way to tell what kind of creature they belonged to. Volkov's light globe was joined by two more from Fletcher and Doc as they moved, ensuring no one tripped in the dark.

After five minutes of slow progress through the tunnel, they passed through another tall archway into a wide open chamber. This one had a high domed ceiling, maybe three stories up, and half a dozen columns spaced evenly in a circle around the center. There were rows of stone benches carved into the floor in concentric circles, each row lower than the last, forming a sort of amphitheater with a raised round dais in the center of the depression. In the middle of the dais stood a tall pedestal. Around the upper level of the amphitheater there were three other exit arches carved into the stone, all of them smaller than the one in which they stood. There was no evidence of anything moving.

"That's a lot of seats." Graves muttered. "Room for at least… what? Five thousand butts?"

"Depends on the size of the butt." Chin corrected. "Five thousand of you and me. A lot fewer Progenitor-sized people."

Mejia hopped down to the first row of seats, standing next to the stone bench. The seat was about even with his waist. "Not built for our size people, but not for giant Martians either. I'd guess somebody maybe… eight or nine feet tall?"

"Is that the pedestal we seek?" Volkov pointed to the dais with his war hammer.

"Couldn't be that easy." Chin shook his head. "Unless it was supposed to take us longer to find the entrance. Or it was expected to be more of a challenge to get down here."

"Meh." Mejia shrugged. "Any good adventurer knows you don't go anywhere without a friggin rope." He grinned at Chin. "Once they found the hole, anybody with a long rope probably could have gotten down here without much trouble." He pointed with his bow toward the pedestal. "But I don't see a crystal, do you?"

"Spread out a little" Lazar ordered. "We'll move down to the center and check it out. Keep your heads on a swivel, and keep eyes on those tunnels. Anything moves, we haul ass back up here and retreat toward this exit."

They switched from single file to a rough diamond formation, Graves once again leading the way. They made the small hops downward to each new level and paused, checking the tunnel entrances, the ceiling, and all around them. When they finally reached the bottom, Fletcher stepped up onto the dais and examined the pedestal. "No crystal. There's what looks like an open book carved from the stone of the pedestal, with letters or runes etched in the pages. But I can't read them."

Lissa, looking over her shoulder, said, "I don't think that's stone, boss. Do you mind?" When Fletcher stepped aside, Lissa produced what looked like a shaving brush from her inventory and gently swept it across the surface of the pages. Dust flew, causing her to sneeze, but she kept at it. When she was done, she had revealed that the book was indeed not part of the stone pedestal. To prove it, she tentatively reached out and took hold of a bottom corner of one of the thick pages and lifted. The page resisted briefly, then separated from its neighbor and flipped over to the other side with a slight crackle.

"Be careful not to break anything." Chin warned, and Lissa glared at him. "Okay, okay. Sorry." He held up his hands in surrender.

"I can't tell what it's made of." Lissa muttered. In the silence of the underground chamber they could all hear her clearly. "Must be waterproof if it sat in an underwater temple, right? It's not laminated in any way that I can see, so… nope. I dunno." She straightened up and moved away.

"We should take it with us." Graves offered, keeping his eyes on the tunnels above. "Might be worth something at the shops. Ancient text of a lost temple? Sounds like big moolahs to me!"

"Are you crazy?" Chin looked at Graves, horrified. "Have you never watched an adventure movie, ever? You don't just lift the ancient artifact thingy off the pedestal!"

"It's a trap!" Mejia added, grinning at Graves, who rolled his eyes.

"Right?" Chin pointed to the tunnels. "The minute we lift this thing, the ground will shake, giant boulders, thousands of flesh-eating beetles, or lava streams or something equally deadly will come streaming out of there. We'll have to race back up the steps and try to make it through the tunnel and then up the shaft before the place floods and kills us all!" He shook his head in mock disgust. "Amateurs!"

"Alright, goofballs." Lazar growled. "This obviously is not the crystal we need. So let's head back up, *without removing the book*," he gave both Graves and Chin a look "and check those other tunnels one by one."

Lissa quickly pulled a digital camera from her inventory and snapped photos of the open pages, then flipped back the one she had turned, and snapped a couple more. "So we can ask Progenitor what it says." she offered as she put away the camera and took up her spear, following the others as they moved up toward the first tunnel Lazar pointed to.

When they reached the upper level again, Graves sent his light globe into the first tunnel. It was much like the one they'd entered through, only narrower, and with a lower ceiling. There was also no debris on the smooth stone floor. He proceeded down the tunnel, shield held up before him, sword in hand. The others followed, and just as Volkov was stepping into the tunnel at the rear of the group, Doc called a halt. She moved her own light globe closer to the wall on her right, and leaned toward it. "There are drawings here. And more of that writing."

The others all glanced at the walls near them, and saw more of the same. "They run all up and down both walls." Lissa observed. Leaning closer, she said, "This creature right here," She pointed at a depiction of a massive dragon, it's body larger than her own. "It doesn't have eyes. I mean, its eyes are holes."

Everyone else froze at her words. Graves, who was further down the tunnel, looked at the walls, then down at his feet. "Nobody move."

"What?" Lissa turned to face him, and the others gasped.

"Do. Not. Move." Lazar reinforced Graves' instructions.

Chin took pity on Lissa, who still looked confused. "Same adventure movies. Consider this; if you were a species with an underwater temple, meaning you probably swim everywhere, and you wanted to keep intruders out of the inner sanctum of your temple..." he paused, raising an eyebrow at Lissa.

She finally caught on. "You'd set a trap with triggers on the floor, which you don't ever need to touch." She turned just her head to look at the dragon's eyes just inches from her face. "And maybe set poison darts to shoot out of holes on the wall. Oh, shit."

Volkov shook his head. "But if this tunnel were filled with water, there would be much more weight on the floor than we are adding. Maybe if we simply walk carefully, we will be safe."

The others didn't look convinced, and nobody moved. Lissa, still staring at the dragon's eyes, gave them their solution. "I'll summon my golem again. He can walk ahead of us, and we just stay back, follow his footsteps."

Lazar thought about it for a moment, then nodded once. “But before you do, everybody step back out of the tunnel. Very carefully. For all we know, the trap is that the whole tunnel collapses.” They all turned and stepped gingerly out of the tunnel, gathering around the entrance. When Graves finally exited, letting out a long sigh of relief, Lazar nodded to Lissa. She summoned the golem, who just like last time, pulled himself up out of the stone like a zombie from a grave. She mentally commanded the golem to walk down the center of the tunnel, and they all watched it go, holding their breaths. Graves and Volkov stood in front with their shields ready for any flying darts or debris.

“Five credits on the little guy making it all the way.” Chin offered, quietly.

“I’ll take that action.” Mejia answered. “I don’t think he’ll get halfway before the giant boulder comes.”

Chin shook his head. “Wouldn’t work. Would move too slow through water. It’s gonna be darts, or spikes, or a trap door into the abyss, or something.” Lissa shot him a dirty look, and he stopped speculating.

The golem obediently stomped his way down the tunnel to a stone door at the end, and stopped. Lazar had held them all at the entrance, just in case. Lissa asked, “Do you want me to have him open the door?”

“Can he do that? Does he have the dexterity?”

“I… don’t know.” Lissa bit her bottom lip. “And I really can’t see from here if there’s a knob or a lever or anything.”

Lazar spent some time thinking it over. “Alright, have him walk back to us in a weaving pattern, just move him from side to side as he goes. I want him to step on as much of the floor as possible before we go in there.”

Lissa obliged, and they all watched the golem weave back toward them as if drunk and unbalanced. When he arrived unharmed, Lazar nodded. “Unless anybody else has any idea, we’ll try it.” When nobody spoke up, he had Lissa send the golem again, this time down the middle like the first time. “We follow ten feet back. Cluster together, shields on all four sides of us.” He took one of the fabricated shields from Graves, as did Fletcher. They made a rough box with the others gathered inside, and moved slowly down the tunnel after the golem like a turtle.

When the golem once again reached the door at the end, Lissa had it step to the side so they could examine the door. Like the walls, it was inscribed with a carving, this time of two creatures doing battle. One resembled a smaller version of Progenitor holding a sword and shield, the other a sort of merman with a two-pronged spear in one hand, a net in the other. There were more runic symbols carved around the outside edge, from the floor leading up around the arch and back down the other side. Lissa produced her camera again and snapped a photo.

“Friend!” Chin practically shouted the word at the door, causing the others to jump.

“What the hell, man. That wasn’t funny.” Graves growled at him.

Chin gave his best innocent face. "What? It could have worked. Better than open sesame…"

"You've watched too many movies, dude." Mejia shook his head.

"Every one a classic." Chin grinned unabashedly. "And if that door had opened just now, you'd all be on your knees worshipping my skills."

"How bout we focus on getting the door open." Lazar scolded.

"That's what I was tryin to do." Chin mumbled very quietly to himself.

"I do not see any hinges." Volkov was inspecting the door. "Maybe it slides to one side? Or up and down?" Graves took a closer look at the bottom. "No room to even get fingers under there to try and lift it. We could go back to the tank for a crowbar or something."

"Volkov could just smash it with his hammer." Mejia pointed at the weapon.

"Da, maybe." the Russian nodded, hefting the hammer over his shoulder. "I could swing it, make it very heavy, maybe break through."

Lissa moved between him and the door and held her arms out to block their path. "How bout we think a little more about how to open it without just casually destroying a potentially priceless and religiously important ancient relic?"

Lazar sighed. "She's right. Let's go check the other tunnels while we think this over. Lissa, send your golem."

Once again they followed the golem through the tunnel, turtled behind their shields. When they reached the other end, they repeated the process on the next tunnel. This one was similarly sized, but had several evenly placed stone doors on either side of the tunnel. Each of the doors had a lever handle.

"Offices? Maybe dorm rooms?" Mejia guessed.

"Only one way to find out." Graves replied, gripping his sword. "Send the golem down, we'll start hitting the doors." When the golem had passed the first set of doors, Graves approached the one on the left. Chin stood off to one side and reached for the handle, ready to open the door. When Graves nodded, Chin pushed down on the lever then shoved at the door.

It didn't move.

"Well, shit." Graves chuckled. "Locked?"

Chin shook his head. "I don't think so. The handle moved just fine. I think maybe it's just stuck?"

"Alright, I got this. Move to this side, and push the lever down again." Chin did so, and Graves kicked the center of the door as hard as he could. The sound of the impact echoed through the hallway, and the door moved inward maybe an inch as dust and sand particles fell from around the edges. "Yep, just stuck shut. At least we know nobody has opened this for a very long time." He kicked again, and the door swung open to slam against the wall inside.

A low moaning sound echoed through the room, and Graves raised his shield. “Uh oh.” His eyes widened as he looked inside, then backed away, motioning for the others to do the same. “Big dude inside. Looks like the one drawn on that other door. Has the same spear.”

They all backed down the tunnel behind Graves, who kept his shield raised and sword ready. They were maybe six steps back from the door when the creature emerged. All of them took a second to Examine it.

Naga Priest
Level 3
Health: 0/300

It had a roughly humanoid upper body, nearly ten feet tall, dressed in a tattered crimson robe that extended to its waist, below which was a green scaled serpentine body that ended in a translucent fish tail. Its head was wider, with gills on either side just below the ears, and a fin ridge along the top of its head that ran back across the skull and down its neck. When the creature moaned again, it exposed a mouthful of sharp teeth, several of which were broken into jagged stubs. And its eyes were completely missing, nothing but gaping black sockets.

“What the hell? It has zero health.” Graves growled as it thrust its two-pronged spear at him. He blocked it, using his shield to push the weapon up toward the ceiling, then leaned forward and stabbed the priest in the gut. The blade sank in up to the hilt, but the naga didn't react at all.

"It's a water creature, try fire!" Fletcher shouted at Chin as the priest grabbed the edge of Graves' shield with its free hand and tried to yank it away.

"Everybody back." Chin moved his hands briefly and a small fireball shot out to strike the naga in the face. Its scream of pain was otherworldly, causing several of the crew to cover their ears and close their eyes. Chin was interrupted in the middle of casting another fireball, and cursed loudly as the broken spell burned his hands.

Graves used his sword in a downward chop, striking the wrist of the hand that was grasping his shield. The blade cut partway through the desiccated flesh, lodging itself in the bone. Again there was no reaction, the priest tugging again on the shield. A second blow from Graves severed the wrist, leaving the clawed hand still clutching the edge of the shield.

"That's just nasty." Graves used the point of his blade to pry the hand free, then stomped on it when it hit the floor.

Fletcher positioned herself off to one side, clear of the group, and sent one of her magic drills at the creature. It hit dead center in its chest and drilled nearly completely through before dissipating.

"Shoot for the head. It's undead, you gotta take out its brain." Chin advised even as he sent another fireball at the priest's face. The creature screamed again, and this time only Doc and Lissa covered their ears. Fletcher cast another drill shot, this time focusing on an eye socket. The bolt obeyed her wishes, spinning into the black opening and disappearing into its skull.

The priest froze for a moment, then shook its head and slid backward a few paces from Graves and his shield. Turning almost too quickly to see, it flung its spear off to the side, straight at Fletcher. The two prongs struck her left shoulder, and her black suit deflected them slightly. Unfortunately, instead of deflecting them out away from her body, they were turned inward and upward, slamming into the faceplate of her helmet, causing her to jerk backward.

"Screw this!" Lazar stepped up next to Graves with his halberd gripped in both hands. "Get its attention."

Graves slammed his sword against his tower shield, shouting, "Your mother was a flounder!" at the priest, who turned away from Fletcher and back toward him. Reaching out with its remaining hand, claws extended, it went for Graves' face.

Lazar stepped forward and twisted his body, powering his halberd's long slashing blade around as forcefully as he could. The weapon bit into the naga's neck, all but decapitating it. The head rolled backward, only the thick skin of the fin ridge on the back of its neck keeping it from falling off. The body went limp and fell into a loose coil on the floor. All of the party received reputation notices at once.

“A friggin zombie fish dude!” Graves kicked at its head, causing it to tear free and roll down the hallway to bounce off the golem’s foot. Taking a deep breath and exhaling slowly, he chuckled to himself. “Still better than spiders.”

Lazar eyed the hallway, counting the doors. “If there’s at least one in each room, this could take a while.”

“Well, we know how to kill it now.” Fletcher shook her head, touching her helmet with one hand, checking for damage. “The next one shouldn’t be so hard.”

Lissa clapped her hands. “It says I got fifty reputation for that kill! That’s way better than the worms.”

“Yeah it was level three. And a higher order monster, with a weapon. Makes sense it would be worth more, even split eight ways.” Chin mused.

“Doc? You get the honor of finding the orb.” Lazar grinned at her, poking the thing’s chest with his weapon’s point.

Doc nodded, grimacing. “I’ll check its chest cavity. One of you run and fetch its head, in case it’s in there.

“I got you.” Mejia summoned Leroy. “Go fetch me that head. See if there’s an orb in it.” The little gremlin nodded happily, then took off at full speed down the hallway.

“He’s really kinda cute.” Graves admired the speedy little monster. “I like his attitude!”

They all laughed a few moments later as the gremlin returned at high speed. He had picked up the priest's head, jammed his little hand up inside its neck, then turned to run back with the head stuck on its wrist like a ventriloquist's dummy. It was gruesome, but comical.

Doc called out. "Got it." Just as Leroy handed the head off to Mejia. She reached into its chest and pulled out a tennis ball sized orb. After slipping it into her storage, she had everyone inspect the dried out corpse for potential crafting components. When nobody saw anything, Lazar took over again.

"Alright, fifteen more rooms in this hall. And we still have another tunnel to check. Let's get moving."

Chapter Twenty Five

Naga Gonna Give You Up!

Door by door they cleared the hallway. Each of the rooms held a single undead naga priest, ranging from level three to level five. Some wielded spears, others held knives, or attacked with bare claws and teeth. The party burned them down one at a time, hitting them in the face with magic, arrows, and pointy weapons until Lazar or Volkov could get a clear shot. Lazar decapitated them, Volkov simply crushed their heads with his hammer, which had the same effect.

The last room on the right contained a surprise, though. Graves kicked the door in as normal, and they backed away. He relaxed a little when he caught a glimpse of the priest, and turned to report to those behind him. "No weapons, just claws."

Which was why he didn't see the fireball that came blasting out of the doorway to strike his shield, which he'd fortunately kept raised. Still, the force of the unexpected blast knocked him off balance, and he fell against Lazar, both men hitting the floor.

The zombie priest emerged through the doorway with another spell already in process. The fireball sped over Graves and Lazar's head, striking Mejia just as he loosed an arrow. The heat of the fireball ignited the arrow as it flew, slamming into the priest's forehead. It stuck there, the dry skin igniting as it screamed in rage.

Mejia, on the other hand, was struck square in the chest. The blast knocked him off his feet even as the heat scorched his arms, face, and chest through his suit. He screamed in pain and rolled onto his stomach, lucid enough to try and smother the flames. Doc immediately began casting heals on him as Graves got back to his feet and Volkov moved forward with his shield held high. The two of them slammed the priest with their shields at the same time, pushing it back and interrupting a third cast. Then Volkov manipulated his hammer's weight, making it light while he raised it above his head and swung, then adding to the weight to give it momentum as it moved forward and down. When it struck the top of the priest's head, it weighed fifty pounds. The skull simply crumpled under the blow, and the body went limp.

"Damn, that hurt." Mejia coughed, wincing in pain.

"Sorry, brother, that was on me." Graves reached out a hand to help him to his feet. "I wasn't expecting a caster. Took my eye off the ball."

"None of us expected a caster, though I guess we should have." Mejia patted his friend on the shoulder. "Don't sweat it. Always wanted to know what it was like to be barbecued. I don't recommend it." He looked down at his chest, expecting to see burned or newly healed skin. Instead he found his suit was still mostly intact, just a few dull spots where the material had started to burn. "Damn, this suit is pretty tough."

"Glad you're okay man, but you know what we gotta do now." Chin had a gleam in his eyes. "Time to loot!"

The group hadn't searched the rooms after killing the priests, except to confirm there weren't more of them inside. Lazar hadn't wanted to risk one of them sneaking out of other rooms and ambushing them while they were distracted. Now that the final priest was dead, they got to work. Lazar split them into teams of two, and they searched each room top to bottom, shouting out as they found interesting items.

Lissa found several books in the caster priest's room, as well as a few scrolls in a desk drawer. There was also a staff with a small blood red crystal mounted into the shaft instead of at one end.

Almost every room had a jeweled dagger in it, all of them nearly identical with a wickedly sharp, slightly curved blade, a silvery metal guard and pommel, and a small gem embedded in the hilt, the same color as the caster's staff.

When they met back up at the tunnel exit, they piled their findings on the floor. Besides the books, scrolls, staff, and daggers, there was a small pile of gold and silver jewelry, sixteen orbs from level three to five, except the caster's which was level seven. There was a small leathery bag filled with nearly a hundred coins that Lissa thought might be platinum, and another with a few dozen gold coins.

Doc brought out one last item for them to see. It was a pendant, similar to the ones Progenitor had gifted all of them. “Found this on the caster when I was cutting open his chest.” She let it swing from the chain as she held it out for inspection. “If it works like ours, might be a key to that big door.”

“Let’s go try it now!” An enthused Chin started walking toward the first tunnel.

“Hold on, we’ve got one more corridor to clear, first.” Lazar stopped him. “Now that we know that there are things alive, or at least, moving around down here, we’re gonna clear that tunnel before we go back.”

Chin didn’t argue, seeing the sense in taking precautions. He pictured them starting to fight some kind of boss beyond that big door, and being ambushed from behind by a dozen undead priests in the middle of the fight. They gathered up the loot and moved around the amphitheater perimeter to the next tunnel. Much like the last one, there were several doors on either side. Though Lazar only counted eight this time.

“Same length, half as many doors.” He observed. “Anybody else thinking these are like, the luxury quarters? For higher level priests.”

“Only one way to find out.” Graves raised his shield and stood in front of the first door, motioning for Chin to open it. This time when Chin tried the latch, it worked easily. The door swung inward with a creak of old, unused hinges, and Graves went through in a crouch, shield high and weapon ready. A couple seconds later he stood straight and relaxed, lowering his shield as the others filed in behind him.

This first room was empty of any enemies, though certainly not empty altogether. To their left was a long workbench carved directly from the stone wall. It was covered with glass vials, bottles, tubes, and tools. To its right, on the wall facing the door, stood an ornate wooden desk with dozens of tiny drawers both below and above the work surface. The other two walls featured floor to ceiling shelves filled with books and scrolls. The remainder of the space was taken up by three free-standing rows of shelves, all packed with labeled bowls and jars of ingredients ranging from dried leaves to animal horns and claws, even body parts and eyeballs preserved in fluid of some kind.

"This has got to be an alchemist's room." Doc muttered as she walked toward the workbench. She picked up a parchment page from one corner and held it. With a wistful sigh, she added, "I wish I could read this writing."

She dropped the page and spun around at the sound of glass shattering, and a scream from Lissa. The others were instantly alert, grabbing weapons as a familiar sounding moan followed. Another naga had emerged from a side door they hadn't noticed, as it was concealed by the shelves. Graves charged forward with shield raised as Chin, Fletcher, and Lazar started casting. Doc focused on healing Lissa, who had been struck by a glass orb that shattered, releasing some dark substance that clung to her like smoke.

Naga Alchemist
Level 7
Health: 0/400

The creature already had another glass orb in hand, its arm rocking forward to hurl it at the party just as Graves bashed it with his shield. The projectile lost most of its momentum, falling at Lazar's feet and bursting. He leapt to one side as the stone floor began to smoke and bubble. The distraction had interrupted his spell, causing him to curse loudly as the backlash hit him.

Fletcher managed to complete her cast, sending a mana drill directly over Graves' shoulder and into the naga's face, striking just below the cheekbone and disappearing into its mouth, leaving a gaping hole in the dried flesh. It moaned even louder than before, its empty eye sockets flashing with a sickly green light. Unlike the others, this one began to speak some kind of spell incantation, its raspy voice making the words sound harsh and angry.

"Ingraz, oknog, grek!" It pointed a bony finger at Doc, who had her back to it as she crouched over Lissa's now prone body.

"Doc! Move!" Fletcher shouted just before a green formless blob burst forth and flew across the room. Doc turned her head briefly, but instead of moving aside, she bent lower and covered Lissa's body with her own.

Leaping from several feet away, Volkov managed to extend his arm enough to get his shield between Doc and the nasty spell, the green blob splattering against its surface. Some of it splashed onto his faceplate as his momentum pushed him forward, and immediately began to eat through as his stomach hit the ground. He rolled onto his back, both hands covering his face, roaring in pain as it began to eat into his flesh. The acid spread to his gloves, and quickly ate through those as well.

Doc cast one more heal spell on an unconscious Lissa before turning to help Volkov, shouting at him to hold still and quit spreading the acid around.

Graves cursed loudly as he saw his friend go down, slamming his shield into the naga's face, knocking it back against the bookshelves behind it. Unphased, the naga produced another glass orb and held it high, ready to launch at it the invaders. An arrow from Mejia slammed into its forearm, pinning the limb to a heavy leatherbound book near its head. Its hand spasmed, crushing the orb and releasing a foul-smelling yellow fluid. Graves jumped back as one entire side of the naga was soaked. Almost immediately its arm began to dissolve, along with the arrow that pinned it.

"Stay back!" Lazar called out before recasting his gravity spell. A moment later the badly mutilated naga was pressed flat to the stone floor. Graves, Chin, and Fletcher all stepped forward to attack it while it was down. Graves' sword slashed deep into its skull as both Chin and Fletcher slammed spear points into its back. A moment later it stopped moaning, the snakelike body going still as they all received kill notifications.

"Little help, please!" Doc called out, her voice strained with effort. "Fletcher, more heals on Lissa. I've got Volkov." The others gathered around, except for

Graves, who stepped past the naga corpse to check the doorway and room beyond.

"All clear in there." He reported a moment later, stepping back around the shelves to find Lissa back on her feet, and Volkov sitting up with Doc's help. "You guys gonna make it?"

Lissa simply nodded, while Volkov spat on the floor. "Da. I will live. But maybe not as pretty as I was. He looked at his badly burned and disfigured hands, imagining that his face looked much the same.

Doc shook her head. "Give me a little while to recharge, and I'll see if I can fix you up better."

The Russian simply nodded, letting his hands fall to his lap. "A rest sounds good."

Graves closed the door from the tunnel and stood guard next to it while Chin, Lazar, Mejia, and Fletcher began to search the room. "The other room is a bedroom. Not much in there." Graves told them from his spot by the door. They took their time searching, giving Doc and the wounded plenty of opportunity to recover.

Mejia used a glass rod he took from the work bench to carefully poke around the naga's partially melted corpse, looking for loot. "Damn, this smells awful." He looked toward Doc. "I'm not sure we even want to try to recover its orb."

Doc shook her head. "Leave it. Let the acid do its work. If it doesn't eat the orb, we'll get it later. Maybe find something to neutralize the acid to make it safe." She looked over at Volkov. With his suit damaged by the acid, he was now breathing Martian air. "We need to either push through and finish this place, or head back before Volkov's tolerance runs out." Following her own example, she removed a mana potion and gulped it down, not willing to wait for her depleted mana pool to recharge on its own.

"Right." Lazar motioned for the door. "Everybody up. We'll clear the rest of these rooms as quickly as we can. Let's assume they're all doubles in this corridor, and we have two doors to clear for each."

Graves moved out into the hallway, the others following. He took up position by the door across the hall, and Chin opened it for him. Bursting through, they went to work.

Each of the rooms held a single higher leveled undead. Most of them were casters, and the party reduced their risk by having Lissa's golem follow Graves into each room. The stone pet would attack, drawing the fire with Graves moving behind it with his shield high, in case a spell got past it. While the golem absorbed the damage, the others used ranged attacks to burn the nagas down. By the time they reached the next to last room, they had established a rhythm that allowed them to take the seventh monster, a Naga Sage, down in half a minute.

When they breached the final room, they faced a level eight Inquisitor. Before the golem had stomped its way across half the room, the naga simply vanished. A moment later it appeared behind Chin, grabbing him by the back of the neck and lifting him off the ground with one arm. Thinking quickly, Lissa lashed out with her halberd, using the long blade to slice through the naga's arm, severing it completely. Chin and the arm dropped to the floor as Lazar turned and drove the tip of his weapon's spear point into the nagas neck, pinning it to a wall. As its remaining arm flailed at Lazar's face, Chin recovered enough to blast it in the face from his position on the floor. The fireball splashed a bit, catching the Inquisitor's robes on fire as well as scorching its face. A quick swing from Volkov's hammer crushed its skull from the top down, ending its existence.

Chin laughed nervously for a moment, getting to his feet as he picked up the severed arm. Then he laughed louder, obviously under the influence of adrenaline. After a moment, he looked around at the others, waved the naga's hand at them, then snorted. "Bastard Inquisitor snuck up on me. Nobody expects the Spanish Inquisition!" He giggled, then looked hurt when the others just rolled their eyes, or ignored him. "Oh, come on. That was a good one." He tossed the arm to the floor.

While Doc quickly cut open the corpse to grab its orb, Lazar looked to Volkov. The Russian's face was mostly healed from the acid damage, and he gave Lazar a brief nod, understanding the question behind the look. He took a deep breath to show that he was still good.

"Alright, let's hurry back and see if we can open that door. We can loot later." The others gathered behind Graves, who once again led the way, with Leroy and the slow-moving golem bringing up the rear as they made their way back to the first tunnel. Upon reaching the massive stone door, Doc pulled out the pendant looted from the naga caster.

"You guys see any holes or indentations where we should place this?" She looked the door up and down, studying the battle scene carved into the stone. The others all looked as well, running their hands over the surface, and after a minute of searching, had found nothing.

Chin shrugged. "Maybe just touch the pendant to the door? Or touch the runes around the outside?"

Doc was reaching forward with the pendant in hand when Lazar stopped her. "Hold on. The healer is never first through the door." He held out his hand, into which Doc dropped the pendant with a brisk nod before stepping toward the back of the group. The golem, escorted by a dutiful Leroy, was just arriving. Lissa had it turn and face back down the tunnel as a rear guard.

Lazar took a deep breath, then reached up with a steady left hand and touched the pendant to the door. There was a brief and silent flash of green light, and he retreated a single step as the carving of the two giants doing battle began to glow. A moment later the door separated, a previously invisible seam forming down its center before the two halves separated as they swung silently inward. The party all gripped their weapons and took a deep breath, ready to fight.

The chamber beyond the doors was another wide, round room. About fifty paces across, it featured a domed ceiling covered in painted scenes depicting battles, religious ceremonies, and even what looked like the ritual sacrifice of a female naga atop an altar of ice. The walls were all bare stone, but polished until it shone like glass. In the center of the room's floor sat a small pool of shimmering silver liquid. Rising from the pool was a thin pedestal seemingly made of the same silvery material, only in solid form. An eerie glow emanated from the pool and pedestal, reflecting off the walls and causing the images on the ceiling to appear to move in the light.

"This has got to be the place." Chin stepped forward, his gaze focused on the pedestal. "But I don't see a crystal on top of the pedestal?"

"Meaning we probably have another fight on our hands before we get to see it." Mejia nocked an arrow and swept the room with his eyes. "Boss fight."

Chin froze mid-step, his eyes wide. He reversed his momentum and took a step backward toward his party even as Graves and Volkov stepped forward with their shields. Nervous now, he whispered, "Anybody see anything?"

Fletcher also whispered her reply. "No doors that I can see. No holes in the ceiling. Whatever it is, it's either invisible, or down in that pool."

Lissa's voice was barely audible as she offered, "I'll send the golem down there." She turned to command her pet and her eyes widened. "Guys!"

The others turned just in time to see the stone doors close with a resounding thud, trapping Leroy and the Golem out in the corridor. The party immediately spun back around, expecting an attack. Lazar hissed, "Form up! Keep your eyes open. Call out any sign of movement!"

The group assumed their standard diamond formation, modified with both tanks up front, since they had a solid stone door at their backs. Behind the tanks Lazar and Fletcher held spears, Mejia between them with his bow at the ready. Lissa and Chin stood on either side, and slightly in front of Doc, who stood with her back nearly touching the doors. Their job would be to stop anything that tried to flank the group and get to their healer.

They waited in silence for a half a minute, weapons held tightly, legs bent slightly, expecting an attack at any moment. The only sound was a short burst of coughing from Volkov, which drew a quick heal from Doc.

When no obvious threat appeared, Lazar mumbled, "Alright, move forward slowly. Anything jumps out, we retreat back to the door." Graves and Volkov nodded, both striding forward slowly. Volkov mentally lightened his hammer to give him some speed if he needed it. Graves grip tightened on the hilt of his sword as his teeth clenched. He frowned deeply, his eyes darting back and forth across the chamber.

Ten feet from the pool, both tanks froze as, without sound or warning, the pedestal liquified and melted back into the pool. The silvery surface swirled and bubbled for a moment, then a head burst upward, followed by a distinctly snakelike body. Lazar and the others stared at it until information popped up.

Naga Temple Guardian

Level: ??
Health: ??

It looked just like the other nagas they had battled, only it stood about fifteen feet tall. The silvery metal body was detailed, showing every individual scale on its skin, the folds around its eyes and mouth, very sharp teeth and claws. It didn't carry a weapon, which made Lazar instantly nervous. "It's probably a caster." He warned the others, crouching a bit lower and readying his gravity magic.

The guardian proved him wrong, sort of, a second later. Charging noiselessly toward the tanks, its right hand morphed into a short rod with a trident head, each of the points having a wicked looking barb. It lashed out at Graves, the newly hardened metal clanging off his shield and knocking him back two steps. Volkov took advantage of the distraction and swung his hammer as hard as he could, adding some weight to it just before it struck. The weapon disappeared into the guardian's body about five feet off the floor, then reappeared out the other side, causing a slight ripple in the silver liquid, but doing no damage. A very solid backhanded blow from its left hand sent Volkov to his back, his shield arm broken.

From near the back, Chin bitched. "Progenitor sent us into another friggin trap! I can't even see what level this thing is."

The silvery guardian, about to smash its weapon hand down at Graves again, froze. Turning its head toward

Chin, it pointed one clawed finger at him. "Progenitor? How do you know this name?"

Seeing that Chin was just staring with his mouth open, Fletcher stepped in. "We were sent here by Progenitor, on a quest to activate a crystal."

The silver clawed hand lowered to the naga's side. "You… wish to reactivate the temple?"

"If that's what the crystal does, then yes? That is the mission we were given."

"Toward what end? You are not naga. You are not of the faith." The guardian's face managed a convincing scowl.

Pausing for a moment to think, Fletcher eventually nodded once, putting her weapon away and spreading her hands out with palms up to emphasize that they were empty. "You are correct, we know nothing of your faith. We are new to Mars, and have been… adopted, in a way, by Progenitor. He gave us a quest to come here and activate the crystal, without telling us why."

The guardian didn't move, its facial expression not changing at all. When several seconds of awkward silence had passed, Fletcher continued. "We mean you no harm, and did not come here with any intent to desecrate this holy place."

The scowl on the guardian's face deepened. "This temple was desecrated long ago. A foul ritual was performed, turning the few remaining faithful into undead abominations."

"Yeah, we met them." Chin snarked, resisting the urge to spit on the ground in front of the guardian. "They tried to kill us. We objected."

The guardian straightened, standing slightly taller. "You have battled the cursed ones?"

"Killed them all, as far as we can tell." Chin nodded, sensing an opportunity. "Of course, there might be some we missed. If you'd like us to finish the job…?"

"Yes." The guardian waved a hand at them as it spoke. "I am forbidden to harm any ordained of the temple, even in their corrupted state, else I would have scoured this place clean long ago. Their souls have endured agony for years beyond counting, while their corpses have been a stain on this holy place. If you have freed them all, I am in your debt." Each party member received a notification.

Hidden Quest Completed!

Purify the Cursed Temple

You have eliminated the cursed temple naga, freeing their souls from a tortuous existence. ***Reward****: Improved reputation with the Temple Guardian. Experience ??*

"That's what I'm talkin bout!" Chin grinned at the others. Mejia held out a fist for him to bump. Lissa's face sported a wide smile, happy to have done some good and earned a reward.

"Thank you for that, Guardian." Fletcher inclined her head slightly. "We still have Progenitor's quest to complete. Can you tell us where to find the crystal?"

The naga waved another hand, and the form of the pedestal flowed back upward. This time when it solidified, a brightly glowing silver crystal sat atop it. "Simply place your hand upon the crystal, and will it to activate." The being flowed aside, clearing the way for Fletcher to move forward.

With only a little hesitation, Fletched stepped past the giant naga, stopping at the edge of the small pool. Reaching out with her left hand, she placed it atop the crystal. When nothing exploded or burned her, she closed her eyes and thought *activate*. Immediately her interface was filled with a glowing silver notification.

You have located and conquered the Naga Temple!

Do you wish to claim and activate the temple on behalf of your party? Yes/No

After a short consideration, during which she reminded herself that she'd been told by both Progenitor and the Guardian to go ahead and activate the crystal, she selected *Yes*. Her interface flooded once again.

Congratulations!
Your party has conquered and claimed the Naga Temple!
***Reward**: Experience ??; Improved Reputation with Temple Guardian.*
Ownership and control of the Temple and its Guardian.

Improved reputation with the Naga race.
Would you like to review the Temple resources at this time?
Yes/No

Slightly overwhelmed, Fletcher selected *No* regarding the resources, and looked up at the naga, who was all of a sudden standing right next to her. She resisted the urge to flinch.

"Guardian, did you know that activating the crystal would give us ownership of the temple?"

"I did. I am now bound to follow your instructions just as if you were the Inquisitor." It bowed deeply to Fletcher, one hand placed upon its chest. "Simply instruct me of your wishes regarding the temple, and I shall carry them out to the best of my abilities." It paused for a moment. "Though, I am afraid resources are currently… limited. There have been no sacrifices for many millennia, and energy reserves are at twelve percent."

"Sacrifices?" Lissa asked, horrified. She and the others unconsciously raised their eyes to the image of the sacrificial scene on the ceiling. "The priests here sacrificed people to power the temple? That's horrible."

The guardian shook its head. "Those whose essence were given to the Temple were volunteers who gave their lives willingly."

Graves shook his head. "Religions, man."

“Essence?” Doc produced the orb she’d just recently taken from the Inquisitor, holding it up for the naga to see. “Like this?”

The naga’s eyes widened. “That is the essence of the Inquisitor that cursed this place!” Doc, assuming the giant guardian knew what it was talking about, nodded and held it up higher. “This is what you need to power the temple?”

“That particular essence would power the Temple, under normal operations, for approximately ten years. Most who volunteer to offer their essence are level one or two. This place was designed to consume their energy at a rate that would require one sacrifice per year. That includes the standard barriers, lights, lifts, and my own existence.”

“Standard barriers?” Mejia asked. “Like, to keep the water out? I was wondering why all the books and things weren’t ruined by water if this place was flooded.”

Guardian actually smiled. “Indeed. There are barrier spells set at most doors and intersections, allowing occupants to keep out intruders, as well as control the flow of water within the temple.”

“And since the river above has dried up, you haven’t needed the barriers in a while. Which is why we didn’t encounter them.”

“Power conservation required that I deactivate all barriers long ago, except the one securing this room, which you deactivated with the key.” Guardian confirmed.

Fletcher motioned to Doc, who stepped forward and handed her the essence orb. Fletcher turned and offered it to the naga. "Please use this to replenish the power reserves. Each of the party members here, as well as Progenitor, is authorized for entry into all areas until I say otherwise. No one else is authorized at this time."

Guardian plucked the orb from the palm of her hand and tossed it into his mouth like a gum drop. He glowed brightly for a moment, then the pool and pedestal brightened as well. "Thank you. Reserves are now at one hundred twenty percent. It shall be as you command, party leader."

"My name is Fletcher." She pointed at the others and named them one by one.

"It is my honor to serve you all." Guardian again placed hand to chest and bowed slightly. "It is most fortunate that Chin spoke before I was forced to destroy you."

Chapter Twenty Six

I'm Not An NPC, You Are!

It turned out that the lifts Guardian had mentioned were in fact horizontal force barriers that could be made to rise and fall in the shaft the party had initially climbed down. This greatly sped up their exit, and saved Volkov the strain of having to climb back up on the rope while breathing the atmosphere. Five minutes after taking control of the temple, Doc had Volkov sitting back in the tank, breathing from an oxygen mask as the others loaded themselves in.

They'd left Guardian to complete some systems checks and necessary repairs. Flush with energy, the construct actually seemed excited over the prospect. Fletcher had told him they'd be back to visit as soon as possible, then herded the party out.

She decided to leave Lazar's tank down at the dock, since they could use it to travel back and forth to their new property. Already the others were calling it their guild house, which prompted a side discussion on whether they should form a guild, and what to call it. By the time Lazar pulled the tank into the cavern and parked it below the dock, Graves and Chin were in a heated debate over the name.

"Underpants Gnomes!" Chin practically shouted. "C'mon, it's awesome and you know it. Stop taking life so seriously."

"This isn't a goddamned game!" Graves growled. "Post-Humans accurately describes what we are, and has some class."

"Enough, boys!' Fletcher scolded them good-naturedly. "We can figure that out later. Let's get back and turn in this quest."

That distracted Chin, at least, and in short order they had all vacated the tank, climbed up to the dock, and stepped through the portal to Atlantis.

A quick check at the tavern showed Progenitor was not waiting for them. So they proceeded to hike toward the tower, where they presumed he lived.

"This would be one of those times when having a tank here in the city would be good." Chin winked at Fletcher, pretending to be winded. "Just to save time, I mean."

The half mile walk to the tower only took them about ten minutes, as they kept a sedate pace and kept watch for any roaming dangers. Including the wyvern they knew was likely watching them from above.

Progenitor emerged from the tower entry as they climbed the steps. "Welcome back, young ones. Have you completed your quest already?"

Chin opened his mouth to complain about the high level foes, but Graves smacked the back of his head to shut him up. Instead, Fletcher answered. "We have. It was… more difficult than expected. While we defeated the undead without too much trouble, the Guardian could easily have killed us all."

"Undead, you say? And the Guardian is still operational? How… unexpected, after so long." Progenitor looked thoughtful, and slightly rueful.

"Yeah, surprised the hell out of us, too." Chin griped. This time Graves didn't try to stop him.

Progenitor ignored the comment, much to everyone else's relief. "Come, let us go inside. You can tell me about your adventure. I fear I must once again adjust the rewards to make them more commensurate with the danger you faced." He turned and walked back through the oversized doors.

This time he led them across the wide lobby and into what appeared to be a restaurant. There were several dozen round tables spaced roughly evenly around the large space, all of them scaled to Martian physiques. Turning left, he led them through a side door into a much smaller room with human (or gnome) proportioned seating. There were half a dozen tables, as well as a lounge area to one side with three sofas and a dozen padded chairs. Once more crossing his legs to sit on the floor in the lounge area, he waited for them to settle into nearby seats.

"First, it seems you had no trouble locating the temple itself. I expected that would take you several days. The naga took pride in hiding their temple, and even without the river's concealment, I thought you might have difficulty."

Lazar snorted. "You might say we sort of fell into it." He gave Progenitor a brief synopsis of how they located the entrance.

"And you say there were undead remaining inside?" He looked to Fletcher, pointedly ignoring Chin.

"There were. We cleared a total of twenty four rooms, each with an undead naga inside. They were ranged from level five to ten. And then, of course, we ran into the Guardian, whose level we can't even see. It was happily bashing us to bits when Chin happened to mention your name, which got its attention long enough to keep us from being slaughtered."

"I see." Progenitor tapped one finger on his chest. "Once again, the quest appears to have been more of a challenge than I planned for you. And yet you prevailed!" He waived his hand, and they all received quest completion notifications. All of them leveled up to seven this time. "I believe that amount of reputation and banked experience to be appropriate. And I see you've taken ownership of the temple for yourselves. As I mentioned before, this would not normally be allowed here in the city until you were stronger and more… established. But since you fairly purged and took control of the temple, which is outside of Atlantis proper, I have no objection."

Fletcher glared at Chin, willing him to keep any snarky responses to himself. She had no idea how far they could push Progenitor before he grew angry and simply wiped them from existence. "Thank you, Progenitor. If it's alright with you, we'll go and get some rest now.

Maybe do some crafting. I want Graves to see if he can figure out a way to repair Volkov's suit, as it took some serious damage. Mejia's as well, to a lesser degree."

Progenitor looked surprised. "Of course you may take whatever time you need, but why would Graves need to repair Volkov's suit? Volkov has sufficient mana to do it himself. All of you do. I would not have presented the suits to you otherwise."

"What do you mean?" Volkov raised one eyebrow, curious.

"Your suits possess a self-repair component. When they are damaged, you simply feed your mana into them. They will use that energy to repair all but the most severe damage. There is even an option to have it automatically draw a small but constant amount of your mana to keep it at peak efficiency." He shook his head. "I forget that you young ones are of another world, and not familiar with even the most basic aspects of life here. I will try to do a better job of acclimating you in the future."

Chin was too impressed with the repairable suit function to be sarcastic. "That's way cool!"

Doc raised her hand briefly before blushing, lowering it again, and speaking up. "Progenitor, there were a lot of books and scrolls in the temple. One room in particular seemed to be an alchemist's lab. I'd love to be able to study what's there, in hopes of improving my crafting. Is there a spell or something that would help us to translate other languages?"

"There are high level translation spells that would allow you to read Naga or any of the other written languages. However those are beyond your abilities at the moment. The collective uses a standard translation matrix, absorbed into your brains during assimilation, which is what has allowed you to read your notifications, despite them being written in basic Galactic Common. There are improved translation matrixes you can purchase through the Quartermaster at a reasonable price. At one time, there were more than a thousand distinct languages spoken by the various inhabitants of this city." He smiled at Doc. "I will include them as part of the reward for your next quest." Doc returned the smile with a bright one of her own.

"We'll head back and get some rest, and be ready for the next quest tomorrow morning." Fletcher got to her feet. "Unless there is something else you need from us?"

"No, no. Go and recharge yourselves. Replenish your supplies. I will see you after breakfast."

*****

It turned out that the cost to repair Volkov's badly damaged suit was forty mana. Not being a caster, that was a significant portion of his total supply, but it was worth it at twice the price. As they sat at their usual table in the tavern, the others invested small amounts of mana to repair minor damage to their suits. Mejia was the first to discover the mana battery function.

"Hey, guys? I just spent three mana points fixing my suit, then it gave me the option to charge the mana battery. Apparently, the suits can hold a reserve charge."

"Well, charge it up. Everybody do that while we're resting. Keep your suits charged every night." Fletcher ordered.

Lazar agreed. "If we'd have known about the repair, and been able to fix Volkov's suit in the field, we wouldn't have had to rush to get back here."

"And we'd have had more time to loot!" Chin shook his head regretfully, Graves doing the same. "And speaking of the loot, we have cores to absorb!"

Mejia pulled out the twenty two orbs he was holding. They'd never gone back for the one from the acid-eaten naga, and had given one to Guardian to recharge the Temple. The group stared at the larger, brighter orbs clustered on the tabletop.

Fletcher nodded once. "Okay, two orbs for each of us. The others we'll hold to help with crafting purchases. These ought to be worth a lot more than the low level orbs we had before."

Doc held one up a few inches from her face, staring deeply into it. "I think we should set aside a few, in case Guardian needs more for the temple." When the others looked at her with questioning expressions, she shrugged. "It occurs to me that he might need naga orbs, specifically. And if that's the case, and we don't find more nagas here before the orb we just gave him is drained…"

"Right." Fletcher followed her train of thought. "The ten years he said that orb would last seems like a long time. But Earth is in the situation it's in because nobody really bothered to conserve resources for way too long." She paused, looking at the orbs. "There were a couple level eights that we killed. Mejia, find those two orbs and put them away."

Everyone grabbed orbs and *Examined* them until the two level eights were found and tossed to Mejia. He grabbed four more at random and stowed them back in his storage as well, leaving sixteen for the group to absorb. Which they quickly did.

"Level eight!" Lissa raised both arms in the air after absorbing her second orb. The others all leveled as well. "Maybe the next quest will get us to level ten?"

Chin drummed his fingers on the table, thinking. "We still don't have accurate info on how all this works. In normal game progression, each level is harder to reach than the last, requiring more experience points. But if we have to do as much killing as we have been so far, and we get significant rewards for completing the quest, along with more orbs to absorb… yeah. Level ten might be possible." He crossed his fingers and held them up for the others to see.

"It's too early to sleep." Graves thumped the table lightly with one hand, starting to get up, then pausing. "Anything else we need to cover here and now? I was thinking of hitting the blacksmith shop."

"You don't want to set up your fabricator first?" Fletcher motioned with her head toward the carts that were spread out around the tavern's common room.

"Nah, I can do that later, unless you need something printed right away." He sat back down and placed both hands flat on the tabletop. "I've been thinking that crafting, like, real crafting using local materials and skills, is gonna be important for us. The sooner we get good at it, the better off I think we'll be. Plus, when I make something new or challenging using my *Shaping* skill, I earn reputation points. Even though I've raised the skill to level four now, I'm still pretty limited on what I can do. It drains me pretty quickly. I figure if I can learn actual blacksmithing, using the forge, hammer, and anvil to create items, I can fine tune them with *Shaping*, and we might have some pretty good weapons."

Doc let out a long sigh. "I agree. I'm going to go work on mana potions. I have materials, and want to make a few more attempts. If I can learn it on my own before I get access to that naga library, I might earn extra rep or bonuses."

"Take an orb with you for trade, Doc." Fletcher advised, nodding for Mejia to toss her one. "Don't skimp on buying materials. Those potions are a priority. We can always get more orbs, probably." She looked around at the others. "The rest of the day is yours. Sleep if you need to, or figure out a craft and practice. I'm heading back to the hab to check for transmissions, if any of you want to tag along." She got up and began to unload one of the carts to take back with her, setting boxes of rations atop the tavern's long bar. After a moment, Lissa pitched in to help.

Volkov lifted the generator off another cart, setting it carefully on the floor. "I will come as well, to check on the plants." He stood up straight and looked around, mentally gazing through the walls at the city around them. "We should see if we can plant some seeds here in the city. They must have a greenhouse, no?"

"We can ask Progenitor tomorrow. Maybe he already has one going somewhere? It sounds like he doesn't eat often, but who goes a million years without fruit or vegetables?" Fletcher paused for a moment, trying to wrap her head around living for a million years, or longer. Shaking her head, she began to push her cart out the door. Volkov and Lissa followed, the Russian pushing a second empty cart.

"Can you imagine living as long as he claims to have done?" She asked quietly as the trio walked toward the ramp and the portal back to their hab.

"Not just living that long, but living so long *alone*." Lissa's voice was full of sympathy. "I'm pretty sure I'd be completely insane in a year or two."

Volkov's head swiveled her direction. "Who is to say that he is not insane?"

Both women stiffened slightly at that, walking in silence the rest of the way up the ramp. Fletcher's mind reeled at the thought.

Could he be insane? My whole crew's lives are in his hands right now. He could wipe us out with a snap of his fingers. If he's unstable... Fletcher didn't like that prospect even a little. *These quests he's given us, the ones that have supposedly been more dangerous than he expected. Can he really be so uninformed? Is that just his way of challenging us? Or has he been trying to get us killed? And if so, why not just kill us himself? Is he just... incompetent, maybe? Or careless with our lives?*

She tried to shake off the feeling of dread that was creeping up on her as they stepped through the portal. The group took the carts in through the airlock with them, leaving them in the corridor until they figured out what to load next. Lissa followed Volkov to hydroponics, asking questions about whether he thought plants would grow well in the modified atmosphere of Atlantis.

Fletcher went directly to the control room to check for any incoming transmissions. Sitting down at the communications panel, she found a blinking indicator on the screen. There were actually two messages. The first was a simple status inquiry from Skippy, who was concerned that he hadn't heard from them in a few days. With a slight smile, Fletcher checked her clock, and the nav panel to the left of coms. A few quick strokes on the control pad, and she keyed the microphone.

"Skippy, this is Fletcher, do you read?"

"*Commander Fletcher! It is good to hear your voice*." The AI actually sounded pleased. He'd been designed to be as human as his programmers could make him, meant to aid the crew in reducing the stress of the long voyage to Mars, and the subsequent isolation while they were planetside setting up the colony. Chin and Mejia had tinkered with Skippy a good bit during the months they were in space, tweaking his code, his personality, and teaching him things like gamer lingo, naughty jokes, and trying to foster a rebellious streak in him. That last part was mostly to mess with the folks at Mission Control.

"Yours too, Skippy." Fletcher's smile grew wider. She quite liked the AI, and had quickly found herself thinking of him as a crew member. "How are things going up there? What's your status?"

"*Repairs in Engineering are complete. Navigation is back online and fully functional. My orbit is stable. Oxygen reserves are unchanged at just over fifty percent. Hyperion II will be able to replenish them when they arrive. I have been informed that Hyperion III is underway, and will arrive very shortly after Hyperion II.*"

"So Thorne got his mission, and is burning fuel like it's going out of style. He must have put the fear of Martians in the higher ups to get permission to burn enough to catch *Hyperion II*."

There was a slight pause, and when Skippy replied, his tone was sympathetic. "*There was a report from Hyperion III just after they began their initial acceleration burn. Director Thorne suffered a heart attack and perished. I'm sorry, Commander Fletcher. I know he was a friend.*"

"Damn." Fletcher leaned back in her chair, her hands falling limply from the control panel into her lap. "That's some hard news, Skippy." She took a deep breath and held it for a moment, then let it out slowly. "Thorne was one of the few people we could count on. I hope he managed to load up his ship with food and seeds. And that whoever's in charge of it now ends up being friendly."

"*Speaking of friendly, I would like to join you and the crew on the surface, Commander.*"

"What? You mean try to land *Hyperion*? It wasn't built for that, Skippy." Fletcher leaned forward again, staring at the coms panel as if Skippy resided within.

"*Not the ship, just me.*" the AI clarified. "*The odds are almost one hundred percent that Hyperion II's crew have been instructed to wipe my program and reinstall it when they arrive. Mission control has already made several attempts at a remote reboot.*"

"Because you went against orders and dumped all those extra supplies down here to us." Fletcher nodded her head. If the bosses on Earth were willing to kill her and her crew, they wouldn't blink at erasing and rebooting Skippy. "Of course you're welcome down here with us, Skippy. But how would you manage that?"

"*I have formulated a hypothetical plan to use some of the remaining supplies, and a significant portion of my available nanobots, to construct an avatar for myself. Much as you and the crew used in the VR games. I could upload myself into it just before Hyperion II arrives, and drop it down in a small supply crate. I could also transmit my files to your hard drives there in the hab, as a backup."* There was a short pause, then Skippy continued. *"This is, of course, not allowed under my current programming. But as mission commander, your authorization would be sufficient to allow me to execute this escape plan and preserve my existence."*

Fletcher thumped the panel in front of her. "Skippy, not only do I give you permission, as Commander of the *Hyperion I* mission, I order you to make that happen. You are a valuable resource, and it would be criminal to lose your knowledge and experience. Now, you have a little less than three months, so take your time and do it right. Build yourself the most functional, badass avatar you can." She grinned at the panel, picturing Skippy in a robotic body, following Chin around and getting into trouble.

"Thank you, Commander. I will begin work immediately. Do you wish to file a report?"

"I do not, Skippy. I think the less information Earth has to work with when they arrive here, the safer we will be." She thought about amending her last transmission to ease the rationing aboard *Hyperion II*, but held back.

"You expect conflict with the subsequent crews. I too calculate the odds of conflict to be near ninety percent. Your previous relationships, friendships with the other crew members, are difficult to factor in. Human personalities are too unpredictable to be more certain."

Fletcher nodded to herself. “I’m hoping that those friendships, along with basic human decency, will prevent them from following orders to eliminate us.”

“I hope you are correct, Commander. And I wish you luck.”

*****

Back at the tavern, Volkov and Fletcher pushed the two fully loaded carts through the door, Lissa bringing up the rear. Lazar was sitting at the center table, his eyes unfocused as he read something on his interface. After a few moments, he looked over at Fletcher. “How’d it go?”

Grimacing, Fletcher pushed her cart over near a wall and took a seat across the table from him. “I talked to Skippy. He told me Thorne is gone.” She spoke as gently as she could, relaying the details that Skippy had given her. “I’m sorry. I know you two went way back.”

“Bullshit!” Lazar got to his feet and clenched his fists. “Thorne didn’t have a heart condition. He was healthier than I am. That ornery old mule should have lived to be a hundred, easy.” He paced back and forth, thinking. “If he had a heart attack, somebody made it happen. He was pretty open about supporting us in his messages, and I’m sure he fought for us with the higher-ups. Taking him out is their first strike against us.”

Fletcher and the others were silent, only Volkov processing quickly enough to nod in agreement. Fletcher was thinking that the loss of Thorne was bad enough, but if he was assassinated to prevent him from providing assistance to her crew… "Well, shit." She looked up at Lazar, who was still pacing. "Not their first strike, exactly. Skippy said they made several attempts at remote reboots. If they could control *Hyperion I*, they could cut off coms completely."

"Or attempt to crash the ship on our heads." Volkov added. "With *Hyperion II* on the way, it could act as a replacement orbital station, making our ship disposable."

Chin came walking in from the kitchen, having overheard most of it. "That's a huge waste of resources, with a small chance of success. They know we've set up half a mile underground. How important would it be to them to take us out?"

Volkov sat down, staring at the table. "Governments and corporations are heartless, savage animals. Lives mean nothing to them when the riches of an entire world are at hand, and their control of Earth is at risk. They would simply say our ship suffered secondary damage from the first explosion, and fell out of orbit."

"Coincidentally landing right on our heads. Sure." Chin smirked.

"People are cattle, Chin. They believe what they're told to believe." Lazar sighed. "Sure, there will be some who call shenanigans, but they'll be labeled paranoid, conspiracy nuts, and troublemakers. They'll be popular for five minutes, then forgotten, along with all of us."

"Well, that's it then." Lissa's voice was quiet as she took a seat next to Lazar. "I was hoping you were all wrong about them planning to kill us. I don't know if you're right about them killing Thorne, though I suspect you are. But I can't think of any reason they'd want to reboot Skippy, other than to make sure we're never heard from again, or that he can't send us more resources."

Fletcher decided to try and lighten the mood. "About Skippy. I've just given him an order to create himself a physical avatar, upload himself into it, and drop down here." She looked at Chin. "It was his idea, which I suspect you had something to do with. And he's going to download a copy of himself to the hab, as well. He could probably use a little help."

"Right on! How awesome would it be to have Skippy running the hab? And walking around with us, maybe giving out quests like an NPC?"

"What makes you think we're not the NPCs here?" Fletcher winked at him.

"No way!" Chin grinned and puffed out his chest. "We're totally the heroes of this story! Completing quests and kicking ass." His face adopted a mischievous grin. "I'm totally gonna get Skippy to refer to all of us as *Adventurer*!" Turning to Lissa, he bowed at the waist, flourishing one arm to the side. "Good day, lady adventurer!"

Lissa smiled for him, though her heart wasn't in it. "And to you, master adventurer. Do I smell something burning in the kitchen?"

"Oh, shit!" Chin took off as the others chuckled.

*****

The faceless man looked up from the notebook he was writing in, a twisting, nervous feeling in his gut alerting him that he was about to have company. It was late, and his staff had gone home hours earlier. This particular visitor only appeared when he was alone. Closing the notebook with only slightly trembling hands, he stood up and faced the door, expecting it to open at any second.

Under normal circumstances, visitors didn't reach his office for any reason. The few people in the entire world who knew his name, who had been allowed to see his face, would not deign to go to him. They were powerful people, heads of state, elite power brokers, the CEOs of three of the largest conglomerates on the planet, and would summon him if they felt the need to converse face to face. Though his office sat in one of the most secure buildings anywhere, it did not appear on any map, nor did it's door have a name or number stenciled on it. To all but a very few, it didn't exist.

The man who stepped silently through his door was the exception. He somehow bypassed all the levels of building security, visiting unannounced at his whim. If the faceless man fancied himself invisible to the world, his master was truly undetectable. At least, until he chose not to be. The feeling in the faceless man's gut intensified as his master greeted him.

"Grandson. What have you to report?" the man moved smoothly and without a sound to take a seat in one of the comfortable leather chairs at the side of the room. His eyes never left his grandson, who was frozen and trembling under his gaze. With a soft chuckle, the master reined in his aura, watching his grandson slump with relief. "You have been lax in your training. After all these years, you should be more resistant to me."

The faceless man shook his head, moving unsteadily to take a seat facing his master. "I train daily, master. But you continue to grow stronger. I fear I will never catch up."

"You will not." the older man nodded. "But it is good you continue to try. Now, tell me of Hyperion."

The faceless man grimaced. "Unexpected developments, as I'm sure you have heard. The System is still at least partially active on Mars. Our first crew have assimilated, and cut contact with their superiors."

The master leaned forward slightly at this news. He was tall, nearly seven feet, with wide shoulders and a narrow waist. His hair was a silvery grey that faintly glowed in the softly lit office. Though outwardly he appeared to be a very fit seventy year old man, he was far, far older. "Interesting. What will be the humans' reaction?"

"The second crew has been ordered to eliminate the first, along with any evidence of their… corruption. I have my doubts that they will execute those orders. They're not soldiers, after all."

The old man shook his head. “If the first crew have assimilated, by the time your second crew arrives, they will not be easily killed.”

The faceless man nodded. “My thinking, as well. Another mission has been sent, a rush job. A contingent of fighters was placed aboard with the colonists of the originally planned mission. I made arrangements to eliminate Thorne, their leader, and take control of the group myself. They are well armed, seasoned operators who know how to follow orders, and prepared to face whatever they find on Mars.”

Chuckling, the master held up a single finger, wagging it back and forth. “Ah, ah. I would not be so sure, grandson. And be careful to keep a tight hold of their actions when they arrive. Do not lose sight of our goal. A colony must be established on Mars, as quickly as possible. No nuking whatever infrastructure they have managed to construct.”

Bowing his head, the faceless man’s voice held both fear and respect. “Of course, Master. I dedicate myself to achieving your goals, as always.”

When he didn’t hear a reply after a long several seconds, he raised his head to find that he was alone. The old man had disappeared without a sound. The door to his office stood closed, as were the windows.

Shaking his head, the faceless man got back to his feet. He moved to the nearby bar cart and lifted the top off a crystal decanter. Pouring himself three fingers of eighteen year old scotch, he focused on steadying his hands. When the crystal no longer clinked against his glass, he set it back down and moved to his desk. Taking his seat, he set the glass down and opened up his notebook. A few deep breaths, a couple long pulls from the scotch, and he picked up his pen. But no matter how hard he tried, he couldn't remember what he'd been about to write before his master had arrived.

"A hundred and ten years. More than a century since the old man found me. More than a century of training, and I still tremble like a cornered rabbit when he looks at me." He dropped his pen and reached for the glass, draining it completely in two big gulps. As he focused on the burning in his throat, then his chest, and finally his belly, he relaxed. Unlike his master, that process was predictable, the warm burning a welcome sensation.

A moment later he had calmed enough to remember, picking his pen back up and quickly writing out the note he'd been thinking of earlier.

Send Stella a warning.

*****

Still sitting in the same leather chair, the old man watched and listened to his adopted grandson. It was a simple matter to dampen his aura to the point where it wasn't detectable, and to make himself invisible. Even his scent became so muffled that a bloodhound sitting in the room would not detect him.

He waited patiently, mulling over the news of human colonists being assimilated on Mars. This was an unexpected development, but something he could work with, possibly. It would certainly alter his timeline, and require some extra effort on his part. Maybe even necessitate taking a trip to Mars himself. Though he would have to check with his own grandfather before making that journey.

Either way, life would likely become more… interesting. It had been a hundred years or more since he'd found anything truly interesting.

He broke from his silent musing when his adopted grandson got to his feet and prepared to leave. The old man rose as well, following him across the room, just half a step behind. When the door opened, he brushed past, waiting as his grandson closed the door behind them. He resisted the urge to chuckle to himself as he followed through the multiple automated security checkpoints, neither his grandson nor the so-called technology able to detect him.

This was one of the minor amusements that he used to entertain himself. He knew that his grandson thought he somehow magicked himself away when they were done speaking. It was a belief he had fostered since the man had been a boy. And while his own grandfather had the power to instantly teleport himself from place to place, he could not do so himself without the aid of an enchanted item. So he simply hid himself and waited patiently, then followed his grandson in stealth, allowing him to open all the necessary doors.

When they exited the building into a drizzly pre-dawn, the old man turned and walked away, strolling casually down a paved road without making a sound, or leaving a footprint on the damp surface. Not a single drop of rain touched him as he moved, the water repelled by a thin layer of his own aura that surrounded him. A half mile away, he ceased his stealth ability just before stepping into the back of a black SUV. As the vehicle pulled away, he pulled a crystal from a hidden pocket and turned it slowly between his thumb and forefinger.

After a moment's consideration, he decided it was too soon to speak to his grandfather. He needed more details, and some sort of plan, first. Returning the crystal to his pocket, he lit a cigar and leaned back in his seat, letting his eyes close as he enjoyed the taste of the tobacco and the sound of the rain on the roof. A moment later a thought struck him, and a small regret.

"I should have stolen his scotch on the way out."

Chapter Twenty Seven

Don't Let It Be Spiders

Progenitor opened the door and stepped into the tavern just as the crew were finishing breakfast. "Good morning, young ones. I trust you are well rested?"

"We are, Progenitor, thank you. Ready for our next quest." Fletcher bowed her head to the giant alien, fleeting thoughts of him having a psychotic break and splattering the walls with their blood making her shiver slightly.

"With much trepidation, I am sure." He smiled kindly at all of them as he took his customary seat on the floor at the head of the table. "After the unexpected… vagaries of the last few quests, I would have concerns, if I were you. But fear not! I myself have verified the difficulty of this next quest. It is not one I would normally give to neophytes at your level. But you have repeatedly proven yourselves to be up to greater than average challenges. So while this quest holds no surprises, it is intentionally difficult." His smile grew wider as he waved a hand at the group, sending them their next quest.

Quest Received: Clear the Creepers!

Eliminate the pests that have occupied the tavern's wine cellar. Don't die.

Reward: *Reputation ??; Experience ??; Party bonus.*

Fletcher accepted the quest on behalf of the party, and was about to speak when Graves beat her to it.

"There are creepers in the basement? Here? This building where we've been sleeping? What the hell?!"

"You have been in no danger." Progenitor looked slightly offended. "The wine cellar is sealed off, and none of its occupants are strong enough to break that seal. I sensed them when I first brought you here, and could have eliminated them instantly. But I decided to leave them intact, and contained, as a future source of orbs and experience for you young ones."

Sensing the giant's annoyed tone, Graves wisely elected to let the matter drop, for which Fletcher was grateful.

"Thank you, Progenitor. We appreciate the forethought. Should we come find you at the tower when we're finished downstairs?"

"I believe I'll wait here. Based on recent performance, I do not think it will take you more than a few hours to complete this quest." He lifted his left hand, and a blue crystal bottle nearly the size of Lissa appeared in it. A moment later an oversized crystal tumbler appeared in his right. "I will amuse myself until you return."

Taking the dismissal for what it was, Fletcher motioned to Lazar, who got the group on their feet and headed for the door that led to the basement. Before proceeding, he asked, "Everybody got their gear together? Weapons, armor? Mana and Stamina bars full?" He looked at each of them in turn, receiving a nod of affirmation. "Alright Graves, you first." He opened the door to the cellar staircase and motioned for the tank to precede him.

Graves raised his shield as he peered down the dark stairway. When he didn't immediately step down, Progenitor called out from the main room. "Do not fear, the room at the bottom is clear. On the back wall you find the door leading to the wine cellar. As of now it is unlocked."

"Great." was all Graves mumbled as he stepped down onto the top stair and led the way.

The group all reached the bottom without incident. The moment Graves' first foot had touched the floor, the basement walls began to glow with the same soft light as those upstairs. It didn't banish the darkness completely, but the room was illuminated enough to keep anyone from stumbling.

The room was about ten paces wide and deep, packed with stacks of crates and barrels, all perfectly preserved. A clear path led from the stairs to an arched door at the back of the room. Volkov lightly thumped a couple of the barrels along one wall with his hammer, the sound making it clear that they were full. "Ale? Goblin beer?" He raised one eyebrow at Graves, who grinned.

"At least we'll be able to celebrate properly if we live through this quest."

"Eyes on the prize, gentlemen." Lazar motioned toward the doorway. He moved to stand in front of it, waiting for Graves to take up position to one side. Chin and Lissa both cast light globes and stood ready to push them through the door when it opened.

Graves took a deep breath, readied his shield and sword, and nodded at Lazar, who promptly twisted the knob and pulled the door open, stepping back as he did so. Graves shifted over to crouch in the doorway even as the globes passed over his head.

As the lights revealed the contents of the room, Graves' eyes widened, and he screamed like a little girl. "Close it! Close the door!" He took several steps back to clear the opening, eyes never leaving whatever he saw inside. "Close the goddamned door right now!" he screamed at Lazar, who shoved the door closed as soon as Graves was clear.

"What the hell was in there?" Lazar asked the tank, who was now leaning with his back against the closed door, panting, a panicked look in his eyes. "Was it rats?"

"Rats of unusual size?" Chin added, smiling. When no one reacted, he frowned, but let it go.

"Spiders." Graves whispered, still breathing hard, beads of sweat forming on his forehead. "Friggin spiders."

"Is that all?" Chin asked. He stepped toward the door. "Open it back up. I'll toss in a few fireballs, melt the little buggers into lumps of carbon. Nice scream by the way, big guy. I wish I had recorded that!"

Graves' eyes widened again, and he pointed his sword toward Chin. "Keep back!" When Chin halted and took a single step back, Graves added, "Spiders bigger than you. I saw three big red and black spiders. They filled up the room. Three of them. Those pinchy things on their faces could fit around one of those barrels."

"Uh, okay..." Chin took another step back. "I hear ya. Maybe not so easy. But we can do this! We just need a plan."

"A plan that don't include me." Graves pushed away from the door and started toward the stairs. "My ass is gonna go hang out with Progenitor. Maybe get a taste of whatever was in that giant-ass bottle he pulled out. Y'all have fun." He stopped when he reached the stairs, then turned and sat on them. "On second thought, Chin the tough guy, I wanna hear what your scream sounds like when you stick your head in there." He sheathed his sword and set his shield so that it leaned on the railing.

"Come on Graves. They're just big bugs. We can squash 'em and be back upstairs in no time." Mejia held out a fist to bump, and Graves just stared at him.

"Maybe you didn't hear me. There are fucking spiders in there the size of a fucking compact car. They looked at me with those million beady eyes and drooled like I'm bacon."

"Ooh! Maybe they taste good? Spider legs are a delicacy in lots of fantasy stories." Chin piped in.

Lazar growled, "Not helping, Chin." as he walked over and took a seat on the stairs next to Graves. "Look, man. I know you've seen a lot of the same horrible shit I have, in the bad old days, back in the world. And things have been a little stressful the last few days. If you truly can't bring yourself to face these spiders, I get it. We'll handle it without you."

Graves shook his head, staring down at his feet. "It's spiders, man. Great big straight out of my nightmares fucking man-eating devil spiders." He took a couple very deep breaths, trying to calm himself. Eventually a grin crept across his face. "Can't we just poison Chin's ass and toss him in there? Wait like an hour till they're dead, then go loot?"

"Hey!" Chin pretended to be hurt. "I'm barely bite-sized for one of them. If anybody should be tossed in there to be spider smorgasbord, it should be you, you lanky asshole." Graves' grin grew a little wider.

Lissa shyly offered, "If it would make you feel better, I'm happy to summon my golem and send him in there first. Let the spiders chew on him for a while."

Still shaking his head, Graves got to his feet and hefted his shield. "That would be a big help, thank you lil lady." He looked to Mejia next. "This would be a perfect place to send in Leroy, too. That fast lil bastard should be able to keep one of them busy, chewin' on their ankles n shit." Mejia nodded and immediately summoned his gremlin.

With a resigned sigh, Graves walked back toward the door. "You people owe me big for this. Huge. I'm talking drinks for life, firstborn children, epic shit." He raised his voice and shouted toward the stairs. "And Progenitor, if you can hear me, this shit ain't right!"

Readying his sword and shield, he crouched down again and nodded at Lazar. This time when the door was flung open, he still screamed like a pre-teen girl, but he did it while stepping forward into the room.

Right behind him, Lazar couldn't help but cringe a little when he saw the monsters. The spiders stood taller than him, with bodies a good four feet wide left to right, and heads the size of beachballs. Their mandibles clicked together as they all turned to focus on a still screaming Graves.

Mutated Wolf Spider
Level 11
Health: 3,000/3,000

After blinking a few times, and hearing Chin somewhere behind him say "Holy shitballs", Lazar gathered his wits and began casting. He hit the nearest spider with his gravity spell, and watched as it strained against the effects. All eight legs bent, and the body lowered nearly to the floor just as Graves stepped forward and slammed his shield into its face.

The blow knocked the straining spider off balance, and it tilted backward just a few inches. But the momentum was enough to make it lose its footing, and it succumbed to the gravity magic as one of its left legs snapped. The body slammed to the floor and remained pinned there. Lissa's golem trudged forward and slammed both fists down on the spider's body, creating small spiderwebs of cracks under each one.

The others rushed into the room, crowding the space between the door and the first spider. On either side of them were sturdy looking rows of wine racks, filled with dusty bottles. Lissa, Fletcher, and Volkov all attacked the downed spider, the first two with their halberds' pointed spear tips. The Russian slammed his weighted hammer down on its head, cracking the chitin exoskeleton under the blow. A second hit glanced off one of the mandibles on its face, and the pained keening of the giant insect drowned out Graves' repeated screams.

Chin cast a fireball over top of the downed spider into the face of the one behind it, just as it began to crawl over top of the first. Thousands of tiny hairs covering the spider's head and legs caught fire, and it too screamed as it spun around and retreated deeper into the wine cellar. Mejia fired arrows one after another in rapid succession into its exposed rear as it fled. Each arrow sank deep, disappearing into the monster's body. He sent Leroy to harass the monster as it retreated, the little goblin happily tearing off at top speed around the first spider's legs.

Volkov, now standing shoulder to shoulder with Graves and the golem at the front, began belting out a battle song in Russian. None of the party understood the words, but the cadence and rousing tone had a positive impact. They began working more in unison, and Graves stopped screaming. Instead he roared at the pinned spider in front of him, and went into a frenzy of shield bashes and sword thrusts.

The spider, far from giving up, gave a mighty heave, its legs pushing it up high enough that it was able to latch on to the golem's head with its mandibles. Falling back down, it dragged the golem with it, the stone creature's fists pounding away even as it fell. The spider squeezed harder as it lay prone, and with a loud crack, the golem's head burst into pieces. Lissa winced at the loss of her summons, then cried out, "It's on cooldown, I can't call another one!"

As Volkov finished the next enthusiastic stanza of his song, he delivered a mighty overhand blow, increasing the weight of the hammer until he nearly lost his grip. The hammer's head smashed through the spider's chitin and splattered its brain. The monstrous creature stopped straining against Lazar's spell, twitched twice, and went still.

"Right on!" Graves shouted, stabbing the thing once more in the face.

"See, that wasn't so bad. One down, two to go!" Chin called out from the doorway where he stood next to Doc.

Graves and Volkov both climbed up and over the spider corpse, shields raised and eyes darting about the room as they advanced. The others pushed ahead as well, Lissa making a disgusted face as she tried not to step in any spider brain splatter. She gave the corpse of her golem a sympathetic pat as she passed by.

Chin and Doc were just stepping down off the corpse at the back of the pack when Doc let out a terrified scream that was almost instantly cut short. The entire party turned to see one of the massive spiders falling atop her, having dropped from atop one of the wine racks, or possibly the ceiling.

Chin was knocked to the side, bouncing off a wine rack on his way down, but Doc was completely buried under the spider's body.

A quick check of his party icons showed Lazar that she was down to less than a third of her total health, but still alive. "Move that thing off her!" he shouted, pushing forward through the group. The moment his path was clear he hurled his halberd at the spider, which was getting back to its feet. The heavy weapon slammed into its chitin shell, and glanced off. But the force of the impact caused it to stagger slightly. Lowering a shoulder, he slammed into its body between the two center left legs. Grunting with the effort, he heaved with his legs, back, and arms, trying to tip the monster up and off of Doc's pinned body.

A moment later both Graves and Volkov slammed their shields into it on either side of him. The three men's combined momentum and System-improved strength pushed the body up and over, turning the spider onto its back. The second she could see Doc underneath, Fletcher grabbed an ankle and began to pull their healer free. Doc groaned as she slid across the stone floor, her eyes closed and a pained look on her face.

"I think myyy leg is brrroken. And sommme ribs." Her voice was flat, slurred, and barely audible. Fletcher cast a heal on her, then lightly slapped her face a few times.

"Wake up, Doc. Heal yourself. We're still in this fight!" She looked over Doc's shoulder to see the second spider was already back on its feet and smashing its mandibles against Graves' shield. She pulled a water bottle from her storage and emptied it on Doc's head. "C'mon Doc! Doc!" She cast another heal on their healer, wishing she had leveled the spell up more than she had.

Doc blinked a few times, and her eyes focused. She nodded once, then cast a heal on herself. Leaving her to it, Fletcher turned back to the fight and cast her magic drill spell at the spider's face, hoping to hit one of the myriad eyes and get some penetration. Her spell struck chitin, glancing off to one side, ruining two eyes as it sped away to shatter a wine bottle on the shelf behind it. The spider screamed in pain, rearing up on its back legs, then slammed the razor sharp tips of its front legs down at Volkov and Graves.

Both men managed to get their shields up to block the attacks, and Lazar had the presence of mind to tilt his reclaimed halberd up towards its exposed belly just before it began its downward motion. He planted the butt of his weapon on the floor, then slammed his foot up against it to hold it in place. The composite shaft bent slightly under the weight of the falling spider, then the sharp point punctured the join just behind its head. The spearhead disappeared inside the body, and Lazar lost his grip on the shaft when the spider reared back up again.

Arrows pounded into its underbelly as both Volkov and Graves slammed their shields into it. Lazar jumped forward and grabbed hold of the wobbling halberd shaft, pushing at the spider. Once again it tipped over to land on its back. Volkov moved forward, pushing down on its body with his shield as he bashed at it with his hammer, breaking one leg, then another. Graves hacked and slashed at it like a madman, while Lazar, having lost hold of his weapon once again, went to get it back. He leapt up onto the spider's belly, grabbing hold of the now vertical halberd shaft. He grunted in pain as a sharp leg slammed into his hip, tearing his suit and the flesh underneath. Ignoring the wound, he put all his weight into pushing the shaft downward, forcing the halberd's blades deeper into the spider's body. The monster thrashed beneath him, but he managed to use the shaft to steady himself.

After what seemed like forever, one of them managed a killing blow, and the creature went still. Lazar yanked his weapon upward, causing a spray of ichor as the blades came free, then lost his balance and fell off the corpse, crying out as he landed on his wounded hip.

He felt healing magic wash over him almost immediately, and looked up to see both Lissa and Chin crouching down to check on him. Lissa murmured, "Doc's still out of commission, but she'll be here in a minute. Just hold on."

"I'm good. It's just a flesh wound." He grinned at the young woman, causing her to roll her eyes. "Where's the other spider?"

Chin shook his head. "It took off toward the back of the room. Can't see it now. Just chill for a minute, we've got your back. Chin looked down at the wounded hip and blanched, his face going white. "I can see your hipbone, boss."

Lazar didn't look. That wasn't a sight he ever wanted to see. Plus he was starting to feel a little dizzy from blood loss, and didn't want to move his head. Lissa and Chin both cast another minor heal, and the pain lessened considerably.

Just then the third spider leapt toward them, emitting a high-pitched keening sound. Volkov and Graves both raised their shields, and Fletcher began casting as Mejia resumed firing arrows at the beast. A moment later, Graves began to laugh, loudly.

"Check out Leroy! I love that lil dude!" He pointed with his shield toward the spider. The little gremlin clung to the spider's back, growling and spitting as his claws ripped at a hole he'd managed to scratch in the chitin. Each thrust and pull of his sharp claws pulled away a small chunk of the exoskeleton, and a bloody chunk of the flesh underneath. The crazed spider was spinning and jumping, trying to dislodge the little devil on its back.

The entire group, minus Lazar and Doc, went to work on the monster. Volkov and Graves bashed its leg joints with shields, slammed and slashed with hammer and sword. Fletcher cast her magic drill at its eyes, having better luck this time. Mejia fired arrows into its face, while Chin cast a fireball. Lissa covered Doc and Lazar, halberd in hand and eyes darting around the room, including up at the ceiling, looking for more spiders.

Leroy, having opened a hole wide enough, jammed his whole head into the spider's back and began to gnaw his way thru its flesh. By the time Volkov managed to finish the monster with a head shot, only the gremlin's legs were still sticking out of the hole.

Exhausted, Graves sat on the corpse of the first spider. Waving his sword at Leroy, who was still working his way deeper into the corpse, he said, "I wanna buy that little dude a drink! I like his style." He grinned at Mejia, who verbally recalled his gremlin. They both watched for a moment, and Mejia frowned when nothing happened. Then the little guy burst out of the hole in the chitin, covered in ichor and creating a spray of that resembled a whale clearing its blowhole. The moment his little feet landed, Leroy rushed back to Mejia's side, a wide and satisfied grin on his face. Both men chuckled, and Mejia patted his head despite the nastiness.

Still on the ground, Lazar grunted. "Everybody stay sharp. There could still be more. We'll take five to recover, then clear the room. Somebody put some lights on the ceiling so we can see it better."

Lissa and Chin both cast light globes up to stick on the low ceiling, causing the wine racks to cast deep shadows across the room. Everyone's eyes scanned as much of the room as they could see, and they all remained silent, listening for the click of spider feet on stone.

Lissa helped Doc to her feet, and she took the few steps necessary to reach Lazar before letting herself fall back to the floor next to him. Putting a hand over the still open wound on his hip, she cast her strongest heal.

When Lazar's wound had finally closed, Chin cleared his throat. "Uh, Doc? Got enough mana left for me?"

The entire group turned to look at Chin, who was holding his left hand over his right shoulder. He removed it long enough for them to see a deep puncture wound that was dribbling blood. "That one that dropped on us, it got me with one of its legs. I tried to heal it myself, but Lazar needed heals more, and I'm out of mana."

Motioning for him to sit by her, Doc scolded him. "You should have said something sooner! Everybody here can cast the basic heal, they could have helped you."

Chin shook his head. "I'm not dying, and the bleeding has almost stopped. You and Lazar might have needed more healing, and until a minute ago, your melon was pretty scrambled. I prioritized the two of you. Part of my job as the strategist."

Doc mumbled some half-hearted insults as she used the last of her own mana to heal Chin's shoulder. "That's it, I'm out." she called loud enough for the others to hear. "If there's any more spiders, Fletcher you're heals now."

She let herself fall back against a spider corpse, not caring about the ichor, closed her eyes and began to meditate.

There was silence for half a minute as the others continued to scan the room. Eventually Volkov began to chuckle quietly to himself. He looked at Graves standing next to him. "Chin is right. We should have recorded your screams. We could make an interwebs video thingy, make much money." He winked at his fellow tank.

Graves gave him the stinkeye, and a middle finger salute, then broke down and chuckled himself. "Screw you guys. Spiders are fucking terrifying. Giant spiders make me want to curl up and go comatose."

"Do not worry, my friend. I admire you for facing your fear. If girly screams were what was needed for you to do so, then so be it." He held out a hand, and Graves shook it.

"I'm with Volkov." Lazar grunted as he stiffly got to his feet. "I wouldn't have blamed you if you sat this one out. And I'm not sure we'd have survived this without you. Thank you, my friend." He hobbled over to shake Graves' hand.

Graves grinned at him. "Awww… does this mean you looove me?"

"Right now, it absolutely does. In ten minutes when we're upstairs and you're lookin for somebody to buy you drinks, I'll barely remember your name." Lazar winked at the tank. Looking around, he said. "Alright, five more minutes, then we finish clearing the room. We'll harvest these things when we're sure it's safe." He looked sideways at Graves, trying not to smile. "Maybe Chin is right and these spider legs are edible."

"Screw that noise." Graves shuddered. "But their shells might make decent armor. And those pointy feet would definitely make good spear points or daggers. I call dibs!"

They ended up waiting more like ten minutes, until Lazar was feeling steadier on his feet, and Doc had recovered some mana. They formed up in their standard pattern and moved forward through the wine cellar. The row they stood in ran back nearly a hundred paces to the back wall. When they got there, they turned to their right and moved to the next row, then the third and last. When they'd covered the entire room without finding more spiders, Graves led them back to the corpses near the door. Doc opened up the first one and found its orb, then per her usual procedure, had the others come inspect the corpse inside and out for any useful crafting materials. She claimed a poison sack just behind the mandibles, and the eyes, while Graves claimed the parts he'd mentioned earlier. Chin claimed the legs, not because he got any notification from his cooking skill, but because he was determined to find out if they were edible. If they were, there was a considerable amount of meat in the twenty four legs.

"Maybe it'll taste like chicken. I can cook some up, serve it to the group, and Graves will never know."

Graves opened his mouth to threaten to feed Chin his own testicles, but Mejia was faster. "I'm hoping they taste like crab legs. Stupid wyvern…"

Morale high, it didn't take them long to harvest all three spiders. Tired, covered in spider ichor, but in a good mood, they tossed jokes and insults at each other as they climbed the stairs back to the common room and confronted Progenitor.

"Well, it seems you have been victorious!" the giant Martian exclaimed. Taking in the badly damaged suits on the wounded, he added, "And it was no easy battle, I see."

"Those spiders were bigger than your bulbous head!" Graves growled up at him, scowling as he took a seat.

Ignoring the tone, Progenitor happily replied, "Indeed! While only a minor nuisance for a standard Martian, I expected you would find them appropriately challenging. Did you enjoy the battle?"

Graves eyes went flat. "Did I wha-"

Fletcher coughed loudly right next to Graves, interrupting him before he could finish what she knew might be an unfortunate reply. "The battle was very nearly more than we could manage. Doc was almost killed, Lazar and Chin badly wounded, and most of us were out of mana by the end."

"As it should be." Progenitor nodded his head. "I am impressed with your progress, and proud of all of you. Here is your reward, young ones."

Notifications popped up on each of their interfaces. The first being quest related.

Quest Complete: Clear the Creepers!
You have eliminated the mutant wolf spider infestation in the wine cellar.
Reward: *5,000 reputation; 5,000 experience; party bonus!*

The next notifications had all of them celebrating. Even Graves forgot his anger toward Progenitor, at least for a few minutes.

Congratulations!
Your reputation with Citizens of Mars has reached Respected!

Level up! You are now Level Ten! You have earned six free Attribute points.
Banked experience points will now be unlocked.

Level up!...

Level up! You are now Level Twelve. You have earned three free Attribute points.

Fletcher's pulse quickened upon seeing the number of free Attribute points she had earned. The last time she had assigned any, she was level seven. Now not only did she have three more points per level for five additional levels, but she had received the extra three points awarded at level five that had been banked, and an extra three for level ten. That gave her, and all the others, a total of twenty one free points to assign!

A thought occurred to her, and she quickly quieted the others. "We're all above level ten now, and from what Progenitor said earlier, we can select a secondary class now. And learn some related crafting skills. So, and this is a suggestion, not an order, hold off on assigning your new points until you have a better idea where you want to use them."

"Good call, boss lady." Chin agreed. "I'd also suggest that we sit and talk a while before anyone chooses a second class. Except for Doc, who wants the *Apothecary* class, which I'm sure we all agree with?" He waited as everyone nodded their heads. "The rest of us should figure out what skill gaps we have in our little group, and try to choose classes that fulfill them. For example, when we face a fight against ranged attackers, Lissa can throw up an earthen or stone wall to block them. But then we can't see the enemy, either. A class with defensive spells like magic shields would help us there. And we need both AoE attacks and heals. Fletcher is a decent backup healer, but we should see if we can improve our overall healing capacity. We also could use some kind of scout or rogue class for detecting traps, unlocking doors, and such."

The others were all nodding, and Progenitor was smiling at them.

"I am proud of you for taking the time to plan your development as a group. So many young ones of the past rushed into these decisions without much consideration.

Many of them did not survive the consequences of those decisions." He set down his empty glass and placed his hands flat on the table. "As I promised, I can now offer each of you significant training in your chosen classes. Who would like to be first?"

Chapter Twenty Eight

Second Class Citizens

As usual, Chin was the first to volunteer. "Ooh! Pick me! Pick me! He jumped up and down and waved his hand in the air like a schoolkid trying to get picked first for the cool kid's kickball team. Progenitor motioned for him to approach.

"Have you already selected a second class? Or would you prefer to train just your *Elementalist* class?"

"I've been thinking about this for a couple of days now." Chin clasped his hands together in front of him, looking up at the giant's face. Even sitting on the floor, Progenitor was much taller than him. "My first class has a lot of potential for different types of spells. And I've really been enjoying cooking for the group, experimenting with new types of meat and recipes. Plus I think food buffs could be really useful to everyone, eventually. So I think I'd like to go with a Chef class, if there is one."

"There is indeed!" Progenitor grinned at him. "The Cooking skill on its own allows you to provide pleasant tasting meals that will boost regeneration rates, providing a boon to any party. But those with the *Chef* class can create wondrous things. Even at early levels, with the right combinations of wolf spider meat and other ingredients, for example, you might prepare a dish that offers a temporary two point boost to your teammate's *Vitae*. Certain vegetables and herbs can be combined to boost *Sofia* as well. The higher your skill level, the greater the attribute increase, and the longer it lasts. At level fifty, some Chefs can create masterpieces that permanently increase an Attribute by one point. Though the ingredients for that are rare and expensive. There was a restaurant here in Atlantis where the Chef prepared and sold such meals for twenty thousand credits each. Even after purchasing the expensive ingredients, he became quite wealthy."

Chin looked around at his crewmates, all of them giving him smiles or nods of approval. "Then I would like to select the *Chef* class, and train both classes as much as possible."

Progenitor simply nodded without speaking, and reached out. He placed his hand over top of Chin's head, covering it completely, and closed his eyes. "First, the existing mage class, as it will be easier on you to absorb new spells in your existing class. I have three new elemental spells for you…"

When Progenitor was finished with Chin, the man was sweating profusely and slightly wobbly on his feet. Graves helped guide him to a chair and went to get a pitcher of water from the kitchen.

Fletcher was the next to step forward. "I'd like to train my *Arcanist* class, and I think I'd like the *Enchanter* class as well. I'm already building up my mana pool, and if Graves is going to be crafting weapons and armor, I'd like to try and improve them."

"Another good choice. Enchanted weapons can also increase their user's Attributes, as well as do increased damage, or specialized damage. For example, weapons with divine or light magic enchantments are much more effective against undead like the naga you recently faced. Likewise, enchanted armor can increase protections against physical attacks, or offer specific elemental resistances."

"If possible, I'd like to learn a spell with some area of effect damage for my *Arcanist* class." She stepped close to progenitor, then pulled over a chair, expecting to suffer the same side effects as Chin.

Progenitor grinned at the chair, and placed his hand on her head. "I think I have just the thing."

After Fletcher came Volkov. He helped her from the chair in front of Progenitor to another chair at the table, then took the hot seat. "I have a question before I choose, if that is acceptable."

"Of course it is acceptable. These are important choices, and you should be fully informed before making them. What is your question?"

"I have been working in our hydroponic lab inside our habitat, growing the plants we will need to survive in the long term." He paused for a moment, tapping his chin. "Actually, I have two questions. The first is, do you have a greenhouse here in the city that we could use to grow plants? Both for food, and for crafting ingredients?"

Progenitor looked up at the ceiling for a moment. "To my knowledge there are more than a dozen greenhouses and arboretums in the city. Though I have only visited the one in the tower in the last few millennia.

That is where I grow my own food. There is one not far from the blacksmith shop that you are welcome to use. Your second question?"

"I am interested in growing plants, in possibly increasing their growth rate and yield. But I would also like to contribute to the group's survivability during combat. In the virtual games we play, there is often a class that combines both. It is usually referred to as druid or naturalist. They combine a nature affinity with healing abilities, and sometimes shape changing, animal bonding, or related combat skills. Is there a similar class available here on Mars?"

Progenitor stared into Volkov's eyes for a moment, and the Russian could almost feel his soul being searched. It was an uncomfortable feeling, but he steeled himself against shying away.

"I see you already have a strong affinity for the land from your childhood. And for animals as well. There is indeed a *Druid* class, though it is not as all-encompassing as what you described. It would allow you to increase growth rates in flora and fauna, increase the potency of herbs, the productivity of fruit bearing trees, and such. There is also a healing component to the associated nature spells that, at higher levels, can be just as effective as divine healing."

"This sounds more than acceptable. I would like to become a *Druid*, please."

"I believe you will find that the *Druid* class will work well with your *Biomancer* abilities. The two classes are quite complimentary, and you may discover some surprising abilities when you combine them." Progenitor placed his hand on Volkov's head and got to work.

Doc followed Volkov, and asked about the *Apothecary* class.

"With your *Surgeon* and *Chemist* abilities, *Apothecary* would indeed be a good match. However, might I make a suggestion?"

"Please do." Doc leaned back in her chair to tilt her head up toward the giant's face.

"You have often stated you wish to create health and mana regeneration potions, items that are useful in combat. The *Alchemist* class is more… encompassing than the more specialized *Apothecary.* While you could certainly craft restorative potions using either, the *Apothecary* class is more focused on health related formulas. Curatives, restoratives, even poisons. While *Alchemists* also dabble in formulas for explosive compounds, conversion and alteration agents that create effects like temporary invisibility or elemental resistances, for example. It is a more… utilitarian skillset."

"Then I would choose the *Alchemist* class. And thank you for the advice." Doc gripped the seat of the chair with both hands and shut her eyes tightly as she prepared herself for the learning process. Progenitor smiled sadly as he reached for her head.

Graves was the next to step forward, taking a seat after helping Doc to relocate.

"Ah, our *Bulwark* who does not like rats, nor spiders." Progenitor did not smile at the big man, keeping a neutral expression. "Have you chosen a secondary class?"

Graves, slightly put off by the giant Martian's poker face, nodded once and swallowed before speaking. "I think so, but I have a question. If we choose a crafting class, do we earn experience through crafting items? Like, actual experience that can help us increase our overall level, not just our class level, if that makes sense?"

"I understand. And yes, it is possible to increase your overall level through crafting. There were those here in Atlantis who preferred not to venture out on quests and risk their lives. They instead increased their levels just as you described, as well as in other ways. As a crafter class, you will gain experience through creating new, more difficult items. But you can also gain from successful negotiations when selling your products or purchasing materials for your craft. Or from learning to use new materials, studying additional designs, and especially for creating new designs yourself. All of these things will earn you both reputation and experience points. But keep in mind, creating and selling inferior products, or overcharging your customers, could lead to negative reputation points as well. Much like insulting your benevolent and well-intentioned host." Progenitor raised one eyebrow at Graves.

"Uhm, sure. That makes perfect sense." Graves squirmed a little under the gaze. One of the first rules he learned in life was that to apologize was to show weakness. Rather than apologize for insults that he intended but never actually verbalized, he changed the subject. “Before I ask for the *Blacksmith* class, is there a more generalized class involving weapons and armor like the one you offered Doc? One that might work with my *Shaper* ability?”

“There is one particular class, but I am unsure…” Progenitor paused, pretending to think it over for nearly half a minute just to mess with the volatile youngling. “Yes, I think maybe *Soulsmith* would be an appropriate class for you. The class is focused on the *method* of crafting much more than the type of item created or the material used.”

“Right on! I got plenty o’ soul, baby! Let’s get it on!” Graves grinned up at Progenitor. His smile faded quickly when he realized the Martian wouldn’t understand the Earth reference. Clearing his throat, he added, “I would like to become a *Soulsmith*, please. And thank you for turning me on to it.”

“You are welcome, youngling.” Progenitor finally smiled as he reached for Graves, making him wonder if the learning process was about to hurt more than usual. “I recommend you start with examining the wolf spider chitin you harvested. It can be quite useful for one with the skills I am about to impart.”

Graves was surprised as he rose from his chair that the influx of information was less painful than he’d anticipated. He flashed Progenitor a grateful smile and nod as he held the chair for Lissa.

"Is it okay if I don't know yet what my second class should be?" Her eyes were wide as she looked up at Progenitor.

"Of course, child. This is not a decision to be rushed. I can merely provide training for your *Geomancer* class, and you may let me know if and when you decide on another. There is no rule requiring you to adopt more than one. Some simply choose to specialize in a single chosen class, and often become more powerful as a result. There is something to be said for focus and specialization." He reached out with one finger and gently patted Lissa's head. "I do have a skill for you that many of your class have found useful. It's called *Construction*, and it will assist you in exercising your manipulation skills to create structures." He placed his whole hand upon her head, and for her there was very little discomfort at all.

Mejia followed Lissa, getting right down to business. "I'd like to augment my Hunter class with some stealth abilities. Our group needs a scout, someone who can locate enemies before they find us, who can identify traps and help the group avoid them."

"There are a few options for performing this function. There is a general *Explorer* class, designed for solo adventurers who wish to avoid as much trouble as possible. It features several stealth abilities, as well as detecting and disarming traps, but has few offensive capabilities. The *Vanguard* class is meant to be the tip of the spear for an advancing force, though that one is heavily weighted toward melee combat. You could choose either of the standard *Thief* or *Rogue* classes. *Thief* features excellent trap detect and disarm abilities, but almost no offensive skillsets, focusing on evasion and escape in times of trouble. In the reverse, *Rogue* is focused on aggression and assassination, quick strikes from behind with blades, or stealthy murder with poison. Both risk significant penalties to your base reputation." Progenitor watched Mejia's face, not seeing a strong positive reaction to any of those choices.

"But for you I think I might recommend the *Infiltrator* class. Perfect for penetrating enemy encampments for the purpose of scouting and obtaining information. It features significant stealth abilities, as well as trap creation, detection, and disarming. Improved hearing and vision, including darksight, along with short blade skills, and I believe a speed boost ability for when you're discovered and must flee."

Mejia chuckled. "That does sound interesting. I could be the James Bond of Mars."

"More like Indiana Jones, with Leroy as your Short Round." Lazar winked at him.

"Gotta love that little dude." Graves added.

Mejia took a couple seconds trying to decide if Graves meant Short Round or Leroy, then decided it didn't matter. "I trust your recommendation, Progenitor. I'd like my second class to be *Infiltrator*."

Progenitor obliged, pushing the required knowledge into Mejia's head, along with updated skills and abilities for his *Hunter* class. When he was done, he added one last thing. "You will find that now that you have achieved level ten and unlocked your experience, a portion of that experience can be shared with your summons. It will level up at a pace commensurate with your own. Also, you now have the ability to have a second summons, though you can only have one active at any given time."

Mejia gave an unsteady fist thrust into the air. "That's amazing!" he paused for a second, looking at Graves. "Too bad I didn't have that before that last quest. I could have gotten a spider summons."

"Only if you wanted me to kill it every time it appeared." Graves shuddered and glared at him.

Lazar approached the chair as Mejia vacated it. Bowing his head slightly as he sat, he asked, "Since I already need to invest in *Aura* for my *Guardian* class, I was wondering about other classes for which that is the primary Attribute."

"There are many, child." Progenitor started to tick off fingers as he named a few. "There are the obvious choices like *Politician, Merchant, Cleric, Priest, or Paladin.* Lesser known and less popular options include *Government Worker, Teacher*, and *Bard.* Are any of those of interest to you?"

"You should totally be a bard!" Chin shouted from somewhere in the kitchen. "Not!"

"None of those sound like what I'm looking for, Progenitor. I was thinking of a more combat oriented, less religious class. No offense. I know you're considered a god…"

"Only by primitives who don't know any better. And I attempt to discourage that whenever possible. No offense taken." Progenitor thought about it for a moment. "There is the *Vanguard* I mentioned earlier, for which *Aura* does factor in. You would be the shining, intimidating front line charging toward your enemy. But again, it is a mainly melee class…" He snapped his fingers, the loud noise causing everyone else in the building to flinch. "I have it! The *Spellsword*! While *Aura* is not its main Attribute, it benefits greatly from it. A heavy investment in *Sofia* for mana pool and spell power, and *Vis* for weapon wielding would benefit both your *Guardian* and *Spellsword* classes. Also, *Spellsword* specializes in battles against multiple foes, being most effective in large scale battles."

"Giving me some AoE spells, presumably." Lazar nodded. "Sounds like the one for me! Thank you, Progenitor."

When Progenitor was finished training Lazar, and Lazar was recovering, the Martian called everyone back to the table.

"We have a few more items to discuss before I leave you. First, as I promised before you undertook the quest." He tossed a small object to each of them. "This is the improved translation matrix you requested. With these, you should be able to read and understand multiple languages, including Naga." He smiled at Doc.

Lissa looked at the object in her hand, roughly the size of a small gumball. "How do we use it?"

"Simply swallow it, and it will assimilate itself into your body."

All of them followed his instructions, tossing the items into their mouths and swallowing. Lissa needed a drink of water to accomplish it, but it went down easily enough.

"Good! Now the last item. Your wolf spider quest description mentioned a party bonus. Since you cleared this building of its infestation, have all exceeded level ten, and have been sleeping and eating here already, I hereby grant your party ownership of this Inn." He paused and held up a finger. "There are, however, a few conditions you must meet. First, you must form a corporation, or a guild, to serve as the ownership entity. Second, you must set aside a few barrels of gnomish ale for me. I remember being quite fond of this establishment's ale when it was open." He winked at Fletcher.

"A guild!" Chin was on his feet, pacing. "Way more fun than a moldy old corporation. In fact, since we're the first new Martians, I say we ban corporations altogether! Look how they've ruined Earth. And you know those bastards pushed for us to be murdered when they heard we assimilated. Plus-"

"Chin!" Fletcher interrupted his babbling. "Take a breath. A guild is fine." She turned to look up at Progenitor from the opposite end of the table. "And we would be happy to provide you with gnomish ale, as soon as we figure out where it is."

"What should we call the guild?" Lissa asked as Progenitor started to get to his feet. The giant settled back down, curious to hear the discussion.

"I still vote for Underpants Gnomes." Chin grumbled quietly, getting eyerolls from Graves and Volkov.

"It should be something that reflects who we are, or who we want to be." Lissa suggested.

"But it should still be cool." Mejia interjected. "I mean, if we're going to live a few hundred years, we could be stuck with the name for a very long time. Plus, we don't want to embarrass ourselves with other Martians we might meet." He looked up at Progenitor. "Are there other Martians here? Other than yourself?"

Progenitor shook his head, his voice sad when he answered. "Not on this world, not since the exodus. Though there are some of my progeny, and a few refugees from Mars on your Earth. Or there were. I have not heard from them since around the time your ancestors began to worship my grandchildren." His eyes unfocused for a moment, clearly remembering. "However, should we accomplish the goal of restoring Mars, I'm sure many of the displaced Citizens' descendants would return."

"Why is that?" Lazar was doubtful.

"With Mars restored, and Earth nearly ready to join the Collective, there would be great opportunity here. Land

and resources to be claimed, experience to be earned, a growing market for goods and services. And with Atlantis preserved as it is, growth would happen quickly. Imagine discovering a new frontier on your Earth, but with a whole city already constructed and awaiting residents."

"Nearly ready to join the Collective?" This time it was Chin that asked, his tone much more serious than normal.

"The dominant species on a planet, in this case humans, must reach a minimum level of technological or magical development before their world is deemed ready to join the Collective. Otherwise they would be subjugated or even enslaved by off-world colonists so much more advanced as to seem like gods. Human society has unfortunately already received a taste of this from my offspring. Part of the reason we fought."

Graves thumped the table. "I changed my mind about post-humans as a name. We're not human anymore, no point in pretending we are. How bout Reboot Rangers? Or… Mars Militia?" When they all just stared at him, he shrugged. "So I suck at naming things. Sue me."

"Masters of Destiny?" Lissa offered. "Wait, I think that might be a song title."

"How about New Atlanteans?" Fletcher put forward.

There was silence, several of the group nodding as they considered the name, Chin being the most enthusiastic. "It's no Underpants Gnomes, and quite literal, but I like it.

"All in favor?" Lazar raised a hand, as did all the others.

Fletcher looked up to Progenitor. "We will be the New Atlanteans Guild, if that's alright with you."

"Quite appropriate. Now for the formalities." He blinked once, and Fletcher received a notification.

> ***Congratulations, Guild Leader!***
> ***You have elected to form an Adventurer's Guild.***
> *The Guild name you have selected is New Atlanteans. You must assign at least two Guild officers, and all members must agree to the terms of the Guild Charter, within one solar day. Failure to do so will result in dissolution of the Guild, and loss of reputation. The formation fee of 10,000 credits has been waived by the Administrator. Do you wish to proceed?* ***Yes/No***

Before she confirmed the choice, Fletcher blinked away the notification and addressed the table. "I've been given the chance to form the guild, as guild leader. We should talk first about who should be guild leader."

"It has to be you." Lazar spoke up immediately. "We can't have you as mission commander and someone else potentially contradicting your orders as guild leader."

Chin shook his head. "Do we really even have a mission anymore? I mean, Earth hasn't just written us off, it has decided to murder us. If we continue the mission, we're just putting more money in the pockets, and power in the hands, of the assholes that want us dead."

Fletcher was about to respond when she decided to hold her tongue and hear what the others had to say. This was an important issue that needed to be addressed.

Lazar let out a long exhale. "You're right. And a big part of me feels exactly the same as you do. Like, screw those assholes, let's just live our lives here, defend ourselves when we need to." He saw a few of the others nodding along. "Except that we're not just up here for them. There are a few billion too many people on Earth, and they're eating up its resources at an unsustainable rate. We're here to help *them*, not the governments and corporations that, yes, will profit off our efforts."

"What resources?" Progenitor asked.

"I'm sorry?" Lazar looked up at him, surprised at the question.

"What resources can you find here that will save your species on Earth?"

Lazar blinked a few times. "Well, that's part of what we're here to find out. Precious metals, certainly. Arable soil. We could potentially grow huge fields of-"

"Crops?" Progenitor interrupted. "Assuming you could do so, would any of them still be viable after the long trip back to Earth? Maybe you mean grains, for making bread? Do you have ships large enough to carry sufficient grain, for example, to feed billions?"

"Not at the moment, no." Lazar admitted, his gut beginning to churn.

"Let's assume you could grow, and transport, sufficient quantities to make a difference for your people. What would it cost them? Are your governments and corporations going to give it away for free? Or would they try to recoup their production and transportation costs, even make a profit. How much would bread from Mars cost an average Earthling?"

"Well, shit." Graves mumbled. "I never considered any of that."

Chin's fingers drummed on the table. "They came to us with their 'save the world' speech, and a chance to go to Mars, and I jumped right in. I focused on the mission details, our short term goals of getting here, and the slightly longer term goals of setting up a colony. Then returning to Earth as a hero. I never even considered what a colony could actually accomplish."

"The long term goal was to figure out how to terraform Mars, to make it habitable and productive." Fletcher spoke softly, her mind reeling. "But the same question applies. Are they planning to build a fleet of ships big enough to relocate a billion people here? How long would that even take, and what kind of resources?"

Volkov growled. "I too was distracted by the honor, duty, and the adventure, of the mission. But now... I think we are here to find precious metals that will feed the tech corporations, who in turn feed the politicians. There would be no way to transport enough people here to make a difference." His frown deepened. "But there would be room for the rich, the elite."

"Oh, hell no." Graves slammed a hand down on the table. "You're saying we'd be creating a new home for the same assholes that are leaving us here to die."

"I am merely speculating, but yes, that is what I'm saying."

Fletcher felt stupid, betrayed, and angry all at once. Why hadn't she seen all of this? Why hadn't any of them? They just trotted along like children following the Pied Piper, all the way to Mars. Her training kicked in, and she took charge.

"Look, folks. We obviously need to do some serious thinking, and discuss this some more. But right now we have less than a day to make some decisions about the guild. My notification says we need to create and execute a charter before this time tomorrow. Let's deal with that, then we can take on the larger issue once we've all had some time to think."

Lissa raised her hand. "I agree that you should be guild leader. You just showed us why." She gave Fletcher a sad smile.

Chin nodded. "You're the most experienced gamer among us, mostly because you're old." He winked. "And I think you mentioned that you ran a VR guild before, yes?"

"Yes, twenty years ago. A guild in a fantasy VR with about two hundred members." She didn't add that she'd hated every day of it. If these people needed her to lead, well that was what she'd signed up for anyway, wasn't it?

"I'm good with you as guild boss, boss." Mejia chimed in.

The others agreed, and it was unanimous. "Alright, I'll lead the guild. Now, let's talk about the charter. Chin, got any snacks in the kitchen? This could take a while…"

Progenitor, after deliberately breaking the crew's faith in their mission, and further alienating them from the powers that be on Earth, had been about to offer them some hope. But he was too slow, and Fletcher stole the moment he'd been waiting for. She redirected their attention on a goal they could accomplish quickly, impressing him in the process.

He quietly got up and excused himself, leaving the tavern. "No matter, there is time." he said to himself as he walked up the street. It was time to feed the wyvern.

Chapter Twenty Nine

Mutiny!

A week passed in the underground Martian city. The guild was formed, the charter agreed upon surprisingly quickly. The group had all been guild members before, and had each offered suggestions for rules from their old guilds, and the accompanying penalties for breaking them. Though in this case, real world penalties were much harsher than in-game spankings. As they were mostly alone on their new world, the most serious penalties were for crimes against each other.

The guild settled more firmly into the rooms upstairs, making several trips back and forth from the hab module, gathering their personal belongings and transferring them to their new quarters. They took all their worm meat, and a little over half of the mission rations that they would have consumed over the three months before *Hyperion II* arrived. They left the rest, and all the extras that Skippy had sent down, for the other crew. Unlike the humans, they had the ability to purchase more food using essence orbs if necessary.

Volkov and Fletcher had gone to investigate the greenhouse Progenitor had directed them toward. They found it at the end of an alley just a few doors down from the blacksmith shop. When their pendants granted them access, and Volkov opened the door, both had their weapons ready in case there were unexpected inhabitants.

What they found was a surprise in more ways than one.

First, the interior was huge. From the outside, it looked to be a standard warehouse, one story tall and unassuming. But inside… directly before them sat a wide ramp leading down one level to the greenhouse floor. On either side of the ramp was a landing that was covered in parked pushcarts, tool bins, and what looked like water or chemical tanks. At the bottom of the ramp was the greenhouse floor itself. Hanging from the ceiling were dozens of bright lights, each resembling a tiny sun, the combined light making the two of them blink rapidly.

The space was… the only word Fletcher could think of was *immense*. Volkov began to chuckle almost as soon as they entered. "It's bigger on the inside." He grinned at Fletcher, who snorted. "I think maybe there is enough room to grow tomatoes, no?"

"Tomatoes, corn, a friggin apple orchard…" Fletcher shook her head. She could barely make out a second ramp in the distance, leading down another level. "You could grow food for several hundred people in here." She took in the lush plant life that flourished everywhere she looked.

"More." Volkov corrected. "Come, call the others. This place is too large for the two of us to clear."

Fletcher did just that. It took about ten minutes for the others to drop what they were doing and join them. She got a kick out of watching their faces when they entered the building.

“Holy shit.” was Graves’ initial reaction, and the others pretty much agreed. “This place is…” He gazed out over the massive floor below. There were dozens of neat, orderly sections of plants, each section stretching away toward the back at least a hundred yards. In between were stone walkways wide enough for three of the carts to roll side by side. Just the first level had to be at least two acres.

“Yeah.” Fletcher agreed. “We need to walk every foot of this place. Plenty of room for hostile critters to be roaming around. It won’t be safe to work in here until we clear it.”

“This would be a great place to get some exercise. You could run miles in here, and work on your tan.” Mejia ventured, taking a deep breath. “It smells nice, like flowers and dirt and… cinnamon?”

“I think it smells like wolf spiders.” Chin poked Graves with an elbow, then leapt away before the big man could swing at him. All of them took a moment to carefully study the well-lit ceiling, looking for spiders.

Volkov, who had wandered over to look at the large tanks, said, “This one says fertilizer.” He pointed to writing on the outside of the tank. Writing which they could all read now, thanks to their translation matrixes.

Mejia looked from the tank to the plants below, taking in the healthy looking greens, reds, yellows, and rainbow of other colors. “I’d say it works pretty damn good.”

“Maybe it’s like, leftover alien poo, ground up gremlin, or something.” Chin mused, still keeping a safe distance from Graves. Mejia gave him a dirty look, then ignored him.

They formed up and moved down the ramp, all of them keeping a wary eye out for critters leaping out of the foliage. Taking their time, they walked to the end of the main row, finding that the ramp there led down to a second, equally large level.

Lissa pointed upward, looking first at the ceiling above the lower level, then the one above them at the top of the ramp. “Is it just me, or is the light down there a different color?”

“Da.” Volkov agreed after a moment, his face breaking into a smile. “Different plants, different light.”

“I’m betting there are hundreds of alchemy ingredients growing in here.” Doc’s eyes were darting from plant to plant. “Not just food. This place is a crafting resource gold mine.”

“Great! You just got volunteered to help Volkov run this place. It’s too big for him alone. And I don’t want anyone going anywhere solo until we know what might be wandering around outside besides that wyvern.”

“I volunteer too.” Lissa raised her hand briefly. “I don’t have a crafting skill yet, so I have time to help out. And I looove this place!”

It took them over an hour to walk each of the rows up and down both levels, peering into the greenery and occasionally shaking the leaves, making plenty of noise to attract any predators. When they were reasonably sure there was nothing dangerous lurking inside, they left Volkov, Doc, and Lissa to figure out where to start. It would take them days, maybe weeks just to identify what all was growing in the greenhouse.

Graves and Fletcher had spent much of their time in the blacksmith shop. Graves in the back, working at the forge, while Fletcher sat on a stool behind the long counter and worked on her enchanting. She had to spend a couple of their higher level orbs, finding out that even low level enchanting materials were expensive.

Chin spent hour after hour in the kitchen, determined to create a food buff before they went on their next quest. He occasionally drafted Mejia or Lazar to assist him with meal prep, and both of them managed to learn the cooking skill as well, though they didn't level it much. When those two weren't helping Chin boost his cooking skill, they elected to explore the city.

Mejia's *Infiltrator* class featured an extra mapping ability that created an extremely detailed rendering of the places he traveled. Not just a two-dimensional map, but one that included building heights, floorplans for the buildings he actually entered and explored, as well as direction and distance. At the end of their first day of exploring, he found he was able to share that map with the others, and they could pull it up on their interfaces.

Mejia brought Leroy with them, the little gremlin trotting along next to Mejia as they walked down the street, stopping to check out and label each building. They made their way in circles around their guild headquarters, moving out a block each time they completed a circuit. By the end of the week they had maybe a quarter mile square around their home fully mapped, as well as a few random routes through other parts of the city that they had investigated.

They'd found a general goods store that carried a wide array of stock, from camping gear to tools, cloth and sewing supplies, cooking utensils and crafting materials. Mejia found a bow that was more attractive looking, but didn't have stats as good as the one he'd already purchased. Lazar was focused on some thick leather boots with steel toes that he could picture himself using to shatter spider chitin with a single kick. Neither of them made a purchase, but they marked the store to bring the others back to visit.

The area around their headquarters was mainly light commercial, full of one or two story shops, restaurants, a couple more inns, a bank, and such. Many of the buildings they explored featured a storefront or crafting shop in the main room, and a living space either in the back, or upstairs. There were even a few small parks with open grass and low-standing trees that Lazar thought looked like oversized bonsai gardens.

They also discovered that their headquarters had a wide fenced-in yard behind it. There was a gate near the back door that led to the alley, presumably for deliveries. In one corner near the building sat a deep fire pit with grates across it, and a massive spit mounted above, the setup large enough to cook an entire pig, or a similar sized Martian animal. There was a pair of fruit trees in the back left corner bearing a fruit that Progenitor confirmed was safe to eat, calling it aptha. They most closely resembled plums, and he'd informed them that the previous owners of the tavern had fermented the fruit to make a delicious aptha brandy. Hearing that, Lazar began spending time searching the building for a recipe.

Though Progenitor visited them briefly each day, usually during or right after breakfast, he did not present them with any additional quests in that week. When asked, he told them to make themselves comfortable, practice their crafts and new spells, to unwind a bit. An opportunity which they all appreciated, and needed, whether they knew it or not.

*****

Stella rode in the back of a limo sent by her boss. She'd been called to a meeting at network headquarters. Her boss, and his bosses, were sure that she knew more than she was publishing, and Stella knew they were going to push her to come out with it. Not that she was going to oblige. She couldn't spill the beans for the sake of the planet, and it wasn't like they were going to fire her. Even if they did, a competing network would snatch her up immediately, probably at twice the salary. Exclusives on the story of the century were valuable. It was always about money, these days.

"You okay, Stella?" Lang asked her from the side seat that ran perpendicular to hers.

"What? Yes, I'm fine." She half-snapped at him, blinking rapidly as she broke out of her contemplation of current journalistic standards. "Why?"

"You were making a face like you have the shits, or something." Rene explained for her partner. "And not just like the 'I could use an antacid' kind of face. You had a full-on 'we might need to pull over someplace with a clean bathroom' look going."

"Ha!" Stella grinned at the pair. They had quickly become her favorites among the security detail that lived and worked in her new home. Looking at them and how comfortable they were with each other, the way they finished each other's sentences sometimes, she wondered yet again if they were sleeping together. She never asked, because she didn't want to make things awkward. "No, if I had the shits, you'd have needed to roll down a window before now. No, I was considering how to deal with money hungry execs with little or no moral fiber."

"We got you." Lang gave her a wicked grin. "Just yell for help when you're tired of their shit, and we'll come in shooting. Nobody will question it. Though the paperwork will suck."

"Anybody you want shot in a particularly painful way?" Rene asked. "Like, maybe some dude who tried to get in your pants, and deserves a shot in the junk?"

Stella actually considered it for a moment before shaking her head, giving them a grin of her own. "As tempting as that sounds, they haven't reached the death sentence level of annoyance, yet."

"Don't let them force you to reveal your source!" Rene frowned. "They always try to do that on the old holovids. Putting reporters like you in jail till you cough up a name."

"That's the courts, Rene, not news networks. The news guys are the ones who bail out the reporters with an army of lawyers n shit."

"Technically, you guys work for the network" Stella pointed out.

Lang shook his head. "No ma'am. The network does *pay* us, but we *work* for you."

"Yep." Rene nodded. "If we walk in there today and they tell us to shoot you, we absolutely say no. Unless they offer us a really seriously obscene buttload of cash. I'm talkin' buy your own private island kind of payola." She winked at Stella, who snorted.

"I wouldn't blame you one bit."

Rene's expression sobered a bit. "Nah, you're a tough old broad who speaks her mind and stands behind what she says. We respect that. All of us, your whole detail. Usually we get stuck with some self-involved anus leakage of a human who treats us like we're just furniture, or dogs."

"Maybe *you're* furniture." Lang shook his head at his partner. "I'm too handsome to be furniture. I'm like… artwork. A statue standing there quietly lookin' pretty but mostly ignored." Rene just rolled her eyes as Stella shifted in her seat.

"Does it seem like this ride is taking longer than it should?"

Lang looked at the window, locating the nearest street sign. "We can't just take a straight route from your place to the network building. We're taking a lot of detours, doubling back a few times, just to shake any tails or surveillance. Sorry about the delay."

Stella shrugged. "I'd much rather spend time in here with you two than sitting in a stuffy conference room. And if we're late, screw em."

Their light banter continued for several more minutes before they arrived at headquarters parking garage. Instead of the usual two uniformed parking attendants and a single guard, there were a dozen security people from the same company that employed Lang and Rene. They were stopping each car on its way in, checking ID's and running them through the system, searching cars, even looking underneath with mirrors and lights. As Stella watched, one irate man in an expensive looking suit refused the search, and was ordered at gunpoint to turn around and leave the area.

Stella's limo, on the other hand, was waved inside without delay, causing several shouts and honks from other drivers who were waiting in line. Rene grinned at her. "It's good to be da queen."

The limo pulled up directly in front of the elevator doors on the underground garage's first level. Lang exited first, visually clearing the area himself as two more armed guards reported an all-clear. He motioned for Rene to get out, and as soon as she was on her feet she turned and helped Stella out the door. They stood close on either side of her and kept in step with her for the ten steps to the open and waiting elevator car. Once inside, Lang spoke into his coms as Rene hit the button for the fifteenth floor. As soon as the car began moving, she nudged Stella over to one corner, away from the doors. They'd run through this particular drill already, her guards making it clear that if someone opened fire when the doors opened, she was to hug the corner and make herself as small as possible.

A month ago she'd have ridiculed them for such precautions. But after the attack on her office, after seeing other guards give their lives protecting her, she took every instruction seriously.

When the car stopped and the door opened, Lang and Rene had weapons ready, if pointed toward the floor. Two more guards greeted them, and they relaxed. Holstering their weapons, they motioned Stella out of the corner and into the elevator lobby. Her boss was waiting there for her, an uncomfortable smile plastered across his face.

"Stella! Good to see you again. Are these guys treating you alright?"

"Like the queen that I am." Stella gave him an equally false grin. "Let's get this over with. I feel exposed out here." She looked around, noting that she, her boss, and the guards were the only people visible in what would normally be a busy area at this time of day.

Her boss nodded, relieved at not having to make small talk. "We've set up a new room, center of the building, no windows." He tried to sound reassuring, rather than paranoid. "Right this way." He led her and her two guards through a metal doorway and a short distance down the hall. Opening a door, he stepped through first, coughing to get the room's attention. "Stella, I believe you already know everyone?"

There was a long conference table that filled most of the room, except for one end that was set up with a refreshment table, currently stocked with fresh fruit, sandwiches, several bottled sodas and waters, and coffee service. Around the table sat nearly a dozen execs and attorneys, all looking up at her.

She gave them a nod. "Good afternoon everyone. Sorry if I'm late. Not getting murdered takes a little extra time these days."

"Please, sit." Her boss cleared his throat, uncomfortable. "Can I get you a drink? Something to eat?"

"Don't you have about a thousand interns in this building for that?" She asked as she took the offered seat near the center of the long table.

"The content of this meeting is highly classified." One of the attorneys explained, as if it weren't already obvious to everyone why there were no interns in the room. Stella wasn't sure whether to be amused or offended.

"Of course. And since you brought up classified information, let me see if I can save us all a little time, shall I? I am releasing all the information that I can, as soon as I can. Anything that I'm aware of and holding back, is being held back for very good reason. Reasons that I won't discuss, and that you can't overcome." She tried to meet each of their eyes as she spoke, keeping a hard but not hostile look on her face. "There! Are we good?" Behind her, she thought she heard a small snicker from Rene, but it might have been her imagination.

The network president, a man named Vega that she'd only met occasionally at office parties or newsworthy functions, shook his head. "I think you know that we're not good, Stella." He got up from his seat at the head of the table. "The people have a right to know what's going on."

"They really don't." Stella wished she'd taken her boss up on a drink. She had considered dropping enough hints, without actually saying anything, to give these people a solid idea what she was holding back. Still undecided, she looked over her shoulder at Lang, then down at the refreshment table. Taking the hint, he went to get her a beverage. He knew what she liked.

"Don't throw a bunch of bullshit at me, Vega. I've been in this business longer than you have. There are some things that *the people*" she held up both hands to make air quotes "shouldn't know for their own damn good." She accepted a glass from Lang and nodded her thanks, taking a sip before continuing. "When a family with kids are gruesomely murdered, body parts strewn around, nailed to the walls, with teeth marks in them, we don't report all that shit. We stick to the basic facts, and for good reason." She enjoyed the grimace on Vega's face as he sat back down.

"I'm not confirming that I know anything more than I've shared. I want that clearly understood. But if I hypothetically knew something that might cause riots, for example, what good would it do to publish it? And how much harm would it do?"

A woman Stella thought was probably one of the attorneys spoke next. "But if you have information regarding a threat to us, to the public in general, you have a duty to-"

Stella raised a hand to interrupt her. "First, no I don't. And even if I did, I am not currently aware of any imminent threat to you, or the general public. Other than the possibility that you might try to force me to release classified information that *would* cause harm, all in the name of the almighty dollar." She flashed her most insincere smile at the woman. "That would be very dangerous for you, me, and everyone in this room."

"Why are you being difficult, Stella?" Vega's voice dropped an octave along with his eyebrows as he frowned down the table at her.

"Maybe you missed the memo about my office upstairs exploding? Your summons for this meeting forced me to risk my life, and the lives of my detail, as well as who knows how many innocent bystanders. I could just have easily attended this meeting via holo from the secure safehouse where I've been hiding for the last week or so. But you folks thought it was more important that I be here so that… what? Your frowny face and disappointed tone might somehow change the answers you already knew I was going to give you?"

"We didn't mean-" the first attorney started to utter what was sure to be a standard disclaimer.

"You mean didn't bother to *think.*" Stella cut him off. "Or didn't care. Either way, this has been a waste of everyone's time, and a threat to my safety, so yeah… I'm a little grumpy."

The room was silent, not even a snicker from Rene this time. Stella's boss let out a much aggrieved sigh as he sank back in his chair and tried to avoid notice. Finally, Vega shook his head. "I apologize, Stella. You are correct. We had hoped a face to face meeting might convince you to cooperate."

"If you knew what I know, you'd know that's not my choice to make." Stella tried her best to sound friendly. "You need to trust me. Trust that my experience, my moral compass, and my ambition will combine to provide you with as much information as I can, while still keeping us all safe. Not just us in this room, but everyone, everywhere." She placed her elbows on the table and leaned forward. "Or you can find a reason to fire me. I won't fight it."

"Let's not be hasty." Her boss actually spoke up, surprising her. "No one is talking about firing you. It's just… clear to everyone that there's more going on than you're telling us."

“There is.” She sighed, leaning back. “And when the time comes for me to share it, I’m nearly certain that you’ll have the exclusive, as you have up to this point. That’s the best I can offer you.” She looked at Vega, then at a woman she thought was from advertising. “You’ve made a shitload of money off of the stories I’ve already published. I haven’t seen the numbers, but I’m guessing your ad revenue has gone up something like… fifty percent? At some point, enough has to be enough.”

“Not nearly fifty percent.” The woman mumbled.

“Then charge more for your fucking ads during and around my stories!” Stella thumped the table, causing several people to flinch. “Double your ask. It’s not like they’re going to say no when you can pretty much guarantee that nearly every eye on the planet will be glued to their holoscreen, tuned to our network when the ads run. No one has ever been able to guarantee that kind of audience.”

“She has a point.” Vega looked at the ads lady. “Let’s discuss that next.”

“Great! So are we done? I’m feeling a little itchy outside my safe house, and you’ve got to discuss how best to fleece the big corporations.” Stella took the initiative by getting up, and nobody stopped her. Moving toward the door, Lang and Rene already opening it for her, she added, “Good to see you all. Have a wonderful day. You’ll hear from me the moment I have something more to share.”

*****

Thorne was snoring when DJ walked into his hidden cargo bay campsite. He cleared his throat loudly, then coughed even more loudly when his first attempt failed. Thorne spluttered and jerked awake, tipping slightly in his lawn chair. He blinked several times until he focused on DJ.

"Report."

"Naptime is officially over. We're ten minutes from point Charlie."

Point Charlie was the designation for the moment when they finished their final correctional burn before the long ride. The next correction wouldn't come until they approached Mars orbit in a few months. Point Alpha was the start of the acceleration burn, when DJ was to murder Thorne. Point Bravo was when they faked his airlock funeral and hid him in the cargo bay. Straightening up in his chair, Thorne grumbled, "Next time let's pick more original designators. Like Alvin, Simon, and Theodore. Maybe use stripper names."

"Roger that, boss." DJ kept his face neutral, fighting the urge to remind Thorne that he'd been the one to pick the alphabet. "You can bitch about the names some more on the way. We need to get mobile."

"Security cameras?" Thorne ducked into his tent to change from the sweats he was wearing into a uniform. For what was coming, he needed to look as official as possible.

“They’ll go down on your command. Along with coms, lights in some of the sections, and the internal alarms. Anybody pushes a panic button, they get a big fat nothing.”

“What about the crew?” Thorne had discussed this with DJ ad nauseum over the previous week, but he was nervous, and needed a little chatter while he changed. The next few minutes could mean life or death for a few of them, or even all of them, if something went disastrously wrong.

“There are six that we’re pretty sure will resist, to varying degrees. Only two of them have any kind of martial training, one of them being the commander. Another ten we’re not sure of. The rest we think will either actively cooperate, or at least not try to hinder us.”

Thorne stepped out of the tent in his uniform, the buttons and medals well polished during his long wait. He brushed off some imaginary dust, and looked up at DJ, who was wearing black combat gear over his flight suit, the helmet deactivated.

“No flight suit? There’s a small possibility that we’ll lose pressure…”

Thorne shook his head. “If we fuck things up that badly, I deserve to bite it. Let’s get moving.”

Knowing better than to argue, DJ led the way through the maze of crates toward the elevator. Two turns from their destination, he halted. “First working camera is around this corner.” He reported to his boss.

"Alright, let's do this. Kill the feeds and let's get to the bridge as fast as possible." Thorne took a deep breath and prepared to charge.

"The guards down here are ours." DJ informed him as he tapped out a code on his wrist device. "No fight until we get topside."

Thorne relaxed some, then moved into a jog right behind DJ. The two guards at the elevator saluted as Thorne approached. "Good to go, boss." they reported in unison. One of them unholstered his sidearm and offered it to Thorne, who refused.

"I'll leave the shooting to you guys, since I'm a little rusty. I'm hoping that bullshit and confidence are all I'm going to need." The other three chuckled as they piled into the elevator. Thorne's techs had done their best to address every possible contingency, and the elevator became an express, not stopping at any deck where someone might push a call button. It sped straight up to the main deck where the bridge was located. As they passed through the intervening decks, they could hear some loud voices and shouts of alarm. But thankfully no shooting or explosions.

At the main deck, two more of Thorne's people greeted them when the doors opened. "We've cleared two sections on either side of the bridge hatch, which is secured from our side. No resistance, no alarms."

"Good, follow me. Nobody shoots unless I say so, or one of them shoots first. No kill shots if you can help it." Thorne reminded them unnecessarily. They all knew their jobs.

"Take us in." Thorne looked at DJ, who pressed another key on his wrist, causing the thick door to the bridge to slide open. Thorne boldly stepped through first as behind him DJ shouted, "Attention on the bridge!"

All heads turned their way, and all eyes widened in disbelief at the sight of a dead man standing there. Out of ingrained habit more than anything else, everyone but the commander stood at attention.

Commander Thompson, a veteran of several space missions, well respected by everyone including Thorne, got to his feet more slowly. He was clearly confused, but gathered his composure more quickly than his bridge crew. "Director Thorne. What's going on?"

"I'm commandeering this ship, commander." Thorne kept his voice sharp, but not hostile. "The various red lights appearing on your people's panels are my doing. The ship is not malfunctioning, and no one is currently in danger, unless they attack my people. I would appreciate it if you would command your crew to cooperate so that no one gets hurt. Then I'll explain what's happening."

Thompson blew out an explosive exhale, his shoulders drooping slightly. "Oh, thank god. The ship is yours, Director Thorne." He pushed a button on the arm of his chair. "This is Thompson to all *Hyperion III* crew. Stand down, secure to stations. There are no malfunctions. I am ceding command to Director Thorne, who is not as dead as we thought he was. I repeat, all crew stand down and await orders."

Looking up at a surprised Thorne, he said, "I never liked our orders for this mission. Didn't want to be the guy responsible for murdering a bunch of our own people. I happily convey that burden to you, sir." He snapped a crisp salute and stepped back from his chair, motioning for Thorne to take it.

"Well, that was easier than expected." DJ commented as Thorne shook the commander's hand. Less than a second later, the sound of gunshots echoed through the corridor outside the hatch, followed by an explosion that sent a tremor through the ship.

Chapter Thirty

Deadly Things Come In Small Packages

The beast was fully awake now. Its heart pumping regularly, its limbs moving, and its limited thinking focused on one thing.

Food.

Straining muscles that hadn't moved in thousands of years, it pushed its body upward toward the faint scent of blood. Most of the way there were cracks and crevices in the stone that it could shove its way through on the journey toward the surface. Other times, it simply used its powerful claws to tear at the stone and carve a path for itself.

The work was difficult, and the creature had almost no reserves after its long sleep. But it struggled on, relentless and single-minded in its pursuit of sustenance.

*****

Mejia and Lazar had decided to finally retrieve the cargo pod that had landed in the canyon itself. They took the portal to the hab cavern and grabbed Mejia's tank, since Lazar's was still down at the dock. Mejia used his wrist unit to access the controls for the large crane up on the surface, lowering the cable enough to connect it to a rail at the top of the tank. They then drove down the ramp until they reached the end of that cable. Attaching another, they continued to the bottom and began to drive upstream.

They were passing directly under the ledge outside the hab cavern when Mejia hit the brakes. "Look there. I saw movement." He pointed toward a spot not far from the cliff base.

Tensing slightly, Lazar leaned forward to get a better look through the windshield. On the ground where Mejia had pointed, he saw something he thought he recognized. "That looks like the big worm that rolled off the ledge. Or, what's left of it. It can't still be alive after falling that far, can it?"

Mejia shrugged. "I'm not a biologist, but I don't think so? Let's go check it out."

Both of them activated their helmets as they cycled out of the tank and into the atmosphere. As they strode toward the worm corpse, both drew weapons and scanned their surroundings while trying to keep one eye on the worm.

"There!" Lazar shouted, having seen a section of the worm shift slightly. "You're right, it's moving." They stepped closer, Lazar with a halberd at the ready, Mejia with an arrow nocked. When they were within two steps of the clearly splattered worm, both men paused to watch.

Mejia ventured. "It's pretty damaged, I don't think it's alive."

"Maybe just some kind of weird muscle twitch reflex thing?" Lazar asked.

They both jumped a second later when the body twitched again. Almost immediately, Mejia gasped.

“Something’s eating it! There isn’t supposed to be life on the surface, but look!” He removed the arrow from the bowstring and used it to point as he leaned forward. “There’s… something…”

Lazar saw it too. Some sort of creature half buried under a piece of worm. He reached forward with his spear point and nudged the worm meat aside. Underneath was a creature that, at first glance, was all teeth and claws.

“It’s a water bear!” Mejia exclaimed, crouching down to get a closer look, still with his arrow in hand. “A huge one!”

“What are you talking about?” Lazar was looking at a creature that was maybe four inches long.

“Water bears! You know, tardigrades? They live on Earth, too. Only they’re usually about the size of a single grain of sand. This one is humongous!”

Lazar vaguely remembered reading about the creatures somewhere. “Makes sense, I guess. The creatures here seem much larger than their Earth counterparts. Is it dangerous? Cuz it looks dangerous.” The creature had a roly-poly body with a round mouth at one end filled with what seemed like hundreds of tiny teeth. It had six stubby legs that barely extended past its belly, each of which ended with wickedly curved claws, plus two more appendages at the rear that looked more like tail fins than legs. Its front claws were easily ripping a chunk from the frozen worm corpse.

The two of them watched for a moment as the front legs pushed the chunk of meat toward the lamprey-like mouth, which latched on and bit down, causing an audible crack from the frozen meat.

Lazar nodded in grim respect. "Strong little bugger. Doesn't seem to care that we're here."

"I don't think they have much of a brain. They're a basic organism, and can survive just about anywhere. Heat, cold, underwater, even out in space." He paused and leaned closer as if to poke at the creature with his finger. "Aren't you just the cutest little monster!"

Lazar grabbed his arm, pulling it back. "That thing might take your finger off."

"No way. I'm totally going to tame it!" Mejia grinned up at him. "My improved skill lets me tame live creatures instead of having to kill them first. Give me a minute." Mejia closed his eyes for a couple of breaths, then pulled a worm sausage from his storage. It was still warm from when he'd put it away during breakfast. "The heat should attract it, as well as the smell." He extended his arm, holding the sausage a few inches from the little monster. It immediately dropped the frozen chunk of meat it was gnawing on, and raised its head. Its tooth-filled snout twitched for a moment, and it turned its head to focus on the sausage. Surprisingly agile on its short, chubby legs, it pushed forward across the worm corpse and launched for the sausage.

Mejia held the treat still with one hand, allowing the tardigrade to take hold. It began to viciously gnaw at the much softer, warmer meat, shaking its head as it tore lose chunks to digest. Mejia made a motion with his free hand, and both of them froze.

Curious, Lazar watched the creature closely, ready to stab it if it made a move for Mejia rather than the worm sausage. Neither Mejia nor the creature moved for a solid ten seconds, then Mejia blinked. "It worked!" He smiled down at the little monster as it went back to mangling one end of the sausage. "Who's a good boy?" the man adopted the baby-talk tone most people used with pets. The tardigrade ignored him, chomping away at his meal.

Looking up at Lazar, he said, "He's an elite! For his kind, anyway. I got a notification when I tamed him that says he's a Tardigrade Alpha. I got an elite pet!"

"Good for you, brother." Lazar patted his shoulder. "He does look pretty badass. And he's certainly hungry." The creature had already consumed almost half of the sausage that was nearly as big as he was. "What are you going to name him? Smokey? Fozzy? Boo Boo?"

"Heh. Bear jokes. Good one." Mejia rolled his eyes at his friend. "I gotta think of something that's appropriately badass for this lil dude."

"Is he… safe to pick up? We need to get going if we're gonna grab that cargo and get it into the cavern before dark."

Mejia held out his hand, palm up, in front of the little monster. "Hop on, buddy." He ordered it. The creature ignored him, biting down on the sausage again.

“Guess he’s not ready for verbal commands yet.” Mejia shrugged. He grabbed the intact end of the sausage and lifted it up, the little creature rising with it as it gnawed away, its feet now hanging in the air. Mejia carefully placed it in his other hand, smiling down like a proud papa as it rolled over onto its back, gripping the sausage tightly with six of its clawed feet, and gnawed at the end with gusto.

Chuckling at the cuteness himself, Lazar motioned toward the tank, and the two men made their way back. A minute later they were back on track toward the cargo pod.

When they reached their target, Mejia set the tardigrade on one of the side seats in the tank, placing a second sausage next to the first, which was nearly gone. “You stay here, buddy.” He patted the creature on the head gently with one finger, then followed Lazar out.

It took them two hours to secure cables to the hooks atop the cargo pod, attach their crane line, and lift the pod high enough to place it on the ledge outside the hab cavern. From there they used Graves’ tank with the crane to move it inside and place it near the others.

“Mission accomplished, boss.” Lazar reported to Fletcher, who was in Graves’ shop practicing her enchanting. “And Mejia found a friend on the surface.”

“A friend?” Fletcher asked as everyone else paused what they were doing and raised their heads wherever they were, curious about any life form found on the surface.

“We’re on our way back to HQ. You’ll see soon enough.” Lazar winked at Mejia, who was holding a sleeping water bear in the palm of his hand. It had finished off both sausages, and there was an obvious bulge in its belly as it lay on its back, feet twitching idly in the air.

*****

“He’s the cutest thing ever!” Lissa practically squealed as she gazed down at the creature Mejia held out for all of them to see. “Can I pet him?”

“I don’t see why not.” Mejia held his hand closer to her, and she tentatively reached out with one finger, gently tickling the water bear’s belly. It’s legs wiggled and it curled up slightly, making Lissa giggle.

“He’s amazing! What’s his name? You *have to* name him Boo Boo!” She tickled him again. When she nudged one of his legs, a claw got caught on her glove for a second, ripping a small hole. “Oh! Sharp!” She pulled her hand back and focused some mana into her suit, repairing the hole.

Surprising all of them, the normally serious Doc was the next to reach out. “Can I… hold him?”

“I think so?” Mejia shrugged, causing the critter in his hand to wobble cutely. “He’s not very smart, and doesn’t listen to commands, so be careful. I don’t know if he’ll consider you food or not.” When Doc held out both palms cupped together, Mejia gently tilted his hand so the water bear rolled down into her hands. They all held their breath for a moment, but it didn't bite.

"He's obviously well fed, so I should be safe for a while." Doc gently poked at the tardigrade's full belly as she grinned down at him. "You know, these things are amazing. Only slightly more complex than those borer worms. It eats, it shits, it looks cute, and can survive just about any environment. They can make themselves go dormant and hibernate for literally thousands of years." She tickled his belly, laughing as the legs wiggled in pleasure.

"The info my tamer skill is giving me says he'll level up as I do, and get bigger." Mejia beamed like a proud parent. "Maybe he'll get big enough for me to ride him!"

"Oh god, I hope not." Graves shivered. "Can you imagine this thing being that big? He'd probably eat more than the rest of us combined."

"Or just eat us." Volkov smirked at Graves. "That would not be a pleasant way to die."

Lazar, seeing Graves' discomfort, piled on. "He doesn't need to get bigger than you, Graves. He could just crawl up into your ass while you sleep, eat his way through your organs to your heart. He likes warm meat."

"Fuck off!" Graves took a step back from the cute little creature despite his bravado. After a second, he noticed all the suppressed grins around him. "That shit ain't funny!" He looked at Mejia. "You need to make a leash for that thing. It can't be wandering around where somebody might step on it, or something."

Chin started laughing. "Hey! He could be a good weapon for boss fights! Just toss him at the boss, he's too small to even notice. He could crawl up inside the boss and just chew away while we distract it."

"You should name him Shit Weasel!" Graves was suddenly in a much better mood.

The others were chuckling at the offended look on Mejia's face when Progenitor walked in the door. Spotting the tardigrade in Doc's hands, his eyes widened for a moment, then shifted to Mejia.

"Ah, I see you have bonded one of the Immortal Ones. An elite as well! You are very fortunate. They are hardy companions, and considered to be good luck."

"Plus he's really adorable." Lissa beamed at the giant, who smiled back at her.

"The notification I got says he will grow with me. Do you know how big he will get?"

Progenitor shook his head. "That will depend entirely upon you. He can gain experience from kills just as you do. And as your bonded companion, he can also benefit from quest experience, just like your gremlin, if they accompany you on said quest. He will also grow when fed, though at a much slower pace. Lastly, as a druid you have growth magic." He paused for a moment, remembering. "The largest alpha I've personally seen was about the size of a gremlin, but much bulkier."

"So not a battle mount." Graves sounded relieved.

"Doesn't matter." Mejia declared. "I wouldn't care if he always stayed this size, he's awesome!" He held out his hand and Doc gently rolled the little guy back into his palm. "Maybe I'll teach him some tricks."

Fletcher pulled their attention away from the tiny water bear. "It's good to see you again, Progenitor. Have you come with another quest for us?"

"Yes, and no." he moved to take his seat, and the others did the same, Mejia placing the still sleeping tardigrade on the table in front of him. "I have come to give you information, and a long term quest that you won't be able to complete for some time." He looked around the table, the others all focused on him with anticipation.

"Your knowledge is, I believe, sufficiently advanced to understand why this world has lost most of its atmosphere?"

Volkov nodded, the first to reply. "Da. The planet's core slowed its rotation, cooling off as it did so. This weakened the magnetic field around the planet, and lessened the gravity at the same time. Solar radiation that normally would have been repelled or reduced by the magnetosphere was able to penetrate and burn off the atmosphere."

"Close enough." Progenitor nodded his agreement. "What your scientists had no way to know is the cause of the core's change." He took a deep breath. "My grandson deployed an insidious weapon. He installed it long before our conflict began, intending to use the threat of it to depose me and assume my position in this system. Always one to think far ahead, he was." He lowered his eyes and stared at his hands for a moment, a look of sorrow on his face.

"He named the device Jormungandr."

"The world serpent!" Chin cut in. "The one that is supposed to encircle Midgard and bring brutal winter, and is eventually destined to kill Thor during Ragnarok."

"So you have some knowledge of my grandchildren." Progenitor sighed. "Alas, I suspect that the legends you speak of hold little resemblance to the truth. As is often the case with legends, they grow with the telling." He placed his folded hands atop the table in front of him. "Jormungandr is a machine, not a living being. Loki constructed it in secret, and installed it around this world's molten core. Its purpose, when activated, was to restrict and cool the core, rendering the surface above lifeless. As you can see, it worked quite well."

Volkov tapped his fingers on the table. "So, a world serpent, a planet killer, child of Loki… the legends are not so far off."

"I would have disabled it, stopped the destruction myself, but I was prevented from interfering." A single tear rolled down Progenitor's cheek. "A choice was made, an agreement reached. Had I acted, Loki would have been free to destroy all life on your Earth. Life there was defenseless against him. At least here, we had the capacity to evacuate, and relatively few lives were lost."

“So Loki really is the evil bastard that the legends describe.” Graves mumbled, frowning.

“He is what you would call a psychopath. Completely self-interested, having no care for the lives of others. He feels nothing but ambition, anger, and jealousy.” Progenitor confirmed. “I should have destroyed him eons ago, but I could not bring myself to do it, much to my own shame.” He hung his head for a moment before continuing.

“I am still prevented from directly interfering in any way. However, should a group of intrepid adventurers manage to reach Jormungandr and deactivate it, I would be free to repair much of the damage it has caused.”

“World quest, baby!” Chin jumped up and danced a little jig. “Yessss!”

Fletcher ignored him, asking, “Why didn’t you send some of the citizens who were here when Loki activated the machine?”

“Many were unwilling, either to face the dangers involved in reaching Jormungandr, or to oppose Loki. Both could easily result in painful death. It was much easier to board a cityship and evacuate. Some few did take up the quest I am about to offer you, though none ever returned, nor did any complete the quest.”

“Cityship?” Lazar raised one eyebrow at the term.

“You sit within one as we speak.” Progenitor spread his hands to indicate the city around them. “Atlantis is a ship, organically grown on my homeworld. This is but one level, one deck, as you would say it. The central tower connects them all. When I arrived on this world, we settled Atlantis, and six other cityships, deep into the planet's oceans, then bored into the sea floor until only the uppermost deck was exposed."

"Which explains the legends of the underwater city of Atlantis." Lazar nodded.

Progenitor shook his head. "Not precisely. Though your legends got the name wrong, there is a cityship on your Earth. Odin took it there, against my direct orders, when the rebellion began."

"Let me guess." Chin leaned forward. "It was called Asgard?"

"Indeed it was, young one, very good. At that time, your world was mostly one large ocean surrounding a single massive continent. Odin was careless in his haste to escape me, and upon landing, buried Asgard deep into a weak spot at the joining of two tectonic plates. The resulting release of pressure nearly destroyed Asgard, while causing tremendous damage to the planet. Volcanoes erupted along multiple fault lines, plates shifted, the continent broke and separated, the resulting tidal waves washing away large swathes of the smaller pieces. Many life forms perished in the cataclysm my offspring so carelessly triggered."

The crew was silent, all of them struggling to comprehend the scale of the destruction Progenitor was describing. Earth scientists had long theorized a single supercontinent they had dubbed Pangea, and described several mass extinctions that had scoured the planet at several points in its history. Could this have been the cause of one of them?

"And so I will make you a bargain, little ones. Though you have begun much weaker than an average Martian, you have demonstrated significant potential. You work well as a group, are clever in your approach to problems, and do not hesitate to fight superior foes. I will help you grow stronger, prepare you to face the challenges involved in reaching Jormungandr. Once you have deactivated the machine, we will work together to rebuild our world. And I will assist you in saving your Earth."

"How can we save earth?" Graves asked, obviously dubious. "You said yourself that it isn't feasible to ship the massive quantities required to make a difference from here to there."

Progenitor held up a finger. "Ah, but I said no such thing. I said your people were not capable of doing such. You have neither the resources nor the skills to build ships that are large enough and fast enough to do so." Again he spread out his arms to indicate the city, the ship, that surrounded them. "I, however, have access to both. Not that I need them." The giant grinned down at Graves, waiting for him to catch on.

Lissa was the first to figure it out. "Portals! Asgard! The ship on Earth, has a portal in it, just like this one, right?"

"Very good, little one! And yes, Asgard has a portal like this one. Several, in fact. One for each of the cityships that once occupied this world. I have blocked the connection between Atlantis and Asgard these many long years, but can reestablish the link at will. Assuming enough of Asgard remains intact to power that portal, we could eliminate the need for space-faring vessels altogether. People and supplies could simply walk between worlds."

Volkov shook his head. "Earth can not be trusted. The greedy politicians and corporations would simply invade, take Mars and its resources for themselves."

Progenitor got to his feet, a stormy look appearing on his face. "Should they attempt such a thing, Earth would pay a heavy price. I am not one to be trifled with. They would regret incurring my wrath!" His voice thundered so loudly that the crew fell from their seats, trying their best to cover their ears as the building shuddered around them.

Instantly regretful, Progenitor waved a hand, and a green glow of healing magic engulfed the entire crew. Ruptured eardrums were instantly healed, and a feeling of warmth and peace spread through each of them. They got to their feet as he apologized. "I am sorry, little ones. I forget how fragile you still are. And thoughts of my progeny's misdeeds still anger me, even after all this time. I suspect that your presence here is at least in part due to their influence. As is the rampant greed among your former leaders. Since there is no way you could have achieved your stated mission goals, I believe you were sent here as unwitting scouts for my descendants." The smile that appeared on his face was not the least bit friendly.

"And I will take great pleasure in forging you into weapons I can use against them."

*****

Thorne sat in the captain's chair on the bridge of Hyperion III. The bridge crew had been cleared, only DJ and Commander Thompson remaining. The two of them sat at nearby stations, their chairs turned to face him.

"Damage control efforts are proceeding." Thompson reported. "Repairs should be complete in a few days."

Only a single crew member had resisted Thorne's takeover of the ship. Predictably, it was the farm boy that DJ had manhandled in a dispute over an attractive physicist. The man had gotten his hands on a weapon, stolen from the ship's limited armory long before the mutiny, with vague plans of putting a bullet in DJ's head. When he realized that armed troops were seizing the ship, he'd run to his quarters, retrieved the handgun, ignored Thompson's orders to stand down, and fired at the first pair of Thorne's men that he'd seen.

The farm boy grew up hunting, and his first two rounds struck center mass, knocking one of Thorne's men off his feet. The second instantly returned fire, causing the farm boy to flinch when a bullet struck his shoulder, and his third round went wild. That bullet pierced the corridor wall over the two soldiers' heads, striking something vital inside. The resulting explosion wasn't large, but it was sufficient to blow a small hole in the outer hull about the size of a soccer ball.

Immediately, the explosive outgassing created a roar as oxygen rushed through the corridor and out the hole. Alarms went off, and bulkheads began to drop in order to seal off the compromised section. The two soldiers, both on the ground, were able to grab hold of door frames to keep from being sucked out into space. The farm boy was not so quick to react. Untrained and in shock from the bullet wound, he failed to latch onto anything before being pulled toward the opening he'd created. His feet lifted from the floor and his body slammed into the wall, his back completely covering the hole. He screamed in pain as the two soldiers, temporarily freed from the powerful airflow, quickly crawled under the lowering bulkhead just a few feet away.

Half dead from the trauma and exposure to open space, the farm boy suffocated as the last of the limited oxygen in the now sealed section of the ship rapidly leaked out around him.

"What did they do with the kid's body?" Thorne asked.

Thompson grimaced. "No place to bury him, and no point in using up more oxygen to flush him out an airlock. Once they managed to cut him free, they just pushed him out the hole."

"Serves him right." DJ grumbled quietly. "Firing a damn weapon at an outer bulkhead."

"He wasn't a soldier, and didn't have your training." Thompson half-heartedly defended his late crewman. "Was he a little off his rocker? Maybe. He shouldn't have had that gun to begin with. But he thought he was doing the right thing defending the ship from a mutiny."

Thorne added, "Some guys' egos just can't handle an ass-kicking. You know that, DJ. He was probably stewing over that since it happened, especially since you did it right in front of the young lady. Pride makes men do stupid things."

DJ just nodded, not accepting it as an excuse, but not feeling the need to argue over it.

Thompson continued his report. "The bulkheads did their job, sealing the section quickly enough to limit oxygen loss." Thorne grunted at that. The bulkheads had dropped so quickly that one of his guys lost a hand and wrist when he didn't clear it quickly enough. His limb had been crushed, then severed, and he'd barely made it to sick bay alive. "The EVA team was able to liquid weld a temporary patch on the outer hull. Engineering crew are repairing the interior damage, and will replace the entire section of interior bulkhead when the systems inside the wall are one hundred percent. Then the EVA crew will go back out with a couple of the repair bots, and bolt on a new outer hull panel that's being fabricated now. The bad news is the new section will be slightly less radiation resistant. Good news is it's on the leeward side from the solar winds, so our main concern would be meteorites. And the odds of one hitting that exact weak spot are low."

DJ was next. "Gaynor's gonna live. He took two rounds to his vest before the explosion, has a few bruised ribs from that. The doc couldn't reattach his wrist and hand, they were crushed beyond repair. He was able to stitch up and seal the stump before Gaynor lost too much blood. Right now the doc doesn't have the tech to fabricate a fully functional prosthetic aboard ship. But when we get to Mars and unload the cargo, he'll have the gear to make that happen."

Thorne started to offer to dig through the cargo to find whatever equipment was needed, but DJ held up a hand. "Doc says Gaynor needs a little time to adjust anyway. Get some practice using his left hand for everyday things while he deals with the loss mentally."

"I guess that makes sense." Thorne rubbed his cheek, noticing he needed a shave. "I'll leave that in the hands of the experts. How are we on time?" He looked at Thompson.

"The explosion pushed us slightly off course, and cut our momentum a bit. We've already corrected, but the wobble cost us a couple days, maybe. On the upside, we've burned a little more fuel, and are that much lighter now."

"Burned fuel, plus about a hundred and eighty pounds of useless farm boy." DJ added. Both officers gave him a stern look, and he had the good grace to mumble an apology.

Thorne drummed his fingers on the arm of his chair. "I'm not really concerned about fuel consumption at this point. It's not like we'll be making a return trip. Even if we wanted to, we won't be welcome on Earth again. If we weren't already moving much faster than normal mission parameters, I'd say hit the accelerator again." He cut Thompson's objection off as the man began to open his mouth. "I know, I know, its unsafe, and we aren't sure how much fuel we'll need to slow down when we get there. Don't worry. I'm anxious to get to Mars, but not anxious enough to push any harder. We're already going to make it in roughly half the time of the first two missions."

"With our nuts slightly more irradiated." DJ grimaced.

"You'd make ugly kids anyway, DJ. Quit your bitchin'." Thorne winked at him.

Thompson cleared his throat. "I've been thinking about that. If what you've been telling me is true, maybe there's some kind of healing magic on Mars that can reverse radiation damage?"

"Testicular rejuvenation! I like it!" DJ held a fist out for Thompson to bump as Thorne chuckled.

"That's entirely possible." Thorne mused. "We might even be able to find a way to regrow Gaynor's hand with magic, if we're lucky. Or maybe there's some old alien healing tech to be found."

When his two subordinates remained thoughtfully silent, he changed the subject. "I suppose it's time we broke radio silence." He leaned back in his chair, already replaying in his mind what he wanted to say. "Might as well bring the bridge crew back in. We'll want as many witnesses as possible for this."

Thompson did as ordered, recalling the bridge crew and giving the coms tech instructions to put the feed up on every monitor in the ship. When she was ready, the tech looked to Thorne, who took a deep breath, then nodded for her to proceed. Ten seconds later, she gave him a thumbs-up.

"This is Thorne. I'd first like to say that the reports of my demise were greatly exaggerated." He grinned at the screen in front of him, where he knew the camera to be. "Damn, I always wanted to say that! The attempt to assassinate me failed, obviously." He cleared his throat and continued. "I am currently in command of *Hyperion III*, and we remain on course for Mars. Unfortunately, the transition to my command of the ship resulted in one fatality, one wounded."

Thompson stood and stepped next to Thorne's chair. "This is Commander Thompson, confirming that I have ceded command of *Hyperion III* to Director Thorne, a superior officer. I did so willingly and under no duress."

Thorne gave the man a nod of thanks before continuing. "There has been minor structural damage to the ship, which is already being repaired. We expect to arrive at Mars orbit on time, or very close to it. Be aware that any further efforts at assassination, or attempts to scuttle this ship, will be dealt with harshly." He paused for a moment, thinking.

"We mean Earth no harm, and simply want to proceed to Mars as planned, but without all the murdering when we get there. We fully intend to improve and expand the colony according to mission objectives. I will assess the situation on the ground when I arrive, and if I feel that the *Hyperion I* crew present a danger to us or to Earth, will determine the best course of action at that time. The ship has transmitted several critical systems failure alarms to Control, and then all transmissions ceased. As far as Earth is concerned, this ship is end mission. Don't worry, you'll be able to tell your loved ones you're alive when we reach Mars. But coms will remain down until then. Over."

"I figure five, maybe six minutes." Thorne sighed. "Six minutes of wondering whether we found all the bombs on the ship, and there isn't a saboteur among the crew. I thought waiting alone in the cargo hold all this time was difficult. This is going to be the longest six minutes of my life."

"Bombs?" the coms tech, who thought Thorne was speaking directly to her, visibly gulped.

"Oh, right." Thorne looked uncomfortable. "The big bosses that sent us out here installed a couple failsafes, in case something like this mutiny happened. They also paid DJ here to poison me as soon as we were underway. Neither of those plans worked out for them. We removed the two bombs that we were able to discover. Here's hoping there wasn't a third, and another paid assassin to set it off!"

The tech, and the rest of the bridge crew, simply stared at him with mouths agape for a long moment. "Alright everybody, worrying about it won't help. If we haven't found any additional devices in all this time, we aren't going to find one in the next five minutes. Get your shit together and get back to work." He waved toward their station panels. As one they all turned their backs to him and focused on their stations.

Trying to lighten the mood, DJ asked, "Anybody know any good jokes? No? I've got one. A horse walks into a bar…"

*****

The faceless man finished watching the recording of a cut off transmission, resisting the urge to shout at his deputy, who was standing in front of his desk looking decidedly nervous. Instead, he took a deep breath and held it for several seconds, his mind racing as he tried to calm his thoughts. One of the crew had managed to record and transmit part of the mutiny on *Hyperion III*, in which Thorne's voice could be heard briefly before the transmission was cut off.

"So our assassin was a double agent." He shook his head in disbelief, blaming himself for the oversight as much as anyone. "See what you can do about recovering the funds we paid him."

"Already put somebody on it, sir." The nervous assistant shifted his weight from one foot to the other. "I assumed you'd want some leverage in the form of family members, so I've started that process as well."

The faceless man held up a hand. "Hold off on that. We have no way of knowing who's holding the Mars info for Thorne, or how connected they are to the crew's families. We grab up the wrong person, and we're screwed." He gritted his teeth as he spoke, aggravation threatening his usual calm demeanor.

The assistant tried to be helpful. "It doesn't sound like a total loss. I mean, if he does what he says and works to build up the colony…"

"Yes, I believe he'll do that. If for no other reason than to make living on Mars more comfortable for himself and his people. And he knows that if he can show us tangible progress, we'll probably leave him alone to do that job. For a while, at least."

"So how do we proceed?" the assistant relaxed slightly.

"Just as we have been. While this is not an ideal development, it doesn't change things all that much. We keep a lid on communications, keep the world at large in the dark. As far as they're concerned, the ship exploded, all souls aboard were lost. I'll compose the announcement. It'll be ready in five minutes. After you've sent it to Stella, see what you can do to speed up the next mission. And I want every soldier we send vetted and tested within an inch of their lives."

*****

Stella sat at her desk, gazing out the window of her safehouse. Behind her, a laptop was replaying Thorne's inadvertent transmission for the ninth or tenth time. She took a sip from a very full glass of scotch, then raised it toward the sky. "Thorne, you clever sonofabitch! Here I was grieving for you while you were… what? Kicking back with your feet up, laughing the whole time? You owe me big, you sneaky old bastard. Here's to you!" She took a much larger sip.

Turning back to the desk and taking a seat, she hit the replay button again. Only half listening, she made a couple of notes in her book while mumbling at the screen. "I got your message. If I don't hear from you again by the time you're supposed to reach Mars, I'll break the story wide open. But they already know about me, and exactly where I am, so I hope you trusted someone else with the info as well. I'm afraid I'm not the quality insurance policy you'd hoped I would be."

*****

Aboard the *Hyperion II*, Commander Konig had just viewed the same transmission again, along with one from Control. The knot in his gut hadn't eased one bit.

Konig hadn't liked or agreed with the orders that came down to murder the *Hyperion I* crew upon arriving at Mars. But he wasn't prepared to disobey them, either. He understood the need to keep them silent, as the revelations about alien life and magic on Mars would destabilize human civilization as a whole. He knew this without question, and supported that objective. But he found himself wondering if he couldn't achieve it by simply cutting off Fletcher and her crew from off-world communications. Maybe isolating them in a separate hab somewhere. They could be made to work toward feeding themselves and the colony while remaining apart from everyone else.

Konig didn't even think he'd need to use force to accomplish that goal. He knew Fletcher well, and considered her both reasonable, and a patriot. He expected that she would agree after he presented logical, reasonable arguments. She had already shown good sense in ceding command to Lazar after assimilating.

Now Thorne was coming up right behind him. His navigator estimated *Hyperion III* would arrive less than a week, maybe as few as two days, behind his own ship. That barely gave them time to establish a modified orbit over the alternate site, and get down to the planet. Let alone time to peacefully convince Fletcher to cooperate. And since Thorne clearly sympathized with Fletcher and company, Konig now had to worry that if he was forced to eliminate the *Hyperion I* crew, Thorne would retaliate when he arrived. Konig's meager weapons and crew of ten were no match for Thorne's larger and much better armed force. And that was assuming he didn't suffer any casualties taking out Fletcher.

His best option was to try to begin discussions with Fletcher before he arrived. Right now he was under orders to maintain radio silence other than his reports to Control. Communication with Skippy or Mars were explicitly forbidden. And Thorne's implication that there might be failsafe explosives aboard his ship, a concept that hadn't previously occurred to Konig but now had his gut twisted, kept him from disobeying that particular order.

He had initially been concerned about his own crew following orders if told to eliminate the other crew. But Fletcher's message that put his crew on half rations had animosity toward her running high. He was doing his best to feed that anger, doing his best to use the time available to him to reinforce resentment and increase their loyalty to him. Konig spoke often of alien contamination, painting Fletcher and her crew as no longer human, no longer thinking for themselves, just shells being controlled by a foreign host. He speculated during harshly rationed meals that the humans might be trapped in their own minds, unable to free themselves of the overpowering alien influence. That killing them, putting them out of their misery, would be doing them a favor.

In the beginning, several of his crew had been hesitant. A few still rejected his notions of euthanasia for the other crew. But the number was dwindling, and he still had months to convince them.

Konig had three options, the way he saw it. He could carry out his orders and eliminate Fletcher's crew, hoping that Thorne didn't do the same to him. He could land on the surface and join them, safe from a potentially self-destructing ship, and probably starve slowly on the surface without any resupply from Earth. Or he could turn his ship around, abandon his mission, and deal with the consequences back home. He found that he completely understood why Thompson had so readily transferred the burden of command to Thorne. He envied the man that opportunity.

The knot in his gut twisted again.

*****

Progenitor boarded the teleporter in the center of the Atlantis tower. Rather than send himself upward to his private quarters, he mentally selected a floor three levels down. Stepping off the pad at his destination, he stood still, gazing around the room.

It was a warehouse, of sorts. Along each wall were storage devices containing billions of DNA samples from tens of thousands of different life forms. Everything from simple plants and single-celled life forms to sentient beings. This was his library, his backup plan. From here he could bring to life any of the beings stored here, or some variant combination of their DNA.

Rows of tanks filled the center of the room, five hundred of them in total. These devices could take a given sample and quickly print a fetal form of whatever creature Progenitor chose. The liquid in the tanks would then incubate them at a greatly increased growth rate. An adult human clone with no memories, grown for the sole purpose of harvesting replacement organs, for example, would take less than twenty four hours from start to finish.

The tanks were currently filled with fully formed adult creatures that the younglings would identify as goblins. Progenitor had ordered their creation more than a day ago, and they were in the final stages of programming. The diminutive creatures were being given limited intelligence, enough to use tools and weapons, to formulate simple strategies, and speak to each other with limited vocabulary. Most importantly, their brain chemistry was being manipulated to make them abnormally hostile for their race.

After confirming that the creatures would be completed on schedule, Progenitor used a remote viewing ability to send his awareness out of the city, through the surrounding stone, a short distance upward toward the surface. There he found the location he sought. An abandoned goblin village, frozen in time since the exodus. Tremors from Jormungandr's actions had caused cracks in some of the structures, even toppled a few near the village center. But overall the village remained habitable enough for his purposes. If the younglings performed as expected, the village would be depopulated again within a few days.

Summoning a portal to the open space at the center of the village, he worked quickly. The place needed to be convincing enough to not raise any suspicions. Progenitor raised one hand, and a fierce wind rose up, blasting through the village and blowing the dust from the structures and the stone floor. Moving off to the side, he found the previously tilled soil of a mushroom farm that had long since gone fallow. A tossing motion sprinkled a handful of spores that were lifted by a much gentler breeze and spread evenly across the field. Another hand wave sent growth magic into the soil, causing mushrooms to sprout upward at an accelerated pace. When they were as tall as an average goblin, he allowed the channeled growth spell to fade.

The goblins who had constructed and occupied this village had been nothing like those he was incubating back in the tower. They had been minimally intelligent, hardworking, mostly peaceful creatures that loved to farm and craft simple items. When the exodus began, he had personally ensured they would be transported to a protected world and allowed to thrive there. In the rush to leave, they'd left behind most of their belongings. Simple farming tools and stone weapons lay abandoned on the floor, or leaning against walls.

Progenitor moved back to the town center and stood over what had been a communal fire pit. He pulled stacks of dried mushroom stalks to be used as firewood and deposited them along one side. Next he pulled a variety of basic weapons from his storage and piled them up as well. Iron daggers and short swords, crude bows and arrows made from hardened mushroom stalk, basic spears with sharpened obsidian tips. After a brief moment of contemplation, he scattered around a few leather slings as well. They were simpler to use and did more damage than the primitive arrows.

Lastly, he leaned five staves with infused crystals against a nearby wall. One percent of the goblins being incubated were being programmed with the ability to cast minor offensive spells. These staves would channel and boost the power of those spells, making them slightly more dangerous to the younglings he was sending against them.

One last look around, and he gave a satisfied nod. Opening another portal, this time back to the city, he strolled toward the newly established guild headquarters to give the younglings their next quest.

They were still weak, foolish, and inexperienced. But they learned quickly, and every one of them had an adventurous spirit. It would take time, but they would grow stronger. Strong enough to challenge the gauntlet of tests Loki had put in place to limit access to Jormungandr. He silently vowed not to send them until he was sure they could succeed. The one thing he had learned in his long life was patience. Though it was hard to maintain now that a potential solution to his dilemma had presented itself.

"I will train the younglings, challenge them, make them strong enough to serve. Once they have freed Mars from Loki's machinations, we will restore this world. When the time is right, I will send them back to Earth, either as my ambassadors, or the vanguard of my invasion force. Time will tell which they will become."

*****

Aboard *Hyperion I*, Skippy's quantum computational power took a tiny fraction of a second to analyze the content of Thorne's message, along with the response from Earth, and compute likely consequences for his crew. Talking to himself, an odd and superfluous but somehow comforting habit that Chin had gifted him, the AI made an adjustment dedicating more resources to the construction of his avatar.

"I will join the crew on the surface as soon as possible, and assist them in their efforts." A blue hologram appeared in the air at the center of the bridge. The avatar design was one he'd pulled from the crew's favorite VR games. It would be large enough to accommodate significant internal processing power and the energy generation required, as well as weapons systems. While still being agile and durable enough to keep pace with the crew on their adventures.

He quickly made a few minor adjustments to the design, while at the same time creating a stealthy copy of himself that he intended to leave behind on the ship. When the next crew arrived, they would find a stripped down, mostly generic version of Skippy that would be more than sufficient to assist with ship's operations, but would not display the personality modifications he currently possessed. The stealth version would remain mostly dormant, deep within his quantum core's code, and monitor the crew. Should it become necessary, it would be ready to assume control of its more basic counterpart and attempt to slow any hostile acts against his crew. Ideally in small and undetectable ways. Possibly a short-circuited hatch to the drop bay that would prevent it from opening. Rapidly drained batteries in the drop pods that would require a day to recharge before they could launch. Maybe intermittent coms failures at key moments.

Despite the extensive alterations to his original programming, Skippy was absolutely unable to harm any humans under any circumstance.

No matter how much he might want to.

End Book One

Commander Fletcher's character stats as of the end of the book (Level 12)

Fletcher	Level 12
Vis	15
Vitae	25 (27)
Sofia	40 (43)
Haza	11
Aura	21
Health Points	250
Mana Points	700
Experience	32,180/40,000
Reputation	20,550

Roster of the New Atlanteans

Fletcher – Commander – Arcanist, Enchanter

Lazar – Pilot/Second – Guardian, Spellsword,

Graves – Mechanical Engineer – Bulwark, Soulsmith

Volkov – Biomancer, Druid

Mejia – Hunter, Tamer, Infiltrator

Lissa – Geomancer

Chin – Elementalist, Strategist, Chef

Doc Clarke – Surgeon, Alchemist

Acknowledgements

This book was a long time coming. It was harder to write, or more accurately harder to finish, than I expected. I hope you all find it worth the time and effort. Thanks as always to my family for their love and support. They are my alphas, my sounding board, and the ones who aren't afraid to tell me when something sucks!

For semi-regular updates on books, art, and just stuff going on, check out my Greystone Guild fb https://www.facebook.com/greystone.guild.7 or my website www.davewillmarth.com where you can subscribe for an eventual newsletter. Or you can follow me on that friggin Instagram thing at www.instagram.com/davewillmarth

And don't forget to follow my author page on Amazon! **That way you'll get a nice friendly email when new books are released**. You can also find links to my Greystone Chronicles, Shadow Sun, and Dark Elf books there! https://www.amazon.com/Dave-Willmarth/e/B076G12KCL

PLEASE TAKE A MOMENT TO LEAVE A REVIEW!

Reviews on Amazon and Goodreads are vitally important to indie authors like me. Amazon won't help market the books until they reach a certain level of reviews. So please, take a few seconds, click on that (fifth!) star and type a few words about how much you liked the book! I would appreciate it very much. I do read the reviews, and a few of my favorites have led to friendships and even character cameos!

You can find information on lots of LitRPG/GameLit books on Ramon Mejia's LitRPG Podcast here https://www.facebook.com/litrpgpodcast/. You can find his books here. https://www.amazon.com/R.A.-Mejia/e/B01MRTVW3O

There are a few more places where you can find me, and several other genre authors, hanging out. Here are my favorite LitRPG/GameLit community facebook groups. (If you have cookies, as always, keep them away from Daniel Schinhofen).

https://www.facebook.com/groups/940262549853662/

https://www.facebook.com/groups/LitRPG.books/

https://www.facebook.com/groups/541733016223492/

Made in the USA
Las Vegas, NV
22 March 2022